Tristan Hawkins

is thirty and lives in nort
advertising and publishing
novel.

ORIGINAL

T RISTAN H AWKINS

Pepper

Flamingo
An Imprint of HarperCollins*Publishers*

| *f l a m i n g o* | The term 'Original' signifies publication direct into paperback with no preceding British hardback edition. |
| **O**RIGINAL | The Flamingo Original series publishes fine writing at an affordable price at the point of first publication. |

Flamingo
An Imprint of HarperCollins*Publishers,*
77–85 Fulham Palace Road,
Hammersmith, London W6 8JB

First published in Great Britain
by Flamingo 1993
9 8 7 6 5 4 3 2 1

Copyright © Tristan Hawkins 1993

The Author asserts the moral right to
be identified as the author of this work

A CIP catalogue record for this book
is available from the British Library

ISBN 0 00 654626 9

Lines from 'Hey Joe' by William Roberts used by kind
permission of Carlin Music Corp., Iron Bridge House,
3 Bridge Approach, London NW1 8BD.

Lines from 'Isis' by Dylan/Levy used by kind permission
of Ram's Horn Music, published by Sony Music
Publishing in the UK.

Author photograph by Douglas Fisher

Set in Caledonia

Printed in Great Britain by
HarperCollinsManufacturing Glasgow

To Oliver

CONTENTS

1

Dappled Things

I've taken a Memory Cocktail.

And if i shut my eyes i can create Pepper.

Her water-and-whisky complexion. Her tea-stain hair. Even the wetness and nutty stipple of Her eyes. My cocktail enables me to picture everything, everything about Pepper, exactly as it is. Inch for inch the coastline of Her eczema – Her sad, lip-red rind – and its emotional and lunar vacillation. Even the way Her right foot errs a fraction inward when She walks, how Her left breast is a degree more pendulous than the other as She crawls over me. The mild crab-stick of Her groin, the intimate essence of a post-garlic fart beneath the duvet, the changed scent of illness. Her greeting me, 'Hi-er'.

It's true, i can even get Her to say things. In Her exact voice. Exactly the way She speaks. And what She says is what i make Her say. In fact, with my Memory Cocktail, i can make anyone i've ever heard speak, say just about anything i choose. For instance, if i'd heard You speak, i could make You say things to me. Things You mightn't normally say. I could lie back, just as i'm doing now, and listen as You whine, 'richard, fuck me. Please, please fuck me.' Or say You're a guy – because i'm not gay (except sometimes in dreams – and only just lately) – i could get You to say, 'I really value your friendship, rich. You're a diamond.' Here, now, i could recall the disaster in all its forms, or play Mahler's Fifth – note for note. With regard to my memory, i'm in utter control.

A fistful of barbs, a nose of pink, a stick and a half of Thai and – if, like me, You can't take being alone at such times – vodka to taste can do this for You. Try it. You'll be surprised at Yourself.

At present i'm halcyon and relatively self-confident. You can probably tell from the calm manner of my speech. My tearlessness. And while i'm like this i'd like to put you straight on a couple of matters. You see, tomorrow (assuming tomorrow) will be quite different. I won't be so level-headed. I'll be a bundle of nerves and regrets. And i'll be so totally alone – even if You're still with me. I may even say some things i shouldn't. So i'd like to square things with You now. Provide You with some timely warnings. Try to get You on my side while the going's good.

Let me open the pitch with an advertisement for myself. It's Pepper. If i can sell you Pepper you might buy me – besides, my life was so good then, a cocktail of passions. It's known in the business as an affinity sell. And right now a splash of affinity could do me the world of good.

So picture Pepper as you first saw her. She was nervous, you'll remember, it being her first day. Hand worrying through shrub of ginger hair. It's got to be gone ten thirty and she still hasn't got the hang of our Sidney. You remember that she wears little puddle-splash spectacles, clay

10

earrings – they're ginger cats, a necklace of round mint drops, a high-necked T-shirt that's pool-table green and pig-pink paisley, black Lycra mini-skirt fitting like an apple skin, zebra leggings and *de rigueur* Doc Marten shoes. Picture her on the verge of tears. She's not, but you don't know that yet (you have to be a right shit to make Pepper cry). The first thing you notice is the sprinkle of cinnamon freckles across the bridge of her nose. Cute. That's your first thought. And it's true – to a degree. Pepper is what you'd call cute. Boyish even – not a word I'm entirely comfortable with, but there you are, it's said. You move closer. You hone in on her humanity. Her too-close-together eyes, her eyebrow neglect, the scarification of historic acne and, of course, the coins of eczema bark behind her ears.

Then you speak to Pepper Furnival for the first time. Say you give her some typing. I don't remember. **One too many vodkas, i fear**. You realize that she says 'OK' too much. But that's OK. She's trying to be 'agency'. You smile rather pleasantly – you've classed Pepper Furnival as someone who needs to be felt sorry for, for a couple of your highly precious minutes, or perhaps you already fancy her a bit – you fancied most things and a lot of women in those days. She latches on to the smile. She needs it, so you reckon – but what do you know at this stage? Then she comes out with it. It's a whisper. She points at her WP.

'Help. Please.'

So, I put children's wear on hold and tell her the things I know about Sidney. Then call Vivienne to show her the rest.

Now, in a manner of speaking, I'm in charge here. I'm not a director or anything like that – yet. But I call the shots. If we're pissing it up corporate fashion, it's my initial on the memo. The birthday fatty-o-gram is on my card number. I arrange for Vivienne to introduce our stream of new secretaries to Sidney. And if someone's taking the new girl to lunch – tell her the ropes, who to suck to, who's a wanker

11

– it's me. Now, I estimate Pepper knows this. By the way people react to me. Directors and all. The way people ask my opinion, my view on the matter. She knows by my enthusiasm – my passion for most everything. And, of course, my malevolent self-assurance, my good, almost middle-class accent. So it's up to me to invite her to lunch. But I think, 'Fuck that!' She's a dippy cow. A sartorial incompetent to boot. And I go to the local with Horace O, my art director.

It's an erratic conversation. Our hangovers have become increasingly recalcitrant of late. We're trying to work out how best to do my twenty-third and, more importantly, the Emily Smith campaign. I'm adamant. It's got to be a speakeasy party. Spats, violin cases, trilbies, martinis and so forth. Horace O thinks Mexican.

'No food, obviously. Just a fuck of a lot of tequila. And champagne. A slammer competition. I'll win. Obviously.' I think Horace O's idea is bad. Unpopular with the women. 'Good point. Women. Or it'll be just like any other night. Get the ales in. I'll do a chaser too.'

'It's eleven thirty, for fuck's sake.'

'I'm on hangover time. It's about three. Hurry! Hurry up for God's sake. I feel the **drink-flu** approaching. And fear.' I fetch Horace O his drinks. There'll be no work done until he's better from the **drink-flu** and fear. **You see, i didn't understand then – when it was beginning – that all the delectable self-confidence offered by the chemicals is on loan. And You're called to repay it in hard currency. Obviously, the other option is keep on borrowing. The choice is Yours. And for my part – well, i'm a child of Thatcher's 'credit age'.**

Some silent time passes. We drink. Horace O suggests a place. Then this happens. I come over rather giddy. Not drunk giddy or hungover giddy, but giddy like you suddenly understand the poem, or like one gets before a premonition – like an amyl hit. And I receive this vivid picture of the new secretary pouring coffee. She's in my white bathrobe, in my kitchen – in my *clean* kitchen!

I'm distracted by the sight of lager streaming down the sides of Horace O's mouth and chin. He belches, smiles like a Rottweiler and emits a loud and polluted, 'AAAGH! Fuck!'

Anyway he's up now and rocking to the tintinnabulation of his coin on the metal of the bar. And a moment later he's back, handing me an exuberant pint and Jack Daniel's chaser. But after last night I don't really fancy more drink. The first did me no good whatsoever. 'Best force it down,' I think. 'Take in some positivity for the task ahead.'

It's midday. The drink's taken an engaging hold. Horace is back to normal and I'm feeling very positive about life in general. So we kick around a few ideas.

Now, you've seen the commercials. But have you ever paused to think? I mean, asked yourself why some are really fantastic – better than the TV they punctuate – yet most are complete crap? Well, this is how it is. All commercials start life, usually in wine bars and pubs, as works of brilliance. But they're dowsed and transmuted by the world's negative forces: uncreative creative directors, account wankers, the Client, budgets, technical feasibilities, tried and tested approaches, narrow-mindedness, legality, the Trades Description Act, the Advertising Standards Authority and the collective lack of imagination and intelligence. (Your average peak viewer has a mental age of thirteen and a half – no lie.)

But Horace O and I think 'Fuck that!' So we invariably get our work bounced back at the first stop – Basil the Bastard. The reason we're over-paid, over-rated and over-confident is that the few ads we have got past the Bastard, the Client and the censor have cleaned up both sales and award-wise – and, of course, there's **The Lie**. So because we're regarded as arrogant shits, we get given the likes of Emily Smith children's summer range – local fucking cinema run.

So what happens when you've been on the piss for the last two weeks and you're expected to come up with a script by tomorrow? Simple, you go to the pub. What happens when you're in the pub and you're stuck for an idea? Simple, you pinch one. Or better still, you rip the piss out of a contemporary genre. And better still, Pepper Furnival comes in whilst you're in full and magnificent creative flow.

This is how it happens. We're browsing through the Emily Smith summer designs with much unenthusiasm, and Horace O remembers, 'I invited the new secretary for a drink.'

'Yeah?'

'Because I propose to lance her,' he whispers conspiratorially and spits another cotton ball into the empty pint pot.

'Yeah, Horace?'

'There's something rude about that woman. Something that . . .' (snort, spit).

'C'mon H. Best we think about bratwear.'

'Yeah – any ideas?'

'No.'

Some empty time passes us. Then this happens. Someone puts 'Hey Joe' on the juke-box and I have this idea. It's a magnesium flare. Vertiginous. I get us some pints and key the song in again. Timing it up to just after the second 'I caught her messin' round with another man' I find it's exactly thirty seconds. But I already knew it would be perfect. My vertigo never lets me down.

CLIENT: **Emily Smith**
PRODUCT: **Children's Summerwear**
TITLE: **Joe**
SCREENING TIME: **30 Secs**
B/W + specials

Vision	**Sound**
1. INT. AB Living room, French windows open to a garden.	Hey Joe: Jimi Hendrix

14

CU. Male toddler's face. Intro. Mean expression.	Hey Joe, where you going with that
Pan down body. ECU. (on 'gun') large water pistol in kid's hand.	gun in your hand?
Pan around room. Colour CUs Cartoon video + squash beaker. Dissolve.	Repeat
Cut back to kid. Move in CU patch on the back of dungarees.	
Kid begins to swagger towards the windows, gun held at hip. Camera follows behind. Pushes open French windows.	I'm going down to shoot my lady, you know. Coz I caught her messin' with another man

2. EXT. AB Garden

POV. Kid. Small girl and another boy at paddling pool.	Repeat
They notice him and look alarmed.	
Pan around to show all 3 by pool. Boy raises pistol. Colour restored. Squirts girl. She shrieks. ECU. Patch on Jeans.	SFX (FVO) Shriek Fade
SUPER: Emily Smith: Kool Klobber for Kids	

'Horace, listen.' I begin to explain, but he waves me quiet.

'I can't hear you,' his corrupt lungs bellow.

So I'm at the bar arguing that the music should be turned down, when Horace barks, 'Hi honey.' He waves to Pepper, who's entering the pub with some trepidation. He bounces up and gallops over to the bar. 'What'll you have?'

Pepper sits herself next to me and the scene shifts to the bar. 'Hi-er.' As she crosses a leg, I notice that her ankles are brown as my forefinger. Her glasses aren't a permanent fixture and red callouses sit where she's removed the ginger toms. We exchange shiticisms.

'You OK with Sidney?'

'We've come to an understanding and he's a real sweetie.'

'So you think you'll stick the day out?'

'Oh, maybe even the week. But if this is the only pub, erm . . .'

'What's wrong with the Intrepid Fox? It's a fine boozer. Ah, H, sit down and don't say a word. I want to run this past the both of you.'

So I explain the brief to Pepper – employing as much impressive jargon as I can manage – and lurch into my idea which, naturally enough, she regards as fantastic. Horace O shoots at it.

'Too expensive.'

'Horse-shit!'

'Badly targeted.'

'Cow-shit!'

'I just don't see it working'

'Pig-dos!' This is Pepper.

So Horace and I spat for a time. And I say, 'OK H, you come up with a better one and I'll finish the campaign with Pepper here.' Now Horace O is sulking and trying to hawk surreptitiously into a handkerchief. And I'm telling Pepper how, if the cinema goes well, it'll run on the box. I'm telling her about some of the famous TV, press and poster work I've done and, of course, some that I didn't – including much

of **The Lie**. She'd like to get into it. She really would. So
I'm telling her (like I tell the whole turnover of our secretaries) that soon we'll need another creative assistant and,
with a bit of flare, it's a cinch to work your way up. She's
buying all of it, which is really sickening Horace O (like it
does every time). And this sickens him even more.

'Right, Pepper. Do you know, "I Ain't Got No Home" by
Clarence "Frogman" Henry?' She doesn't, so I sing: 'Oooo. I
ain't got no home. No place to roam. I'm a lonely boy' etc. She
gets the picture and rubs her sandpaper hands in anticipation.

Reluctantly, Horace bungs me the catalogue and I indicate some clothes. 'OK, there's a kid. Male one. A boy, like.
In this hat. Yeah, it has to be this straw hat. He's black or
blond. Cute specimen. You feel maternal to him already.
Maternal, don't you?'

'Do I?'

'Yeah. Hands tiny. Fingers chubby as profiteroles.'

'Yuk!'

'Legs like little balloons.'

'Yuk!'

'He's nibbling a piece of straw. Dead maternal, yeah?'

'I'll take your word.'

'Now he's sitting in the street, back against a dilapidated
wall. Alone. Aah . . .'

'Aah.'

'The song. "I ain't got no home . . . I'm a lonely boy". Aah.'

'Aah.' Still sarcastic.

'Right, he's looking at a frog.'

'A frog?'

'I dunno, maybe it's a cuddly frog. Yeah, he picks it up,
stands up and you see that he's not in the street but an AB
– a middle-class – garden. He walks to the back door. His
mother hands him milk and a biscuit. Perhaps he gives her
the frog in exchange. Otherwise he ignores her and walks
off. End of commercial. What do you think?'

'Why the frog?'

'There's a frog in the song. Trust me. It's dead witty.'

'I'm not sure,' she ponders, 'It sounds OK. The joke is that he *has* got a home really?'

'Yeah, well. It's rough at the moment. It needs some kicking around. Fine tuning. But, you know?'

When Pepper pops away for a pee, Horace says to me, 'There's something wrong with her skin. I've changed my mind about her.'

As for me, I revel in the imperfections of us life forms – the tricky caprice of nature. I'm also fancying Pepper like hell. So I say, "Glory be to God for dappled things – For skies of couple-colour as a brinded cow."'

Horace empties a nostril on the floor, clears the remaining string of albumen with a beer mat, and says, 'It makes you sound like the Bastard.'

Sure we struggled. But around pub-shut we more or less finish the first draft of the two commercials. Partly through bad luck and partly because we stayed in the pub until five, we couldn't source 'I Ain't Got No Home', so Basil the Bastard will have to sit through an abortion of a recording featuring me on the guitar and Horace O singing. To get right, I needed some time in the bathroom – fingers tickling epiglottis. Horace O needed wine and slimming pills.

Enter Basil the Bastard, salami complexion, fat as a cake and two-thirds cut.

'Good evening, gentlemen.'

In unison, unenthusiastic. 'Alright Basil.'

'So much industry. Such dulcet tones. I trust you have another work of genius to justify your inordinate salaries, your creative time-keeping, your . . .'

'Actually it's fuckin' brilliant,' says Horace matter-of-factly. 'But the bin's over there. So shall we dispense with the formalities?' He lobs the cassette in. 'Goodnight Basil.'

'Faith in your unquestionable abilities, gentlemen. As

ever, your creative director is all ears.' He thumps down and tips himself a tumbler of Horace O's wine. 'Château Landsdown? Gentlemen, because we sell the muck, it doesn't oblige us to suffer it. Despise *me* if you must. But spare a thought for my ulcer.'

I protest, 'Basil, we agreed tomorrow. You can't just barge in . . .'

'Like a fat sod in a cake shop,' whispers Horace, and spends the next minutes crunching back mucoid hysterics.

'Young man, tonight I am the quintessence of affability. Tomorrow I shall be hungover. It's my recommendation that you call into play the little common sense I suspect you possess, and present your ideas tonight. Moreover, I propose a small wager. Should I find a modicum of worth in your labours, we shall adjourn, in a merry threesome, to L'Aquila. That is unless your sybaritic engagements demand your presence elsewhere. Should I find your work typically atrocious, I dine alone.'

So we run through our ideas, our positivity pissing away at each change of story-board. Basil takes more wine. We finish and he stares at the table – and I'm reckoning on Basil doing pasta solo.

'Tell me Richard. Now this isn't meant as a criticism – God forbid I offend you – sensitive creature that you are. But by way of observation, why have you seen fit to omit the very thing that is central to advertising – a selling proposition? What on God's earth would persuade anyone to part with hard-earned money for these products? Because they like nigger music?' Horace turns his gaze to the ceiling fan.

'C'mon Basil, you've read the brief. We're repositioning the brand. Out of the catalogues on to the high street. We're talking *designer* kids' clothes – not Landsdown discount washing powder. This is good.'

'And laddie, the tag: "Kool Klobber for Kids", it smacks of illiteracy. What happened to the days of *Never Knowingly Undersold*?'

'Are you buying us Italian or what?'

'I'm not hungry,' says Horace.

'In the days of CML Chicago. It must have been in '65, Herman Lorenz said to me . . . Your puerility notwithstanding, you *have* heard of Lorenz?'

Simultaneously. Bored. 'Yes.'

(Affects crap American accent) '"Young man, always remember the four Necessities of a good advertising campaign." Have you heard this?'

Simultaneously. Bored. 'Yes.'

'Well it'll do you no harm to hear it again. "The first Necessity is to sell, the second is the Necessity to establish or reinforce brand awareness, the third is the Necessity to sell the first two to the Client, and the fourth, and most important need of all, is the Necessity for a drink when you've satisfied all other Necessities." This time, and conceivably this time only, I'll bow to your better judgement – so needy am I of the fourth Necessity. Fetch your coats gentlemen.'

'Yo! Good man B.'

So we're in the restaurant. The Tenuate Dospan has attenuated Horace's appetite and I've become too drunk to be hungry. Basil, gorging a second plate of *escargots*, sluicing down garlic grease with the shells, doesn't help. I'm pawing something reminiscent of bird's guts and breathing deeply to try and still the room.

Funereal waiters importune with Chianti and grappa and wield baseball bat pepper pots. And in my mind the words *Pepper Furnival* lilt back and forth like a mantra. When I'm bombed I sometimes think in words (a garrulous stream of rubbish – it can be unbearable at times). Even when it's my turn to slur in and out of the conversation – which isn't often, as Horace is whizzing and Basil is roaring – the name plays on and on, just below consciousness, like guilt.

20

My crushes are like colds. They fell me with an infuriating regularity. Then I put paid to them with a screaming jag and get back to my day-to-day, night-to-night concerns – put the volume control back on my *joie de vivre*, so to speak. But this stuff is quite different. Not even this much drink can snuff her. And I realize that Pepper Furnival, with her eczema and too-close-together eyes, has mown me down like a summer flu.

Then I hear, 'Richard *something, something* arrogant little shit too.'

'Sorry Basil?'

'I'm saying,' splutters the Bastard (he's really rat-arsed now), 'that you're too arrogant for your own fucking good. How long have you been in the game?'

'Five years.'

'And how old are you?'

'Twenty-three next month.'

'You see. You see, you're not even a graduate. But you think you know it all. Och, don't get me wrong Richard. It's meant as friendly advice. An avunc . . . alvuncurar word of warning. But you do. Don't you?'

'Do what?'

'You think you know it all. Admit it, you think you know better than *me*. I *know* ye do. You think you've got more *natural talent*. Natural talent ha! I'm telling you it's shit! There's no such thing as natural fucking talent. Thirty years. You're looking at thirty years' top agency experience. All I'm saying is – watch it! Learn from those around you. Those with experience. Do you understand what I'm saying? A little humility in this business will get you further than I'd like to tell you.'

'Basil, fuck off.'

'You see. You see. You can tell *me* te fuck off. You can get away with that sort of shit with me. You don't know it now, but one day you'll realize I was the best CD you ever worked for. And you'll be knocking at my door. Begging me to take you back – when you meet some of the other bastards out there.'

'A bit of respect back from you once in a while would be good.'

'Listen Pal, I've *earned* the right to be arrogant.'

OK here's a cross-section through Basil Colquoun's book: here are some typical examples of thirty years working in the 'top' agencies here and in the States:

CLIENT: **Universal Encyclopedia Corporation**
Poster + Single Page Press.

1: CHILD. Visual: Sixties style photography colour added.
Small child (V. American-looking) engrossed in a volume of encyclopedia.
Copy line:
 'I know my soul hath power to know all things'
 Sir John Davies 1509–1626

2: FATHER. Visual: Father with hand on son's shoulder, son looking up at father through thick specs. Encyclopedia in foreground.
Copy line:
 'My little son, who look'd from thoughtful eyes'
 Coventry Patmore 1823–1896

3: PLANT. Visual: Small boy reading encyclopedia. Open page shows botanical diagram. On table next to encyclopedia is the same plant, freshly cut.
Copy line:
 'O how much more doth beauty beauteous seem
 By that sweet ornament which truth doth give!'
 William Shakespeare 1504–1616

Same period:

CLIENT: **Blenerhasett's Candy**
Single Page Press.

POP. Visual: Santa, hood and beard down, revealing he's
really 'Pop'. Behind him is this vulgarly decorated Christmas
tree and he's surrounded by wrapped presents. He's picking
out a chocolate from a Blenerhasett's box that's recently
been unwrapped. The gift tag in the foreground reads:
  'To Mom from Santa X X X'.
Copy line:
  'Give unto others as you would have others give unto you'

Admittedly – we're in seventies England now – there *was*
Basil's famous Blake's Curtains commercial. You must have
seen it. The one where the commando sets the flame-
thrower on the Blake's curtain mounted on a metal frame.
Of course, the frame melts but the curtain fails to ignite.
And I will concede that that commercial was brilliant. But
I'll bet it was the art director's idea.
    Since then he's done nothing of worth. I mean ads like:

SEE SCENTS! – Picture of a bottle of some or other perfume –
AT HALEY'S YOU CAN BUY 100ML (BRAND NAME)
FOR THE PRICE OF 75ML.

Or there's:

WE CAN'T MAKE YOUR CHILDREN MORE INTELLIGENT –
Photo of kid at computer – BUT WE CAN INTRODUCE THEM
TO SOME INTELLIGENT COMPANY –
Tag line: XANADU: THE INTELLIGENT COMPANY

They're hardly a passport to arrogance – are they? In all
honesty, I reckon that the best stuff in the Bastard's book is
the stuff Horace O and I have produced under him.

23

Anyway, we heft the Bastard into a cab and take him up on the offer of staying in the restaurant with the agency plastic. Horace orders a £240 bottle of cognac which I agree to share with him. But balancing here, both hands firmly clasping the table, swallowing hard to postpone the volcano of hot puke, I'm struggling with what I need to say.

'H, gimme something to pull out of the lag.' H connects and rolls a *Rhubarb and Custard* my way – which is better than nothing. Though I have to say, in my experience, Es and crushes don't exactly mix. And thankfully I don't have the woman's number – yet.

When it comes to doing things to birds Seb is worse than useless.

He can't even shoot straight. Even when we're sighting up on cans, Seb can't hit one. So he's got no chance when it comes to the real thing.

It's good when you can do something markedly better than your older brother. It's also dangerous. But for now, as long as Arnold sticks around, I'm OK. You see, although Arnold's my brother's age, when it comes to doing things to birds, I'm his friend – not Seb. Age and bodily strength don't figure when you've got a gun. Besides which, Seb has no imagination for inventing new and better fates for the birds when they're dead.

When we scored open the sparrow, to see whether it was Arnold's or my slug that got it down, and its guts flopped out like macaroni, Seb puked and couldn't eat his supper. Ha, ha, ha. And when we make holes in them and put bangers in, so they explode all over the shop, Seb goes indoors. He also thinks that wearing a crow's foot in bed brings bad luck. He's inside now because he considers it cruel that we've strung out a blackbird to find out how long it is inside.

I feel a deal safer when Seb's indoors. Besides which, he

24

certainly wouldn't approve of what we're trying to do this afternoon. It involves a crow. A live one.

Arnold, who really knows what he's doing, has rigged up a variety of crow traps. The first consists of a simple fish hook, baited with a piece of stewing steak, hung at low crow height in one of the oaks. Trap number two, and we both think this is a long-shot, is constructed out of a tea-chest, supported at an angle with a stick. Attached to the stick is a length of string. The idea is to pull the stick away and trap the unsuspecting crow in the box. But, as I said, it's a long shot – crows are shrewd. The third, and most elaborate of our traps, is really a full-scale version of the second. It involves cordoning off and heavily baiting several square feet of prime crow-feeding grass with yards of green netting. The netting is draped over a semicircle of long canes and weighted with rocks on the ground and stones along the diameter of the roof for rapid collapse. Lengthy deltas of string run from the bottoms of the canes, through the grass, to us crouched in our bush.

We've tested it. It works. Now all we need is for the crows to come.

We've been waiting, silent, for perhaps half an hour. It's so exciting I fear that I'm going to wet my pants. And I'm so scared that I'm not going to pull my string in time. That the crow will get away and it'll be my fault – and I'll be as useless as Seb. Now it's starting to get dark and soon I'll be needed at home for supper. Still no crows want to explore our trap.

'Reeechard,' calls Mother with an embarrassing shrillness. I arrange to meet Arnold here at seven the next morning, hopefully without my git brother.

This evening Seb's being a pain. Literally. He's giving me Chinese burns, dead legs, arm twisters, and nipple scrunches. Of course, he's punching my arm and kicking me up the arse as usual.

'You're a bloody little liar, Richard.'

'Leave me alone. I'll tell Father.'

'Well, I'll tell him what you've been doing to the birds.'

'I'm allowed to. They're our birds.'

'They're more mine than yours. I'm older.' He punches my arm. Hard.

'Get off, you bastard. I'll call Father. I will.'

'You do and see how bad you get it tomorrow, and the day after, and the day after that, and the day after that, until you die. You bloody, fucking little sneak.' He pushes me over and sits on my chest and arms and pokes my face and pulls my hair.

'What were you doing?'

'It's a secret. Piss oomph.' He holds my nose and places a hand over my mouth.

'You're going to tell me or you're going to die.' After many minutes (so it seems) my mouth is taking involuntary sucks at Seb's hand. And I'm trying to lift my head but it's banged back against the floor. Seb is rising and falling with my diaphragm. Now I'm giddy, giddy like I know something is about to happen. I know what it is. I'M GOING TO FUCK-ING DIE! But then I fade back into the frozen time. There's nothing I can do about any of this. Then this happens. But I didn't do it. I don't remember wanting to do it, considering it even, nor opening my mouth. But it seems I've bitten Seb's hand. He's thrashing around the room holding it, shrieking and shrieking. And my mother's in the room too.

'Look! look!' he screams. 'You can see the tooth marks. Look.'

I'm in my room, with a stinging arse and I'm still finding it a labour to breathe. Is it because I've been crying or because of Seb? Anyway I'm planning revenge on Seb and Mother. And I smile when I think of the crow trap.

I wake in time and flee the house to meet Arnold. He's brought some gardening gloves (to hold the crow with), a bowie knife and some wire. The petrol's still in place from

26

yesterday. He tells me that we must snare the crow then cut it from the netting before setting light to it and letting it go.

So we wait and wait. Soon it's afternoon again and we're cramped, hungry and thirsty and, I consider, about to give this up as a bad plan. Then it happens. Three crows descend simultaneously, just within the semicircle of our trap.

'Wait for it,' whispers Arnold. 'Wait for them to go in more.' It's a decent while before one crow proves sufficiently foolhardy. 'One, two . . . three,' Arnold hisses. Together we jerk our strings. And the trap collapses nicely to surround the bird.

We leg it over. The crow's flapping insanely. It's taken off and is dragging half of the trap behind it. But it's well ensnared.

'The rocks. Move them in. We'll weigh it down gradually.'

Now if you've ever been close up to a crow, you'll know just how bloody monstrous they are. Eagle-size and dead scary. But after all this there's no way we're going to let it get away. And if I bottle, I'll be worse than Seb. So with caution, and I guess a worthy degree of respect, we pin it in with the rocks that surround the trap. The crow is well frightened and, no doubt, a deal pissed off. And soon it becomes evident that we're not going to be able to get close enough to snare it. 'Look, we'll throw petrol on it from here. When it sets on fire it should burn through the net and fly off – on fire!' I run for the petrol. But walk back because I'm winded. It feels as though my trachea's tightened to a straw's width and won't let the air in. 'Hurry up,' yells Arnold. 'Run.'

'I can't,' I wheeze back. Arnold's pretty pissed off when I return. 'I'm sorry, Arnold. I can't breathe any more. Seb did it.' Arnold moves as close to the bird as he dares and pitches ribbons of petrol at it. Some lands on the crow, but not enough, I reckon, for it to go blazing spectacularly into the sky. The tin's empty and we back off. We both have matches, of course, so one by one we strike and lob them

towards the patch of fuel. But it's no good. Then Arnold lights the remainder of his matches and tosses the box in. And whoosh – a corner of my family's field is on fire.

Anyway, the crow manages to escape. It's a little bit alight. And it starts running from the scene. It seems unable to fly. So we give chase – trying to kick it and throw stones and the like at it. Then it just opens its massive wings and pisses off into the sky. And I collapse – with no panic, just a child's quizzical concern that there no longer seems to be any air in the world.

2

Arsenal vs. Pepper

My vertigo never lets me down. From where I sit half up in bed I can see Pepper in my spotless kitchen, in my white bathrobe, pouring us coffee. She's showered and minty-breathed and the sheen of her leg tan is softened with talc. Rumours of summer have reached the flowers and trees of Islington. At the window my Venetian rattles with a breeze that's almost warm and Mahler's Fifth quietly wakes me. In a month or so we'll be seeing the Emily Smith commercials on TV – they did so well in research that it looks like the Client might make the investment without the cinema test. Basil has upgraded Horace O's and my wheels as a result. Emily, my black BMW, is parked out front – smiling at passers-by. It's Saturday and I don't have a hangover. And it strikes me that it's about the best it can be without drink or drugs. That is except for one frustrating thing. But that'll come my way in time. Everything always does. Oh, and in case you're wondering, I skipped throwing a speakeasy or Mexican party for my twenty-third, and let Pepper cook me something with aubergines and we canoodled our way through a bollocks video.

She places the mug on my bedside speaker and walks around to climb in beside me. I'm stroking her damp hair and thinking that wet hair certainly suits Pepper Furnival. Scraped back (she's growing it) and neat, it gives her face agreeable definition. So I kiss her pepperminty mouth and tell her my prediction.

'It's going to be a good summer this year.'

'It's all those greenhouses,' she says.

'It's nothing to do with the greenhouses – it could piss down for all I care. It could fucking . . . sorry. It could snow. It's going to be a good summer because you're going to leave the other Richard and give me the job full-time. I've been pitching for this account for over a month now.'

'Making me feel guilty won't help your cause one iota.'

'We're going to fly away to somewhere that's dead hot. Like Barbados or Australia. And drink champagne cocktails in the setting sun.'

'Can I have a strawberry iced daiquiri, please?'

'If you insist. We're going to drink those until we feel good.'

'I feel good now.'

'I mean really good. Really very good. Shall I tell you how good I mean?'

'How good do you mean?'

'Right. We're hand in hand.'

'Hand in hand.'

'Yeah. And we're slowly walking from the taverna . . .'

'Where they serve strawberry iced daiquiris?'

'Yeah . . . along a beach lit by the silver Caribbean moon.'

'Not if we're in Australia.'

'It's the same moon, twit. Slowly I begin to undress you.'

'Undress me – whatever for?'

'I'm undoing each button and removing each piece of your clothing with my teeth.'

'Won't we look silly? Me standing in the middle of the beach, smiling at passers-by, as you tug away at my buttons with your teeth?'

'You'll be lying down at the time. Overwhelmed. In a frenzy of moistness.'

'With all that sand in my clothes and hair – hardly. And that's disgusting, Richard.'

'You won't mind the sand after all that champagne or strawberry goo.'

'If you want to get me drunk and rape me, why take me all the way to the Caribbean?'

'Different rape laws.'

'It's not something to joke about.'

'I'd rape you nicely.'

'Richard, that's not bloody funny.'

'Shut up and give me a Pepper kiss.'

'No, I don't want to. Besides, you haven't cleaned your teeth. You taste like a pub ashtray.'

'I don't go in pubs these days.'

'You liar! You and Jeez were totally – what do you say? – rat-arsed the night before last.'

'Yeah but it *was* a Thursday. I get pissed in moderation now.' It's a fact. Since I've been seeing Pepper I've cut back on 'bad' living somewhat. I've switched to low-tars, I've steered clear of powders, slimming pills and Es, and I only get lagged four times a week maximum. Sure I puff. But so does Pepper. Besides which, it's well known, puffing isn't bad for you. And show me a Londoner who doesn't get pissed three or four times a week and I'll show you a bad haircut and saffron robe. Even Pepper's not adverse to a spritzer or five of an evening.

Let me take you back a month or so. It's evening and we're in the wine bar. Pepper's on spritzers. Horace O and Jeez are on bottled lager – the type that's stored long enough for the sugar to turn to poison – and, of course, sour mash chasers, and I'm on weak Mexican shit (and I've only had five or six). And frankly I'm getting embarrassed at the way Horace and Jeez are carrying on. Alright, Jeez's raconteur bit is OK when you're as pissed up as him. But Horace looks like he's about to throw any second.

'My next venture,' Jeez goes on, 'will certainly be into publishing.'

'Yeah, books?'

'No, no, Horace, my friend. Magazine publishing. I intend to publish a monthly, free, aspirational magazine for London's young Epicureans, entitled *Young Wino*.' Horace totally pisses himself – even Pepper chuckles. 'Each issue will contain a listings section. A guide to establishments with a wholesome disregard for licensing laws. It saddens me to say it, but there are people in our good city, who trundle home at two o'clock believing that they've had a night out. That that is all London has to offer a dedicated young wino. Years of practice wasted – through nothing but sheer ignorance. Look! Look at him sitting there . . .' Jeez points with a straight and conspicuous arm. And, oh my fuck, the geezer's only looking. '. . . A young wino if ever one walked. But I'll wager that, as he staggers out of his taxi at one or two this morning . . .'

'Stop pointing at him, Jeez,' whispers Pepper.

'. . . he won't have the merest clue that within half a mile there's more likely than not a kebab vendor with keen under-the-counter interests.' He raises his voice. 'Kebab shop, sir. There's a kebab shop in your area that does late ones. Trust me. Cheers. You see, Pepper. You see. He's grateful.'

'He thinks you're bonkers, more like.'

'What about a section on how to pull out of a lag?'

'Excellent, Horace. Where to purchase essential, trustworthy pharmaceuticals in Soho at three a.m. And, of course, "Jeff's jolly Gin tips","Kingsley's killer cocktails". And, naturally, we will drag a bum from the street each month, bribe him to pull his overcoat open a tad and, hey presto, "Page Three Wino".' At this H spits beer over the table.

'Sorry Pepper, man. I mean girl. Woman. Yeah. Hey Rich, you OK?'

Now the fact is, because I'm off the strong stuff I've lost most of my self-confidence. I've been trying to think of good things to say to Pepper but nothing's coming. I mean, under normal circumstances, this would be my type of conversation.

'I'm sorry, man. I'm going down with a cold or flu or something.'

'Well, well, my man. We all know what to take for that.' Horace O laughs, '**drink-flu** man – we've all got **drink-flu**.'

'It's not **drink-flu**, H. I can tell. I'm just a bit out of it. I'll be fine man. Really.'

'You can tell?' Horace O is really chuckling now. 'This is the man who is, four o'clock Sunday morning, spewing out the window of the cab. Says to me in all fuckin' seriousness – in complete and utter seriousness – 'It must ha' been somethink I et.' Now this is all I need. And even Pepper's smiling. So I smile too and five minutes later make the excuse that I have to fetch something from the office and dash out. But I go into the Fox and swiftly down three pints of Lowenbrau and a triple Jack Daniel's, enough, I consider, to give me the balls to say something profitable to Pepper.

'. . . So I said to him, "My good man, the only criminal record I've got is a CD, ruined by the merest hint of a sharp B flat in the andante." So the humourless fucker nicks me.'

'You'll get a stretch, man.' says Horace.

'Of course, Horace. But doubtless my QC will ensure that I'm kept in the lap of luxury. And think of the contacts I'll make. Three months in low security and I assure you, my client base will be doubled within six.'

'Well, I think you should be put in prison for longer.' Everyone stares at Pepper. 'I mean, you think it's clever to sell your drugs. But actually, it's murder.'

Of course, Jeez maintains his composure. 'Pepper, my dear. Were I a hardware merchant and a customer purchased a knife from me, and subsequently saw fit to sever a proprietorial artery, would you regard me as a murderer?'

'That's a ridiculous analogy.'

'Quite the contrary. And I take offence. Not that you accuse me of murder – a truly honourable pastime in many respects. But that you regard me as having such little respect for my fellow man, that I would deign to interfere with his freedom of will.' He takes a haughty swill of his beer to emphasize the genuine nature of his huff.

Now, Pepper's like anyone in this respect. She's infinitely more desirable after you've had a skinful. So again, I'm watching myself from the outside, waiting for myself (or rather Pat), to say something worthy. Only this time I know that I'm pissed, so I'm staying silent. Riding the tide, so to speak. Then Pepper says this to me – sort of quietly, deliberately out of the others' earshot, 'Richard, you're being quiet tonight.'

Of course, it doesn't register first off. I'm concentrating on the silk of her breath on my face. And by the time it does hit home, the pause has been great enough for my autopilot – my built-in intelligent answer device, comedian, charmer, thank you God for *Pat* (*abbr.* patter) – to cut in (which is precisely what I've been trying for all fucking night). Coolly, Pat says, 'I was at his house with Horace one night and they were getting unbelievably wrecked. Unbelievably. And Horace says to Jeez, "Hey man, I'm bored. Turn the telly on." So Jeez crawls over and offers it the spleek.' She chuckles and I continue for a good half-hour in a similarly witty manner.

So we're upstairs in the Crown and Two Chairmen – just Pepper and me, that is – swapping disaster jokes. And I'm trying to get Pepper to drink more. She's saying things like, 'I'd better have a pineapple juice this time.'

And I'm saying things like, 'If your train skewers off Victoria Bridge tonight you'll be glad I talked you into another wine.'

And she's saying, 'OK, but just the one more. Then *I really have to* get my train.'

And as we're leaving L'Aquila, bloated and in love, at

about forty-five past midnight, Pepper says, 'I'm not going to make it back to Sutton. Am I?'

Later, as we lie nose to nose in my spring-balanced king-sized, she giggles, 'I feel so guilty about this.'

'You *know* I'd have given you the cab fare.'

'I know.'

'So you craftily engineered your way back here.'

'I did no such thing – you got me drunk.'

'Are you happy?'

'I might be.' At this point Pat steers my hand up inside the back of her T-shirt. And she's says, 'Please, don't do that.' So we move apart. And it seems to me that the other Richard (the 'proper boyfriend' that is), although he's three hundred miles away, is lying between us.

So as is wise in such situations, I spend the next few days ignoring her. That is until the following Thursday morning when she, somewhat bravely I feel, re-opens negotiations in the lift.

'What's up with you then?'

'I'm sorry Pepper. It's this Landsdown job. I've been plum high in soap powder. But, even if I do say it myself, the campaign – it's the cat's arse. And it should be over by tonight. Maybe sometime – not tonight, I mean we could go out for . . .' And the lift door slooshes open. But Pepper doesn't move. No, she's waiting for me to finish. I hesitate. She smiles. I hesitate more – psyching the girl good.

'Maybe what?' she grins.

'Maybe . . . I'll do something thoroughly unpredictable in a second.'

'Richard?' So I press the ground-floor button, wait until we're resealed and lurch over and shove my tongue into her face. Dead suave like. Like I'm in some goddamn film. And what an inspired move it is – for she reciprocates whole-heartedly.

Of course, we should have pretended we were nipping out

for something when Basil got in at the ground floor. Then again he seemed too hungover to notice my hand placed awkwardly in a trouser pocket and Pepper's ninety per cent magenta cheeks.

So for the rest of the day they're back: the conspiratorial smiles, the meaningless Post-it messages, the accidental hand-brushing. And I'm considering that both of the campaigns I'm working on are going rather well.

Then, as is the nature of this glamorous profession, just as Horace and I are about to piss off for a well-earned high strength or ten, we're hauled into a meeting.

'Och, c'mon. Ye can' sey tha noow. It's six already,' moans Basil to Robert – the Account Director – head suit. 'It's yer oown fuckin' fault. Ye should have briefed it in sooner. We've had fuckin' no time at all.' It's rare but, obviously, Horace O and I are in total agreement with Basil.

'You wanna be here till midnight. Again?' I contribute.

'If necessary,' he says, 'Look. Do you want to keep the account or . . . ?'

'Listen, smarm bucket,' this is Horace getting dead pissed off – thumping pissed off, I'm hoping. 'You saw the work in progress. You've been poking your greasy head in all day. Why didn't you say something earlier? Eh? And . . .'

'Look, I've just . . .'

'Don't fucking interrupt. And none of us got out last night. We didn't get out at lunch and we're not going to get out tonight.'

'Yeah,' Basil and myself – simultaneously.

'As I was saying. I've just spoken with the client. She's been out all day – alright? And when I indicated the way we were going, she said she thought it was wrong. Now, it's not my fault. I'm just conveying what the client said.'

'Tha's just i'. Glorified fuckin' messenger boy. We do all the fuckin' work and you on a hundred grand or more an' a fuckin' Porsche an' ye canni even communicate with a fuckin' junior a' the client's. Listen. Ay'm the creative director an' I say i's

36

good work. Ay'm heppy wi' i'. So pu' tha' in yer pipe an . . .'

'Listen, listen, listen!' I shout. 'Compromise. Why don't you call back? Use all your highly paid skills to get the meeting put back a day or preferably two and then we'll all be happy.'

'Because, Richard. Their MD is, as we speak, working up a dose of transatlantic jet lag. Does that answer you?'

'No, Robert. He's going to be in London for more than a day. Surely he's got other things to do. Can't his agenda be shuffled slightly? I mean, the presentation is only going to take an hour – max. He's not coming all the way over from Miami for this, is he?'

'Trust me. I know how the organization works. And that, incidentally, is one of the reasons I earn my salary. Now we've wasted enough time. I suggest we get cracking or we really will be here all night.' And he pisses off out of the room.

Of course, it's a fuck awful feeling. Knowing that for a third session running we're going to miss opening time. Really, it's enough to make each of us weep. Obviously, it's slightly different for the Bastard – he did lunch and, judging by the accent, he's still got a little fuel left. But sure as hell he's crashing down.

Because we're all thinking the same thing, nobody speaks. Basil gets three beakers and shares out the last of his gin. There's a little knock at the door. Pepper pokes her head in.

'Alright if I go now?'

'Och, Pepper. I'd be grateful if ye'd hang aroond for a wee bit. There's still some more to do.'

'I was arranging to meet someone. Should I phone and cancel?'

'I think that might be a good idea, if ye don' mind.'

And I'm thinking that at least one good thing has come from all this. You see it's poor Pepper's job to copy up all the documents, bind them up, then do colour stats and package up the presentation – after we've done our bit.

Now I'm in two minds here. I half want to get everything done by closing time – obviously. And I half want it to be too

37

late for Pepper to get home so that I can suggest that she comes back. But thinking about it, there's no way in hell she'll come back if she's sober.

If you're an advertising creative you'll know all about this type of situation. The art director is going to go with absolutely anything the copywriter suggests because it takes so long to scamp up then create half-acceptable layouts. Then he/she's going to look in advertising books and *Creative Review* to nick a hot idea. And, of course, you're going to go with anything that the creative director, or advertising books suggest. But at the end of the day – and I promise you this – you'll have something absolutely out of this world.

At nine o'clock, we've finally got Robert to agree our concepts. So now he's a bloody good bloke again and we're on the same side. At ten thirty I'm still struggling with the body copy. All I need is three or four drinks to loosen up and I'll be fine. But nipping out to the pub just isn't on. Not when your art director is chucking colour markers around and shouting because he can't find the right stock shot to pilfer.

People are feeding Pepper documents like she's some sort of machine. I go up to her. My plan is, of course, to tell her that, if she's going to have difficulty getting home – being a lone woman, like – she can always . . . you know. I mean, I'll go on the sofa, and that.

'What?' she asks angrily.

'Nothing. I just came over to breathe some words of encouragement. And say, I'm as fucked off as you. And that if we get out before closing time, I'll get you a large one if you want. Nothing heavy.'

'How long do you think we're going to be?'

'I dunno. You know what it's like here.' She growls and tears well up behind her glasses.

'I wish I'd never taken this bloody job. It's hell here.'

'Huh! Then you'd never have met me.'

She touches my hand. Then she says, totally out of the blue, like – and shy with it, 'Richard, if we have to work

38

really late, would it be OK if I, you know, stayed at your place? I mean, I could go on the sofa.'

'Pepper, it would be an absolute pleasure.'

'You sure? I wouldn't want to put . . .'

'I'll call the butler and have him prepare the guest suite.' She laughs. And I'm wondering if the frustration of the evening has disintegrated so totally and instantly for her too. Someone hands her a document and she tuts.

Back at my desk I have reason to do some thinking. Now, don't get me wrong. I think sexual assaults and muggings are as fuck awful as you do (assuming you're not a rapist or mugger, obviously). But listen. I can't count the number of times I've been out with women in town and it's gotten late and I've managed to get them back to my gaff because it's too dangerous for them to go home alone.

Then it clicks. Bosh! like that. It's like cracking the head-line when you're on the can. Understanding the poem, so to speak. Pepper Furnival (and the others, for that matter) could easily take a cab if she wants to. She could dial an account car, at any time of the night, and she'd be back in Sutton in an hour.

Then I get to thinking about cabbies. If no one got mugged or raped and that, then half of them would be out of a job. I wonder how they feel. And what about charity workers . . . ?

See how your brain reels after more than twelve hours on the same ad? So I ask Horace, 'Horace? Blackcab drivers. They're worse leeches than solicitors. Think about . . .'

'Black cab drivers? What you on about? Most of them's white.'

'No black taxis. You know . . . ?'

'Is this important?'

'No, not really.'

'Then please, do me a favour and shut the fuck up.'

It's around twelve thirty and we're nearly done. Pepper is still scurrying around like a puppy trying to get the documents in order. But we've all got that good, deservedly knackered feeling. The work is totally fucking brilliant as usual. And it's all been worthwhile.

When Pepper's finished and the presentation is complete, Robert says, 'Ladies and gentlemen. Did you really think I'd let you down?'

'You what?' I say.

'Wait,' he commands and goes into his office. He emerges hefting a crate of wine. Basil gets the corkscrew and beakers from the water machine and says, 'Now gentlemen.' Basil's sober by now. 'You'll forgive me if I'm entirely mistaken. But am I to conclude that, by virtue of your efforts tonight, you are entertaining thoughts of perhaps not lending your efforts to the agency for the greater part of tomorrow? If so, I should warn you to think hard and think again.'

'You what, Basil?' snarls Horace.

'You see, I've taken the liberty of booking a wee table at L'Aquila for twelve o'clock.'

'Yo. Good man, Basil.'

'Unfortunately, Robert, you will be otherwise engaged. But you will, of course, have every opportunity to enjoy our company at a later stage. Shall we say next week?'

'Yeah, yeah. Lunch on me next week. It's a promise.'

'Diary it now then,' says Horace. 'You owe us about ten lunches this year.'

'And, I trust that on both occasions, we may be privileged by the presence of the both charming and beautiful Miss Furnival.' Pepper gacks back a whole beaker of wine and I'm figuring that she's going to say something like: 'Not if you ask like that, you arsehole.' Or do a fingers down throat routine. But she's learning.

'That would be very nice, Basil, Robert. Thank you.'

We're tipping back wine like it's some sort of race. It's almost down in one, pass the bottle, etc. And I figure that this must have reawakened Basil's lunchtime supply because he says, 'Richard, now you don't have to answer – really you don't. But are you boffing my secretary?' Then – thank fuck

– Pepper walks into earshot. 'Pepper,' the Bastard only continues, 'I was asking Richard . . .'

'Basil man, leave it out.'

'No Basil, persist at your leisure,' contributes Horace. 'These are indeed questions that must be answered.'

'Pepper, my dear.'

'What?'

'You and Richard. Are you . . .'

'Fuck off Basil,' I tell him. 'It's none of your fucking business.'

'Ah so. Pepper. Tell me. Are you and Richard here, how shall I put it? . . .'

'Fucking?' says Horace.

'. . . something of an item?'

Pepper scowls at him good and hard and for a fair while before answering. Then she turns to me, grabs my head and smacks a major wet one on to my cheek.

'As Richard said, it really is none of your fucking business, Basil.' The point here is – I haven't even got past her T-shirt yet.

'More wine, Pepper?'

Then a week or so later this happens.

As I think I've told you, I'm a copywriter. As such, I've got a PC to do my writing on. And like all the PCs in the office it's networked up to Sidney. Anyway, my secret is this: I've managed to mole, via Sidney, into all the luscious agency files. Payroll files: so I know what the likes of the Bastard are on. Personal files: so I know who the likes of Vivienne are fucking. Accounting files: so I know what the agency really turned over last quarter. But more importantly, I can hack into Pepper Furnival's personal file. And how delicious is it? It's like pawing through her knicker drawer, or reading her diary – all from the safety and comfort of my desk.

41

Anyway, I'm in Pepper's menu and I notice she's set up a new file, MARI.LET.

Dearest Marianne,

I've done it again. Fallen head over heels for a bastard! He's called Richard (he'd have to be) and he works where I've got this job.

I'll tell you the good things about him first (there aren't many) so you might forgive me. Firstly, he's bloody gorgeous-looking. Medium height, dark hair, skin wow! Except for some ugly gouge marks on his hand and about a dozen or so round scars on his forearms, his skin is out of a soap ad (God! did I say that. Am I getting like them? If I say 'OK' too much when I next see you, or 'absolutely' even once, don't ever talk to me again). Then there are his eyes. Oh my God! His eyes. He makes me laugh, he's intelligent, he's got money (not that I give an iota – well not much of one), and well, that's it. Oh, and he doesn't seem to mind my dragon skin. Apart from that he's an absolute shit.

The worst thing about him is his friends. I can't begin to describe his friends. Imagine Matt, with his rugby friends in the Union. These guys are ten times worse. I mean, they don't undress and they're not particularly sexist (they are in the normal way, of course) they're just SEEDY. Horace O, his best friend, drinks as much as the entire rugby team. I'm not exaggerating. And Richard consumes at least half that much. And when he's drunk he's disgusting. He swears a hell of a lot when he's sober, but when he's drunk it's every other word.

He's also totally selfish (my type – eh?). I don't know quite how to explain, I mean, he's generous with his money. It's just the way he acts. He walks about here as if he owns the place and expects everyone to drop what they're doing for him. I can't think of an example right now. But you know when you're talking to someone and all they want to talk about is themselves. Oh God! That's what I'm doing now, isn't it? You know, I could cheat and put the next bit at the top if I wanted to.

How are you Marianne? How's the MA going? How's Ciaran? (Lovely man that Ciaran. Give him a hug from me.)

Anyway, I spent the night with him. We had to work until about midnight. I couldn't be bothered getting a cab. Besides I was a little drunk. No, no, no, *of course* we didn't do anything.

(Of course I didn't want to. Of course I didn't. Of course I did – lots and lots and lots.) Did he try anything? Of course he did! But, and you won't believe this after what I've said about him, he took 'no' for 'no' like a good boy. And he still talks to me.

I've got to go now. Some pig has brought me a mile and a half of figures to type. I'll write again tomorrow.

Hello. It's me again. It's tomorrow.

Oh dear I feel so guilty about (Newcastle) Richard.

And guess what? I spent last night with (London) Richard. No, no, no, of course . . . we only snogged a bit . . . a lot!

But it's Pepper the prostitute from now on!!! On our way into work he offered to buy me a new top so no one would know I'd spent the night out. And, I don't believe it, I accepted . . .

Good news, wouldn't you say? Apart from the odd libel. I can drink more than Horace, any fucking day!

I'm up now and dressed and still trying to get Pepper to agree to come on holiday with me.

'Why don't I pay for it for your birthday!' Pretending, as one does, to come up with the idea on the spur.

'I don't want you to spend that sort of money on me.'

'Pepper, many hundreds of women would lap up the chance of spending a fortnight in Barbados with me and my credit cards.'

'They're called whores. And you're free to take one on holiday if you want. I don't care one iota for your money. I'm bloody well not for sale.' So I zap on the telly to watch *Saint and Greavsie*. Pepper makes her boredom obvious. And to annoy her the more, I light a cigarette from my smouldering butt and fetch a tin from the fridge. I belch loudly as I swallow the first sublime half. She says she's going. I say nothing. So she just goes.

Now, there's nothing that irritates me more than feeling

43

uncomfortable about things, letting situations or other people get in the way of my love of the here and now. I mean – how fucking dare they? It's my fucking life. So I drink a few more tins of beer and some vodka to get some positivity back inside, and go to Highbury to watch the Gunners play Man U. But Man U don't figure. No, this ninety minutes is Arsenal vs. Pepper. The fact that Arsenal are losing isn't helping. There again, there was a half-decent fight in the Clock End, which cheered me up for a few minutes. I decide to call Pepper and apologize. Then Arsenal score and I think it best to play pool and have a few drinks in Finsbury Park.

It's kicking out time. I'm steaming and broke. I lost a great deal of money by being over-confident of my pool-playing ability with the shrewd Irish drunks.

Now, if you're like me, and shit scared of things that bite, it's always better to be loaded when you're in this manor. A drink or two inside me, and I don't cross the road, like I normally do, when I see a hard dog or group of youths approaching. In fact, I believe I'm dead tasty. I really reckon I can take on anyone and their fucking dog. So I don't regard it as a problem that I'm singing, 'We Love You Arsenal', at the top of my voice as I stagger down Seven Sisters Road.

It's around four a.m. when I wake up with a routing head-ache in a shop doorway on the Holloway Road. My first thought is that I'm recovering from a disaster. I must have been mugged or attacked by Spurs fans or a dog. But I'm alright. I've still got my credit card and I reckon the dried blood on my hand and arm is from my fall. I vomit once, take a leak in the doorway, do a pulse count (105 – shit!) and head towards home like a broken robot. And I vow, as one does, to quit drinking, smoking, going to football, play-ing pool, having casual sex, singing football songs when I'm alone and pissed, making cigarette burns on my arm and being nasty to Pepper. Yeah, and I'll be honest with you, I'm weeping a little. I just feel so terrible. Having dog-shit up my trouser leg doesn't help. All I want is to be in bed, curled up with Pepper, not feeling all this fear – and for the world to be a beautiful place again.

I pass an abandoned mattress. And yeah, I'm feeling just too low to light it.

It's leaden dawn when I get home and the birds are mocking me with their stupid optimism. I clean up, vomit half a pint of red wine into the bidet (although I don't recall doing any wine), take five or so anti-diarrhoea tablets and build a stick to calm down. But this makes me paranoiac and convinces me that I'll die in a disaster if I carry on partying. This is desperate. Being bombed is wondrous. Being sober is sublime. It's the in-between bits, the shadow-times, that are so unbearable.

Now, the way I've painted it, you probably think that, by now, I'm sleeping with Pepper Furnival. It's true, I am. And that's the one frustrating thing. That's all. Sure we kiss a bit. We may even fall asleep clutching one another. Leastways, Pepper is happy to drop off in my arms. I find it rather harder. But I'm working on it. Still, when I think of her in Newcastle, being nailed by the ideologically sound and moderate-drinking other Richard, it gets me like an uppercut in the diaphragm. And it also makes me a deal resentful towards the self-righteous Pepper – which doesn't help the pitch. Say I've taken her out for dinner, maybe even some crappy musical as well, and I'm lying snuggled up against her with a hard-on that's trying to pull my rectum out (trying to get into hers). I only need to think of that tosser up North, with no money, too lazy to visit her in London, with his licence to touch her in all the places that are off bounds to me – and I won't get to sleep for another hour. So these are the things I do for revenge. I dial my own number with my mobile under the duvet and pretend I'm asleep when the phone bleeps; I get up, take a really jangly piss with the door open and pull the chain; I gradually second the duvet, so that she wakes up and has to get it back; I scratch the bottom of her foot with my toenail then pretend I'm asleep. Then I fall asleep – more often than not waking, half an hour later, in a torque, as the ladle of goo flushes into the front of my boxers.

First the bad news. I downed two cans of Super, along with a lot of milk for my stomach, to get right. It means that I'll get the shadow-time tomorrow. Now the good. I noticed that I had some messages on my answerphone. Three were from Pepper and she sounded pretty upset. They went like this.

First: 'Hi-er Richard. If you're listening please answer. Please call me as soon as you get in.'

Second: 'Hi-er. I'm really sorry about this morning. I really need to talk to you.'

Third: 'Hi, it's me again. If you're not phoning me because you're angry, I understand. But please do. Look, about the holiday. About everything. You know. It's alright. It's just, I dunno. I'm sorry Arsenal lost. Please call me, Rich.'

There was also one from my git brother Seb, telling me not to be so immature and get in touch.

So I re-record my answerphone message so she knows I'm in and go back to bed. Yeah, I'm buggered if I'm going to call her. I'll let her sweat for a bit. Ha! But lying here, imagining all the excellent things I'm going to get up to with Pepper, I recall what she said about Arsenal. You see, I was *there* and they drew. So I zap on the teletext and learn of the disaster.

3

This Mountain Water Feeling

It's unlike I expected. I'm referring, of course, to the disaster. In fear, in premonition, it was always so much worse. I mean, there's only so much pain a human body (or is it a human mind?) is capable of dealing with. After that you just get the limit of pain – the worst pain there is. Press a lit cigarette tip to your skin and after ten or so seconds it stops hurting. Then again, if you're lucky like me, you keep falling unconscious. It really is best to try and relax – to blackout for a time. Don't even think about how long they're taking to dig you out. And fill you with lovely opiates.

Some people are obviously hurt less badly than I am. They must be or they wouldn't be awake. I can hear them moaning, shrieking at times. My body's anaesthetic takes me out of all this – as soon as I regain consciousness and start to feel the pain. It means that I must be hurt quite badly. Occasionally, I'm thrust into consciousness with the certain realization that I'M GOING TO FUCKING DIE! Then I fade back into the frozen time of the accident. There's nothing I can do about any of this. This dark then light then dark then light then dark, except passively hope that I'll wake in the light.

I wake to the light of the TV. I'm sharing the pillow with the intestines of a doner kebab. And it's still there. I didn't fucking dream it! Three-one to United. So I shove the dead kebab to one side, count 103 beats per minute and roll back over – and try to forget my problems by concentrating on anonymous and gratuitous sex. But I'm temporarily impotent. So I do some sound hangover sleeping.

Perhaps five hours later I wake and fumble for my inhaler. Fuck! I must have done a hundred cigs yesterday. The phone's cawing and I'm about to answer. But I realize it's probably Pepper and I leave it to hear her message. But it's not.

'Horace. Yo. Well I'm feeling pretty shit right now. I'm gonna turn on for a bit. And if I can get my pulse to under a ton I'll cab round.' So I build a six skinner, swallow a 5 mg Diazepam and go for a bath-smoke. Then as I'm settling down the phone goes again. This is Pepper's teary message, 'Fuck you, fuck you, fuck you, fuck you,' etc.

HEALTH TALK
Dr Cathy's Casebook

Each week Dr Cathy Smith answers some of your
health questions

● **I suffer from cold sores on my lip when I'm run down or it's particularly cold. A friend of mine told me that they can cause genital herpes. Could I infect my boyfriend during unprotected sex?**

Cathy says: Your friend is right. Herpes simplex one (facial cold sores) can be the cause of herpes simplex two (genital herpes). But don't worry, infection can only be passed on when a cold sore is open and it has direct contact with your partner's skin. You should certainly avoid oral sex when a sore is active. And if your boyfriend doesn't suffer from cold sores himself, then you shouldn't kiss him on the face or anywhere during that period.

● **I've read a lot lately about RSI. I'm a secretary and use a word processor for seven hours a day. Is there a big danger of me developing it?**

Cathy says: RSI stands for repetitive strain injury. When RSI is caused by typing, the symptoms are sharp pains in the hands and wrists, a stiffening of the joints and, in severe cases, the inability to pick up everyday objects. Unfortunately, anyone who does a job which involves repeated movements is at risk. It affects tennis players, factory workers, journalists and secretaries alike. So far the only known cure for RSI is rest. In extreme cases, up to two years off work. And I'm afraid that the only preventative course is to avoid repetitive strain, i.e. change jobs. Switching to a job that involves more clerical work and fewer hours typing would certainly reduce the likelihood of you developing RSI.

● **About a month ago I tried LSD for the first time. I didn't really enjoy the experience and don't plan to take it again. My problem is that from time to time I still hallucinate. It's awful and I'm terrified that the LSD has given me permanent brain damage.**

Cathy says: LSD stands for Lysergic Acid Diethylamide, a drug which if taken in sufficient quantities can cause hallucinations. It is illegal and you've behaved very irresponsibly. But I think you must realize that. The first thing you must do is to stop worrying. It's unlikely that you have brain damage. Although the main effect of the drug rarely lasts for more than twelve hours, it is common to experience . . .

This bath is good and giddy-hot. I'm supine and stoned and slooshing the water back and forth to the rhythm of Mahler. In fact, it's so sublime and womby that I can't even be bothered to reach for my lighter to explode the occasional bubbles of fart. And I reckon that the time's right for me to consider a couple of important developments. Psychological developments. My symptoms.

The first, I've named, **disaster-fear**. There was a time when the disasters happened at a safe distance – when, apart from the fact they were on the news, they were fictional. The third world has always been a prime arena. The Soviet Union is another favourite. And you get the odd hurricane in the States and Australia, a scattering of pit collapses in the North or Wales. But never anything serious in London. I mean, a London disaster is a footsie avalanche or a Labour by-election win.

But now! London's getting a share of the real fuckers: the slow and cruel scythe of AIDS (Hell, I turn the ads off), hurricanes, tube fires, train crashes, boats going down. And I'm convinced I'm going to be in one.

Maybe it's the drink and chemicals making me paranoiac, but it seems that the disasters are honing in on me. Trying to pinpoint my exact location. I mean a bloke went under the tube at Angel last week – an hour before I was there. I mean I could have *seen* it. Or worse still . . .

Now, I told you about my prescience – my vertigo. Well my vertigo tells me that I'm going to be in a disaster. I mean, the way I stagger home sometimes, setting light to abandoned consumer durables, the way I drive, swear at strangers – I *deserve* to be in a fucking bad disaster.

But the worst thing – the thing that most convinces me – is my recurring dream. In each dream, as I'm lying waiting for the rescue workers to cut me out, I *know* this is the disaster that I've been waiting for. The real one. And I get a vertiginous recollection of the past dreams – the premonitions.

The second development is the birth of *Gary*.

Gary is Pat. Pat mad! Gary is Pat on a crash-down. Gary is someone who needs to be physically suppressed, caged up – but at times it's impossible. He's my garrulous drunken inner-speak – escaped. The big problem with Gary is that he says things, terrible things – out loud! And I can't stop him.

Now, the way I look at it, we've all got a little bit of Gary in us. You can hear him speaking loudly when you shouldn't. So loudly that you wonder whether you actually said it or not. But he's in your head. He's safe. Gary is the man that likes to abuse hospitality, shatter love, ridicule bombast.

Let me give you a situation from my own experience. I'm in a dead important new business presentation. The boardroom's been polished, right down to the leaves on the yucca. And we're all bowing and cock-sucking to the Client. The directors who are usually obnoxious and arrogant are vomiting urbanities and bonhomie across the table. And I've got to play along. So I'm introduced as 'our find' or 'our young genius' to the chairman of some place that could shove millions our way. I'm shaking his hand and I get this overwhelming urge to whisper something like, **I wouldn't get too close mate. I picked up a nasty dose of crabs the other night**. I mean, obviously I don't say it. But I feel I've thought it loud enough for him to hear. So maybe then I'll blush. Then I'll get dizzy because I'll think of more things to say. The meeting could have reached the point where the Client is showing a little doubt. And there's this intense silence. Everyone's trying to divert their eyes from the imaginary stacks of notes on the table. And I might get an unbearable need to say, **Holy shit! Has someone guffed?** It's OK, I'm in control. Then, it's like when you're a kid – when you really want to laugh. Fuck! I'm trying *so* hard not to laugh. Then I think what it would be like if someone really did produce a rasper. And it makes me want to laugh even more. So I can't look anyone in the face. I mean, even if a little laugh came out, obviously, I'd be out. (Not that getting another job wouldn't be a piece of piss.)

Try this for size. I was with Pepper. She'd been lounging at my place all weekend. It was Sunday. And I was feeling hot and claustrophobic. A bit sick from my hangover, and all. And she was being over-the-top affectionate to me. Clingy. Trying to hug and kiss me all the time. All I wanted was for her to go. Just to leave me alone for a time. Stop touching me, you know? I mean, I knew I'd become lonely if she left – but I could always go to the pub or a mate's – catch a party somewhere. Anyway, internally, Gary was saying some very loud things.

She'd just cooked for me and gone out and bought wine and cigarettes – she even got me fags! – and I considered, you can't get much better than that on a Sunday. Under normal circumstances Pat should have been doing the talking. But because I was sobering up – because Pat was coming down – Gary was trying to speak, urging me to yell, **This is really disgusting. Please, fuck off.** And things like, **C'mon Pepper we're not having any fun. Why don't we call it a day and you go home?** Things that would really destroy her. I mean, I was seriously trying to contain an impulse to dab her with my cigarette end. And then after each impulse I'd feel so guilty. Like I was responsible for this beautiful and frail child, and the last thing I would ever consider was hurting her. Anyway, the things Gary wanted me to do were getting worse and worse. Like throwing the food at her or even roughing her up a bit. Then it just came out. From nowhere. And Gary just said, 'Pepper, I love you.' It's the last thing I wanted to say. And you can imagine the fucking trouble it got me into. She's round now virtually every night – legs crossed, obviously.

Oh yeah, I quit my job.

The point is, things at work aren't going particularly well at present. Yeah well, there was a balls-up on the Emily Smith job. We couldn't get permission to use the music, or it was too expensive or something crap. I mean, it was something that we – not necessarily me, well, definitely not me – should have checked out. So the Client's thinking of pulling the whole fucking thing. Of course, it's me that takes the stick. And, of course, there's the other thing – **The Lie**. So one morning the stress was getting the better of me. Basil was laying into some of our work. And ripping up from my subconscious were words like, **We're fakes. We can't do the work. Just leave us alone**. But I controlled him.

Then: 'Fuck you and fuck your job,' just flew out. How sick did I feel? Imagine puffing a quarter of Skunk on half a bottle of vodka. Horace O was aghast. I had no option but to storm out – or tell them about Gary . . .

No, no, I'm not unemployed. Horace came into the pub – where I was supping mournfully and testing my bravery with cigarette tips – and informed me that Basil had refused my resignation and wanted to take me for lunch.

The message. Huh! Looking back, I reckon it was a dose of Gary on Pepper's part because, when I fell out of the cab that night, she was sitting on my doorstep just wailing her eyes out and shaking like a beggar with a sodden blanket. Now Pepper being the sort of person who generally has her hands on the reins, the situation was enough to sober me up almost completely – after I'd thrown up (more red wine as it happens). Of course, I'd forgotten how much of a shit I'd been and kept saying, 'Who's died? Who's died?' As I've said, I'm expecting a disaster.

OK, this is the story. The other Richard: horse-shit! He was Pepper's *Lie*. He was her excuse for not consummating our friendship. Why didn't she want to go that far? Embarrassment. The eczema. Pepper's scared to take her top off lest I think her repulsive. Oh yeah, and she's also almost a virgin. (I'm not sure I should have told you that.) So what happened? Nothing. I just spent the night holding her while she did a heap of grizzling.

Now, you know what it's like in bed the next morning when you've opened your hearts the night before. Yeah, you're breathing the fresh air of honesty and feel close as kittens in a box. So we both rang in sick and Pepper looked after me because I had bad stomach cramps and vomiting. In fact, I was so bad, I threw up on the pub floor at lunch. But I forced some drink down in another pub, to get right, and we went back to take Pepper's top off.

'When I'm happy, sometimes you can't really notice it. And Richard, I do feel happy.'

'It wouldn't have mattered if you had scales.'

'I do sometimes.'

'Scales!'

'Well sort of.'

53

'Well you're a mullet then.'

'A mullet?'

'Yeah, tough scales outside but dead nice inside.'

'You really are lovely. I've been so silly, haven't I?'

'Shut up, Mullet.'

Ah, the sweet novelty of having the lovely Pepper Furnival whimpering beneath me – all soft, warm and almost smooth. And even more novel is this mountain water feeling of having been *totally* off the pills, booze and cigarettes for over a week. And as I heave up into Pepper's warmth, hear her give a little gasp, then lift her back slightly and gently work the white Betnovate across the archipelago of her shoulders – I'm thinking, 'Yeah, I could happily never pick up another pint glass, drop another E or suck another reefer if life was like this full time.'

'Good comes from bad.' That's today's motto. You see, even as we're reaching the thrashing stage – that comes from making love several times before in a morning – I can't feel it. I'm referring, of course, to my ulcer. It's the reason we took the week off and drove Emily to Devon and I stopped my bad living. The way I look at it is: my bad living was to do with the stress of my work – **The Lie** not helping – and the stress and bad living together conspired to blow a hole in my stomach lining. A potential disaster if ever there was one. But, as ever in my life, it's all worked out for the good.

All anyone has to do is suffer the shadow-time: the come-down. Take it for the shit it is. Realize the necessity of shit. That there are positive aspects to shit. And once you're man enough to swallow just a couple of days' negativity you get given this whole bunch of positivity. It's a different kind of high than cruising on drink and pharmaceuticals but it's just as good. Nar, better. You see, it's *moral* hedonism.

I mean, I've slowed right up. I'm *seeing* things now. Silly things. A couple of seconds ago I was noticing the way the breeze was making the lace loops on our bedside lamp do a Mexican wave. And it just made me want to laugh out loud. I'd never have wasted my life with such trifles before. But the real point is: it's the trivial things that are the most important. Let me give you an example. At the moment my hand is resting next to Pepper's neck and we're just touching. And the really important thing is, I can feel Pepper's pulse. It's the tiniest sensation. But it's everything. It's responsible for all the years of her being the excellent Pepper Furnival: her capricious answerphone messages; her cradling hot coffee in two hands; the way she clings to my arm in her sleep; the nascent ponytail that she half wants to lop off and half wants to grow; her in one of my shirts, down past her bum, collar sticking up; her cracking the face-pack with a laugh; the way she can't eat tagliatelle without first cutting it up; her animal-free make-up; her ever-clipped nails – so that she can't scratch; the way she greets me with, 'Hi-er', her arms outstretched and smiling; her trying not to cry by growling and, of course, the way she holds me so tightly when we make love that I fear she's going to crack. I'll tell you what this *seeing* caper is like: it's like being born a painter or a writer, it's like doing your first acid.

In fact, I feel so together (pulse – below 90) that I may even chance a tipple tonight and then again I may not – ha!

'So what does Pepper want to do today?'

'I'm too sore to do anything.'

'It's one o'clock, you know.'

'I'm still too sore.'

'But it's a nice sort of sore – isn't it?'

'Mmm. I'm not so sure. Can we drive to the sea please? I think I need one of those creamy ice creams. But you must promise not to frighten me.'

'But Emily gets so uptight if I don't drive her fast. She might throw us into a field if I drive her slow.'

'Please. I won't go in her again unless you promise. Now.'

'How fast is fast?'

'Speed limit fast.'

'Pepper, I haven't had a drink all week, I haven't even had a cigarette, no pills, no hoogs. You must allow me one vice.'

'It's up to you. Drive your bloody car as fast as you like. I'm not going in it.'

'You going to get a train home?'

'I'll get the bloody train home now, if you raise your voice again. Besides . . .'

'Don't poke me!'

'Besides, you've had your vice. All week with me.'

'That's a vice, is it? Taking a week out to make you happy.'

'Who said I was happy about it?'

'What, in the name of all that fucks, do you mean by that? You weren't enjoying it? Is that what you mean, Pepper?'

'Look, stop trying to argue with me. God, you're so sensitive. Of course I enjoyed it, you . . . you . . . male! It was lovely. Richard, it was really . . .'

'Get off.'

'Richard, I was only joking. C'mon silly, let's drive to the sea. Sensibly.'

'I don't know if I want to go to the fucking sea.'

'God, you can be a baby at times.'

'Alright, let's go to the pissy sea: the radioactive; sewage dump; fish fuck in it; snot green; dead sailor; smelly oil; used rubber; mullet scale; slime round your legs; puke bucket of a sea.'

'Give me a kiss first and say you're sorry.'

So I wheel-spin a salvo of stones over the hotel and screech on to the Devon road then decelerate to no more than ten miles an hour. Half a dozen or so cars follow like rolling-stock, and – ha ha – none of them can overtake me because their crappy road is barely wider than my BMW. I'm expecting someone to hoot or yell some abuse but no one does. People aren't like that in the country. Pepper, being from Sutton, *is* giving me some abuse. And I'm saying, 'Pepper if you're concerned, why don't you get out and tell them the problem?'

'Please, please, please, please, please don't do this to me Richard. Please, please.'

'Do what?'

'Fuck you, fuck you, fuck you,' etc.

Anyway, I have a talent for knowing just how far I can push something, so I speed off to lose the other drivers, and continue on sensibly.

We take our ice creams into the dunes. Pepper's walking quite a way in front of me and we haven't spoken since we left the car. So I think: 'Fuck her!' And I lie down to smoke one of the cigarettes I've just bought and reflect on matters.

Now, I'm of two minds here. It's perfectly feasible that this life of fresh air, denial and taking time out to appreciate things is the best way for a person – well, me – to live. It seems morally sound somehow. Guilt free. Since I've been out here I haven't once dreamt of the disaster. And it's also feasible that the reason I'm so irritable is because I've been entombed in a room with Pepper for too long. (Shit, this cigarette is good.) On the other hand, I've only been here a week and I'm piss bored. Sure, it's a good change, bouncing to exhaustion six times a day and waking up without a hangover. But I'm beginning to miss the nirvana bliss of swilling in a dark pub with Horace O, then snorting a line of chaz and surfing on the delirium of London's bacchanalia. I'm young, confident, good-looking and rich. London's a couple of hours down the road with its clubs full of champagne, chemicals and good-looking women. And here I am, in a poxy village full of daft yokels, with the moody Pepper who's nothing that bloody special anyway. I don't know. All I want is to be turned-on – the whole time. And it strikes me that this is a shadow-time. A hangover from drinking too much sobriety and virtue.

So I'm staring up, trying to detect pornographic images in the voluptuous cumulus. And out of the blue, it hits home. If the other Richard was a lie, how come Pepper mentioned him in her letter? At once the clouds writhe into a disgraceful orgy and I find that I am in need of a long reflective jag.

'Give me money. There's got to be a fucking buffet somewhere on here.'

'So you're talking to me now.'

'Are you happy? First fucking class. Are you fucking happy now? Are you going to lend me some money or what?'

'Look Richard, it's not my fault. I'm genuinely sorry about everything but it's not my fault.'

'I'm too bloody cross to argue about it. So just leave it. Alright? Gimme your handbag. I need money and aspirin.'

TALK TOPIC
Headaches

Women have more headaches than men – especially at bedtime. It's a joke as old as the hills. But a disturbing report published in Germany last week reveals that women really are prone to more headaches than men. On average women suffer eleven per cent more headaches lasting twenty minutes or more than men of the same age.

This week we take a look at the phenomenon of headaches and attempt to answer some of the questions most often asked.

Q **The headache at bedtime syndrome. Is it a total myth?**

A *Obviously a woman should be free to refuse sex at any time whether it's with her husband or not. However, men can put undue pressure on women to have intercourse. Such pressure could indeed cause the woman a very real headache. So men, next time she says she has a headache, she probably has.*

Q **What is the best 'cure' for the occasional head-ache?**

A *A number of simple remedies can be used. These include a glass of water, mild exercise or temporary change of physical environment. Painkillers such as aspirin and paracetamol are effective. However they can cause gastro-intestinal irritation and indigestion. And remember, only take one or two. More than this will usually give you no extra relief at all.*

Q **What can I do about frequent headaches?**

A *There are two main causes of frequent headaches. The tension headache, which is caused by muscle contraction, and the vascular, migraine-type headache, caused by dilation of the cranial blood vessels. In either case, you should consult your family doctor. You may be advised to change your lifestyle slightly (for example your GP may suggest that you do more exercise or practise a relaxation technique) or you may be prescribed a tranquillizer or sedative that will combat the tension itself. Alternatively for a migraine-type head-ache, you could be prescribed one of many drugs, depending on the severity and type of migraine you suffer from.*

Q **Are any types of headaches warning signs of some deep-seated trouble?**

A *Yes. Frequent headaches; headaches which always occur in the same location; headaches which resist previously effective medication; headaches accompanied by personality changes; headaches which are sudden and severe at the onset; headaches accompanied by neurological changes such as hallucinations, convulsions, fainting, weakness . . .*

An hour later Pepper tries to put her arm around me but I shrug. And then she starts to blubber. And that really is about all I can take. I mean there are other people in the compartment by now. 'Stop it Pepper.'

'I'm sorry. I can't help . . .'

'Pepper, look! There's a bloke there with some tins. The buffet must be that way. Stop crying by the time I get back. OK? . . . OK? Pepper by the time I get back you'll have stopped crying. OK? Don't fucking answer me then.'

When I'm back, with a box of those whisky miniatures and

some tins of Kronenbourg 1664, Pepper's stopped crying. I sit down and she starts again – really loudly. The couple opposite are staring out of the window pointing and naming the things they pass.

'Oh! A horse.'

'And if I'm not very much mistaken that is a Chinese necklace poplar.'

'You know, I think you're right.'

'And there's an orchard' etc. But they keep glancing over. And *I'm* getting fuck furious. I need to stop Pepper from crying. Then have a go at her for last night. I'm getting that hangover anger, you know, that really impatient, itchy scrotum anger. I'm whispering things like, 'C'mon Pepper. Please stop crying. Alright, it's not your fault . . . only it is. A bit.' And thumping in my head are things aimed at the ABs opposite. Things like, **There are plenty of seats. Would you mind awfully just fucking off**? And, of course, just plain **FUCK OFF**! In between, I'm whispering, 'Oh please Pepper. Please cheer up . . . God you're making me really angry now . . . Sorry I didn't mean that. It's just last night and everything.' Anyway, I'm obviously not going to say anything to the couple, but if I were it would be a toss up between, 'Tut, cancer,' and 'What do you reckon: abortion or marriage?' I break open a tin and the bloke turns. Our eyes meet.

'A drink sir?' I offer him the tin. 'Or would you rather watch the show with a clear head?' Instantly Pepper stops grizzling and stares at me. No it wasn't in my head. Gary said it. Out loud. Now, I'm staring at the bloke – out of surprise at my loss of volition, I reckon. But he obviously construes this as me wanting to make trouble. And he mutters, 'Sorry. I'm sorry. Sorry,' and they shuffle out.

Obviously, I feel a mite awkward. The knowledge that the mendacious Pepper Furnival is probably still seeing the other Richard – and there's nothing I can say or do about it – isn't helping. Nor is being on this fucking train. Pulse at 104.

*　　*　　*

'It's happened. It's past. Get light. Feel good. Drink more and smile,' smiles Horace O ethereally – or rather, bombed. 'It's a pisser. But it could happen to anyone. And the Bastard, he can't say a thing . . .'

'Yeah I know, he's on five years.'

'C'mon, drink more. We're celebrating.'

'I'm not in a very celebrating mood H.'

'Rich, your heart still beats out the rhythm of your life. Drink and be merry for the day before yesterday you nearly totalled yourself. Splat! Like a ripe, red plum. Splat!' He hammers a fist on the table and the butts in the ashtray leap up – like their team's scored. Jeez comes back with the round. He puts a hand on my shoulder and says, 'In my not so humble opinion, I believe the patient to be suffering from mild shock. Fortuitously, the pharmacist . . .'

'Cut the crap Jeez. I'm not interested.'

'Seriously Richard, I have some exquisite Barbie dolls.'

'Yeah, and I still have about two hundred units of liquor in me.'

'You'll be fine. Just the one. Go on.'

'No no. I'm trying to cut down on that shit. I'm serious. No offence, Jeez.'

'None taken, my friend. And if you change your . . .'

'Cheers.'

'Take one,' advises Horace, 'It'll make you better fun.'

'I don't want to be better fun.'

'Now Rich, there are many plus points.' After poking one good and hard up his nose Horace begins laying matches on the table for the plus points. 'One: You're alive, not even scratched. Two: You've a fine and legitimate excuse. You had a couple of drinks because you did arguing with your scaly girlfriend. Show *her* to the beak, man, and you'll definitely be let off.'

I'm shouting above their laughter, 'Four fucking times over the fucking limit!'

'It was a big row. Three: No one else was involved man.

Four: You can drink wherever you go now. Five: You can show pictures of the car at parties, if it's as bad as you say it is. I believe they take pictures for evidence.'

'Do you think they'll make me pay for the wall? And the fucking tree? I could even get banged up. Second DD, and all.' And, of course, there's my other previous to consider. Oh my fuck.

'Six: You won't get banged up. Seven, and this is a good 'n: Play your cards right and you might even get a salary rise in lieu of the motor.'

'Get real, Horace.'

'I mean it. When we move job.'

'Move job.'

'Move job. I got a call when you was off.'

'Shit! Who?' Wow! I've always wanted to be head-hunted. 'Tell me about it.'

'I don't reckon I should tell this guy *nicht* until he gets more fun. Waddya reckon, Jeez?'

'Well Horace, far be it for me to press a man into drinking. But you have a certain point. He is – how can I put this nicely? – rather fucking up the evening. No offence, Richard.'

'None taken, my friend.'

So I drink some shorts and narrate what I said to the old couple on the train and about being so wrecked that I left a football match at half-time.

'Excellent, my man,' says Jeez after each bit. I drink faster to stop him being irritating. And Horace O tells me that some two-bit head-hunter has *hand-picked* us for a lucrative opening at an undisclosed agency. Jeez tells me that I probably haven't got an ulcer and if I have it's only small or else the pain would be much worse. But he'll give me some Andursil which means I can drink as much as I want without puking blood. And Horace O informs us that `drink-blood` is perfectly normal.

Anyway, we've wound up in this club. It's not so much a

nightclub as a members' drinking club – you know, snow-thick carpets, marble table-tops and leather armchairs, brown and soft as cowpats. Of course, when you're with Jeez, you're a member everywhere. The crowd is bohemian-Sloane, the drink: champagne. And the chemicals: bad cut candy (mostly whiz – leastways, if you're buying from Jeez it is – unless, of course, you know him). We're at an art preview, I think. But there are too many people here to get a view of any paintings. Jeez has business to attend to – so Horace O and I are slumming it at the bar in the snooker room, getting pretty shit-faced and eating Es like they're M&Ms. Horace is ejecting little sprays of saliva like one does on the street and I'm **forgetting-drunk**. Do you know what I mean? I mean, Horace staggers off for a piss and I wait here wondering where the fuck I am ('Hey, what pub am I in, mate? . . . Ah, fuck you too!') and who I'm here with. I mean, I know whoever it is will be back. And I remember whoever it is, is one of my good friends. But I just can't remember which one. It could be Jeez, Richard Juggler, Horace O, Pepper, or even someone I haven't seen for a time. Of course, part of being **forgetting-drunk** is that you don't give a fuck. Yeah, I'm really steamed. I mean, I had all that whisky and 1664 on the train, didn't I? So how is it that I end up spending so much profitable time with an art student on this Sunday night? Maybe I put an E in her drink. My normal tactic when time is short.

4

Lime Jelly and Pig Liver

I hit my menagerie of alarms off – bell, bleeper, radio and fog horn.

'Oh my God! Oh my God!' screams the art student, wiping herself with my bathrobe. 'Oh my God.'

'Oh fuck,' I moan, wiping my eyes and reaching for my inhaler and a cigarette.

'Oh my God. You bastard.'

'You what?'

'You've only fucking wet the bed.'

'Oh my God! Fuck-shit. I'm sorry.' (Gary helps – or am I still drunk enough for Pat?) 'Charlotte.'

'So you remember my name?'

'Sorry?'

'Well you asked me it about ten times while you were trying to screw me.'

'Did I? Sorry.'

'Do you remember anything?'

'Not much. You're an art student, aren't you?'

'That's what you kept calling me. Remember? "Wanna drink Art Student?" You fell asleep while we were doing it, you know?'

'Shit, I'm sorry.'

'Did you have a bad dream, just now, when you were wetting the bed?'

'Yeah, fuck awful. Listen, I've got to get to work. Can I get you a cab?'

'Is this it then? I just come round, you piss on me then

64

tell me to piss off? No numbers, nothing?' Now I'm looking at her. She's smooth and naked as an eel and her good looks are piercing my hangover. And I'm thinking that I actually wouldn't mind seeing her again and being less drunk. Still, I don't mean it when I say, 'Give me your number then. I'll call you later in the week.'

'Take me somewhere nice?'

'I find it hard to believe that you're actually prepared to see me again.'

'Do you always get that drunk?'

'No, of course not.'

'Yeah, I'll go out with you again. You're an interesting case.'

'OK, I'll call you. Later in the week.'

'No, I think I'd better take your number. You seem un-reliable to me.' She heads purposefully towards the bedside phone.

'No don't call me here. You can't. I'll give you my card. Ring me at work. But not today, eh? And er, sorry about things.'

It's around eleven when I arrive at work. And the strangest thing happens. I lock myself in the khazi, scare the shit out of myself with a pulse check, then dissolve into some purposeful weeping. It's the fucking accident. It keeps replaying itself over and over. Only each time I don't just get out and casually stagger off towards the hotel. It becomes the disaster. And it's my side that's screwed up like a chew-ing gum wrapper. Bits of me are trapped or severed and I'm waiting for the rescuers, in unspeakable pain. What are the worst things you can possibly imagine happening to you, physically? Please, imagine them now, if you can. I mean it. It's those things that are so vividly bursting into my mind. Only, now, I'm not like you – I can't control it. Suddenly, I realize that a shard of metal has pierced a testicle. I can see my lap because an eye swings over my chest. I'm para-lysed. One of my hands is hanging off. Or worse still. Much worse, I think. Pepper's in the passenger seat and I'm OK. And I'll admit it, I'm thanking God – actually talking in my head as if I believed in God – for sparing my fragile life, my soft skin, my delicate organs, my friable bones. Shit, the dreams should have been warning enough that the disaster is catching up with me. And I vow that I really am going to quit misbehaving for good. As soon as I've gotten right over lunch.

It's not that I really need another drunk, especially after last night and all. I mean, I could quite feasibly take this hangover on the nose and come in tomorrow feeling regular. But I have a couple of delicate matters to deal with and, frankly, I'd feel a heap more confident with Pat doing the talking. Also I've got clap-fear after my unsafe encounter with the art student.

Horace O, red-eyed and mulatto pale is hiding behind a mountain of colour markers, reading a book called *The Varieties of Meditative Experience*. Huh! I nod and he grabs his coat and we amble off to the Intrepid Fox.

I order our drinks and realize that my hands are shaking too much to carry them. So I go and join Horace.

'I can't do it.'

Horace understands, there are days when he can't pick things up. He brings us our drinks and I half say, half sob, 'Oh my dear God, I'm so fucked. I'm so fucked.'

'Shhh. Drink.'

A couple of pints later I'm OK enough to light my own cigarettes and my fear is subsiding. In fact, I'm feeling the confidence of a man who's lain someone new and good-looking. As soon as I can be bothered to talk, I'll boast to Horace. Then the worst possible thing happens. Basil the Bastard walks in. Of course, the police informed the company first thing this morning, didn't they?

'Basil can we talk about it after lunch? I'm not in the fucking mood.'

Basil's laughing. 'Richard, there's nothing to say.'

Basil and Horace O are both laughing at me now and I'm a touch concerned that I'm going to cry or something.

So I ring Pepper from the pub and she says, 'Richard, there's nothing to say.' So I lock myself in the pub shitter to nurse my fear in solitude and perhaps burn a few holes in my arm.

An hour later I hear Horace growling to the relief of an overdue piss.

'Alright, Rich man?'

'Yeah. Shit, I was just doing some thinking.' I open the kludgie door to a well-looking Horace O.

'Thinking! In the crapper? For an hour? Huh. What about?' he demands.

'Nothing, H.'

'The scab woman. Huh?'

'No man, about when I was young.'

'Shit uh?'

'No like whether something happened or whether I dreamed it – it's weird.'

'Huh. Like I said, shit.'

'H man, do you ever remember things?'

'Do I owe you money?'

'No, no. I mean things that happened a long time ago. Things that you'd thought you'd forgotten. Childhood things.'

'The speed and the puff they unlock many doors. Doors of perception, doors of paranoia, doors of ecstasy, doors of creativity, doors of memory. A Saigon Rose Stick courtesy of the Bastard. Taste it.' And as I inhale the sensemelia and feel the smile begin to rise from the pit of my stomach, Horace says: 'You're in trouble. Big trouble. Woman trouble. Scaly came in with this.' And he hands me a note. 'Me and the Bastard both reckon you should kill it. The scabby one is a no-good woman.'

'So you've both read it? And why the fuck do you insult my girlfriend so much?'

'Man, you'll be insulting her good when you've finished that. Ah, ha, ha, ha.'

Dear Richard,
   The reason I didn't want to say this to you face to face is because you frighten me. You get so angry, I think one day you're going to hit me.
   I don't suppose you remember much of the train journey. Insulting that couple, making cigarette burns on your arms, insisting passengers take your pulse every five minutes, throwing cans at people at the station, nearly punching the guard, and trying to pull the communication cord when they wouldn't serve you any more drink.
   I'd say you were an alcoholic, I'd say you were a drug addict, I'd say you were a lager lout – but you're not. You're worse! I seriously think you might be mentally imbalanced. You seem to lose control of yourself at times. One minute you're so lovely to me (although you've only said you loved me once) the next you're calling me a scaly mullet and telling me to get out of your head. I can't handle it. I can't handle you.
   Richard I'm so confused. I'm almost crying as I'm typing this. If someone talks to me I expect I will. When I woke up this morning I was an explosion of red – and it had almost cleared by the end of the holiday.
   I do love you so much and I don't want to dump you because you've got problems. But I don't see any alternative. If you want to talk about it with me that would be great. But please, please, when you're sober. If not, I guess I'll have to hand in my notice.
   With love Pepper X X X
   PS. You're the best boyfriend I've ever had. I really do love you.
   PPS. If you don't want to talk about it, could you bring my things into work sometime?

'You absolute bastards, reading this.'
   'Entirely the opposite. Your allies. Now, best drink.'
   'Best be sensible.'
   'You know it's good for you.'

'Besides.'

'Exactly – besides.'

In unison, 'The one never hurt anyone.' We do a respect and resume things.

And of course the letter was utter bullshit. Three days later, Pepper Furnival's saying, 'I really don't know why I'm doing this.'

'What?'

'Don't talk with your mouth full. But if I'd have known you were such a good cook.'

'The reason you're doing this is because I'm a lovable rogue. I admit I have been roguing a bit much of late. But from now on I'm going to behave. I promise. And the reason I'm such a good cook is because I've got a microwave and the Italian on City Road delivers.'

'So, do you love me then? Scabs and all?'

'Please Pepper, not while we're eating.'

'If you love me and you're going to behave, you won't open another bottle.'

Pop.

'Whoops.'

You know, in candle light, Pepper looks really quite good news. She's arranged her hair so that her ponytail is on top of her head, like a whale spout and she's wearing the tom cats. And as I sit here, drinking fairly moderately (OK, I had the one bottle before Pepper got here. But this is a dead important occasion. You see, I'm going to confront her about the other Richard), I'm reckoning that I really have got life sussed. I mean, I've got a cinch job, a decent posse of mates, and I know how to control things. Take drink and drugs, for example: sure I do more than my fair share of hard parties – but the point is I can control myself. I never let it affect my work. Drunk, sober, up, down, stoned or straight, I write brilliant stuff. In fact, apart from Gary, I'm in utter control.

Two days ago, Pepper passed on her stupid note. We had

a brief chat after work, and she said that she'd give it another try on strict condition that I visited Drink Crisis. So last night I met a DC counsellor. I told him about my lifestyle, not pulling any punches. And do you know what he said? He said in the first instance, I don't drink regularly enough to be an alcoholic; secondly, I don't drink enough; and, thirdly, I'm not secretive – alcoholics are very secretive. In short I'm just a kid making hay. He even gave me a 'To whom it may concern' note on official letterhead. Do you believe that? Pepper did, until she saw the logo artwork on Horace's desk yesterday and dumped me again – on a fucking Post-it note. I ask you. So how is it she's here eating dinner and drinking wine with me now?

The answer is romance. A couple of hours ago Pepper had a visit at home from one of our account cars. She took receipt of a cassette and a key to my flat. On the cassette was my suicide message. Of course, I made it quite clear that the onus was on her to save me.

'You have (retch, phlegm-up, hawk, barf) my key. And, by the way, I told the cab to wait ten minutes for you.' Well, you know how anger can switch itself to affection like that. Especially in the face of a candle-lit dining room bedecked with bouquets and perfumed with hot garlic.

You see, I know how to control things. Take the Emily Smith Children's Summerwear. For whatever reason, we couldn't use the original version of 'Hey Joe', so Jeez (who's our R&E man when he's not doing business) does what he thinks is the next best thing. He hires some session players to impersonate it. It's dire. Like a fucking busker with a practice amp and car battery. Anyway, with all the legal wrangles, we were overshooting the deadline and were forced to show the commercial to the Client, who naturally enough coughed fur balls. A few days later I'm splitting cans and snorting snow with Jeez in the studio and, ding! I'm on an amyl hit. I know the solution. Take off the vocal and rip through the melody with a guitar and sample in bits of the original vocal track. Of course, it works. Dead SOA. And it's really fucking subtle. Better than the original in my book. And, of course, the Emily Smith mob buy it. And how about this? – 'Lay Lady Lay', same treatment (imagine sampling that for fuck's sake!), with a couple of kids on sun loungers? Yeah, of course it'll get pulled first airing but it'll get Horace and me in *Advertising Week* – which is what it's about after all. The other ones feature a kid in some groovy gear in the back of a Land Rover – SFX: Instrumental and sample of Iggy Pop's 'The Passenger'. And a garden party with loads of kids all dancing away to 'Everything Begins with an E'.

Now, Pepper thinks that we're going to finish our meal and settle down for a nice little canoodle on the sofa, but she's wrong. You see, I've got us both on the guest list to see some mates of mine, the Plum Jugglers, at the Town and Country Club. In hindsight, I reckon this idea is probably bad – us getting on so well and that. But it's too late now. The lift'll be here in twenty minutes.

We're sitting backstage with Richard out of the Jugglers, having a puff – and Pepper's really unimpressed. I'll give her her due, she put up a good show of being grateful for the night out and everything – but she's really not very taken with Richard at all. He's arrogant because he's almost famous (if you're into indie music, you'd probably recognize him), he spits on the floor, he drinks bourbon from the bottle, he's permanently bombed and he puts on this fake mid-Atlantic accent. I like the man. So we're talking about the normal sorts of things: bands we've seen recently, fights we've done, whether he's fucked anyone interesting of late, the old Es vs. Charlie debate etc., and Pepper decides she's had enough. Right, remember what I was telling you about control? We could drink back here for at least another hour and probably go back with the band and get properly wrecked, Richard has a permanent spliff on the go, we're surrounded by good-looking women and semi-famous men, and I agree to leave with Pepper – after just the one more drink.

And as I lie in bed, smoking a post-coital jade, I feel glad that I didn't broach the issue of the letter. I mean, it's true she lied to me, but I lie all the time. Moreover, she hasn't had a chance to escape to Newcastle. She's not mentioned him. And she never writes to him on Sidney – I check every day, obviously.

I cup her crusty shoulder and wonder if I could be nice enough to her for long enough to make it clear up completely.

'You'd think that he'd have the decency to offer her his seat.'

'You talking about me?'

'I'm sorry. I'm sorry, you were reading, after all. Maybe you didn't notice, but the woman standing next to you is pregnant. It might be a nice gesture to offer her your seat.'

'Well don't look at me. I didn't put her up the duff. Besides, it might be a beer gut for all you know. You shouldn't go around commenting on people you don't know.'

'Well, really!'

'Look love, do you want the seat? Go on, have the seat.' The fat woman ignores me so I go back to my reading.

TALK
Life Begins at 92

Interview by Georgina Prate

[Caption] *'People expect gems of wisdom, but I'm as foolish as I was at seventeen'*

[Caption] *'Of course all my heroines are based on me. Though I employ touches of imagination when it comes to some of the more exotic romantic passages, if you get my drift.'*

Feisty as ever, Beatrice Smith will be celebrating her ninety-second birthday next month. The month also sees the publication of her fifty-third romantic thriller, *The Pallbearer's Daughter*.

'Perhaps as death grows ever nearer, I'm growing morbid,' she chuckles. 'I do hope so. No, no, quite seriously, I see a profound affinity between love and death. I'm far too close to the edge to accept that death is a loveless abyss.'

At just over 1,200 pages *The Pallbearer's Daughter* certainly demands a commitment from readers. But fans won't be disappointed. The plot weaves its way through murder, betrayal, romance, sex, not to mention incest, grave-robbing and, of course, Smith's great love, history.

'Of course my novels are historical,' she says. 'I'm historical.' And she's off cackling into her coffee . . .

'Superb. Thoroughly superb. Look I don't need to see any more, your reputation proceeds you.' I could kill Horace O. I could fucking kill him. 'So shall I put you up for it?'

Horace, 'Yes definitely.'

Gary, 'You mean *precedes*, ignoramus.'

'Yes, quite. So I'll arrange an interview. It really is a fantastic place and I'm sure they'll love you.'

Fifteen minutes later, in the pub Horace says, '"You mean precedes, you ignoramus." Why the fuck, eh?'

'I didn't like him. He's an arsehole. And you. Why the fuck did you show him the **Lie** work? I thought we'd agreed. A clean start and everything.'

'It's bullshit that counts in this game, man. Besides he's only a pissy head-hunter. Stella?'

'I'm not drinking with you, you fucker. I don't believe it. I just don't believe it. I could fucking kill you.' He raises his arms kung fu style.

'You could fucking try.'

'He's obviously going to mention some of the numerous accounts we've worked on to the agency. I really can't believe you did that, Horace.'

'Trust me. Two Stellas, my good man.'

Of course, truth always triumphs. Even if you need to lie through your teeth to get to the truth. Let me explain.

Quite simply, we got away with bloody murder. We've been offered the job as senior team at Rocastle, Upton and Tyrone (RUT) at preposterously more money. It's a wet dream come true.

So how did we navigate our way through the complex map of **The Lie**?

The Lie, as I'm sure you've gathered, is Horace's and my book – our portfolio. I mean, we are talented, we've done some fantastic work in our time. But to get the job with the Bastard, we needed some live work – not scamps and the stuff we'd done on pissy placements. So, quite simply, we created a book of other people's work. Middleweight TV, radio and press ads. We even took polaroids of posters that impressed us at the time. Obviously, we genned up on the agencies that had done the work. What various people were like, so we could say we knew them. And we presented it as our own. We figured that, by the time **The Lie** was rumbled, we'd have our own book of live work and could make a clean start. Anyway we managed to hold on with the soused Basil for over a year. As for the clean start, the greedy Horace O saw fit to perpetuate things with the head-hunter and we sank further into the imbroglio at our meeting with RUT.

For a couple of days prior to the interview we scoured libraries for trade magazine back issues and association journals and wove a filigree network of sub-lies. Obviously, we had to claim that we'd worked at the agencies that actually did produce the **Lie** work – only this time, we split the work up and claimed we'd done it separately. We simply told Imogen (our new creative director) and Keith (the executive creative director) that, previously, we were each teamed up with various other people – the people that actually did the work (yeah, we named names, 'I think he's at Martyn, Thomas, Wright now.'), but we broke our teams up because we discovered that we really sparked together. Of course, we chucked in a few details for good measure. 'Yeah, I worked with her for a time. And you shouldn't believe everything you read. The split was in fact very amicable. Oh, you didn't see it? And Horace O, stupidly, broke up one of his early teams to take a position in New York, but you know

how they treat their art directors like studio boys over there
– yeah, screw the septics . . . Joke, joke . . . No, we didn't
think Kurt Tyrone was a Brit . . .'

And so, with a month to clean up, dry out and get sharp,
Horace O and I can look forward to life without the Bastard
and the prying Pepper Furnival. But again, we're inextri-
cably tied to **The Lie**.

Now, I'm supine here, tied to the bed, a lot less bombed
than the last time I saw Charlotte. And shit, is she kinky?
Lime jelly and pig liver! To tell the truth, I feel a mite
vulnerable. I mean, there are books from the Female Press
on her shelves. And I'm wondering about the safety of my
credit cards and inhaler, and how hard it is to get biro off
dick.

Pepper's due at my flat in half an hour. And doubtless
she'll arrive having slow-cooked her stew of gripes: not been
sober since we made up; forgot to take me to lunch – or
more likely, too drunk; never listen to me; puked in my
boot; all take and no give; hang around with perverts and
junkies; don't put CDs back in covers; deliberately hide my
Bob Dylan CDs so you can listen to the Plum Jugglers, Zola
the Gorgon and Sisterectomy; just use me for sex; wet the
bed, etc. etc. Anyway, I've had it with Pepper. And this is
my way of telling her she's been dumped. I'm going to be
richer now. I can probably afford to rent in Bayswater or
Knightsbridge. I really don't need the clinging Pepper to
interfere with things now they're going so well. I mean, I'll
be able to do Chaz now, instead of Whiz, crappy slimming
pills and Es – imagine what that'll do for my social standing
and come-downs.

Now, as far as I'm concerned, this little session with Charlotte is over. But, as you know, I'm at a slight disadvantage
and can hardly take my leave at present.

So I tell Charlotte, 'My turn to tie you to the bed,

Charlotte.' You've probably guessed my plan. I mean, I'd put a blanket over her before leaving.

But she says, 'It's not my thing.'

'Well, I'm not sure it's mine.'

'Oh, I think it is,' she rejoins, clambering on to me. And I decide to stick around a little longer.

'If you don't piss off now, I'll call the police.'

'C'mon Pepper, get a beaker and have some champagne.'

'I mean it Richard. And you Horace.'

'Listen sis, if he wants us out, he should have balls enough to say it himself.'

'He's too angry and I'm just doing what I've been told. Now pack your stuff or I'll call the police. I will.'

'I'm going to see him.'

'Don't do it, H,' I say.

'Please Horace, I'm just doing what I've been told. Don't cause any trouble.'

'What about our money and P45s?'

'I'll sort it out. I promise. But just go. Now.'

So Horace O and I put our few possessions into a couple of boxes and are set to leave the employ of Basil the Bastard for good, when the Bastard himself leans round his door and shouts, 'Oy, you two.'

'Yo! Basil.'

'Och, fuck off! You ungrateful bastards. Especially you, Richard. Especially you.'

'C'mon B. No hard feelings.'

'Fuck off!'

Now, I can appreciate the Bastard's sentiments at this moment. I mean, a month ago when Gary made me resign, Basil stood me a five-hour lunch and persuaded me to stay. Because I'd resigned by accident, it shouldn't have been a hard job. But I'm shrewd and have a talent for knowing how far I can push a thing, so lunch cost him dear: a 2K pay rise

76

(back-dated, cheque made out for cash) and a little more fucking respect – eh, Basil? So you can imagine his indignation upon receiving this.

MEMORANDUM
TO: Basil   DATE: 1st June
FROM: Richard
RE: **Stuffing your job up your fat arse**
Please accept formal notification of my resignation.

So I hack into Sidney one last time to see if Pepper's written any letters to Richard – not one – and piss off to The Fox.

Six hours later – pulse reading dead on the ton – and we're in the wine bar with most everyone from the agency (except the Bastard and some of the jealous creatives who never liked us anyway) being offered good luck and congratulations on the cavalier manner of our resignation. And I'm wishing that Pepper wasn't here tonight. More than that I wish she wasn't making it so bloody obvious that I'm *with* her.

'I bought him that.'

'It's lovely, Richard.'

'Yeah.'

'It was a little *I'm sorry* present.' Whispers, 'I blew him out for dinner.'

'Oh Pepper, you naughty thing. Were you waiting all on your lonesome, Richard?'

'Driven to pig's liver and lime jelly.'

'And,' Pepper whispers at me angrily, 'drawing on your thing. You sicko.'

When you drink enough, you can fuck yourself so badly that you can get seriously shit-faced on a couple of lagers. Unfortunately for me, I'm not at that stage yet and replenishing my *joie de vivre* is a costly and time-consuming business. In fact, I've developed such a stubborn tolerance of late that I can drink export lager – which is near on twice as strong as regular lager – from opening time to closing, and only be pretty pissed. I mean, we've been on the sauce since the Bastard – or more accurately the leech, Pepper – ejected us, and the rest of the crew, who arrived at seven, are a deal more pissed than us.

Indeed, would that I were now nullified, for these are Gary's disturbing urges: first, to rip my new shirt and tell Pepper about Charlotte; second, to say that I don't want to see her any more; and third, to lift up Pepper's top and show everyone her eczema, or push a cigarette into her arm. Of course, these things simply serve to make me guilty and in love with her. So I'm kissing her cheek and squeezing her hand and other clingy things, things which almost make her giggle with delight. Yeah, she reckons that I'm going to sacrifice the better part of my leaving party and stay sober enough to do shagging. Fat fucking chance, Pepper. Another of Gary's humourless impulses involves saying something quite degrading to the waitress (I won't say what). She's got the confidence of the over-beautiful and deserves to be brought down a peg or two. Another is tripping her up when she scurries by with her over-confident tray. And the other (actually suggested by Horace O) is – no, I can't tell you that.

Jeez suggests that we consummate the celebration with a line or two of C in the kitchen. I think this idea is bad. It'll make me self-assured and likely to neglect poor Pepper in favour of some of the good-looking women at my party who I never got round to fucking. There are some things you should never do in the company of a girlfriend you don't really like, Charlie is one (trips, of course, is the worst).

It's about ten and I'm feeling mighty warm and affable. I reckon I've killed Gary and am unlikely to shove my hand up the waitress's skirt. (I mean, I'm not a pervert – like Horace O – it's just, it really would have been the worst thing.) Anyway as I said, I'm feeling really up, and Pepper, who I haven't left for moment (except for my five-minute pisses – amphetamines can give me **bladder-fear**), whispers:

'Richard, I love you.' And I'm in such a good fucking mood that I whisper it back to her. Only I don't. You see, much as I feel terrific, I can't move. It's not a problem, rather a temporary inconvenience. So I try to smile instead. But I'm not having it. 'Are you OK Richard?'

Yeah, I'm fine.

'Are you OK? Say something. He's not moving.'

It's not a problem, I'll move when I'm ready.

'Horace, Jeez, he's not moving.'

'He's probably dead,' says Jeez matter-of-factly.

'Dead,' agrees Horace.

'Oh for fuck's sake! Call an ambulance. Call an ambulance.'

Don't cry Pepper, I'm saying.

'AN AMBULANCE!' Pepper dashes through the drinkers to telephone the emergency services and I realize that I could do with another piss. So I get up and walk down to the men's. I'm midway through and I realize that Pepper's in here with me. And I remember what I wanted to say.

'Ah Pepper, I love you too, so I do.'

'You bastard. You bastard. I've called a fucking ambulance for you.'

'Don't cry Pepper. I'm always making you cry. I'm sorry.'

'How could you do this to me?'

'Do what to you, Pepper?'

'Pretend you can't move.'

'I couldn't move then, I'm alright now. Pepper help! Will you help me?' A blanket of fetid lager flings itself over the wall. Over the floor. Over me. Over Pepper. And I'm on the floor of the men's in my puke, too ill to move, and Pepper's crying deeply and desperately. So starts my month's holiday.

'I can't go on holiday with you. Look.' She raises her top. And shit! – she's redder than tandoori. Like one of those shots on the news that 'some viewers may find disturbing'. I do some hard swallowing then make myself smile.

'It'll clear up when you're on holiday. When you're relaxed and happy,' I say rather hopefully.

'I can't be relaxed and happy with you. What about our last holiday?'

'What are you saying? Are you saying that I'm responsible for your eczema? Are you saying *your* eczema is *my* fault?'

'Well there does seem to be a distinct correlation between your behaviour and my skin.'

'You fucking what?'

'Look, don't get angry. It's just that you have a stressful personality. It's not your fault. It's mine for staying with you.'

'You mean, you should leave me?'

'Of course I bloody should. No one should be expected to put up with you. Look at you. You're totally out of control.'

'Go on then, fuck off. Leave me.'

'If I was going to leave you I'd have done it by now, wouldn't I? C'mon Richard, we're both mad. I'm mad for staying with you and you're just plain mad.'

'So you love me?'

'You know I do.'

'So you'll come on holiday with me? And listen, there'll be no Horace, no Jeez, no temptation to party.'

'But you do it on your own.'

'So you'll come?'

'God, Richard. God, God, God.'

'Go on say it: "Anything for a quiet life." Yes? Yes? Go on a little "yes" for me.' She throws up her hands and slowly shakes her head.

'Good one, Pepper. You can always wear a T-shirt on the beach.' And at this juncture it strikes me that I really have landed myself a peculiarly unattractive girlfriend.

'"Oh we're going to Barbados,"' I'm singing in the pub on the way to the travel agent's. '"La la la la la la la." Horace is going to be shit jealous. Are you OK?'

'Just for a week.'

'There's no point in going just for a week, Pepper. We'll need a fortnight.'

'Look Richard, I'm not sure . . .'

'Pepper, be quiet. I'll book it, it'll be too late then, and you'll have the holiday of your life. Just don't say anything. Don't even think anything until it's booked. Cheer up. For fuck's sake why are you crying? I'm buying you a fucking holiday for God's sake.' Pepper scurries out of the pub in tears. 'Ungrateful sow!'

Naturally enough, I down the requisite number to make me half like Pepper again. And, as one does after a couple of strong ones, I feel mightily cocky. Consequently I'm employing some expertise in chatting up the snow-haired cockney behind the screen. And when she comes to type in the second name for the holiday I read the name on her badge. Now the way I look at it, I haven't been harassing her in any way. But when she calls the manager, I'm wondering whether Gary has said something or perhaps I'm a little drunker than I calculated.

'No! Please, don't do that.'

'I'm sorry, sir.'

'Don't cut it. Just give it back and forget the booking.'

'I'm afraid it's the law, sir. I have no option.'

'I won't allow you to do it. It's mine. It's my property, you bastard.'

'It belongs to the credit card company and they've instructed me to destroy it.'

'Look, there's a mistake. Give it back and I'll call them.'

'I'm very sorry sir.' Clip.

'Fuck you and fuck your crappy holidays.'

I leave via several brochure stands and head home for a smoke and a weep. But when I get there I change my mind because Pepper bounces off the sofa and flings her arms around me. She smells of alcohol.

'I'm sorry, I'm sorry about the things I said. Last holiday

was brilliant except for the end. I'm cooking for you and I've bought some wine and a present for you, and I'm feeling really horny.' I'm reminded of my dream: *dark then light, dark then light*. In my mouth, her tongue flickers molar deep, she's pulled out my shirt and her nail-less fingers manipulate the taut skin of my midriff. But I'm really not in the mood for Pepper. I'm far too concerned about getting hold of some money.

'Sit down Pepper.'

'Mmmmmmm. Kiss me, Richard.'

'Pepper, I've been thinking.'

'What. Kiss me here.'

'My life. The reason I party so much and everything. There's no structure. It just goes on and on. Bits and pieces. Like a never ending hip-hop mix. I'm drunk. I'm sober, I'm at work, I'm not. There's no story to it. And do you know what, Pepper . . . ?'

'Do you like that? Hang on! I'm sorry. Darling, would you like some wine? I've bought some.'

'Yes. Were you listening to what I was saying?'

'Uh-huh. You'll have some wine, lover.'

'Pepper you're drunk, aren't you?'

'Yes.'

'So you don't want to hear how boring my life is?'

'It's **drink-boredom**.'

'Where did you get that from?'

'Horace O says it. "Aaagh the **drink-boredom**!"' I'm taking lengthy draughts from the bottle to try and tune into the idea of doing sex with Pepper. I could quite easily handle Charlotte now, or the blonde travel agent, or anyone smooth for that matter, but not Pepper.

'Pepper, do you have any money?'

'Do I have to pay to fuck you?'

'No I mean it. Have you got any money saved up or anything?'

'Fuck me – please, Richard.'

'Hang on I need to make a call. Wait there.'

'Oh bloody hell, Richard. Please be quick.' So I go upstairs and, for no particular reason – because I've forgotten about borrowing money – call Horace O. I tell his answerphone that I've got **drink-boredom** and that my life is a one-dimensional monologue – a fucking hip-hop record – I wish the football season hadn't gone, and that my current pulse rate is 104. After a few minutes Horace cuts in and says, 'Quit wasting my tape, man,' then hangs up. So I lie on the bed and smoke to try and get horny for Pepper. But you know what it's like, the more you try, the more other things become appealing. The spliff is making me more bored. What I need is something to entertain me. So I'm rooting around under the bed for some hard-core visual aid when this happens: Pepper walks into the bedroom, entirely naked.

The **drink-boredom** evaporates and I put on my CD of Mahler's Fifth.

Three hours later we're sober and in love. Well, about as in love as I can be, devoid of seed and hungover. To be honest, I'm a little bored and fancy a few jars and a game of pool. I always play well after sex. It seems a waste to have all this recently-laid confidence and just eat dinner.

'I'm afraid it's a little burnt round the edges, like me.' Conspiratorial smile.

'Wine, Pepper?'

'I've already been drunk once today.'

'And look what happened. Anyway it's a Saturday.'

'Here's to our holiday.'

'Our holiday. Pepper, listen to this. Which one do you think is better? Right, there's a visual of a woman catching a ball in a swimming pool while another woman sits on a lounger looking jealous.

83

'The headline reads:

What's the difference between these two women?

And this is the body copy:

Frankly, there shouldn't be any difference at all.

They're both having their periods and they both enjoy having fun.

The difference is, one of them has discovered Femtamp from ClairCare.

So why doesn't her friend tell about absorbent, super-absorbent and ultra-absorbent Femtamp with their handy "Three second" applicator?

Femtamp – a girl's best kept secret

'Right this is the second: two pictures. The first is a glass of blue water being poured on a white panty liner. The second is the panty liner – still white – being sent through a mangle. And there are no drips.

'The copy line simply reads:

A somewhat dry account of why you should try Lady Confident panty liners.

'Which one, eh?'

'Richard, why do you always buy that crappy magazine?'

Because it's normal. It's comforting. Because it's real. 'I don't know. It's so crap, it's funny. So, which one then?'

'Hell, I don't know. I need to see them.' I show Pepper the magazine. 'The one with the mangle, I suppose.'

'Why?'

'I don't know. Richard, we're eating. Do we have to discuss sanitary towels?'

'The second one's better because it demonstrates up-front the USP of the product. The more I think about it the better I think it is. I mean, ask yourself, if you ran one of your jam rags through a . . .'

84

'My God, Richard! I'm trying to eat. Please.'

'Right. Fine. Change the subject. It's only my job we're talking about. But if you don't want to discuss it . . .'

'Richard. Shhh please. Listen, I bought you some shorts for the holiday. Those bright lager lout ones.'

'Because I'm a lager lout?'

'Precisely.'

'How kind of you.'

'I'm sorry about before. I really can't wait.'

Don't be, because we're not going, you daft bint. 'Yeah, me too.'

'Is the food alright? It's not too dry, is it?'

It's dry and crispy like your skin. 'No, it's fantastic.' **Aubergines, aubergines – I'm fuck sick of aubergines**. 'You have a way with the egg plant.'

'I love you, Richard.'

I hate you, Pepper. 'I love you, too.'

'Just think, if you hadn't sent the key round that time, this afternoon wouldn't have happened.'

Pepper, will you marry me? 'Serious foresight on my behalf.'

'You don't mind me letting myself in like that, do you?'

Of course I fucking do. What if I was playing wheelbarrow with Charlotte? 'Not when you're in a mood like today's.' **Pepper, be my wife**.

'You're thirsty. Sorry, I'm not nagging.'

Yes you fucking are. Besides, I'm trying to kill my demon. The one that thinks you're a scabby whore. 'It's good wine.'

'We can cuddle up and watch a film tonight. There's bound to be one on. Or we could rent a video.'

Go screw yourself. Waste your own life watching videos, I'm going out to get fuck-faced. 'Sounds good.'

'Richard, why did you ask me if I had any money saved up?'

Because I've run out and quite fancy a party. A couple of grand should see me through the weekend. 'No reason. I was just thinking.'

'If you need to borrow some or need me to pay my way for the holiday, I've got a little.'

Bingo! Fucking bingo! Marry me, Pepper. 'No, no. I'm fine.'

'It's really my father's. I'm supposed to use it to put down a deposit on a house or something.'

So there's lots. I love you. 'I love you.'

'I love you too.'

'Marry me Pepper.' **Oh my fuck!**

'Pardon!'

'Sorry it was a joke. You know. You tell me about your father's money and I ask you to marry me.'

'Oh.'

Actually Pepper, it wasn't a joke. 'Pass the wine.'

'Richard!'

Ah, fuck off. Wine's wine whether you drink it from the bottle or a poncy glass. 'Oh Pepper, Pepper. I've got such fucking weird things in my head.'

'It's Jeez and Horace O's drugs. I wish you'd stop taking them. And, I'm not nagging, but you do drink so much.'

Actually it's got fuck all to do with partying. I'm called Gary and I'm Richard's demon, but you wouldn't understand. 'Not drug thoughts.'

'Richard, please use a glass.'

'Stop fucking nagging me. I shagged you stupid didn't I?'

'I'm sorry.'

'No, I'm sorry. I didn't mean to snap like that. I really didn't. I expect I'm a little nervous about the new job. Sorry Pepper.' **I guess you're right. I've fucked my brain right up with all the lovely drugs and drink. And I want to fuck it up more.**

'It's just I don't want you to become like Jeez and Horace O.'

'What's wrong with them? They can handle their medicine. They're OK.'

'C'mon. Horace is a total junkie. I saw a hypodermic needle in his drawer.'

'We only use it for amphetamines.'

'Oh my God! You don't inject drugs?'

'No, of course not.'

'Why did you say *we* then?'

'Slip of the tongue.' **Oh yeah?**

'Promise?'

Ha, ha, ha – Sure I do. 'Yeah.'

'You promise?'

'I said *yes*, didn't I?' **Bitch.**

'And what about Jeez?'

'Jeez is in control.'

'I don't like him. He's a total fake. He just reckons it's cool to be bi-sexual and pretend he's a drug-dealer. He doesn't even need the money.'

'He prefers the term "fringe pharmacist".'

'Huhh. He's going to prison for drugs, isn't he? I expect he thinks that's cool too.'

'Yeah, well. I'm too tired to do arguing.'

'We're not arguing. I just don't like either of them. It's my prerogative. That's all. I like you though, Richard.'

'That's something.'

'Richard, I think I'm a little bit drunk again. Do you really not mind my tits?' In a shamefully amateur seductive pose she peels up her top.

'I think you're on heat, woman. Sit down and finish eating.'

'Shut up and kiss me.'

'Pepper, sit down.' She emits a sudden, horrified shriek and pulls her top back down.

'Oh my God!'

'What?'

'The window.' There's a clack on the glass. I turn to the

fine sight of Horace O and Jeez waving bottles and smiling. And Pepper looks as though she may well cry. But I don't feel sorry for her. Not at all. You see, it's clicked. The other Richard. Obviously, he's moved to London.

The serrated metal saws on my skin if I so much as whimper. The wall seemed to buckle, momentarily bubble in under the impact, then tear in half with a natural ease, making the glass of the window splash out and the wood lash in, like a baseball bat into my head. I think my eyebrow has been cut off and hangs to the side of my eye, but it could be anything. And I can taste blood pulsing from somewhere tender and meaty inside my cheek.

And I remember! I remember what it is. Why I deserve this. Gary pulled the communication chain. I crashed this fucking train.

'WAKE UP, WAKE UP.' She bellows. 'Oh my God, Richard, you've . . . again. A-bloody-gain, Richard.'

'Listen Pepper. This is important. Say you pull the communication cord on a train, right? . . .'

'Richard, for fuck's sake shut up and get up.'

'But do you reckon it could buckle up when the wheels lock?'

'No. Now move. I want the sheet.'

'I'm sorry Pepper.'

'Don't apologize, it's a marked improvement on last night. All men shit on women. You've just developed the talent to do it in your sleep.'

'It's not funny.'

'It's not, is it?'

'I'm really very sorry, Pepper.'

'Just shut up and make some coffee. I'm not going to get back to sleep now. Put that in the washing machine.'

'Look, Pepper.'

'For fuck's sake, take it. And put the hot water on so I can get washed.'

Now, Pepper's in the bathroom. And I, presumably still pissed – judging from the excellence of the hard-on I've just sprung – decide to call Charlotte. Yeah, I have this vague recollection of pissing her off last night. And I want to clear things up before the morning's guilt sets in.

'Fuck off, you unbelievable creep,' bellows Charlotte.

'What?' I whisper.

'I don't believe you've got the gall to phone me, after last night. And at bloody six in the morning.'

'I don't understand.'

'Don't try and pretend you've forgotten.'

'Charlotte, I don't know what you're talking about. I'll make it up to you. Let me take you out or something.'

'Oh yeah. And are you going to take him out? When he gets out of hospital. You and your friend. Just see if you don't get . . .' There's a male voice in the background. 'Yeah, but leave it . . . Which one? . . . The white one, but leave it . . . The cunt. Gimme the phone . . . Please, leave it.'

'You total cunt,' he yells. 'You and your mate – you're going to fucking die for this.'

'You fuck off.'

'You're dead.'

'Oh yeah,' I bellow back. 'You so much as fart in my direction and I'll shoot your fucking legs off. And you'd better believe that I'll do it – coz I do things like that, me. Understand, smeg scrape? I'll muller yer. Get the fucking message?' I smash down the phone and still I'm shaking when I feel Pepper's hand on my shoulder.

'Richard darling, perhaps you ought to see someone. Can we talk about it? Please.'

'Will you take my pulse, please, Pepper?'

*　　*　　*

89

It always makes me throw. Smack that is. But, apart from that – by fuck! I'd recommend it to anyone. Try it. Just the few times, mind – when you deserve a treat. But don't die without puffing the magic dragon.

I'm lying naked in Jeez's bath, the shower head oozing warmly on my stomach, rinsing away the vom, and it's giving me time to reflect.

All the problems of my life – Gary, Pepper, the other Richard, **drink-fear**, creditors – seem so insignificant. I mean, one day on this beautiful planet of couple-coloured skies is worth any amount of debt and mind-fuck, isn't it?

And there's this. I don't remember who said it. Horace O, I think, but it relates directly to my mire – my misbehaviour: 'How can I be substantial if I fail to cast a shadow?'

'Substance needs shadow?' I point out to Horace.

'Yin needs yang.'

'Good needs evil.'

'Moderation needs excess.'

'Self needs others.'

'Your round.'

'No can do. Wealth needs poverty.'

'Poncing needs patronage. Lowenbrau?'

'Cheers H. You're a prince.'

It's a rare situation, this, for a number of reasons.

First: I haven't had a session with Horace O for a couple of weeks now. Not since he attacked Charlotte's friends. In fact, of late, he's been living a life of painful moderation.

Second: I haven't had a proper session without Horace O for a couple of weeks. Not since my credit card was killed. Of course, I've bounced a couple of cheques in unfamiliar off-licences – but with a fifty quid cheque limit how much of a session can you have?

Third: The interfering Pepper has put me on probation for a month. Can you believe it? She had my final salary cheque paid into *her* account and she issues me with 'pocket money'. Admittedly, it was my idea. I had a morning dose of loneliness-fear because I'd swamped the bed – again.

Fourth: It's warm enough to drink outside.

All in all, a rare and satisfactory situation.

From where I sit on Charing Cross Road I can see five beggars. In a doorway there's the teenage girl with scag-addict burgundy hair who might or might not fuck for money yet. There's the crimson mohawk a couple of cubicles up. Now this guy's got *beggar chic*. Oily khaki jacket, oily black scarf, oily army boots, oily dog. You know the dogs I mean? Wiry rattish rags, who do sod-all but sit in door-ways being thin – the essential nineties beggar accoutre-ment. Beggar three, a normal piss-head bum, is mobile and petitioning passers-by with little success. I can't tell you much about beggar four as he or she is asleep or dead beneath a blanket. And beggar five is me – poncing drinks off Horace O.

Horace O weaves his way through the lunchtime crowd with the ales. He sits down. We drink. Beggar three lurches up to us and mumbles something about spare change.

'FUCK – OFF – YOU – BUM,' we shout simultaneously, close up against his face. It's our standard line. We laugh and do a respect.

We drink more. And I get a mild anxiety attack about Horace O. Maybe he'll get pissed off with my economic situation and bugger off after this one. Maybe he'll remem-ber he's supposed to have given up drinking.

Then I smile – I remember the advertisement in my pocket. It has the paradoxical headline:

'INSTANT CASH – FAST! No questions asked.'

Then something else of fiscal nature catches my eye.

'Still reading that shit, man?'

91

'Listen, H:

'I'm a mother, a housewife and a millionaire

Let me tell you how I did it.

'That's a darn fine idea, honey. Why hasn't someone else tried it?'

'They have,' I said. 'John Zeigler. And he spills the beans in his book *The Lazy Millionaire* for just £9.95 + P&P.'

'It's a scam, honey. Don't waste your money.'

SIX MONTHS LATER and my husband is saying . . .

'I never figured we'd be rich enough to live in Palm Beach. But just why did John Zeigler give away his foolproof secret for just £9.95?'

'I guess he's like us, honey. He just doesn't need to make any more money.'

Scrubbing dishes, taking out the trash, fetching the groceries, cleaning up after my family. I barely had time to catch my breath, let alone make any serious money.

Then I saw an advertisement in a paper just like this one. It said, **It Takes Just an Hour a Day to Make a Million Bucks in Six Months.**

"Who are you trying to kid?" I thought. But when I read that real people like me, from Connecticut, Jersey, Buffalo and Vermont were making thousands just by sitting on their butts, I thought, "Why not give it a go?"

"Besides," I figured, "what's a measly £9.95 . . ."'

'It's the five pints I just got you.'

5

My Strange Attractor

'It's fine, we'll take it.'

'Richard, can we please talk about it?'

'What's there to talk about? It's perfect. Sex on a stick.'

'Richard, I want to talk about it. We'll call you back.'

'Christ, Pepper. Hang on, mate, I'm sorry about this. I'll give you a dog this afternoon.'

Of course, the bitch sulks all the way to the pub.

'Racism. That's what it is.' I angrily funnel in my first Export.

'Richard . . . Richard . . .' But I'm at the bar scowling hard.

'Fuck you, racist.' I mouth back. An Export and triple Jack Daniel's. Cheers. 'Racist. Bloody racist.' And I've got Pepper Furnival by the ideological short hairs.

'Richard,' she whines, 'I'm not a bloody racist. Don't ever call me that.'

'Racist.'

'Listen to me, you git. Hear me out for once.'

'Fire then.'

'Richard, it's not the black faces. That was just an observation, not a criticism of anything. Not the area. Not anything. But this place is a rubbish tip.'

'Rubbish. It's good here. There's a pool club by the station and Highbury's within gobbing distance. The place is full of ethnic colour. Take Stroud Green Road on a hot Saturday. It's seriously funky. All soca and fried fish. Geezers in regal dresses and unusual hats. And there're some poncy restaurants and wine bars up the road in Crouch End for snobs like you. Although I will concede that Finsbury Park backwards is krapy rub snif. Ha, ha.' No reaction.

Doubtless, you've sussed the reasoning for my talking Pepper into relocating. Yeah, one hundred per cent fiscal. I owed five months back rent, not to mention Poll Tax, fuel, overdrafts, credit cards, charge cards, mail order demands, TV hire, milk bills, lost videos, etc. And the way I look at it, with the new job, a modest decrease in partying and the shared rent, I should be able to pay off the 'Instant Credit Fast' loan in a couple of months.

And then there's the other little problem.

Picture Pepper and me, drinking – not to excess – in the Hen and Chickens on Highbury Corner last Sunday evening. Admittedly, Pepper's trying to convince me that I might be wise to seek some manner of professional help for my various idiosyncrasies. And though I'm getting somewhat ratty – perhaps my voice is raised a fraction – we're harmless enough. So imagine Pepper's utter surprise when I empty my half-full pint on to the floorboards and pitch my glass at someone standing in the centre of the pub, then violently grab her arm and lunge her out of the door, screaming, 'RUN PEPPER, RUN!'

Charlotte's posse give up the chase somewhere on Upper Street, but we carry on until we collapse (at the City Road junction, as it happens – no mean sprint by any standards). Obviously, Pepper's crying. And when she's finished that, she's demanding explanations and her coat and handbag back.

So between long bouts of inhaler, pulse counts and a shaky strong one or six, I explain how Horace O, for no particular reason, demonstrated his mastery of kung fu on several of them, putting one of them in hospital. Obviously, I omitted details such as me making a drunken hit on Charlotte – much to the chagrin of her suitor – and Gary's rather crass collective invitation to 'have a go if yer think you're hard enough'.

'Richard, I counted five dogs on the way to that flat. Three of them were pit bull terriers, I'm sure.'

'It's just a trend. Besides they only go for kids. And there's jazz in here in the evenings.'

'The streets are filthy. And I don't feel safe here. It's not like Islington. And I don't know, us moving in together. I know we spend most nights . . .'

'You're having second thoughts? I don't fucking believe it! And here's me thinking at last I've found someone I can trust. I'm lost for words.' And I prove this by heading off for the fruit machine.

'Oh Richard . . . Richard. I thought we were supposed to be talking.'

'Gimme a break, Pepper.' On the first spin three bars click up, the machine does some victorious synthesized music then gobs out a fortune in aluminium. 'Yes! Drink tokens. Rock and fucking roll, or what? Pepper, look! It's a sign. If that's not a sign then I'm a Yid . . . Spurs fan, I mean.'

I tip the tokens into her leather hands and kiss her.

'Trial period? A month? Say *yes*. Please. Pepper sweet. I love you. Really. Go on, say *yes*.'

'A month?' Quickly I kiss her and go to the bar.

'Celebration drink?'

'Orange juice, I suppose.'

I order a large vodka with orange, a pint of Holsten Export (So what if they sponsor Spurs? It's a fine ale) and a triple Jack.

*　　*　　*

CLIENT: **AIDS Education Trust**
TITLE: **Dispenser**
SCREENING TIME: **50 Secs**
B/W + specials

Vision	Sound
INT. Modern pub/wine bar. Atmosphere dark & moody semi-crowded.	'Tonight I celebrate my love for you' Played on a moody Sax
CU. Young couple, not overtly good-looking facing each other at table, talking intimately.	
Boy smiles and gets up.	
POV. Girl. Back of boy as he walks towards men's room.	
CU. His back. Camera follows him. He fumbles for a coin.	Music volume drops accordingly
Pan around side view. He places coin in condom machine.	
ECU. His hand as he releases the knob and feels for condoms in tray. There are none.	SFX
Camera back He pulls the ejector handle and feels for his money. There is none.	SFX
He hits the machine in frustration.	SFX
POV. Girl	Music to original volume

Front of boy leaving
the men's room looking
disappointed.

Cut to original camera
position.

He sits and the couple
exchange words. She points
at the bar. He smiles and
shakes his head. She rises.
He tries to grab her arm. He
looks mortified.

POV. Boy.
She goes to the bar and
stands between some
drinking men.
Cut to side, aerial view. She
begins conversation with the
barman. She points at the
men's room.

He walks to the till and
takes out a £1 coin and
offers it to her. She shakes
her head. He lifts up the bar
hatch and she follows him
toward the men's room.

Cut to original camera
position. She sits back down
and looks disappointed. Then
smiles and drops half a
dozen condom boxes on to   Music builds to climax
his lap. He laughs.

SUPER: Make condoms a   Music ends on long note
way of life.

Right, how about this? It does an intense two week run. You're sick of it. You're watching *News At Ten*. The bloody commercial comes on again. Exactly the same music, etc. Yawn. Except this time . . . the machine works and the kid pockets his box of onion rings. Value for money, or what?

OK, it meets the brief. Tackles embarrassment-generated market resistance and it's unlikely to terrify the one-off holiday indiscretion market into mass HIV testing which previous campaigns have. But the campaign isn't brilliant. At least it wasn't until we talked our client, Peking Tea, into doing their bit for national prophylaxis.

You know the campaign. The oh-so-fucking-twee soap opera, with the sophisticated couple who want to shag badly but have little in common, bar drinking Peking Tea. The flimsy drama is strung out by the fact that all of their retentive trysts end prematurely, due to the frustration of *their* brand of tea not being available in the best restaurants. Naturally, each has a supposed partner at home, so the tea-drinking can't take its obvious route to the bedroom. The acme of the campaign led our stars to Peking, where they revelled in an orgy of tannin swilling, only to discover they had still less in common. Then Tiananmen happened, and the commercial was canned. Enter Horace O and Richard with the scam of scams to get Peking Tea and French letters onto the front pages.

Again the coy lovers meet under the intolerable circumstances of after-dinner coffee. Then the guy announces that his other half is away on a course. The woman smiles with restrained lechery and enquires, 'Of course you have . . . ?'

'But of course,' he smiles.

'A condom?'

SUPER: Make condoms a way of life.

Fucking brilliant, or what? See if you don't see my face in the paper. In *Advertising Week* even.

Naturally, Imogen Rocastle thinks that Horace O and I

are the cat's arse. Naturally, all the junior teams wish us dead and CVs are oozing from the laser. This is good. I plan to recruit a crack department – of export lager drinkers. And naturally, we've earned the right to resume our old agency stance – propping up bars from eleven to four.

'You know what I like about this pub, Mum?' She's talking about the White Lion on Stroud Green Road.

'No dear.'

'You can actually have a conversation. There's no music.'

You know what I hate about this pub, Mrs F? They open all the doors and tell you to fuck off out dead on eleven. Well legal this gaff is. 'That's rare these days.'

'And they do vegetarian food on Sunday lunchtimes.'

Now, I've struck up a very stupid deal here. I agreed not to drink in the pub tonight. Leastways, not until we've got shot of Pepper's mother. The deal is, Pepper's bought me a bottle of bourbon that I'm allowed later. Also, I figure some fairly perverted sex is in the offing if I keep my end. A bargain, you may well think. A bargain it should be, but for Gary.

There again, there are some pretty tasty slags here – usually.

'So Richard, what made you decide on Finsbury Park?'

But I've never got near tugging in here. I mean, they're always all with blokes. Blokes in polo necks.

'Richard, Mum's asking you something.'

'So Richard, what made you move to Finsbury Park?'

Take a look at the couples. Bored shitless with each other they are. And the smug foursomes: 'I usually detest football. But I must confess I was riveted to the World Cup.' 'Well, the highlight of our weekend was the Senegalese music night in the King's Head, on Friday.' 'Deputy assistant in charge of family and marital services co-ordination. A bit of a mouthful but I assure you it's glorified pen-pushing.'

The White Lion tonight, with my orange juice and Pepper's fat mother, serves as a timely warning. It makes the disaster look positively attractive. I could be wasting my life more profitably watching a crappy sitcom.

It's obvious, I must ditch your daughter, Mrs F.

'Richard?'

'Yes, yes. I was thinking. Lots of things recommend Finsbury Park, Mrs Furnival. Lots of things.'

'Yes?'

It's piss easy to score here. I got hold of some plausible Chaz and some quite excellent New Yorkers last week. 'Well there's the park for one. It's ten minutes into town. Cheap rents. Cultural plurality.' **And of course there's the Red Army. ARS – A – NIL.** Yeah, I know, I'm sounding so polite it seems like I'm taking the piss. But it's the only way I can get a handle on Gary. Think hard about every word before you say it. Let nothing slip by on automatic.

'Patricia tells me you're a copywriter. What exactly does that involve?'

For fuck's sake woman, shut up – can't you? 'Well you know television and radio commercials, and the posters you see, and the advertisements in newspapers and magazines . . .' and I go on in this way, explaining about art directors, suits, production and media departments, above, below and through-the-line, and just about everything I can think of until I'm convinced she's bored shitless and will leave me alone.

Take a look at the crushed cotton of her cheeks. The spidery blue hieroglyphs hanging beneath the great ditches of her eye sockets. How her bear-size arse fills the chair. Add eczema to that and we're talking tertiary syphilis. Is Pepper going to turn like that? Sure, she looks OK now – until she gets her kit off, that is.

I mean, Mrs F, she asks the inane questions. And small ripples of cellulite are already dripping from her knickers.

100

But it makes no odds. I intend to ditch her as soon as is convenient.

'. . . Emily Smith, a total success story. Branches everywhere. High Street Recession. What recession? But in all honesty, I think it had more to do with business planning, a good brief, than creative . . .' A drink! a drink! my kingdom for just one fucking drink. '. . . No, dogs are related to bears.'

'Rubbish, Richard.'

'They fucking are. Can't I please have a drink yet?'

'Richard, please. Please, please. You've been so good.'

'Do you reckon she still wanks?'

'Richard! She's coming back.'

I can handle you, you fucker. Do you hear, Gary? I've got you licked.

You reckon? Just for that, I'm going to make you say: 'Oh thanks very much for the curtains you made us. They're fucking crap.' And then, 'Pepper, fuck off and take your pox-ridden tits with you.'

'Mum, Richard reckons that dogs are related to bears and not horses – he's wrong, isn't he?'

'I'm right. And horses are related to rhinos. And in terms of DNA we're closest to rats.'

'Chimpanzees, obviously.'

'I thought it was pigs.'

Well in your case Mrs F.

'Don't be silly, Mum. Apes.'

And like this we waste our lives . . .

'And, Mrs Furnival, we'd love you to come around for dinner. Wouldn't we Pepper, Patricia? Oh, and thanks very much for the curtains. They're . . .'

The ten-minute bell sounds. And I'm reckoning that I can get a good four in before kick-out time, if she fucks off pronto. And, of course, there's my bottle at home.

. . . fucking gross, woman. '. . . lovely. They really go, like. And match with everything.'

101

Pepper returns from seeing her mother to the car. I've done two pints – belching a lot, obviously, to make room – and double chasers. I'm about to tackle the other two. People are looking at me as if I'm some sort of a nutter. But fuck them.

'Richard! You were brilliant.' And Pepper's on me. Dabbing her cold lips around my face. I decide that Pepper is, after all, a pretty good-news girlfriend.

'I won't have another, man.'

'H, we're celebrating.' So when Horace nips down for a pee, I buy him a couple of drinks. I refuse to be subjected to lone drinking when everything's going so well.

'Rich man, it's gone four.'

'Fuck it. It's Friday and I'm a free man.'

Horace takes a long tug of his pint and repeats, 'I still don't believe it, man.'

'Listen H,' I joke 'you're going to be the first man I take out, when I'm on the highways.'

'Can't wait, Rich.'

RUT is in Covent Garden, so our local pub is the Round House. It's on Garrick Street, well outside the piazza, and apart from it being circular, there's little else to attract the colourful Swedes and bickering Italians. For the privilege of tourist-free drinking, the pub charges tourist prices. But we don't mind – we're in advertising. Besides, the poncy wine bars charge even more for their bottled piss.

It being late and us having long passed the gallon marker, we're sitting at a window leering at the smooth brown limbs of passing tourists and celebrating that I didn't get bird for Emily's attempt to nuke Devon.

The magistrate took a right shine to Pepper when she stood up and swore that I'd been on a sobriety jag, was level-headed and had been forced to tank up due to her cruel and insensitive behaviour. And you should have seen the probation officer's report: broken home, problem child, worked his way up from nothing, doing some important work for the AIDS Education Trust, would be a crime against society to impose a custodial sentence, even a lengthy period of community service for that matter. Truth always triumphs in such circumstances and I got off with a 2.5K fine, two years' probation, the insistence that I attend Drink Crisis meetings and a ten-year ban. Suits me. It's one less disaster to contend with.

Can you imagine my fear during the five-hour train journey? Not only did my infallible prescience tell me that, in reality, the disaster would involve cement floors, slop buckets and murderous encounters with rhino-tough bugger boys, I had the threat of Gary to contend with. I mean, in the sombre magistrates' court, with so much at stake, how could he resist?

So despite Pepper's unbound protestations, I evoked the spirit of Pat in a pub before the trial.

And, of course, the magistrate read out my previous before sentencing. So I got 'Why didn't you tell me before?' all the way home. So Pepper knows about the five scars on my hand. It's no big deal. And I trust her not to mention it to a soul. Of course, I remoulded the truth somewhat and told her that I did my stretch in Feltham for doing someone over in my village.

'Rich man, I'm giving some serious thought to quitting this poison.'

'Fuck off, H!'

'Get into some meditation or something. Life re-adjustment.'

'And I'm a Spurs fan.'

'No shit, Rich – I'm meaning it.'

'It's shit, H. You mean nothing of the sort.'

But as we leave the boozer, I know Horace O is right. It's time to grow up, jack up on some work ethic and pay back the overdraft of a hard summer.

And all in all there really hasn't been a better time to get long-term right. Condom-wise, everyone is on my side. And as for Pepper, things couldn't be sweeter. She hasn't spent an evening out since we moved – I phone to check.

I really owe it to me – to Pepper, the loan companies – to sort out. I may well paint some of the flat, get an HIV test even, maybe try and read a book. Then again I always get this back-to-school feeling around the beginning of September. Memories of kissing goodbye to the blissful freedom of summer.

'You must have noticed there was no furniture.'

'When I woke up the place did look a bit bare.'

'So why didn't you come home like you said?'

'It was a leaving do. I forgot. I was intending to go for just the one. Horace was there. I'm sorry, I guess I haven't got much self-control. I'm sorry, I should have called.'

'There's no bed. You must have noticed. Where did you sleep.'

'In the bath.'

'In the bath!'

'I often used to sleep in the bath.'

'In the bath?'

'Yes. In the fucking bath, Pepper. It's a good place to sleep when you're puking your guts out.'

'And you stayed asleep until now?'

'Yes. I was very drunk. I admit. Rat-arsed. I'm guilty. I'm very sorry. What else can I say? I'm sorry, Pepper.'

'Anyway, you've been drinking.'

'Leave it out, I feel shitty.'

'Exactly. You always drink when you feel shitty – *to get right*.'

'What utter crap.' I touch two fingers above my head and walk in a straight line to prove this.

'You stink of it.'

'It's probably from last night. I did drink a lo . . .'

'No it's fresh alcohol.'

'How the fuck do you know that?'

'I've known you long enough to know the difference between stale and fresh alcohol on your breath. I get a mouthful of stale when you kiss me goodbye in the mornings and a mouthful of new when you kiss me goodnight. Or worse still, I have to breathe it for an hour or more while you're trying to come in me.'

'Fuck you, Pepper.'

'Richard.'

'Fuck off.'

'Christ! Richard, I need to use the bloody loo.'

'Fuck off.'

'Richard, please. Come on. You're being really silly.'

Now, this is true. In order to reflect on my situation, I locked myself, an eight-pack, twenty cigarettes and a magazine in the bathroom and it hasn't been much fun at all. The problem being, the bloody flint's gone in my Zippo and I'm finding it near impossible to think of anything, bar needing a cigarette very badly.

Three weeks ago when we moved in, Pepper and I were a real team. I mean, I was going to do it anyway, but it was on Pepper's suggestion that we loaded the fully furnished aspect of my flat into Jeez's van and took it to Finsbury Park. After three or so trips – her head on my shoulder in sweet fatigue during the last – we had everything inside and sat down to discuss how to arrange our new home. Then Pepper whispered, 'Let's sort the bed out first.'

And that was that.

For a fortnight . . .

'Richard please, I've got cystitis. I need to go.'

. . . it was lovely. I barely went out at nights. My pulse

dropped below 90. And we took it in turns – Pepper cooking and me forking out for takeaways. I even suffered her Bob Dylan records in silence. Then after the news at nine or ten – except when football or *Prisoner: Cell Block H* was on – we'd slink off to *our* room and make love in the Indian summer breeze. Either that, or we'd do perverted sex in one of the other rooms.

Then last Friday things started to . . .

'Do you want me to piss all over the fucking dishes?'

. . . change. The Client provisionally accepted the condom creative and we celebrated. Ebullience shone through my Saturday hangover and I celebrated more, etc. etc. (a short break to appear in court) etc. etc. until last night – when this – amazing thing – happened.

Hell, I wouldn't blame you for not believing a word of it. Then again it's the sort of thing that happens . . .

'I swear I'm going to leave you if you don't open this door.'

. . . once in everybody's lifetime.

Like I told Pepper, I did a leaving do. And like I said, I was so fuck-faced that I forgot I'd moved and let myself back into my old gaff. What I didn't tell Pepper was that there was someone there.

'Hello Richard,' said Linda curiously, as I staggered into her living room.

'Hello . . . er . . . Linda.' I probably said.

'What are you doing in my flat?'

Anyway to cut a long story short, we fucked. I drank her wine, she undressed me and let me be unconscious in her bed – which I didn't shit, piss or puke in – and I woke in the morning with her . . .

'Oh Richard, please. Please. Please.'

. . . playing rocking horse on me. Then, basically we fucked all day, then I went to the pub to play pool and stop Gary saying anything dangerous to Pepper.

'Fuck you. Fuck you. Fuck you. Richard, you bastard.'

Oh Linda. She was one of the women at my last agency that I didn't get round to fucking.

'My God, Richard. What is wrong with you?'

REAL LIFE TALK
The Day My Husband Came Back from the Dead

[Caption] *With a loving wife and beautiful son and another one on the way, he had everything to live for.*

[Caption] *When they told me he was dead I didn't know who to turn to . . . It had never crossed my mind before, but now I know there's a God . . . Paralysed from the waist down, Tom's still the same man I married three years ago.*

Two years ago disaster struck the Campbell family. Tom, loving husband of Julie and father of eighteen-month-old Henry, was involved in an accident and pronounced dead shortly after arrival at Mayday Hospital in south London. Had the experts made a mistake? Or did the priest really bring Tom back from the dead?

'It was my birthday. Tom had come home especially early, weighed down with roses, the biggest box of chocolates I'd honestly ever seen and a painting I'd said I liked in passing, maybe a month before.

'He'd secretly arranged for a baby sitter and booked a table at our favourite restaurant.

'During dinner that night I broke it to Tom that I was pregnant. He was over the moon. At that moment I felt more in love with him than on our wedding day. I knew I was the luckiest woman alive. I was in heaven and nothing could spoil it.'

Little did Julie know that, in less than twenty-four hours, her dreams would be shattered. And life for the Campbells would never be the same again. The dreaded phone call came at three fifteen the next afternoon.

'When it rang I knew. Call it telepathy, call it female intuition, but I knew something dreadful had happened to Tom before the voice at the other end had said a single word.

'I'll never forget that voice, cold as ice. "I'm afraid there's been a motor accident. Your husband was involved." "Is he dead? Is he dead?" I pleaded. "Please come to the hospital immediately, Mrs Campbell," was my answer.

'After that, all I could think of to say was, "He's a rep for

Paynes. He's a good driver. He's a rep for Paynes, the chocolate people."' . . .

. . . Julie was taken to see the body and was shocked to see a priest with Tom. Tom wasn't a Catholic. The St Christopher that the ambulance men had found hanging on the car mirror had been given to him by a hitchhiker. Julie asked the priest to leave.

'I've never prayed before. Maybe it was because I'd seen the priest, maybe it was desperation, but I said, "Please God, don't let Tom be dead," over and over again in my head.'

Two and a half hours later nurses advised Julie to return home to little Henry. Having given up all hope, she rose to leave.

What happened next nearly caused her to jump out of her skin. Tom sat bolt upright and blurted, 'Are we having sausages for tea, then?' . . .

'I'm sorry. I'm sorry.'

Bingo! that's what I was waiting for. Now all I need to do is make like I've been crying, do a little apologizing and all will be good again.

'I'm sorry,' she's crying. So I splash some lager on my cheeks and unlock the door.

But she doesn't charge in. Nor is there any calculated, nor less calculated abuse.

She sits cross-legged on the landing floor. Crying pathetically – as her pathetic piss tries to decide on the stain it'll make on our new carpet.

Pepper's forgiven me in the quiet, hurt way women sometimes forgive. She doesn't cry. She doesn't smile either. She's being routine. And I think it's dangerous.

I estimate that we haven't shagged for a fortnight. And this despite the fact that I've been off the beer and trying to pamper her. Yet for all my smiles and coddling, I'd get more warmth from a stuffed cat.

Pepper watches some daft fuckers with tambourines and I watch Pepper.

DAFT FUCKERS:

 I see Him in the flowers of Spring,
 When blossom paints our Earth.
 And each new bud unfolding,
 Brings promise of rebirth.

ME: Some shit this is.

PEPPER: Go to the pub then.

DAFT FUCKERS:

 I feel His love in summer's warmth,
 And bright blue summer skies.
 As each new dawn lights up our world,
 I see my Saviour rise.

ME: Will you come?

DAFT FUCKERS:

 Open your eyes, look to the skies,
 Witness the wonderful truth.
 On every day, in every way,
 Our planet's the living proof.

PEPPER: I don't feel like it. I'm trying to watch this.

ME: C'mon, Pepper. We haven't been out together for aeons.

PEPPER (*snappish*): No.

DAFT FUCKERS:

 I see Him in the gentle leaves,
 That do in autumn fall.
 And when the leaves a-rustle
 I hear my Saviour call.

ME: Waddya say, Pepper?

PEPPER: I don't feel like it tonight. Leave me alone, can't you?

ME: Go on, you'll feel fine when we're in the pub. (*Passing her the spliff*) Have some. (*She shakes her head irritably*)

PEPPER (*snappish*): No.

DAFT FUCKERS:

 I feel Him in winter's chill,
 When bright snow cleanses all.

109

ME (*to the tune*):
And you can watch this shit alone
Pepper Fur-niv-awl?

Spliff can make me hungry. Not just *munchies* hungry. Hungry for other things. Things like normal human contact, for pubs, for Pepper. And supine on the bed, I'm thinking rationally about such things. I'm weighing up exactly what the things are that I want. And more importantly, how to get them.

I want three things. And because I'm stoned I want them badly.

1. I want Pepper to come on to me. A trifling token of affection would do. I mean, her touching my shoulder and smiling would be enough to hold on to. My ideal in this wish category is for her to ignite spontaneously, like the old days, and rape me. (Yeah, I know I always turned off when that happened – but I wouldn't now. No way, Pepper.)

2. I've been pretty much off the sauce during the last week, trying to get Pepper to like me again. (Horace won't drink with me any more.) What I wouldn't give for a hit.

3. I've got the munchies badly. I need Indian.

The obvious solution seems to be: put the Pepper problem on hold, fill up with strong boys at the Worlds End, then do a vindaloo in the curry house, drop five Imodium to tamp the morning outburst, and sleep on the couch.

But me, well I'm paid to come up with non-obvious solutions. Here's how my mind works. I trot down to the take-away, order buckets of scram for Pepper and myself – a quick half a gallon while it's being made – pick up a carrier of beers and spritzer materials on the way back then crumble a generous eighth into Pepper's vegetable curry and wait for her to grow amorous. If that doesn't work, tomorrow, I'll break an E into her fruit juice.

I really will have to do something about this.

An innocent police enquiry could turn into a full-scale bust.

I mean, you don't notice when you've been inside all day. But when you open my front door from the outside, you're knocked back by a rolling carpet of viscous and illegal fog.

The immoral seasoning complete, I carry in our dinner.

'Wow!' shrieks Pepper. 'You absolute lovey.' She dowses her spleek and turns to embrace me. She's in my white bathrobe. Only that. It's undone. 'Mmmm. I love you.' Her tongue tastes like a lump of Sputnik.

She's trying simultaneously to talk and spade in curry heaped on naan bread.

'We really must try and get on,' she's spluttering. 'I'm sorry. You've been good all week. I'm not going to be moody now.'

Consequently I'm taking a purposeful tug of the wine and thinking 'What a bloody waste of an eighth.' And I'm noticing that my desire for her drains as she speaks.

'I'm sorry too, Pepper. I'm glad we're friends again.'

'Lovers,' she growls and her teeth grin greenly at me.

Pepper breaks off mid-blowjob.

'I'm sorry. God, I feel stoned. I'll be OK in a bit. Please, your hand.' Her vagina sucks greedily as I retrieve my hand. 'Oh God. Oh God, I've got pins and needles in my head. My head's going to blow up. I mean it. Richard, help me.'

'Quiet, Pepper. You'll be alright in a while. I'll get you a glass of water.'

'A bucket.'

'I'll get you a pint glass.'

'A buck . . . I'm going to.' She does. And continues to spew for a long while.

'Pepper, let me get you the bathrobe. You're freezing.'

'I'm boiling. Don't go. Hold me.'

'Like *this*?'

'That's fine.'

111

'Are you sure *this* is OK?'

'Yeah.' I'm holding Pepper as she kneels, her head down in the bath. The *this* aspect is that I'm unbuttoned and working myself off between her snowy buttock cheeks. Each time she retches it's fabulous.

'I'm going to sue the fuckers.'

'It wasn't the food.'

'Of course it was.'

'It was the dope.'

'But you only had half a spliff.'

'Maybe, I made it a little strong. I was very stoned when you came back.'

'Did you mean what you said? About us getting on.'

'Yeah.'

'I'm glad Pepper.'

'So am I. Richard, will you get me the robe now?'

'Hang on. I'm nearly . . .'

'Richard! I'm bloody freezing.'

I take Monday off to help Pepper get over her food poisoning and to shampoo our carpets. Our carpets say what her eczema can't. They say I've managed to bring Pepper down to my level of physical functioning.

By about midday she feels just normally stoned. So we go to the World's End for lunch.

'The theory is illustrated by what has come to be known as the *Butterfly Effect*. Simply stated, it means that the minutest disturbance of air caused by a butterfly's wing could initiate a chain reaction capable of causing a hurricane on the other side of the planet. Here's a weather report from October 1987 . . .'

'Oh Richard, do we have to watch this?'

'Don't you think it's fascinating?'

'I don't really understand it. And I don't think you do either, to tell the truth.'

112

'Of course I do. I always read *New Scientist* at work. I think it's all quite excellent. I passed physics CSE, you know.'

Pepper crawls over to me. She rests a hand on my thigh. 'Richard, come on. Come to bed. You're not interested in *Open University.*'

'You go. I'll finish this tin and join you after the programme. Go on.'

'Oh Richard,' she whines. Hell, the woman pisses me off at times. 'I want to fuck.'

'I'll do you after this. Please, be quiet. Please, Pepper.'

'. . . Push the pendulum the merest fraction harder and a quite remarkable phenomenon occurs. Its behaviour becomes quite unpredictable. Chaotic.' A bearded septic comes on.

'Now there's no question that the pendulum is still subject to Newtonian laws of motion. But its movement is now quite unpredictable. It's now following what's known as its *strange attractor*. Perhaps it'll become clearer if I show you on the computer . . .'

'Richard.'

'What?'

'You're *my* strange attractor.'

'What?'

'Well you're strange and I'm attracted to you. And look.' She opens the robe. 'That's what that is – on the computer.'

'A Mandelbrot set. Chaos.'

'Yeah. It is chaotic sometimes.' She begins to massage my torso. I'm twitching with irritation. Then she undoes my jeans. I really don't know why I'm putting up with all this. But you know how moods can swing – quite unpredictable they can be at times.

'Look Pepper.' I laugh, 'I seem to be defying the laws of Newtonian physics.' I set the video and put on Mahler's Fifth.

6

A Lone Rubber

TALK TO TARA

Readers talk to Tara about their Personal Problems

• **Our six-year-old can't seem to leave his penis alone for five minutes. For the last two months it's been his favourite toy. Is this normal or should I discourage him? It's particularly embarrassing when we have company. No one knows where to look.**

Jane, Chiswick

Tara says: Come on Jane, you should know by now that it's every man's favourite toy. But seriously, it's quite normal for toddlers to go through a phase where they are fascinated with this newly discovered part of their body. However, six does seem to be a little old, especially now he's expected to mix at school.

You should explain to him that it's perfectly acceptable behaviour when he's at home and alone. But not when he's in company. And this includes Mummy and Daddy.

• **Do some people never sleep? Well, there are me and my husband for two. The lad who lives below us is a DIY enthusiast. From when he arrives home from work to the early hours (often three or four o'clock) all we can hear is drilling, sawing and hammering. Once I think he even hired a pneumatic drill.**

We've tried reasoning with him but he says it's not that loud. We even threatened to call the police, whereby he promptly produced a warrant card and said, 'No need, they're already here.'

Is there anything we can do?

Nikki, Teeside

Tara says: Ever heard of ear plugs or estate agents?

But seriously, what can be done depends on the by-laws in your area. My advice is to visit a Citizens' Advice Bureau and arrange a visit from a noise pollution officer. Your neighbour may be in for a £2000 fine if he defies an injunction – policeman or not.

● I suspect that my boyfriend is sexually abusing my seven-year-old daughter. But I daren't approach him about it in case he's entirely innocent. My daughter clams up at the mere mention of his name.
Name withheld
Tara says: Readers will forgive me if I don't preface this answer with my usual quip.
    Cathy, you must . . .

The arrival of the 10.32 to Edinburgh is announced. I pocket my mag, get my Newcastle ticket checked and board.

Let me tell you how all this came about.

For a week after the OD incident, Pepper was on to me like an infection. Now, I'm not complaining. It's how I scammed it after all. But you know what it's like with someone's hot, all too human pants on the back of your neck? When they want to cuddle up to you at every opportunity, seduce you when you get back from work – when all you need is a large drink and a cool smoke. Pepper was doing things like leaping out and kissing me as I left the khazi. She even asked me to teach her how to play pool. Exactly – fuck that! It was like being a kid and having to wear your school blazer in blazing September. *Infuriating* isn't the word. Add the fact that I'm developing crush symptoms over a suit at work, and you can appreciate why I didn't get shirty in the slightest when she announced her plan to visit Newcastle at the weekend.

Now, come Thursday, I call Pepper to ask her whether she fancies going out, it being our last night together, and that. She declines, saying she has to pack and leave early Friday morning. I go for a couple of ales after work. I grow lonely for Pepper (high-frequency sex is ten times more moreish than puff). So I head off home to discover Pepper absent and note saying 'We decided to leave tonight.'

115

WE!

I snatch a tin and stomp into the living room. There are two glasses on the table. One smells of bourbon. There are two high-tar cigarette butts (not my brand) in the ashtray. Make what you will of it. I'm on my way to Newcastle to sort matters. Sort them for good.

These were my initial theories.

1. The other Richard lives in London. He picked up Pepper to: (a) Travel to Newcastle with her; (b) Take her to his house for the night; (c) Fuck her in my bed.

2. The other Richard still lives in Newcastle (the letter on Sidney). Somebody else picked her up and she's going to meet him there. It would explain why she suddenly snapped out of her huff and got friendly with me.

3. There's a perfectly innocent explanation.

Too sober to make any reasonable judgement, I check my bed for evidence and go to the Duke of Edinburgh on Fonthill Road.

I decide to pace myself with the drinking – i.e. drink at consistently rapid pace – and assess the situation rationally. The inner-speak's rapping fast.

Look man, you're best shot of her. Remember how you felt just yesterday when she wouldn't let hold of you in bed. Face it – it's a bad relationship. Besides there's her at work now. She's obviously hot on you.

And this is countered by a deeper inner-speak. The slow purposeful voice of the heart, which says: **She's a beautiful, fragile and precious creature and you mustn't hurt her. You love her. And you really can't complain if she's seeing someone else. You brought it upon yourself – twat. You're a bad human being. Let's face it – you'd sooner she was killed in an accident than fucked the other Richard.**

By rights, I'm far too skulled to be playing well. In addition I'm bang out of practice and my confidence gauge is on red. But I'm wiping the baize with this geezer – I even chanced a double off the flat of the pocket. Why? I knew I'd get it in. You

116

see, each time, my opponent is the other Richard. And I'm letting him into just what he's dealing with. Eight games later, twenty balls crowd the table and the laws of cause and effect have called it a day. To the cheers of everyone I go seven up. Then I go outside for a ten-minute piss and a thirty-second puke and I don't give a sod about Pepper or Richard. I'll go clubbing and pull something better.

I'm in the Arsenal Tavern with Fishburger, Seamus, Richard, Mark and Mac the Spoon – my new mates. The band hack their way awkwardly through covers like 'And a Bang on the Ear' and 'Hi Ho Silver Lining'. My stomach fires jets of neat hydrochloric up into my mouth. I drink much – pissed logic tells me that more drink will cool the flares.

On the way home I barely break stagger to vomit. I have a purpose. I must load up on amphetamines, shit hardeners, ulcer medicine, then pack. Later today I'm going to find out about the other Richard for sure. I stop only to torch an abandoned sofa. Sofas go up a treat. Try one, you won't be disappointed.

9.30 Friday morning. I attempt to call in sick but there's too much fear. Pulse, irregular – approx. 107 BPM.

10.30 Friday morning. I'm spewing and weeping into a toilet bowl in King's Cross Station. Yeah, I ran off the train. The 11.32 struck me as an infinitely preferable option.

17.00 Friday afternoon. I wake up hugging toilet bowl in King's Cross Station.

19.30 Friday. Back in the Duke of Edinburgh. Nearly gotten right.

Now I wouldn't say I was a particularly jealous person but on Friday night I didn't manage a wink of sleep. Each time I closed my eyes I'd get this ECU of Pepper smoking dick.

On Saturday, I figured my best bet was to drink hard and try and get some sleep during the afternoon. The plan works and I catch up on the latest instalment of the fuck awful disaster. In this particular version I could actually see Horace O and Pepper. Crushed up together between two

117

seats. Yelling and moaning and struggling – like they're doing deranged fucking or something. Of course, I was thinking – shit, that should be me there, crushed up against Pepper like that. But what do you expect from a disaster?

Obviously, I've got stats of the cunning woman's diary and address book. So on Saturday night a dinner party in West Jesmond is interrupted when the phone rings.

'Is Richard there?' asks a thick Irish accent. She says that Richard and Ciaran are camping on Lindisfarne. I tell her it's bloody madness and hang up.

Do you remember those new mates I told you about? Well they're not exactly my mates now. They beat the crap out of me outside the pub after time. I believe that Pepper's infidelity and my subsequent efforts to anaesthetize my understandable anguish have made me a less than convivial person of late.

I smoke nearly a quarter of Sputnik to cheer me up and help me get to sleep. Bad idea.

TALK TOPIC
Alcoholism

Last month's news that approximately 5% of the British population has a drinking problem shook the nation. However, according to the results of an independent survey carried out by Glasgow University this figure is wildly inaccurate. The disturbing conclusion is that in England and Wales the actual figure is between 17–22% whilst in Scotland between 23–25% of adults had drink addiction problems.

This week we investigate alcoholism. And answer some of the questions most commonly asked.

Q **What is alcoholism?**

A *Alcohol is an addictive drug. And quite simply, alcoholism is an addiction to the drug alcohol. Like all addictions, it means that the body's physical and mental processes can no longer function normally without the drug. For example, someone with a mild alcohol addiction may suffer from insomnia if they don't have a drink at night.*

Q Is alcoholism a disease?

A *Yes. It has all the symptoms and behaviour patterns associated with a disease and often it requires medical treatment. According to Drink Crisis it is a contagious disease – although not like mumps or chicken pox. By associating with heavy drinkers people tend to drink even more, thereby increasing their tolerance to alcohol, which causes them to drink more. This can lead to a dependence on alcohol.*

Q If you only have one drink a day can you still be an alcoholic?

A *Yes. Our traditional notion of alcoholics is that they drink from sherry bottles on the street, or conceal bottles of spirits at work. However, an alcoholic is anyone for whom alcohol has become a part of their metabolism. The Glasgow University survey didn't focus so much on how much people drink, rather how deeply people craved for what little they did drink.*

Q How can I tell if I've got a drink problem?

A *Your doctor prescribes you medication and tells you that you are not to drink for a month. How do you react: 1. With panic? 2. With mild anxiety? 3. It causes you no anxiety whatsoever? According to Drink Crisis, only people who can honestly answer 3 do not have a drink problem of some sort.*

Q Can alcoholism be cured?

A *The only 'cure' is to abstain from alcohol totally. However this isn't an actual cure. One of Drink Crisis' mottos is 'An alcoholic is an alcoholic for life.' It means that an alcoholic could give up drinking for ten years and still be addicted to alcohol. Just one drink could . . .*

'Richard! What the hell's happened to you?' Pepper screams as I stagger in on Sunday night.

'Welcome home. It's nothing. Did you have a good time?'

'Thank you. And yes, I had a great time. Richard, have you been in a fight?'

'Pepper, I've got a present for you.'

'You've been drinking. And fighting. Are you OK?'

'Of course I've been drinking. But you'll forgive me when

119

I show you what I got us.' I untie and carry in the new animal from the hall.

'Oh Richard, it's lovely. But we can't – we haven't even got a garden.'

'He's only a few months old. Look how big the little fucker is.'

'Richard we can't keep a dog. What about when we're at work?'

'We'll get a litter tray. I'll exercise him mornings and evenings.'

'You! Huh.'

The dog lifts its sandy head and blinks at Pepper.

'Hello, you,' she croons and lowers her face down to it. *Don't you dare bite her. She'll never let me keep you then.* It springs on to her lap and begins to French kiss her face.

'Look, he likes you. If I didn't take him, he'd have been put down.'

'Richard, he's lovely, but we can't keep him.'

'What shall we call him? How about Slugger?'

'That's horrid.'

'How about Arsenal or Gunner? What about North Bank?'

'Yucko. I'm going to call you Buttercup, until we find a home for you . . .'

'Buttercup!' I'm buggered if I'm going to scream *Buttercup* when I'm in Finsbury Park with my pit bull terrier.

'Have we got any food? Any meat?'

'Buttercup's going to be a vegetarian – aren't you lovey?'

'Get serious, Pepper.'

'I mean it. You can get vegetarian dog foods. Rich's dog is a vegetarian.' My diaphragm bounces and the weekend's party threatens to evidence itself.

'Rich? Who's Rich?'

'Richenda. She gave me a lift to Newcastle.'

*   *   *

120

Twelve o'clock Sunday and the **drink-fear** is bad. I go to the Park Tavern to medicine up and get the pulse down. In the pub I use my hands to muzzle in Gary – whose threats are many and unpredictable. The Gunners are playing later and it's being televised on the *Match*. This is good. It means an extension. In Finsbury Park a by-law allows pubs to flout prescribed opening times on St Patrick's day and when Arsenal are on the box.

After about five or so Extras I'm feeling a deal harder. I decide to watch the match down the road and, if I see them, muller the fuckers who slapped me.

I walk in John Wayne style and look around. At once, I'm pushed down into a chair and told not to try it on with any more women or I'll get it even worse.

Arsenal win – I think. So we drink much.

It's dark. Everyone's had a good laugh at the expense of my face and I'm outside because I can't be arsed to walk round to the pisser. Nearby, there's someone I've met once or twice before. A rough little kid with a thick Windie accent. He's hanging on to his dog like he's water skiing. It's a dead impressive animal. A hard animal. An American pit bull terrier the size of a small pig. We get talking. He informs me that recently his dog made some new pit bulls. Like most things around here they are for sale. Gary asks to buy one. An hour later the kid meets me. I hand him a ton and he hands me a rope with a piglet-sized mammal tugging at it. I name my £100 insurance policy Slugger.

From the bedroom, we hear Buttercup smashing about in the kitchen.

'He's probably looking for more cornflakes.'

'He ate them, didn't he? I told you he was a vege-tarian.'

Pepper tells me that the girly weekend nearly went wrong when Ciaran – Marianne's boyfriend – arrived back, bedraggled from his foolish adventure on Holy Island, and started this bastard row. 'Like men do when they come in drunk.' But they made up and things were OK.

Do you ever make deductions in your sleep? At four I'm flung awake with a stomach cramp and the sickening realization that Richard must also have come back with Ciaran – and spent the night in the house. Fucking Pepper.

Later that morning I'm woken again as Buttercup burrows and snuffles against my body under the duvet.

When Pepper leaves, she canoodles with Buttercup for five minutes and pecks me on the forehead. Pepper thinks that Buttercup's a Staffordshire. She also reckons that Staffordshire bull terriers are dead safe.

I call in sick, apologize for not calling in on Friday, and buy dog food, a hard-looking harness, sleeping box, ball and dog training video and set about mastering my new dog.

'Sit,' I shout and heave its lower back down as instructed by the video. It rolls over. 'Stay,' I yell and walk off. It hops after me. So I lock it in the kitchen, grab an ale and go for a rummage in Pepper's luggage bag.

The things I find – that I consider relevant to the case – paint an ambiguous picture.

1. Tampons. Of course. I forgot. Excellent.

2. Betnovate cream. Second only to the influence of my behaviour, her skin follows her lunar cycle. Bleeding and scabby – of course my Pepper behaved. Then –

3. A lone rubber! In a three-pack!

'Oh Buttercup, Buttercup, what is she playing at? The woman's trying to kill me I swear,' I say as I walk my dog to the pub. It bounces about like a badly balanced, oversized yo-yo and ignores me.

'Heel boy.' I yank the leash. It yelps. As people pass by it jumps up at them – affectionately.

Supping and ruminating over the other Richard, I hear the Voices:

Dump her before she dumps you. Even if she's not having an affair, she'll ditch you when she finds out about your next little project.

Rich, Rich, play it cool. Put a lid on all that poisonous jealousy. Pretend you don't suspect a thing – until you have proof.

Animals were put here for the benefit of humans. And that includes minks, Buttercup and Pepper for that matter – ha, ha.

An old dude in bad clothes enters. Buttercup flies off my lap and makes a bee-line for him. He head-butts the man's knee and polishes his dirty trousers with his ears. The man bends down to pat him. Buttercup opens his incipient jaws and wipes the man's hand with his tongue.

'Buttercup,' I call, and turn cerise. He streaks over and back onto my lap. So I'm nuzzling Buttercup and reckoning that maybe I've been sold a defective pit bull.

Owners of hard dogs defend their dogs by saying: 'There are no bad dogs just bad owners.' Maybe they're right. Maybe Buttercup's a blank piece of hardware that needs to be programmed. So I consider the ways in which I can be cruel to it. Let it know who's leader of this pack. Give it some attitude. It looks up then burrows its brick of a head in my pocket. I lift him out and kiss his tiny truffle of a nose. What sort of a fuck-up could fuck up a beautiful creation like Buttercup? I ask you.

The old dude walks over. A fuck-up, if ever one walked.

'Gi's a ciggie, son.'

'Go on mate.' I hand him a cig and light.

'Con ye spar us e poond? Oor e'en stoond us e pint?'

'Go on, have a couple of quid.'

'Och, cheers, son. Yeer a geent.'

'No worries.'

'Fuck off!' he shouts suddenly and loudly.

123

'You what?'

'Eem sorry. Eem . . . fuck yer arse. Eem dead sorry. Coont. Coont dog. Ee ceen't . . . Ee'm fucked in the heed. Wanker!' I'm stood nose to nose with the bloke.

'If you weren't such an old . . .'

'Coont . . . Coont.'

'Exactly, I'd drop you.'

'Eem sorry. Ee ceen't halp maseelf.' He drops the two coins and runs out. And I'm regretting squaring up to him and wondering what he calls his demon.

Buttercup doesn't understand about long grass. Instead of barging through it like more knowledgable dogs, he jumps over the tufts like a spring lamb. And when I call him, he comes to me.

Would you do it? Write an advertisement for a fur company, I mean? If you do, you could be in for a stonking bonus and a heap of brownie points and, more than likely, you'll be allowed to sack the junior teams – who refuse to do it. If you don't write it, your own position may well be on the line. And, let's face it, you badly need the money. Then again, if you do it, you stand to lose your girlfriend, art director, and much face in the industry.

'You wear leather, hypocrite.'

'Richard, I'm not going to argue about it. Do it and we're finished.'

'Pepper, it's my job.'

'I don't know how you can even think about doing it. Buttercup, come here. There's a good boy.'

'I reckon Buttercup's grown in a week.'

'Buttercup's fat because you feed him kebabs. And don't change the subject.'

'I'm going to have a pint and mull it over.'

'I won't be here when you get back.'

'Pepper, in the name of all that fucks, it's only an ad.'

'It's something I feel very strongly about indeed. You go out and I go.'

'OK, Pepper. OK.'

'Thank you.' She kisses me. And though I could construe this as some sort of invitation, I become imbued with a coldness, a feeling of infinite self-sufficiency. I fetch a Scotch. Pepper tuts. I ignore her.

'Pepper, I want to tell you something.'

'Yes?'

'About when I was young.' Appetite fills her face.

'Yes, yes do. You never tell me anything about yourself. Tell me.'

'I had, when I was a boy, a gun.'

'A gun!'

'An air rifle. You pumped it up. It could either fire ten slugs in succession or one at an incredibly high velocity. I used to always use just the one. One was all I needed. The gun had a telescopic sight which could guarantee accuracy for up to a hundred metres. It was absolutely fucking incredible.'

'Richard, why are you telling me this?'

'Listen.'

'I'm listening.'

So, and for the life of me I don't know why, I tell Pepper about how I shot, dismembered, decapitated, disembowelled, plucked, skinned and ignited the various fauna that lived on our farm. And I spared her nothing. The bolognese of their guts, the set yogurt of their brains, the bleached sticks of their bones. The dull thud of a slug smashing through a gull's breast cartilage, the stench of a cigarette burning fur, feather and flesh. I told her of my dried crow's-foot neck thong, the rat I tried to preserve in pickling vinegar, the bird skeleton collection, the fox's tail that stretched across the handlebars of my bike.

And when I'd finished, she walked over and held me, for half an hour or so, lifting the whisky to my lips, feeding

125

me my inhaler and drying my eyes with the sleeve of her blouse.

'Richard,' she whispered, crushing my head to her body, rocking me like one would a baby, 'there's something you haven't told me, isn't there?'

7

She Kisses My Hair

Horace O sits sculpture-still. It rams home my own twitch-
iness, general unease and bad pulse. At the moment I'm
suffering from nose-fear. No amount of probing, blowing and
wiping will convince me that I haven't a bogey peeping out
of one of my nares. Horace's calmness is insufferable. It's
due, he reckons, to quitting chemicals and learning Transcendental Meditation. According to Horace, TM changes
your whole perspective on things. Regular practice elimin-
ates the need to party and allows you to immerse your psyche
in the oneness of creation – it improves you morally. Have
you ever heard so much tosh? Obviously, Horace has caught
a barb habit.

'H, I've decided. The fur thing. I'm not going to do it.
You happy?'

'It pleases me greatly, Rich.' He takes a sip of mineral
water with an unusually steady hand. 'Richard, take a look
at this.' He hands me a copy of today's *Advertising Week*.

'How the fuck did they get hold of this?'

'I don't know, man. But it pleases me.' Everything
bloody pleases Horace O at the moment. He behaves like
he's been converted to God. Mark my words – this cannot
last.

'Why, H? They've exposed our ace card before the campaign.' I'm looking at some stills from the Peking Tea/con-
dom film. After we'd finished shooting the male actor only
produces a rubber from his pocket and then, like a twat,
pulls it down over his head so he looks like a foetal X-ray.

127

Then he blows it up with his nose until it pops. 'Huh, they don't even mention us.'

'They will. Have faith.'

I bell Pepper to tell her that I've broken news of my decision to the agency and I'm told that she's got the day off. Obviously, it's news that makes me want to vom. I settle for head-butting my WP monitor. It hurts. It hurts the WP more. It topples from my desk and pops.

'You've had a rather good morning, haven't you, Richard?' sneers Imogen Rocastle.

Eat shit, you talentless sow. 'I guess.'

'First you make bloody fools of us in the industry rag . . .'

Fuck off! That wasn't me, Imogen. 'Now, that wasn't me.'

'Then you destroy several hundred pounds worth of computer.'

I'll head-butt you in a minute. 'The cleaner must have moved it.'

'Now you tell me that you've changed your mind about the damn pitch.'

If you're such a pro, you write it. 'Look, I'd lose my art director and my girlfriend.'

'OK Richard, I've got a proposition for you . . .'

Fuck your proposition. 'What?'

'I'll hire a freelance team to write it.'

'Yeah, cool.'

'Only that team will be you and Adrian . . .'

I'm not working with that twat.

'. . . and you won't be paid any extra. But you can do it anonymously. At the weekend. No one will be any the wiser and we'll forget the problems you've caused us.'

Problems! My girlfriend's playing the double-backed beast with someone as we speak. Now that's what I call a fucking problem. Don't you?. 'Yeah, OK.'

'Good, then it's settled.'

'No, hang on. No.'

128

'I'm sorry?'

'I won't do it. I can't.'

'Why?'

Because of Buttercup. That's why. 'I'm sorry Imogen, it's a question of conscience.'

'Richard, if you wanted a career with conscience you should have become a bloody nurse, not a professional bullshitter. Did you take the long way home last night? Via Damascus?'

'I'm sorry Imogen'

'Look Richard, perhaps I'm playing this the wrong way. Let me run it this way. One: You're a bloody good writer. The best we've got. You know that. Of course you do. Two: We're slap bang in the middle of a recession. Three: It's a bloody rare chance to win a new piece of business. The Knightsbridge Fur Company is worth the best part of a million to us. And we'll not be ungrateful to you if we win it. Richard, what's good for the agency is good for its employees. That's *always* been my philosophy.'

'Listen. I take your points. But, you know, it mightn't be all that good for the agency, long term. Picture the headline in *Advertising Week*: 'RUT Branded Bloody Murderers'. They'll dig out all the anti-fur ads, get quotes from industry hot-mouths, pressure groups. They'll ask us to defend our actions. We'll get fuck all new business for years and it could piss off our current clients. I mean the guys at AET – they're all pinkos.'

'Mmm, Richard, here's one. Junior copywriter circa 15K.' She's scanning the appointments in *Advertising Week*. 'Here's another. Oooh this one's 20K.'

'Are you sacking me?'

'I'm not sacking you. I'll leave that for Keith to decide. But you'd be wise to keep your eyes open. Now fuck off out of my office.'

Charlotte (not that Charlotte – an account handler at work) accepted Gary's invitation to lunch. But after a few drinks

129

– obviously, I downed a couple after my meeting with Imogen – all Pat wants to talk about is Pepper and my work situation. Charlotte's well fed up.

'Richard, they won't get rid of you after the condom stuff.'

'Yeah, but they can make life bloody difficult.'

'You could easily get another job.'

'You reckon?'

Really long awkward pause – the type where you can hear yourself masticating and gulping.

'Richard?'

'Yeah.'

'Can you keep a secret?'

'Sure.'

'I mean promise not to ever tell anyone. Not to mention it ever again. Even to me.'

'Yeah, yeah, tell me.'

She leans forward. I lean forward to hear her secret. But she says nothing. Instead, I feel her hand spider over my groin.

'I'm testing something,' she grins. Her test proves positive. 'Don't worry about your girlfriend. Let's fuck sometime. Yeah?'

'Charlotte, you know, you have exactly the qualities I appreciate in an account handler: insouciance, alcohol tolerance and a firm grip. Waiter, more wine.'

This is the theory. If you take a downer you become calm. If you've taken a downer and want to get normal, you simply take an upper.

This is how it works in practice. Mix barbs and speed and you feel pretty weird.

This afternoon, cruising on the cocktail of the drink, Pepper's infidelity, Imogen, and the promise of Charlotte, I feel mighty weird.

I leave early to try and catch Pepper and Richard at it. I go via the Duke of Edinburgh for fortitude.

On approaching the living-room door, I hear much rhythmic sighing and moaning. Or to be more precise – Pepper having a fuck big orgasm.

With burning eyes, clenched fists and a bag of cement in my stomach, I fling the door open. I'm figuring I'm about to see the worst thing it's possible to see. But you know what it's like? You pass a road smash-up and you've got to slow down for a good old gawp.

'Richard!' screams Pepper. 'Meet Rich.' Pepper's well lagged.

'Alright?' says Rich.

'Hi.'

'It's Richard's turn,' says Pepper. 'Do an impression of a male orgasm.'

'Hang on,' says Richenda – she's dead pissed as well. 'This is a male orgasm: uh .. uh .. ooooowww. Goodnight. Snore.' They cackle themselves into tearful hysterics. I forcibly overcome my relief and don a look of gross distaste. As I leave the room, Pepper springs up after me. I hear Rich shout, 'Oh, leave him.'

'Don't I get a kiss?' I kiss her perfunctorily. 'Are you OK? I'm sorry, she's drinking your whisky. I'll buy you another bottle. Are you alright, lovey?' I kiss her again and squeeze her hard – and for a brief moment I don't believe in the other Richard.

'I'm just fine, Pepper.'

'You don't mind me having friends round?'

'Your friends are always welcome.' So long as they're female.

'You do still love me, don't you?'

'Stupid question. C'mon Buttercup.'

The wanker who swaggers down the pavement – his pit bull unleashed and trotting ten yards in front. You must have come across him. Well, that's me. Buttercup's looking

131

mighty tasty these days – and no one meets eyes with me now. Of course, I stare hard at them. And most people cross the road when they see my fawn street-weapon is out of its sheath. Yeah, they mistake his *I'd like to be friends with you* grin with an *I want to get us in the local paper* look.

'Two meat harmonicas,' I tell our kebab man. Obediently, Buttercup sits at my legs and looks up, as our man in his surgeon's garb operates on the dripping cylinder of lamb.

'No cheelee sauce fer ve dorg. Thes right, yis?'

'That's it. Butterballs, you keep an eye on that harlot, Pepper, and I'll keep you in kebabs.' The dog looks up in agreement, despite his limited grasp of English. Buttercup understands 'Buttercup' (or rather thinks that anything beginning with B is it's name), 'Sit', 'come', 'walkies', and 'veggie din-dins'.

We kill our kebabs and head off for a couple of jars like old mates.

An unusual metaphor, possibly. But if you puff you'll quite understand. This spleek that I now hold is a microscope. And it enables me to focus on the deep chaos of my life. Its skies of couple-colour, its shadow and substance, its dark and light. With each toke I descend deeper into my own peculiar Mandelbrot set – which is both beautiful and horrific.

It's like this. Point a video camera at the monitor. Add a touch of light – the tip of this joint for instance – for a fraction of a second. Then watch the monitor and wait. First off, all you'll see on the screen is the red tip of the cigarette. But as the camera re-records the image and plays it back over, on top of itself, things begin to happen. It's called 'period doubling'. It means events overtake themselves and an infinite and unpredictable replication is initiated. Yeah, chaos. The spontaneous creation of breathtakingly eerie patterns. And this is precisely what I reckon's happening to me. Feedback. Naturally, if you've ever been in my sort of shape you'll know all about feedback. The accelerating merry-go-round, the shriek of tinnitus, the whorls of fearful eidolons – culminating invariably in a *fractal cluster* of vomit.

OK, sure. This is stoned logic. But isn't everything these days?

So I follow the rule of my *strange attractor* down into the formula and take a look at the lie of the land. Establish some of the light sources and, of course, the shadows. And sure, there's light here. But, as is typical in my life, there's also a load of shadow to fuck things up.

First, the light sources. The initial round of condom commercials. Well, you'll have seen them. And you'll know that everyone's talking about them. Go on, tell me you haven't mentioned the campaign. And the best news of all is that Horace O and I were mentioned in *Advertising Week*.

The sax version of 'Tonight I Celebrate My Love for You' is scheduled for release next week and is expected to chart immediately. And Imogen apologized about the fur thing and said she's looking into more money for us. Even the tabloids are on our side – 'Give us your funniest condom machine incident and win a year's supply of Love Condoms.' 'Inside the result of our readers' poll – where is the worst condom machine in Britain?' 'The message from the paper that cares is: Make Condoms a Way of Life.'

The other light of my life is the gorgeous Charlotte. Lifts, lavatory cubicles, cars, her flat, my flat, Imogen's office, a bus. It sounds good. Yet, true to the dictates of stoned logic, it is and it isn't.

The reason, predictably enough, is Pepper.

Picture Pepper and me drinking moderately in the White Lion, the posh pub in Finsbury Park. Now I know bugger all about architecture – I mean this could be restored Victorian, or fake – but whatever it is, it's making me uneasy. No, I'll be fair, it's not just the woodwork, the faded prints and the spinning-wheel tables that are pissing me off. It's the whole gizmo. The dozen or so *real ales* – so we're talking beards, cardigans and daft opinions. Sure there are a few trustworthy types on Guinness or strong lager at the bar. But I mean, there's no pool, no pinball and – can you believe this? – no music. In fact, I'm thinking, the only saving grace about being here is that we're in a pub, which is obviously better than not being in one. Oh the football machine is good news.

Now listen to this. Pepper's started drinking Guinness. In pints – which is, in itself, fair enough. Leastways it would be if she were drinking it for the right reason. To get good. But she's still on her first and, frankly, she's struggling.

Because there's no music you can hear other people's conversations. It means, theoretically, they can listen in to ours. I say *theoretically* because we've barely grunted to each other since we arrived.

'Toby, it's definitely your shout.'

'Listen, matey, I got one when we arrived. It's hardly my fault if you arrived half an hour late and missed out.'

'That's Toby. Tight as one of Nabokov's women.' They laugh and Pepper titters.

'What's funny?'

'Oh nothing. Just something they said.'

'What? Tell me, won't you?'

'Richard.'

'Tell me, Pepper.'

'Richard, please. Don't embarrass me.'

'So why earwig?' I'm whispering. 'Why don't we have a conversation of our own?'

'OK. What do you want to talk about?'

Why you haven't let me fuck you for a week. Why I've been staying in (mostly) and you've been out most of the time. 'I dunno. Anything.'

It's a fact. I came in pretty bad a week or so ago. Admittedly, Pepper didn't give me a hard time. She just said, 'Hello,' like I was a flatmate or something. And I wasn't too

134

out of order. I didn't try to cajole her into sex or anything. You see, I'd been doing some thinking on the way home. My work looked as though it was set to soar out of its trough, I'd done some good infidelity – flushed it out of my system, so to speak – and, well, yeah fuck it, I suppose in a way – in an unconventional way, mind – I love Pepper Furnival.

So I sat down soberly and said: 'Do you mind if I turn off the television? I'd like to say a couple of things to you if that's OK.' I figured I'd start like this so as she'd think I was about to dump her and be even more pleased about what I was about to say next. But when she said, 'Yeah, I s'pose,' she looked nonplussed.

So I told her that I loved her truly and that it was about time I grew up a little, got right long-term, got more responsible like – with money and that – and did some staying in with her. Of course, she ranked my speech on the same level as my similar all too frequent speeches. Consequently, she said, 'That's nice,' and went to bed.

Next evening, no pubs, wine bars – nothing. I came straight back from work. No Pepper. Naturally, my first inclination was to go out. I still had a lot of hangover. But I didn't go. I just watched TV. I say *watched*, more accurately I *looked at it*. Obviously, the only thing to think about was where the fuck Pepper had got to.

She got back at eleven thirty and said, 'Hello, you're back early.'

'I stayed in,' I said with some pride.

'Nice change. Goodnight.'

Where the fuck have you been? Where? You've been fucking someone, right? My namesake, by any slight chance? 'Goodnight, Pepper.'

Now the thing about stopping drinking suddenly is that you can't sleep anyway. But with Pepper next to me – in a T-shirt and panties – you can imagine the sort of night I had. All the poisons exiting via my sweat pores, the **drink-fear** rising and diffusing out, projecting fuck awful

135

pictures into the darkness. And right there, here in my bed, the epicentre of my fear (was it **drink-fear** or justified suspicion? I was in no state to tell), infidelity incarnate, purring contentedly, sated.

Normally, in a de-tox situation such as this, I'd have gladly doubled my debts to have Pepper Furnival in hugging distance. But not this night. In times past, when an arm of mine momentarily roused her, she might murmur, *Mmmm*, sink towards me and drop back off immediately. Now I was too afraid to wake her. Oh, I did try the once and her semi-conscious response was a moan. Of displeasure. And even if I touched her lightly so as not to waken her, perhaps just a knuckle brushed against the lowest slope of a buttock, I gleaned fuck little comfort. No, I was fired through with the most intense rage. Rage that shocked me with it's raw physicality. Rage that made me need cigarettes – badly.

Of course, I didn't get up. I just lay there vainly hoping that she might turn in her sleep and place an arm around me. Touch me of her own volition. Just the tiniest sign that our relationship wasn't terminally fucked. And all the time I'm getting the maniac Voices. Rolling over and over themselves.

What if she is fucking the other Richard? I'll muller them both.

Maybe I won't. I'll carry on getting right and dump her civilly. Or maybe, if she's unreservedly contrite, I'll forgive her and try and get things back to how they were.

No, fuck that! No one takes the piss out of me. I'll do them both. I'll use her for a fucking ashtray.

No, listen Rich. Get better evidence. Be sure. Then hit her in the crotch with Charlotte.

Why even wait until you're sure? Just get the fuck out of the shadow-time. The not knowing. Wake her up and ask her where the fuck she was.

Nar, nar man, get real. Ask her if you can do talking tomorrow.

But definitely give her some slaps if she's been misbehaving.

At around three, I think I did some dreaming. You know the sort. Where you dream that you've been in bed for hours and can't get to sleep.

At seven forty-five when Pepper gets up I'm awake. I pretend to be asleep to see if she'll kiss me or something. She doesn't. When she gets back from the shower, I'm sitting up in bed. I want to run a check on whether she'll disrobe and dress in front of me. She does. Just like that. It's routine. Not sexy in the slightest.

'Bye.'

'Don't I get a kiss?'

'Sorry.' She pecks me on the lips and turns.

'Pepper?'

'Mmm? Tonight. Can we stay in? Maybe watch a vid or something?' And I'm thinking that this is exactly the sort of thing Pepper used to say in the mornings. Exactly.

'Not tonight. I'm busy. Maybe tomorrow. See yer.'

There's still much poison floating around in my system. I can tell by how pig sick I feel on the first fag. Even by six o'clock cigarettes are making me shaky. There's still fear. I stay home a second night. It's not good. But I'm kept going by the fact that I'm sorting out and that we're going to talk tomorrow.

Tomorrow comes. Pepper remembers to kiss me goodbye – which pleases me. I say, 'See you tonight.'

She seems to have something on her mind but says, 'Yeah.'

At work, Horace O and I are briefed to create a press ad for the launch of a series of part-work magazines that build up into a set of books. Pre-recession, it's the sort of thing that would have run on the box. Understandably, I'm rather fucked off by the imposition – especially when the condom stuff is going so famously. But then, you know, I've got a living to make. The title of the series is *Incredible But True*.

'Well H man, we've got a few days on this number. What say we spend today reading the magazines and do some creative *dovetailing* tomorrow, darling?' Obviously, I can't do any work today.

'What yer sayin', Rich, is that you wanna spend this whole day in the public house reading magazines?'

'Oh how mistaken you are, my friend. Not a drop has passed my lips in over two days.' I hold out my hand. It still shakes, unfortunately. 'Well, it takes a bit of time. But I'm not lying, Horace.'

'Man, you should be in the book of *Incredible But True*.' The first magazine in the series – the one we need to concentrate on for the launch ad – concerns itself with death. And it's good. In fact I'm going to have to do bugger all work on it. I can simply headline the ad *Incredible But True*, write a bit of *part 2 free with part 1* and *at your newsagent now* and then pull out quotes from the text. It's as good as sold out. People like death. Horace can have the problem of choosing some inoffensive pictures to reproduce. Some of the dead Egyptians and the woodcuts of patented coffins look OK. Obviously, it would sell better if we could get a lardy-limbed autopsy shot in or go centre page with Jeremy Bentham. But there you are.

Cigarettes aren't so bad for me today. Maybe it's the coffee that's making me shake and palpitate. My real problem, of course, is thinking up an excuse to call Pepper and confirm. I mean, you can hardly call up your girlfriend and confirm a night in, can you? Fuck, maybe I should have booked a restaurant to give the date some importance. Then again, she could well think it profligate of me. And let's face it, I'm hardly going to stick to the four or five polite wines.

I finally find the courage to call Pepper. Sure it's after five strong ones at lunch. But listen, it's twenty-four hours later.

'So where the fuck were you? . . . At a friend's? Which friend? . . . Of course it's my fucking business. I was up half

138

the night worrying about you. I was going to fucking call the police, the hospitals, the . . .' I'm looking at a picture of a Stilton-coloured cadaver on a slab. 'That's not the reason I was worried.' Obviously it was. 'You could at least have called.'

'If you were so worried why didn't you call me earlier?' she asks with some sarcasm.

'Well, I was waiting for you to call. With some sort of an apology . . . Well no, I'm not sure I do accept it. Are you coming back tonight? I mean early . . . Tomorrow night? . . . Right, a definite no-excuses date Thursday after work. Or . . . Or I s'pose I've got a lot of thinking to do. No, don't say: *what thinking?* Just thinking. Alright?' Of course, Horace O is tittering throughout all of this.

I retreat to the khazi and detach my shirtsleeves from last night's cigarette assault.

So here we are. It's Thursday. And Pepper's scammed it so it's impossible to do a heart-to-heart. She's staring at air. Turning occasionally as if she's expecting to meet someone. The bitch seems totally unfazed by things. And I'm hoping that someone I half know comes in and saves me from this bastard situation.

My advice to myself at such times is to get the fuck out (I even did once). Turn the tables. Leave *her* to look the daft twat. And I would, but for the maddening hope that, given time and drink, she's going to say something useful. Touch my hand. Smile even. It's like when you're bad and trying to get right. Sure, you know, somewhere below the rising oblivion, that each drink, each cig, each slimmer you take is merely condensing the pollution – and no matter how long you stick at it you're not going to pull out of the chaos today. But you drink, feeling that after the next – if you do it fast enough – you're going to feel OK – that your piss will somehow go from its poisonous brown to yellow – and end up clear and clean. So here I am, shredding beer mats. Doing endurance.

'Pepper,' I snarl-whisper, 'Do you understand what you are doing to me?'

'I'm not doing anything to you.'

'We need to talk. I don't need to sit and watch you staring serenely at passers-by.'

'I asked you what you wanted to talk about. You said you didn't know. Do you know now?'

'Yes, yes,' I'm still whispering, leaning over intently. 'Us.'

'What about us?'

'I never see you any more.'

'God, Richard. One night.'

'I don't mean that. I mean in the evenings and weekends.'

'But you're always out in the evenings and at weekends. We never saw each other much anyway. Just because I've got some friends now.'

'But we saw each other more.'

'Be honest, Richard. It's fine if you're out with your friends having a good time, just so long as I'm safely at home waiting for you to return? Yeah?' But she doesn't say this angrily. She says it like it's some sort of fact.

'It's not that, Pepper.'

'Then what is it?'

'I dunno. Look.' I'm really shout-whispering now. But she's behaving well. Calmly. Like we're not having a scene or anything. 'Pepper, do you still, you know, love me, like?' She looks at me for a couple of seconds. Smiles like she might to a Client or the Bastard and calmly says, 'Yes.'

'That it?'

'What else do you want me to say?'

'Well, if you still do, like you say, why don't we ever, you know, make love any more? Well lately, like?'

'You're usually too drunk.'

'Well I'm not getting drunk these days. Yes, I was very pissed off last night because of – you know.' She nods. 'So can we do it a bit more? Please?'

'OK.'

'Do you mean that? I mean, really?'

And then this happens. She puts a hand on the back of my neck, draws my head towards her, kisses me on the nose and says, no almost growls, 'Yes, Richard.'

'And maybe when we're in bed. Sort of just sleeping, you know? Maybe we could . . .'

'Hello,' she cries gleefully. And immediately I'm filled with this urge to do something that'll get me in the launch issue of *Incredible But True*.

These women. Oh man. They look like they've just fallen out of a documentary on Temgesic abuse. Or those *hippies* that get on the news each summer for fucking up someone's farm in the West Country.

'Richard, you know Rich, don't you?'

'Yeah. How you doing?' She nods.

'And this is Char.' This is Char. Doc Marten eighteen-holes. Disgraceful leggings that may once have been white – the holes reveal her legs to be hairier than mine. Jacket I can't describe – unless it really is a potato sack. Scalp shaved at the sides crested with pond-coloured natural dreads. Nose-ring.

'Hi.'

'Alright mate?'

'And this is Linda.' Linda's better. She's similarly cropped. But, you know, that kind of hair sometimes suits black people. She still wears shit clothes though. Some kind of cowl or jellaba. Fuck knows. Same boots and nose-ring. Absolutely no respect for herself (or the people who have to look at her) in the slightest.

'Hello there. Pleased to meet you.' She offers a hand. Obviously, I have to take it.

'Who want's a drink then?' asks Rich. 'Pep?'

'Mmm. Guinness please.'

'Richard?'

'Me!'

'Would you like a drink?'

141

'No, no. I'm fine thanks.'

'Don't be silly. You've only got a dribble left. What do you want?'

'Becks . . . ta.'

Sure they invited me along too. I supplied the gear, after all. And I suppose it doesn't feel all that bad. At least I know where she is. At least she's with women. And she did indicate that we were still on shagging terms.

Then again, the look she gave me when they asked. It said: 'Don't even think about coming back with us. This is a part of my life in which you sure as hell don't figure.' Reasonable enough. Leastways, reasonable enough when it's three a.m. and you're midway through a bottle of Irish.

Obviously, come morning, when I wake alone and unwell, my attitude will be somewhat different. I'll be piecing together all the crap I said, getting shit bad guilt and loneliness. But listen – I wasn't that out of order. I made a right effort to be civil. And that, I figure, is what pissed Pepper off. Now, under normal circumstances, if I had remained sober and polite and refused an after-hours invitation to smoke and drink, Pepper would be giving me hugs and congratulations and the rest. But tonight, it was like she wanted me to play the arsehole. And because I got on well – or tried to – with her friends, it's like I let her down.

And you know what? Pepper was telling them things about me. Not lies as such. But things well out of context. Things that I figure were designed to make them dislike me. Make me live up to the monstrous picture she'd painted of me. You see, Pepper's not like them. She's never lived in a squat, raved on Es, lobbed bottles at Nazis – I mean, can you imagine Pepper using the crappers at Glastonbury? No, she's in advertising and wears normal – if somewhat tasteless – clothes. The only way she can get them to like her is to paint a hard-luck story about an evil boyfriend.

Right. At one point the conversation was books. (Books that seemed in the main to be about adultery or fruit.) And

Pepper said, 'Richard doesn't read female authors.' And this is true. But before I had time to counter that I didn't read any male authors either, they were asking me what I did read. Pepper answered for me. 'Magazines.' And then, of course, the bitch went on to tell them about the sort of magazines I read. 'Those ones you get in the supermarket. For menopausal housewives,' she laughed.

'I read lots of different types of magazines. *New Scientist*, *Viz* . . .'

Sure, it's nothing. Maybe the Irish is making me read too much into things. And Pepper's friends remained non-plussed. But you know? It's about loyalty and that. I mean, God knows what else she's said.

Anyway, Pepper fucked up well and good. Rich asked her where they could score on the manor. Pepper looked at me, obviously. So I gave them an eighth – just like that – buckshee. And they started asking me what else I could get and for how much and that. As you know, I can get anything. Now that might not impress you, but it sure as hell got them going. So we did drug talking for a time. That's to say, I delivered a lecture that they were all – with the obvious exception – well into.

Also, Pepper retold the quip she'd overheard about the Russian politician and they didn't understand either.

It's seven a.m. I slept. And it's unlike I expected it to be. No fear, no retrospective shame, no malaise. Obviously, I'm still drunk. I exercise Buttercup and go to work. I rattle off the page ad in a couple of hours. And because I'm not expecting another brief until Tuesday, I arrange to take an early lunch with Charlotte and forestall the come-down – besides it's Friday. Then this happens. I'm emptying my ashtray and putting on my jacket and my phone goes. And for the first time in fuck knows I get a call from Pepper.

'What are you up to tonight, Richard?'

'Why?'

'Well, it's just that I've had a lot of late nights and been drinking too much and my skin's suffering, and I wondered if you fancied a night in. I mean, you said . . .'

Now, the obvious thing to do is to plead a prior engagement. Tip the balance, so to speak.

'Well actually Pepper . . .'

'I mean, if you've arranged something . . .'

'No, no. I'll cancel.'

'Thank you. It'll be nice, won't it?'

'Pepper?'

'Mmm?'

'Last night. I mean, was I OK? I didn't misbehave or anything? Say anything out of line, did I?'

'I don't think so. But I can't really remember. I got horribly smashed. I reckon if anyone misbehaved, it was me. I spent half the night puking into the loo.'

On the way to the pub, arm in arm with Charlotte, I hum 'Perfect Day' by Lou Reed.

Eight thirty. I get home. Sure I've had a few – but the promise of having Pepper to myself, at her behest, is keeping me well sober.

'Hi-er.' She's on the sofa, arms outstretched for me. We hug. She lets go after normal hug time. But I hang on in. 'Arr,' she whispers and wraps me up again. It's good.

We lie on the sofa, tongues in each other's heads, hands in each other's shirts. I break snog and move my head back to look at her face. It's puffed and blotchy from drink. Her back and breasts are leprous. Out of curiosity I pull off her leggings and caress a knee. As I suspected, almost fully calcified. In fact, right now, Pepper's pretty bad news.

So why is the volcano already trembling?

At six thirty I took Charlotte back to the empty office. And we did what we'd always said we would. Yeah, we fucked on the boardroom table – and it was good. I've probably done a gallon of strong ale. So what in the name of all that copulates is going on?

Pepper – and she's grinning like she used to, almost –

144

limbo dances out of her knickers. She's working at my belt. I'm thinking hard about Arsenal vs. Leeds. But it really is no good. How am I going to raise the cash for a season ticket or a bond, if needs be, when Highbury goes all-seater? She's got the button undone and her fingers are on my fly. Everyone around here agrees. The North Bank will never be the same. We should boycott it, we say. Obviously, we won't. I'm so terrified. Her hard hand trickles into my boxers and she pulls me towards her.

'Good grief!' she exclaims, wiping her hand on her T-shirt. 'It must have been a long time.'

'Oh God, I'm sorry.'

'Don't worry. These things happen once in a while.'

'I'm so sorry.'

'Don't be so silly.' She takes my hand and coaxes it down. 'It doesn't matter. Really it doesn't,' she whispers. 'Go on, go on. Please.'

I start gently, as one does, then begin to squelch away like pastry-making. And it pleases me that soon she's good and sloshy. Yet, her sighs and facial expressions appear disingenuous – or maybe it's just that I never noticed before. Then she puts her hands on my head and urges me down. An uncharacteristic move for Pepper – but, obviously, I comply. In minutes I'm ready to have a second bash at lovemaking. Yet loose and expansive as she is now, and replete as I am, I feel sure that it's going to happen again. And Pepper's not helping. She's gritting her teeth – swimming against the tide of her orgasm. Then she can delay things no longer and as ever she clings to me with all her strength. I continue. It's only going to take a couple of seconds. And then I just lose interest. I mean, there's no longer anything at risk.

Normally, in situations such as this, I want to be in a pub – badly. All at once Pepper seems too close – too hot. Sure, I know the form. I've got to stick around for a while, say I love her and that. But it's not like I really mean it – at that exact moment leastways. But now, fuck, I don't even want to break this embrace for a cig. And yeah, I'm meaning the things I say. So when the telephone rings and she says, 'Don't even think about answering it.' I don't regard it as a heaven-sent excuse. 'Anyway, the answerphone's on.'

Then I remember Charlotte. How I buggered off without doing any of the aforementioned. I wouldn't put a hurtful answerphone message past her.

'I won't be a sec. I'll be back I promise. I love you.'

'Good God.'

Now, obviously I should have told him she was out. Obviously.

Ten minutes into the call I walked up behind her and began to massage her shoulders. She put a hand over the mouthpiece and said, 'Please, Richard. I'm trying to talk.'

After about an hour she comes back into the living room. She takes the wine bottle from me and sits across my lap. Then she kisses me – really quite nicely – and strokes my face.

'Look at this.' She indicates her T-shirt. 'I'll have to change. Richard, I've got to go out.'

'What do you mean, *go out*?'

'What I mean is, pick up the telephone, call a minicab, walk out of the front door, get into the taxi and go to Hornsey Road.'

'What the fuck for?'

'That was Rich's man. They've had a fight. He's pretty cut up about it.'

'So you're going to comfort him?'

'If you like.'

'In the name of all that . . .'

'We're just going to talk. Don't be so silly.'

'So who's going to comfort me?' She hands me back my wine bottle. 'Will you be back at all tonight?'

'I hope so. I'm shagged.' She smiles and kisses me again. 'Bye, you.' And she gets up.

I knock myself out with wine and Columbian and inhale the pungent vapours of my arm hairs as they sizzle into nothingness. Obviously, I dream about fuck awful disasters for the rest of night.

At midday there's no sign of Pepper so I head off to the pub like I always do before football. But on the way out, I'm halted by a high voltage force-field. A letter for Pepper. Postmarked Newcastle-Upon-Tyne, indubitably male script on the envelope. Writing, in fact, that bears a startling resemblance to mine – albeit legible. Same name, similar handwriting – it really is quite sickening.

Of course, waiting for the kettle to boil, my voices bicker over the ethics of the matter. But as my hand starts to burn and drip in the steam, it's not the voices that convince me to leave the envelope intact and hide it under the bed. No, it's sheer cowardice. A delicate matter such as this must obviously be approached shit-faced.

By kick-off the pub is more or less empty. My pulse certainly isn't up to football. So I figure, best drink, go outside for a little puff and catch up on some thinking. But all I get is my fuck awful Voices doing thinking for me.

Suppose you have a choice. You can either be in a fuck awful disaster, or Pepper's fucking someone else who may or may not be called Richard. Which would you choose?

Suppose you have a choice. You can either have Pepper in a fuck awful disaster, or you can have her fucking someone else who may or may not be called Richard?

Are you finding the choice difficult, Richard?

Are you?

'Only because I'm bombed,' I tell them.

Perhaps they're one and the same.

And I'm thinking – wrecked as I am – that this might be a relevant point. Did the **disaster-fear** precede Pepper?

'Fuck stupid voices anyway.'

'You alright, mate?' says someone. I look up horrified and pull away the joint that's become attached to my arm.

The walking's good. But the eating's a problem. You see, if I don't eat soon I'll be forced to disgorge my lunchtime session. If do eat, I'll obviously chuck it up. And if I make myself sick, I'll be too sore to eat even if there's room. Then it clicks. Slimming pills!

So you can imagine the sort of mess I was in when Buttercup knocked me over and back into the street early Sunday morning. Now, by rights, Buttercup should be locked in the kitchen – it means, of course, that Pepper still hasn't come home.

I do a couple of hours kip in the bath and wake, not hungover, but reeling again. I feel confident that the undercurrent of drink cascading beneath the Whiz is enough to put me out a second time, so I crawl towards the bedroom. I lunge up at the handle and fall into the room on my stomach. The bedside light goes on. I kneel up. The bloke in my bed sits up. We stare at each other. Oh sweet Jesus, this really isn't the way I wanted it to happen. Meeting Pepper's lover in this kind of state. On my knees for fuck's sake. If you have but a milligram of self-possession, find it now. Please, whatever happens, don't cry. And don't even think about fighting.

'Richard,' he says.

'Hello. I'm, er, Richard as well. Pleased to . . .'

'Richard,' says Pepper again.

In the morning – could it have been that I wasn't up to doing tact? – I asked, 'Holy shit! What in the name of all that fucks have you done?'

'It's *my* hair,' she retorted. No spat.

'But I'm the one who's got to be seen with you, right?' Then for no apparent reason she freaked. I mean crockery-chucking freaked.

In the evening she stayed in and watched television. And I did a lot of highly shameful apologizing – which I certainly don't intend to go into. And finally, when David Attenborough had said his piece, a hand came down to where I was sitting below her. And she said, 'I'm sorry too. About the plates and that. I'll get some new ones. But Richard, you don't half say some stupid things.' I agreed. And after she'd gently bandaged my arm, we kissed and she smiled and said. 'Let's drink some wine and make friends properly.'

We did. It happened again. She was slightly less understanding this time around.

And I'm forced to ask myself what, in the name of all things that fuck, is going on? I mean, I've been sacking with Pepper since the spring – so why now? Why now, when her hair is short and her responses curt, do I find her more desirable than ever? So desirable that I'm – yeah, well – you know. And it's bad. I just can't do it with Pepper any more. You'd have thought I'd have been OK, seeing Charlotte on a fairly regular basis, and all. And you know what? I reckon it's got something to do with the other Richard. (Does that sound weird to you? Does it sound at all gay?)

Anyway, in the uppers and downers equation, Pepper's bad medicine near extinguishes the whole of the rest of the celebration.

So I've made my decision. I must gain some parity in this cold war. Let her know that I too have nuclear capabilities. That is to say, she must learn something of the gorgeous Charlotte.

Equanimous at the prospect of facing a few months government hospitality for cocaine possession, Jeez is having a party. And if you've never been to a Jeez bash – well, what can I say? There's isn't a better rave inside the M25.

'Is it alright if I bring a couple of friends to Jeez's party?' Pepper asks me.

'Pepper, if you've got tickets, do what you like with them.' She protests.

'You know it's sold out. You can get tickets, can't you? You're supposed to be my boyfriend.'

'You didn't take me to your party last week.'

'But that was different. You wouldn't have known anyone. You wouldn't have enjoyed yourself. I've been looking forward to this party ever since you told me about them. Please, Richard.'

I turn my back on her. In the picture frame, I see her poking two fingers up at me. What the fuck has gone wrong with the woman?

The thing about one of these raves is that the fortnight before is damn good too. You have to go into training if you're going to do the party properly. If you don't it could prove fatal. Well, if you're like me it could.

'Richard, why don't you want me to go?'

'C'mon, I'm going to be in a right state. With all my mates – those creeps you hate.'

'That's why I want to take some friends.'

'I'm not walking in with you and your coven of viragos.'

'Richard, you're a bastard. You really are. Who are you taking then? Your new girlfriend? Someone from work is it? The new secretary? No, no, silly me. You couldn't possibly be seeing someone else, you wouldn't take two seconds to fire off if you were.'

'And what about you, eh?'

'What about me?'

'The Richard you went out with at Newcastle.'

'You really *are* absolutely crazy. You really are. I told you, I MADE THAT UP. Have you been suspecting me for all this time? Of course I've been faithful to you.' She lifts her top.

'Shit – it's bad.'

'Do you really think that anyone, barring a sicko like you, would want to get within spitting distance of that?'

'I don't fucking believe you just said that.'

'Well I did . . . But yeah, I shouldn't have. And I'm sorry. All the same, the tickets admit two. What if I didn't go with

150

anyone else? Just you and me? What do you say to that?'

'Look, Pepper . . .'

'Look Pepper nothing. I don't want to go to your seedy parties. I don't care if you are knocking off the office tart. I've given up. Had enough. I'm going out.'

'Where? Are you coming back?'

'Would you notice if I didn't? I could put a pig's carcass in the bed and you wouldn't notice for a month.'

'Look Pepper, I'll take you. I'll take you.'

'Fuck you, Richard.'

'See yer round, Pepper.' She stomps out but turns back. She's still shouting.

'And Richard, you git. I've just found out.'

'Found out what?'

'You haven't paid any bloody rent at all since we moved in. No bloody wonder you wanted to do separate direct debits instead of that budget I suggested.'

'I just forgot, that's all.'

'You're bloody pathetic.' Slam.

TALKBACK
Letters

• I read your tips for giving up smoking with interest. Here's how I did it. I limited myself to one cigarette at eight o'clock each evening. It meant that I always had something to look forward to and never felt entirely desperate. When, after a few weeks, I no longer looked forward to my nightly smoke, I stopped. It was entirely painless.

   D. I. Norton, Maidstone, Kent

Peg says: If any other readers can shed light on how to stub out the habit, please roll up. We'll be happy to hear from you.

• Living in London, I can't help noticing that there seem to be more blind men than women. Is it that more men lose their sight through work or is there another explanation?

   E. Micklewright, Wimbledon, London

Peg says: Can any readers provide an eye-opener regarding this interesting observation?

I hear the front door open and Pepper storm in. She flings the living-room door into the wall.

'Sorry.'

'Hey look, it's fine. I'm sorry too, Pepper. Maybe we should . . .'

'I meant about the door. Listen, I've just remembered. Your brother Sebastian called . . .'

'WHAT! How in the name of all that fucks did he get this number?'

'He called the agency and got through to me. He asked. I didn't think there was any harm . . .'

'My God. My God, Pepper. I can't believe you could be so . . .'

'WHAT?'

'Tell me, please tell me you didn't give him our address.'

'No, no. Why are you so . . . Richard, it sounded really important.'

'Right, Pepper. Listen to me. Listen to me good. The answerphone stays on full-time. You don't answer until you know who it is. Under no circumstances do you pick up the phone.'

'Richard, do you owe him money?'

'Christ, no.'

'What is it?'

'Just do as I say.'

152

'"Do as I say. Do as I say." I come back because I remember a message that I think is important and what do I get? You are turning into one arsehole.'

Leaves leave the trees. Foreigners leave London. And Horace O leaves me to drink alone.

'I hate it when autumn really gets going,' I said as he calmly sipped his orange juice.

'You're supposed to,' was the guru's esoteric reply. He went on to explain. Some nonsense about Jung – coming into consciousness, archetypes of death and rebirth, and ancestral memories of winter. Some crap my art director talks these days. He stops abruptly.

'Tell me what you've done since the condom stuff,' he demands.

'What d'ya mean H?'

'Workwise.'

'What have *you* done?'

'Plenty my man, plenty. I've been working with another writer. One that writes.'

'Cheers, H. Cheers very much. I wondered what you were doing.'

'C'mon Rich, you haven't been with the living for the last six weeks. You must sort yourself out. Be wise, Rich.'

'Horace, you're the one that's gone weird. TM. Baldness. Shaving your head's not normal.'

'Possibly, but my blood's blood.'

'Yeah well, I cook on gas.'

'Rich, I want you to do me a favour.'

'Oh yeah. What's that?'

'I want you to come to a TM class. Rich, it'll help you get off the poison, improve things with Pepper.'

'That cow.'

'Rich, I don't want to lay down ultimatums but it's either that or some sort of alcohol or drug dependency therapy. If you don't sort yourself out soon, we're going to break up.'

'C'mon H, let me buy you a pint.'

'Have you listened to a word I've said?'

'Look, I'll sort out after the party. One last bash and I'll clean up. I promise. Now let me get you that pint.'

'I mean it, Rich. You're heading for a disaster.'

'Come on, Richard. Mind the door frame. Don't cry now.'

'Peffer. Peffer.'

'Be quiet. Down you go. Into the shower. That's right. Give me your foot. That's it. Lift your arm. Let me get this jacket off.'

'I'm sorry, Pepper.'

'Be quiet.'

My body is showered and my clothes are in the washing machine and Pepper is trying to communicate something.

'Pepper, you're so nice to me. Your love is boundless.'

'Richard, can you understand me? Nod if you understand what I'm saying.'

'Who's that, Pepper?'

'It's Rich, she's helping me pack.'

'For Newcastle?'

'No. I've been to Newcastle already. I'm going to stay with her for a bit.'

'For good?'

'Richard, listen. I've put everything down in a letter for you to read when you're sober.'

'Did you say I was a rapist, Pepper?'

'I didn't say that at all. Now go to sleep.'

'I'd never do . . .'

'No, I know you wouldn't, Richard.'

'Will I see you in the morning?'

'No.'

'Tomorrow night. I'll take you out. That'll be nice, won't it?'

'Richard, I have to go now.' She kisses my hair. 'Goodbye, Richard.'

8

Crawling with Spiders

Buttercup loudly snoozes where Pepper usually does quietly. I shut my eyes and think: 'Father in heaven, if you exist and are at all a good bloke, make Pepper come back and stop being such a fucking hag.' **Fuck you! Give me the accident I deserve**, says Gary. I fall back asleep and do some predictable dreaming, predictable enuresis, etc.

Dear Richard,

If you haven't already gathered, I've left. I'm going to stay with a friend until I have somewhere else to live.

Richard, you have, quite genuinely, been very kind to me, and I'm sorry to have to hurt you. Then again, you've been unspeakably cruel. I won't pain either of us by listing the instances I can remember, suffice to say I think you know what I'm talking about.

I've been planning to make the break for some time – even before we moved here, if the truth be known.

I know you'll think my new friends have put ideas into my head, poisoned me against you. Maybe they have. But it's been coming for a long time. If you're cruel enough to an animal for long enough, it'll grow hard.

What made me decide to go tonight was the message on your answerphone. Anyway, it didn't hurt me, it just made me realize what wretched creatures most men are.

I pity you, Richard, you must really despise yourself to commit suicide in such a slow and painful way.

And I actually think that there might be a very nice person somewhere beneath all the pills and alcohol. Someone who'd take on a girl with rhino hide instead of skin.

And Richard, do yourself a favour. Take a look in the mirror. When was the last time you weighed yourself?

Anyway, I have to pack. Obviously, I can't take everything, and I'll continue paying my share of the rent until I can move it. Oh, and if you're 'rat-arsed' one night and you think it's a good idea to damage any of it – it will of course be a police matter.

Kind wishes

Pepper

PS. My love to Buttercup. You can call him Slugger now.

Imagine copping a Doc Marten in the stomach from a mate as you hand him a drink. Sickening isn't the word. Especially when you consider that the sow didn't even have the gall to come clean. I mean, the lies are more transparent than one of the woman's spritzers. So when I've finished puking, I say, 'Butterballs, we deserve a drink.'

'The one never hurt anyone,' I growl for him.

'But first . . .'

Click. Beep. Hiss. 'Richard darling. It's me. Charlotte. Just a short message to say I won't be able to see you for a week because I'm going on a surprise holiday to . . . er . . . Lar . . . Touket with my parents. But I'll be back in time for the party. Love you.' Beep.

Yes. Obviously, I regret getting Charlotte to do it. But you know, when you're lagged . . .

'Walkies. Pub walkies.' Anyway, I'm not going to let a hiccup like this put me off my training.

Working out in the Duke, last night begins to fall into horrendous focus. And I'm wondering if Buttercup ever has difficulty in separating real events from dreams. Or if he ever feels deeply guilty about the things he's dreamed – or hopes to shit he's dreamed. Yeah, I produced a tantrum. A magnificent one at that. A smashing things one. In front of Pepper and her friend. Then I did a Niagara vomit and collapsed.

The debate I interrupted was about whether or not all

157

men are potential rapists. Richenda maintained they are. Pepper saw the main strength of the proposition as lying in the word *potential*. Obviously, I was having none of this. And I just went nuts. Not aiding my cause much, I must say. Rich beseeched Pepper to leave the more than potential violator be, but then remained content to watch her revive me, strip me, shower me and put me to bed.

You probably shat in the shower, says Gary matter-of-factly. Gary's drink tolerance is well up these days. Pat is virtually out of the picture.

'A couple more Buttercup, then we're off. I have a plan.'

HAIR:

Pepper – Crinkly, hueless ginger, with no particular game plan. Lately cropped out of all femininity.

Charlotte – Jasper smooth, jasper black, hair you can take anywhere.

SKIN:

Pepper – Insipid tan with small freckles in places. You know the rest.

Charlotte – Caramel smooth, caramel tan, three small moles so far discovered – I have the rest to look forward to.

FACE:

Pepper – Too close-together eyes rescue it from thorough normality.

Charlotte – Could easily be a make-up model if she wanted – easily.

FATTY BITS:

Pepper – Soft and pillow-like. Buttock cellulite beginning to escape from panties. Folds already sketched out their intentions on thighs. Beginnings of a stomach precipice in tight jeans.

Charlotte – Firm as a pit bull's rump.

FINGERS:

Pepper – Short chipolatas, cicatrices due to compulsive nail biting.

Charlotte – Pornographically long and smooth. Blood-red
   nails, clean and shapely as beetle backs.
LEGS:
Pepper – Too short to fit comfortably around me.
Charlotte – A circus act.
PROBABLE REACTION TO MY ANALYSIS:
Pepper – 'It's typical of you – comparing women's physical
   features.'
Charlotte – 'Shut up and fuck me.'
CURRENT LOCATION:
Pepper – Fuck knows – probably at work or at Richard's.
Charlotte – On my bed.
CURRENT ACTIVITY:
Pepper – Typing or waiting for Richard to finish on her (she
   never was very inspired).
Charlotte – Masturbating into my camcorder.

But it's not working. All I want is for her to go – leave me
to work on a way to convince Pepper of my innocence.
   All of this is, of course, a minor problem for someone with
Charlotte's talents and I soon forget about my wicked ex.
   Then it's morning and I'm sore and outraged as a beetroot.
I think about the condom in her luggage, the letter on
Sidney, the letter from Newcastle that I'm too scared to
open, and the wrong person next to me, and piss Charlotte
off with some serious crying. She grabs me like a kid grabs
a cat's tail. I scream. It really is too painful to bear. This is my
view. Unfortunately it's not the view of the priapic madman
under the duvet. Before she'll get up, I need to spend half an
hour, my hungover face gorging her into salivating epilepsy.

Rottweilers grin and slaver as we trek up the drive. The
ultraviolet sensors reveal an angry dick. Our tickets are
good. We enter Jeez's and our ribs clatter to deep house.
Charlotte takes advantage of the crowd and strobe to shove

a tongue in my mouth and a hand into my trousers. A week later I'm still not better and I'm thinking that this could be bad news.

The hall scene's not for us, so we find somewhere to get a drink and spin a stick. Charlotte wants to try an E. I give her a Microdot, but tell her it's an E (for obvious reasons) I also give her a Black Bomber to give her tripping a decent surge. I eat two Es and a Microdot. I'll use some Bombers to get me right later.

We find a room with ashtrays and bean-bags and just smoke and drink and talk and wait for the chemicals to change us. I'm one hundred per cent content here and now with Charlotte, and rarely think about Pepper. I no longer think I keep spotting her in the crowd. We're both having a good time. I need to drink as much as I can before the Es take effect. After that, I'll probably slow up a little or, worse still, go on to beer or soft drinks. I've drunk two-thirds of my bourbon bottle already. But it's OK. Tomorrow I'm going to sort out long-term, like I promised Horace.

I take Charlotte into the garden where the stage is. I tell security that I'm a friend of Richard's, from the Plum Jugglers. He lets me through.

Richard lies unconscious in a pillow of vomit. His sick seems to have it's own peculiar mauve halo. Do rock stars, I wonder, have superior sick to the rest of us? Both Charlotte and I are transfixed with Richard's vomit. It really is quite exquisite.

'You've noticed it too?' She says.

'Yes.'

'It's beautiful, isn't it?'

'It's wonderful.' Richard is hauled away but Charlotte and I stay to take in the sick some more. I get us a bean-bag. Periodically, I fetch a beer or soft drink from the cooler behind the stage.

Now Charlotte's eyes are on me. Her pupils are big as five-pee bits.

'You're so very lovely,' she says and caresses my face. I look at Charlotte and, really, she is so fucking beautiful. I stroke her face. We kiss a bit. My pecker feels like it's being pumped up with acid, ground glass and nails. Yet I can't help my hand from descending into Charlotte's culottes. I'm feeling so good.

'It's no good,' she smiles, 'I can't feel a thing.' Speed can do this sometimes. 'Shall we look at the sick again?' So we do. But it's dried a little and lost much of its colour. 'It's not as good as I remember.'

'It's not, is it?'

It seems only a short while later when I say, 'What time do you reckon it is, Charlotte? No don't look. Guess.'

'Mmm, around two?'

'Wrong. Twenty-five past five.'

'My God! It can't be. Has everyone gone?'

'There'll still be people dancing inside, maybe.'

'Oh my God, dancing. I can't even get up to pee.'

'You can.'

'No way.'

'Honestly, I know about these drugs. Once you're up, you feel just as cool up as when you're sitting down. You think you can't do it. But you can. Trust me.' I get up and pull Charlotte up. And because there's no one left backstage we both take a long piss.

Then I remember about Pepper. And it's like she's laughing at me for wasting the whole of this fucking party looking at a piece of sick. I neck down a heap of bourbon.

'C'mon Charlotte, let's dance.'

'No, no Richard, I'm feeling totally gross.'

'But we've wasted the whole party.' We emerge from behind the stage. It's dead. 'Shit, shit, shit.'

'What's wrong?'

'It's all over. It's not like it used to be. In the old days people'd stay until, I don't know, Sunday night maybe.' We leave Jeez's and amble around, hoping to chance upon a

161

cab. Obviously, we won't get one with me swigging whisky, but it's good out here.

Central London. Totally deserted. Misty, beautiful dawn. Take away the parked cars and it'd be like a fucking oil painting. Our conversation dries so we drop another BB each.

'I really enjoyed that party,' says Charlotte.

'Well, we missed it. But yeah, I know what you mean.'

Periodically, Charlotte stops talking and kisses me – like she's on a fucking E or something.

'Richard, you're so fantastic to be with. And you know why I enjoyed the party so much?'

'No?'

'It's because . . . promise you won't be cross?'

'Scout's.' I do the stupid sign.

'It's because I'm falling in love with you.'

'Don't talk silly, Charlotte. It's the drugs.'

'Yeah, maybe.'

And because the speed is making me talk some crap, I say: 'Besides my girlfriend only left a couple of days ago and I miss her like fuck.'

'You poor thing,' she says. I seize the opportunity and do some crying on her.

We've both got a fair amount of come-down and we're speeding, so the question of us separating doesn't arise. But as the cab splices through dawn's gauze and we bounce around, and into each other, I'm getting my stock going-home thoughts – 'Maybe she's changed her mind and I'll find her at home in bed.' I also know that if I take a dive from the Whiz before the pubs open, I'm going to want rid of Charlotte's cloying company. But hell, it's so unusual to be with someone these days, it's worth the risk.

Charlotte goes to the bathroom and I hunt for liquor. Not finding any enrages me. My first instinct is to bawl Charlotte out. I don't though, obviously it's not her fault (well, *prima facie* it's not – but I blame her somewhere along the line

162

for this shit). But when she emerges all fresh and smelling like Pepper, I go off the fucking handle. But come-down rage only lasts a second or two.

Charlotte, as I think I've said, is bloody gorgeous-looking. And to see her face collapse in big tears – oh, man. I was almost tempted to ask if she'd let me video her before I apologized.

'I'm sorry. I didn't . . . It's not as if she's died or anything.'

'It's OK. Look, I'm really am fuck sorry. It's just – I suppose it's because I couldn't find any drink. And it's only six thirty and there's no way I can do sleeping.'

'Richard, I've still got a bottle of wine I bought for the party. I'm not up to drinking any though.' And I'm figuring that it's about the best it can be without Pepper. Rationing myself with much discipline, I manage to maintain a degree of mellowness until opening time. I also manage to get rid of Charlotte – who I'm beginning to suspect thinks that she's something akin to my girlfriend.

By three, the Whiz has worn off – or I'm too lagged to notice it. And I get a sudden and violent panic attack. It says I'm going to make a career of drinking tramp brew on the streets. And I'm wondering what Pepper's reaction would be when accosted by me in bad clothes, dog-shit for hair, wielding a tin on the street. Sympathy? Is it possible? Is it, fuck! She'd be pleased. It's then that I make the purposeful decision to dry out.

Except I don't.

Listen to this. Everyone's buying condoms. But more importantly, *Advertising Week* want to do an interview with Horace O and me.

Picture Horace O, Charlotte and me in the Round House.

'Picture the Bastard's face when he sees it.'

'Picture Pepper's.'

'Cheers, Rich.'

'Cheers, H.'

'Becks and chaser?'

'Good man, H.' Just like old times, eh? – I'm thinking –
It's about bloody time I had a break.

Then this happens.

The journalist from *Advertising Week* is disappointingly
young and dishevelled. She also appears to be quite unimpressed by our (well at least my) youth, professional distinc-
tion and the state-of-the-art boardroom. In fact she comes
over a touch disdainful if anything. But I'm reckoning she
fancies me all the same.

I'm wrong. I discover this when I prelude an answer with:
'Listen dear,' and touch her hand. This is how she takes
revenge.

'I know you work as a team. But there must have been a
moment when one of you came up with the big idea. "Let's
use the Peking Tea couple!"?' she asks.

Horace O smiles and points at himself.

'Hang on H,' I say.

Then it happens.

We have this bastard row, there, in front of the journalist.
When we've finished, she clicks off her recorder.

'Thank you gentlemen,' she says, and pisses off.

'I don't believe that bastard,' I say to Charlotte over dinner.

'Don't worry, they'll probably gloss over that bit.'

'That bit! That bit was the whole fucking interview.'

'I suppose it's a bit of an unfair question to ask. How can
you remember who suggested what?'

'No that's wrong, Charlotte. I *always* come up with the
ideas. That tart just draws them up. He might make the odd
suggestion once in a while but . . .'

'Richard, you're getting boring. I'm sure it's not the end
of the world.'

I'm in the Worlds End because Charlotte was wrong – it is
the end of the world.

Of course, the cow put the knife in, then gave it a good firm twist. She reproduced the argument verbatim. Nothing else. But listen to this. Having cut out our guts she displayed them on a full-colour DPS for the whole industry to gawp at. She only asked that dog Imogen about our pedigree, our CVs, **The Lie**!

So on the next page there are a number of samples from *our* book, and next to them the team and agency that had really done the work. Picture the Bastard's face. Picture Pepper's. Horace O will be here in a couple of minutes. We must discuss our future.

I replace my jacket to hide the blood that's started to soak through into my jumper sleeves.

'Yo, H man. Buttercup come here. What'll you have?'

'Richard, if I'm staying, you must tie the dog up outside.'

'I've told you about Butterballs – he's a fuck-up. He's friendly.'

'They can turn – just like that.'

'Look I'll put my hand in his mouth.'

'You can put your testicles in his mouth, if you wish. I don't drink with it.'

'But it's freezing outside.'

'See yer then.'

Apologizing profusely to the dog, I attach him to the railings outside the pub.

'Export and chaser?'

'Just a regular brew, half. I'm not so used to it these days.'

So I get my friend Horace a pint of Export, thump him on the shoulder, laugh heartily and say, 'Whoa man, how embarrassing. What a fuck bad situation. So, *quo vadis*?'

And he says, 'Look Rich, you're a good friend and that. And we've done some stonking work together. But I think we're going to have to call it a day.'

'You what, H?'

'C'mon face it. Look at you. You were going to dry out after the party . . .'

'Yeah, but things happened.'

'Things will always happen. Look at you. Have you seen yourself in a mirror lately? Look how many glasses there are on the table.'

'They're usually good about clearing them here.'

'They probably have cleared them a couple of times already. Richard, you're beyond help.'

'C'mon. We can start over in the States. They'll love us over there. We'll have such a laugh. The chicks . . .'

'Rich. Listen. They kept me on.'

'They fuckin' what?'

'Look, I'm really sorry.'

'What the fuck am I supposed to do?'

'I'm sorry, Rich.'

'But, H . . .'

'I've got to go.' At once, I'm consumed with the most intense **loneliness-fear**.

'Hang on. Just because we're not working together, I mean, we can still be friends. Let's have a few for old times' sake. Just one. C'mon H, mate. The one never hurt anyone.' Of course he hasn't touched the first.

'I've got to go, Rich.'

'One for the road?'

'See yer.'

'See yer soon, H. Soon? Yeah?'

Obviously, I get fairly fuck-faced and go home to call Charlotte. My only friend. Charlotte isn't answering. I try masturbating to her answerphone message. It's none too satisfactory. I remember the video. It makes things worse.

I drink some tins and go to bed. But tins don't work.

I pretend that the dog asleep next to me is Pepper. (I mean, I just imagine it. I don't do anything to it. Obviously I don't.) When that gets too sad I change it to Charlotte. But that's never good for long – so I go back to Pepper. I get to sleep at around seven a.m. and wake, most unwell and fearful, at midday. To test my courage I set light to the hairs

166

on my right arm. None remain on the blood-red moonscape of my left. The pulse has machine-gunned up to 108.

Dr Cathy's Casebook

Each week Dr Cathy Smith answers some of
your health questions

● **A friend of mine told me that you should have two flannels and use one for your backside only. I bathe twice a day and I wonder whether this is strictly necessary.**
Cathy says: Nasty little micro-organisms can be carried from your anal region to your vagina if you use the same flannel for both areas. This can cause a number of problems including thrush and cystitis.

However, if you shower or enjoy a relaxing bath with a splash of Dettol each day you should be fine.

But remember, however thorough your personal hygiene programme is you should ask your doctor for regular smear tests.

● **I regularly gargle with a mouthwash after brushing my teeth. I've been using the same brand for years but lately it's been making me feel slightly sick. What could this be?**
Cathy says: It may well be that the company that makes your mouthwash have altered the contents slightly and that you are suffering from a mild allergic reaction.

Nevertheless, my advice is to consult your doctor. If you feel nauseous after eating, are experiencing stomach pains or have noticed that your stools are unusually dark, you should see your doctor immediately. It could be that you are developing a mild stomach ulcer.

But don't worry, 99% of stomach ulcers can be cured with a course of tablets if they are diagnosed early enough.

● **In the last couple of months my six-year-old daughter has become listless and virtually lost her appetite. She's also developed bluish rings around her eyes. I've kept her away from school. But I love her so much that I'm afraid to take her to the doctor in case he says she's suffering from something serious.**
Cathy says: I'm rarely this frank with readers, but it's you who needs the doctor: a psychiatrist! How can you say you love her . . .

167

I manage to get through to Charlotte at work the next after-noon. She says she's busy this evening and doesn't know when she'll be free. But she'll call me soon. Within a minute of my replacing the receiver, the phone goes. I run out to hear who it is. It's only my git brother with his third petition of the week. I re-record my answerphone message omitting 'and Pepper' and adding the codicil: 'If that's you, Seb – [loudly] go fuck yourself with a kebab skewer, you complete cunt.'

So it strikes me that, quite simply, my life couldn't be worse. And I conclude that it's time. Yeah, I'm going to read the letter. After a couple of ales, obviously.

Seven (or was it eight, maybe nine) jars on, my hands are still quite spastic when I try to slide the knife under the envelope flap. Now, the temptation is to ignite my leg hairs – prove I'm still courageous in some way or other. Then, I just do it.

Dear Pepper,
    This morning I saw a poster for the Royal Mail. A simple affair. A pretty girl with a smile across her face and a tear in her eye reading a letter. The line read, 'I just wrote to say "I love you."'
    There you have it.
    Richard XXXXXXX

I know not whether it was the shock or the nauseous fawning of the man, but a torrential outpour of seven (or eight per-haps nine) pints of premium strength occurred.

There is of course only one sensible course of action. Don a smile and get on with the important matters of my life. And, as I'm making my last remaining kite out to the off-manor vintner, I'm considering that, were I a man of lesser fibre, I would surely have topped myself by now. Then again, fuck knows how I'll fare when I've finished this lot.

Three days on and I'm thinking that perhaps I should have allocated a portion of the cheque to some food. But I guess I'm just too fucking low to eat at the moment. All I seem to be able to do is pace the house (often all night), chain-smoke, chain-drink, chain-nose pick and chain-wish the phone would go. (Yeah, at one point it got so serious, I doubted that I'd even be up to my annual mushroom-picking outing.) Tragedy's like a bad time on amphetamines in many respects. I mean, the things you want most when your speeding is going badly are sleep and other human beings. I haven't slept for days and no one's phoned me for a couple of weeks now. And my calling anyone is out of the question. In fact, frolicking with Buttercup's the only human contact I get. Naturally, it's somewhat substandard. These letters I'm fingering constitute my first instance of human communication in two days. They communicate: 'Pay us money now – or else. Apologies for inconveniencing you if you have paid within the last ten days.' Obviously, I haven't.

As for this bath. Well, it's the first I've had in God knows how long. As for the Mahler's Fifth you can hear – I seem to be chain-playing Mahler of late. I find that pop music brings me too close to tears. All that meaningful stuff about love and shagging and that.

Of course, I should have known better. Never do mushrooms when you're in my kind of shape – especially not three hundred.

Things started off well enough in the bath. The tiles spiralling around and kaleidoscoping into themselves, the bathwater turning into Dali's *Salmon Fishing*, the taps reflecting and refracting like Jean Michel Jarre at the Docklands. The tripping turned sour when I left the bath and decided to go carpet-speeding on the bath mat. (You must have done it – lie face down on a long carpet and race through the forest.) Now, I was doing fine. Steering at 200 mph like a pro. Then on to the horizon lumbered a big and crispy house spider.

Suffice to say, I'm staying here – under the duvet – until I finish coming down. I mean the flat is crawling with spiders. The type that streak into your peripheral vision, then disappear when you focus.

> *She just stopped running. It was useless anyway. He was far faster – and stronger. She held her forearms over her ears and turned up the volume on her screaming. Her animal noises. And my thoughts said – my daft voices, rather – how good it is that us animals have built in alarms. Come to think of it a burglar alarm was clanging most of the night and no one went to see what that was about either.*
>
> *The idea came to me in an instant – and froze me, so strange it was. 'Go on Richard, DO SOMETHING ABOUT THIS BAD EVENT.' I pondered (as his big labouring arms belted her head from side to side) that maybe this is what they normally do. A piece of their intimate ritual. They're far too passionate about things to be strangers. I mean, he's not raping her. He's just giving her a good hiding. Perhaps she deserves it.*
>
> *Cars rolled by. One actually sounded its screaming device. DO SOMETHING HE'S HURTING HER BADLY. You've drunk away your fear of life. If you don't intervene (he kicked her in the belly and she folded like broken celery) it's cowardice pure and simple. He looked riled. Dangerous. I crossed the road – obviously. And left him to aim his kicks in to the gap she left in her foetal position.*
>
> *He wasn't raping her, I thought, as I crossed back over to my front door. If he had been, I'd have definitely done something.*

Are you guilty for something you do – or rather don't do – in a dream?

My hangover is spiked with the guilt of my dream. As the afternoon wears on, the poisoning grows with the suspicion, then the certainty, that this was no dream.

Yeah, I'm lying. All that happened a week ago. I was too ashamed to say anything. And it's like, well, like Pepper was watching everything.

But look Pepper, I am brave really. Could you hold a cigarette in your fist for thirty seconds?

On twenty-three seconds, I'm not sure what happens, perhaps the tip burns clean through to a nerve. So I shout and fling it. Of course, the fiery bullet shoots off and lands where the sofa cushion meets the sofa. And as cigarette tips are wont, when I lift the cushion it dives down further. I gouge around, feel its sting and manage finally to hook the angry little bastard out. The point of my relating this drama to you? I only find three cocks, don't I? Thirty fucking quid! Obviously, I offer up a prayer of thanks and perform detailed autopsies on the sofa and armchairs – raising a further seventy-three pee.

So here's the plan. Drink until I'm not too scared to leave the flat. Get some more drink for the flat. Then what? Play it from there, eh? One thing at a time. Maybe there'll be a message on the answerphone when I get back.

I won't bore you with statistics. Suffice to say I found myself in a pub and drank more beer than I have blood. Unfortunately, I vommed most of it up on the way home so I'm relatively sober.

From the landing, I hear Buttercup whine and scratch behind the kitchen door. The poor sod must have been in there all day. I unhook his harness from the wall and let him out.

'C'mon BC. Midnight ramble.' I make for the front door. But he won't follow. No, the fucker just sits outside the bedroom door – sort of squeaking. 'You want to do sleeping, Buttercup? C'mon, man, I could handle a nice old walk.' He scratches at the door. 'You must need a shit or something. What's up, man?' Clearly, my dog is unwell. I haul his dead weight into the kitchen and check his eyes, tongue and things. 'Cough,' I say and he licks my nose.

171

I open the door and he skids in and up onto the bed.

'Oh God. What? Buttercup. Hello. Please go away.' she moans.

'PEPPER!'

9

Isis

'Oh Richard, Richard, please. Don't . . . don't be cross. Don't throw me out. I'm dying.' And she sounds completely out of it. Like on 'Hunky Dory' when Bowie's having problems saying 'Warhol' – well boxed. I flick on the light. She does more moaning.

'Pepper?'

'Oh God. Oh God. Please let me stay. Please let me sleep. I feel so awful.'

'Hell, what the fuck's wrong with you? What is it? OD?'

'No . . . no.' She's slightly more awake now. 'Flu.'

'**Drink-flu**?'

'Flu flu. Fever. Please be good to me. Please let me be.'

'Why here? Why did you come back? Are you locked out? Do I sound drunk? I'm not, you know.'

'Please, Richard, we'll talk in the morning. Please. Will you be a lovey and get me a glass of water? We'll talk in the morning. I promise.'

I fetch water, and surprise myself with what I say next.

'Shall I sleep on the sofa then?'

'Just for tonight, if you don't mind. I feel so terrible.'

Her words sloosh back and forth like a deranged mantra, bouncing over themselves, feeding back, shrieking. Mere words, sure – but they splash over the fractal landscape of my consciousness, contorting and transmutating in cabalistic significance.

173

Or to put it another way: What the fuck did the woman mean by *just for tonight*?

Will she allow me to cot with her tomorrow night? Or does she plan pissing off in the morning? And so, yet again, I remain awake for much of the night, tossed hither and thither by the derangement of uncertainty.

The fact that Pepper's in my bed and she's too unwell to go anywhere for the time being burns clear through the cloud of this morning's hangover. And as I lean over the railings trying to gob on the ducks in Finsbury Park pond, I'm thinking that maybe, if I play it consummately cool, I can get her to stay for a while. But I figure it's like this. One fuck up, a word out of place, Gary mentioning the letter, and I've lost it. A brown pearl of sputum and cigarette tar wends its way over the birds and wobbles, still intact, just before hitting the water. Then one of the ducks only fucking eats it. I go home.

This morning I entered the febrile stench of my bedroom to see how she was – well, in truth, check she was still satisfactorily lame. I held her hand for a while and she half returned the pressure – indicating, at the very least, that she didn't mind. The eczema had softened from a night's sweating. She asked for more water. But when I'd returned with it she was asleep. I took a polaroid – to remember her powerless and dependent on me, then I took Buttercup out and we bought tea, milk and orange juice for Pepper.

I place the orange juice on the speaker and she asks me to hold her. When I do she says, 'I'm sorry. It's making me too hot.' And I'm wondering whether she means psychological or calorific hot. Of course, I must watch myself – one can, after all, be too nice to a person. Create too much heat, so to speak. Then she moans, 'I can't go to school today.' Obviously, the time is not right for us to do down-to-earth talking.

'Pepper, I figure you should get up for a bit. Air the duvet. Open a window.'

'Mmm. In a bit. Richard, I might need you to help me across to the loo.'

174

'Look, I think maybe I should call you a quack.' And I'm reminded of the time when Basil the Bastard thought he was having a heart seizure – obviously it was indigestion – and he asked me to call him an ambulance. So I said, 'Basil you're a fat, fucking ambulance.' Of course he laughed lots and loosed up sufficiently to do a deep and resonant belch and was OK again.

'No, I'll be fine. It's just flu. Rich had it. It goes after a couple of days. Help me up please.' I help her up and she hobbles into the bathroom, catching her balance on the wall and resting at the door for breath. And I receive a vision of Pepper old and infirm – and still with me. It's good. She emerges from the bathroom in my towel robe and asks if I can lend her some clothes. Of course, I haven't done the washing for weeks. I remind her that she left quite a lot of clothes behind.

'Yes, but they're horrible. Your clothes are much nicer.' So I stick some in the washer. I certainly appreciate it when Pepper wears my clothes – her bum fighting for room in my tight-arsed 501s, her bra-less chest dancing around in one of my work shirts.

Pepper's lying on the sofa. Her head is on my lap and I'm stroking her hair. She's not objecting. She shifts her head back further into my groin and collides with the tent pole.

'You,' she laughs.

The television proves too brash for her fever so she asks me to read to her.

'I don't mind what. One of those silly magazines, if you like. I think that's about all I'm up to.'

I get up and fetch my copy of *Incredible But True*.

Real or artificial teeth. From one to an entire set, with superlative gold pivots or springs, also gums, sockets and palates formed, fitted, finished, fixed without drawing stumps or causing pain.'

That was the advertisement London dentist, Martin Van

Butchell, placed in the *St James' Chronicle* in 1773. Unfortunately it generated little business.

So when his wife died two years later, he hit upon an unusual marketing gimmick. He embalmed her body and displayed Mary in the waiting room of his surgery and introduced her to patients as, 'my dear departed'.

Mary had the desired effect and business boomed like never before.

However, the embalming job was less than satisfactory. And five years on, customers began to complain that Mary, who was no longer in the prime of death, had ceased to look (and smell) her best. Perhaps it was time to bury her?

Van Butchell wouldn't hear of it.

Finally, after much protest, his new wife gave him an ultimatum. One of them had to go. He opted to keep the living wife and Mary was given a Christian burial.

'That's absolutely horrid.'

'If you die from your illness, that's what I'm going to do with you.'

'Huh.'

'Then you won't be able to walk out on me again.' Pepper doesn't respond. I remain silent. No, I shouldn't have said it.

'Thank you so much for looking after me,' she says. 'I didn't want to be ill at Rich's place. I wanted to come . . . home.'

'*Home*. Do you mean that? *Home*.'

'Oh God, Richard. I'm not up to one of these.'

'But, you know, if I stopped going out on the lag, like? Totally. And was dead nice . . .'

'God, Richard. I feel so ill. Will you get me some water, please?'

'Pepper, that message on the answerphone.'

'I don't want to talk about it.'

'Look. I got her to do it to make you jealous. Honestly. I honestly did. Because of everything. And you . . .'

'Please, I don't want to talk about it. Now, be a nice boy

176

and get me some water. And, go on put one of my CDs on for me.'

When Pepper wakes me in the afternoon one of my hands is inside the robe. And her hand is on mine in sweet consent. Bob Dylan, who's been automatically replayed several times, wails about Sara.

'How are you feeling?'

'Like a cup of tea, please. And maybe mashed potato with cheese and baked beans for tea. Please. I think I'm feeling a little better, you know.'

'That's good,' I obviously lie. 'How do I make that?'

'Why *do* people get ill?' Pepper asks me as we sit up in bed.

'I dunno. They just do.'

'But, I mean, it seems like a sort of design fault in life.'

'Yeah well, in my book, the whole life package is sub-standard. I mean, look at all the fucking disasters – acts of God – that happen.'

'Mmm. But on the whole, life is good.'

'I reckon there's just as much darkness as light. The same amount of good and evil. For every action there's an opposite and equal reaction.'

'It's just that it's all a bit unevenly spread. I mean, not that anyone deserves to be in a disaster. But, I suppose some people deserve it more than others . . .'

'Like me. I deserve to get my balls crushed in a fuck awful disaster,' I ejaculate – or was it Gary?

'Don't be so silly.'

'Actually, yeah.' I see my opening. 'It's like in relation-ships. There's a lot of good. But to get that good you need some bad. But overall they're good. I mean like you being sick. It's good.'

'What?'

'Well, look at us. We've been friends all day . . .'

'Yes, but Richard . . .' I put a finger over her mouth and say it.

'Pepper, listen to me. Are you going to stay?'

'Don't ask me that.'

'It's a fair enough question. I mean . . .' But she looks afraid. Like when I'm all fuelled up and about to blow at her. 'Sure. Don't answer. I'm sorry.'

'Well,' she says smiling again, 'if you catch my disease, I'll have to stay to look after you.'

'You'd better kiss me then.' We snog and I guide her hand down.

'Richard, I really am too weak.'

'I don't think it'll take very long.'

'Tomorrow.'

At about one in the morning Pepper's too hot, so she takes off her T-shirt and knickers. She's got nothing against me putting an arm around her in principle – it's just that she's too hot. I can respect this. Although it's not just this which gives me insomnia. I've had no drink or smoke all day. And like Pepper, I too am sweating out my ample poisons.

My nose touches Pepper's neck. It has the familiar comforting scent of Pepper, yet is tinctured with the alien, yeasty aroma of her virus. I'm gorging on her vapours. I want to catch her illness. Not just because it'll make her stay. But because it's been inside her. I want all of her. All of her.

Besides, I probably wouldn't notice if I did get her flu. I feel like that most of the time.

Three a.m., and Pepper says, 'Richard? Are you awake?'

'Mmmm.'

'I can't sleep. I think I slept too much in the day. You know when you're really, really tired but can't sleep because your mind's got too many thoughts in it?'

'What thoughts are those, Pepper?'

'Oh just rubbish. Fluey thoughts. Richard?'

178

'Mmm.'

'Did you really get that girl to leave the message on purpose?' I'm sitting up now.

'Yeah, Pepper. I wrote it on a piece of paper. She was someone from work. Do you remember how she pronounced Le Touquet – Lar Touket?'

'Mmmm? Daft boy.'

'You do believe me, don't you?'

'Daft boy.'

'Yeah.'

'Oh God, I really want to get to sleep.'

'I have the answer. A couple of Mogadon.'

'What's that?'

'Sleeping pills.'

'I don't think so, Richard.'

'You'll be fine.'

'Are you going to have some too?'

'Well, I would. But, you know, I don't know how much alcohol is still left in my system. You wouldn't want to wake up in the morning lying next to a stiff.'

'Oh, I'm quite used to that.' Her hand comes behind her and she gives the stiff a squeeze. I fetch the pills and convince her to take them. I have a plan.

It's despicable, I know. But, well, she might go again. I need a memento. Something of sentimental value.

If she wakes and asks why I've taken the duvet off, I'll say that she was burning up. If she asks why the light's on, I'll tell her that I'm looking for the pills because I can't sleep. If she asks why I'm taking photographs of her with the polaroid, I'll be in River Shit.

She doesn't wake and I'm toying with the idea of changing her position – getting some decent *pickle* shots, so to speak. Obviously, I don't. I'm not that depraved.

I put the photographs in the envelope with the other Richard's letter. To dilute it some.

I get to sleep at about seven and am woken by Pepper at

179

around midday. She's warm and naked and, sober as I am, I feel unusually horny.

It only takes about ten seconds and I nearly drown her. And by her disgusted expression I think that she couldn't help but swallow some – which pleases me.

My first cigarette brings malaise. Unfortunately, I think it's toxic rather than viral. And I must face facts. A poxy influenza virus wouldn't last thirty seconds in my blood.

Pepper calls work. She also calls Rich – which I consider inauspicious. But when she returns she says, 'It's so nice to sleep in a proper bed again. All toasty warm and snugly. Rather than a smelly sofa.'

'With me?'

'Might be.'

'That's good.'

'You know, when I first arrived and got into bed, I could smell you. It was quite comforting. Like you being there to look after me.'

'So how did it smell? Of my natural, irresistible musks?'

'Huh. More like you hadn't changed the sheets since I was last here. Stale cigarettes and beer.'

'Cheers. So what are your plans, Pepper?'

'What are yours? You haven't been to work for a day and a half.' So I explain how I was made redundant. And she tells me that work said that she should take the rest of the week off, so we should spend today and tomorrow sorting me out.

'Fuck me mate! How many weeks?'

'I'm sorry, it's the same for everyone. You can get emergency payments if you're really desperate. You should have come to see us as soon as you became unemployed. And I suggest you contact your ex-employers if you've had no notice payment whatsoever.'

'Talk to those fuckers? I'd sooner stick pins in my eyes.'

As I leave the unemployment centre on Medina Road and trot out on to the wide drag of Seven Sisters Road with Pepper and Buttercup, I feel a sense of achievement – albeit a low-life one.

Pepper says she quite fancies a drink. But she's drinking with Rich tonight so it would probably be unwise. Obviously, I more than quite fancy a drink – especially in the face of this. Then right there. Outside the Sir George Robey, in broad daylight, Pepper stops walking, grabs hold of me and kisses me.

'I'll cancel her,' she announces, 'and take my poor, unemployed ex-boyfriend out to lunch for being so nice to me.'

And so over Malaysian and wine – not much wine mind – we have our down-to-earth. Which culminates in Pepper saying, 'Well, I've had time to think and, frankly, I'm still confused.'

In Pepper's book, there's more to life than shacking up with a boy and being a secretary. And when I suggest that I dry out totally and behave – which is about all I have to offer – she says, 'Then things really would be mundane.'

That afternoon and evening we stay in and fuck – a lot. Pepper's astonished at how horny I am. But it's not that. It's something different. Something I can't explain. It's Friday morning and – unfortunately – I don't seem to have caught the virus. I'm raw as hell but I need more Pepper. But she's not like she was yesterday. It's like I've used up all her emotion or something. So she just lies there – acquiescing. Then she begins to cry. Not that good post-shag stuff – but upset crying. So I stop.

'What is it?' The crying becomes more intense. I slide out. She catches her breath.

'I'm not sure. I think it's the design fault.'

When I first got the job with Basil the Bastard, got into advertising, I became what I'd always wanted to be – a

181

proper *copywriter*. It defined my existence. In the mirror I saw an advertising professional. Perhaps fifty per cent of all arts graduates – even the ones who profess socialism – tell the careers advisor that they'd like to go into advertising. They get told about the agencies that run graduate recruitment schemes. For the next few weeks they dream of swivel chairs and getting pissed up on cocktails. Then they end up binning their dozen or so photocopied 'good luck elsewhere' letters and approach magazine companies. And here was I – fuck-all degree, yet good enough to make the grade. 'What do you do?' – 'I'm in advertising.' – 'Nice.' And I even felt good on Sundays – because tomorrow I'd be in advertising again. Then, obviously, I found out just what unglamorous shit it was, got used to the idea and didn't give a toss any more.

Today, it's Pepper that defines my existence. The problem is, I can't get used to it and give a very big toss. True, she left again. She said, 'Richard, I don't want to see you at all. Well at least not until I've fallen out of love with you.' But she's watching my every move. Making sure I sign on every other Tuesday, checking how much I drink, reprimanding me for letting the flat disintegrate, reminding me to walk my dog, choosing which shirt I wear – yeah, I even ask which shirt she likes me in. So I wonder how she's taking this. Badly I hope.

Click. Beep. Hiss. 'Thank you, Richard. That must be your first instance of communication with me in over six years. Richard, it was all so long ago. Everyone but you is more than prepared to bury the hatchet. But if you're determined to be so heartless as to keep up this wall of silence with me, perhaps you could at least see your way clear to telephoning Mother and Father.'

*   *   *

I've been behaving in the most despicable manner of late. Yeah, buying halves, getting into conversations and being included in the round. People are beginning to notice, and I'm becoming known as a ponce.

I hit on Horace O and Richard Juggler for a few quid (Jeez's answerphone informs callers that he is 'temporarily indisposed') and buy my way back into North London's unemployed lagging circle. It's pitiful. We arrive at the pub soon after opening time. And drink slowly until life seems a little better – which is usually about closing time. It's like a co-operative. Whoever's got a giro or has managed to shift some blow gets the round. If we're running out of funds we get as much £1.99 wine as we can afford from the supermarket and share it. There's talk about sorting out. Chipping in for a bar of hash and knocking it out on a different manor. Or getting work. It's like we're waiting for something to happen. Expecting someone to come into the pub and ask us to crew a yacht to the Caribbean. No one says too much. As if we're conserving our energy for the big one. Then again, we're not as bad as the slags who tap you for wedge on the street – to buy their tins of loopy brew.

Loneliness swells in my belly like starvation. You can smell it on me – like sweated out garlic. I'm exuding anti-pheromones. So when, sometimes, I talk to women, it's barely surprising that I get nowhere. But, you know what it's like, after a day on the juice you've got to try it on with the barmaid.

And then something happens to change my whole life picture. Convince me of an eternal beneficence. An Epiphany, so to speak. I remember that in my box of pills, Dear Johns and other crap is a building society book. A remnant of a time when I actually did things like save for hi-fi equipment and holidays.

Sure, it's been well pillaged like the rest of my life. But a sum like twenty, thirty, or even – please God – fifty quid, well I wouldn't have bothered with. Now, of course, it could make all the difference. *All* the difference.

Twenty-two pounds, forty-six pence. Fourteen pints of Extra. Just winking at me from the dusty childhood savings book.

I consider investing it in a quarter and turning it into £30. But I don't. I buy some anti-shit pills (obviously, my guts are shot), and invest the remainder in Pepper.

So I take a shower, remove the film of filth from my teeth and drag a comb through my hair knots, then head off for the West End.

I change my mind about fearlessly barging into the agency with the flowers and making a quip about her perfume. The romance of the drama would certainly be lost if I ran into the Bastard. So I down a few in the Intrepid Fox and wait for five thirty. OK, so I look a right twat standing on Wardour Street with this major splash of flowers, and I'm needing a piss – badly. But it really is the obvious course of action.

It's ten past eleven and I'm back in the local, arguing that people have still got full pints so why won't they sell me one? I'm still wet from the thunderstorm.

A couple of us chip in for a two-litre bottle of red and we go back to someone's house to drink it. And because I'm hammered and have got to tell someone, I explain about my folly and how I got my first glance at the other Richard – in a fucking polo neck he was. Obviously, they point out, I should have slapped the bitch some, and spent the money on getting us drink. Obviously.

He takes a tiny sip of his orange juice and soda and coughs deliberately as my cigarette smoke oozes over.

'So what do you do, Richard?' I ask with intensity. As if trying to appear interested in what people in Fair Isle sweaters actually do.

'I'm fund raising manager for "Friends of the Planet".'

'Worthy,' I say and Pepper, smiling softly, touches his shoulder. I feel a fire-ball of jealously spin in my abdomen.

'You couldn't point your cigarette in the other direction?' says Pepper. I tip down my pint, my eyes boring into her.

'Of course,' I say maliciously. I take a final pull of the cigarette, inhale deeply and exhale downwards. Smiling as the nicotine marries with the amphetamines and alcohol.

This is the other Richard: dark-haired – like me; sallow-skinned – like me; handsome – like me; no red blotches or alcohol-smashed blood vessels – unlike me. This is me on philosophical parable: 'So he faces a moral dilemma.' This is Richard: 'So she faces . . .' This is me on philosophical theory: 'Leave it out. It's like this . . .' This is him: 'I'm of the opinion . . .'

I waggle my left hand and ask Richard, 'Why should all women masturbate with this hand?'

'I don't know. Is this a joke?'

'Because it's mine. Ha, ha.'

'What's smellier than an anchovy?'

'What?' he says with emphasized boredom.

'An anchovy's cunt.'

Pepper's smile speaks of understanding my sense of humour still, of a well of tolerance; of knowing precisely why I spat that most excellent of Anglo-Saxons at him. It's something that we share, and Fair Isle sweater is unable to grasp. It's the merest of grins but it suffuses through my body more warmly than an E rise.

When Richard leaves for the pisser she sighs, 'He's really boring, you know?'

'I gathered.'

'But he's easy going.'

'And I am the forest and night of dark trees.'

'Call me, Richard.'

185

I wake and resolve to call Pepper. But not yet. When I'm sorted – with a proper job. When I've made enough to put down a deposit on a respectable gaff – pay off some debt – sort out long term.

So this is what I do. Skull a couple of tins for fortitude and begin to leaf through my phone book. And yeah, I get down to it. Do some networking, so to speak. Call up just about every contact I've ever met and not fallen out with in my career.

The 'friendly' contacts total five, and two of them tell me to get fucked. The other three are head-hunters. I'm told that things are 'dead out there' at the moment, but there might be some 'movement' in a few weeks, happy to take a look at the CV. I head off for the pub to celebrate.

The pub is empty (except, of course, for Pepper and Richard holding hands and laughing at me in the corner).

This is what happened with Kat (my girlfriend before Pepper). She left. I was pissed off and got drunk for a fortnight. Then I hated her. Simple. She made no ghosts. And I remember her exactly as she was. All the ugly things about her – the inside of discarded knickers, the stench of her trainers, a tampon swelling in the toilet bowl, all the crap things she said.

But – and the drink's making me quite rational now – the eczema, the Shredded Wheat hair, the bed farts, the smell of her puke, the caprice – none of these figure in my picture of Pepper. It's like she's turned into some sort of fucking angel.

And I figure this. What I need is a way of remembering her. Exactly as she is – with all her bad adjectives. Of course, to do this properly I need to research the other Richard. He is, after all, her worst adjective. I buy another drink and try to do some more remembering. And I remember this.

'H man, do you ever remember things?' I once asked.

'Do I owe you money?' he replied.

'No, no. I mean things that happened a long time ago.

186

Things that you'd thought you'd forgotten. Childhood things.'

'The speed and the puff they unlock many doors. Doors of perception, doors of paranoia, doors of ecstasy, doors of creativity, doors of memory.'

'I wonder how it works,' I say when we're back in the bar. 'I mean, you'd have thought that you remembered things better straight. You know? Dope and drink are supposed to fuck the memory right up.'

'The chemicals do nothing to you, man. They add nothing. Take nothing away. With the chemical you see only what is already present. They merely enable you to . . .' And he leans over and whispers as if to impart an awful wisdom, '. . . explore the awesome landscape of the mind.' And he explains about the Memory Cocktail. Take the precise amounts of uppers and downers and you go neither up nor down – you travel backwards. 'However,' he raises a foreboding finger, 'this is most, most inadvisable.'

'Why, man? I quite fancy doing a test drive.' He necks back the remainder of his pint.

'When a man's life is shown before him, it is for one reason. Because he approaches death.' I get us more ales and decide against the Memory Cocktail.

'Listen, H. Suppose, you took a different cocktail. Do you reckon you could travel forwards, like? Tell the future. I mean, like see if you were going to be in a disaster or something?' He looks at me intently then breaks into deep and hollow laughter.

This is my room.

On first entering you wouldn't be blamed for thinking, 'What a fuck awful mess.' But on closer inspection, you'd see. You'd realize that it's a sort of laboratory or incident room – designed to crack a problem. Paint a picture. Enable me to remember Pepper exactly as she is.

On the wall next to the bed, I've stuck up the polaroids I took. But they're not too hot. I couldn't use a flash so you can't really make out the skin complaint too well. They actually look a bit *Readers' Wives*.

The floor is carpeted with various pages ripped from grot mags. CUs of girls with epidermal blemishes, acne ghosts, small red blips, tiny fawn freckles and the like.

You'd also notice that the room smells rather overpowering. There's a reason for this. I've soused one of the pillows with her perfume. And I've underlaid the director's chair with a thick coat of her deodorant – it's that hypo-allergenic stuff, so it doesn't smell much. Then there's the apple and banana shampoo on the curtains. And that patch in the corner that looks like a runny dog-shit stain, that's half a bottle of her aloe shampoo.

Obviously, items of her underwear are randomly bestrewn – as I remember them best.

As for the tinny fairground music that you can now hear, that's Pepper's 'Highway 61 Revisited' by Bob Dylan.

And let me tell you. As memory aids, these changes to my environment work quite excellently. The obvious problem is, they fail to give me the type of picture I need. You see the eczema, the farts, the design faults, all of that sad humanity – it all appeals to me. For, as I have said on more that one occasion, Glory be to God for dappled things . . . etc. And yeah, I'll admit it. I'm even starting to like old throat cancer himself.

And I figure, what I need is a nice long session with someone pretty grotesque. Someone who can remind me what a human is really like.

This is Kat or Cat (short for Kathy – or Cathy – funnily enough, the name of Pepper's predecessor): stocky (well, obese under less desperate circumstances – but the only female contact I've had in three weeks is when bar staff, handing me change, accidentally touch my hand), nouvelle blonde, porridge complexion, dirty pink bra-strap dislodged from shoulder, two kids, nearly divorced, boyfriend inside for GBH with intent, breaks filters off high-tars, drinks Guinness and Jamesons, pissed, has fucked most blokes in pub at one time or other – so she reckons, wants to fuck me, wants to get more pissed first. What a find?

This is me: hand in pocket and concentrating on football to quash desperate anticipation, dropping pound coin in vending machine, nothing, hit machine, unamused with irony of it, reconcile self to catching VD – or worse – if I haven't already got VD. Which I think I have.

This is Buttercup: grinning in that doleful sort of pit bull way, charging over to welcome us, retreating at the none too steady advance of big Kat.

Understandably, it was hard pretending that she was Pepper – but I belly surfed on Kat many times last night. She left early – in a panic to check her babies were still alive – astonished and grateful that one so young and handsome could spend so long on her meticulous attentions. Over breakfast beer she grew philosophical, and said that I had taught her something valuable. She, in her turn, taught me a couple of things. That two human beings, however wretched, can generate degrees of comfort and happiness just by being human beings. And that it's true what is said about fat women – they do indeed have tighter beavers.

And what do you know? For a few short seconds last night Pepper took her eyes off me.

The stale waft of Kat's gynaecology turns my gut when I draw at this cigarette. Still, I don't wash my hands. The pungent dampness of the bed, the bloody butts in the ashtray, the pink and greasy kisses on the glass – all of it helps. As a disgraceful reminder of feminine humanity, all of this is quite excellent. Yet, try as I might, I fail to pin any of it to Pepper. And it seems to me that Pepper, like a great thespian or rock star, has the unique talent of being able to take her humanity with her when she exits the stage. It being a condition of my sanity that I make Pepper human, ugly and the bad-news girlfriend that she was once more, my mind turns again to pharmaceutical solutions.

But fuck being up at ten o'clock in the morning. I'm back to the manifold scents of my bed.

I'm midway through the train disaster when this happens. I'm woken by someone talking outside my room. I retch, roll out of bed, pull an arm off the director's chair and fling myself out of the door.

And, what do you know? The voice emanating from my answerphone is only that of Pepper Furnival. Fuck, I'm so excited I need to hold my foreskin to avoid pissing on the floor. It hurts. As I think I've told you, I have a slight condition.

I lift up the handset and switch off the machine.

She wants to come over and collect her stuff on Saturday. Is this OK?

'Sure,' I mumble. Any more and my voice would crack. **Sure. I've turned my room into an Egyptian burial chamber for you. All perfumed and decorated, it is. You'll love it to death – so you will.**

'Are you alright?' she asks – almost sympathetically, as if something inside her still cares about me. I do one of those instant calculations and decide it's better not to break down and tell her that I'm quite fucked up about her, actually.

'Sure. See yer Saturday.' I put the phone down and do some crying on the carpet. But I don't piss myself. The hard-on takes care of that.

I nip out for a couple of jars. And I'm thinking of that geezer who embalmed his wife. You know, I can understand it. I really can. Then I buy six tins of Super to assist me in dismantling my shrine.

Now there're a number of ways I could do this. I could play unaffected. The good loser. And pack all her stuff in

190

boxes and bin liners and leave a little note saying, 'Sorry I couldn't be there, no hard feelings', etc.

I could OD and let her find me and have to look after me.

Or I could break down and just plain beg.

I smoke the remainder of my ganja and come to a number of wise and well-thought-out conclusions.

Firstly. Obviously, if she has to pack, she'll spend longer here. Secondly. She hasn't got a motor. It means that she'll be arriving with someone else. Could this be my chance to clue up on the other Richard? Get a handle on her fuck-worst adjective. Plainly, this all means that I will have to do Saturday sober and civil. It's Wednesday today – so I can afford to stay wrecked until Thursday night.

I play the beginning of Pepper's message on my answer machine a few more times, rebutton my fly and go to the pub.

True to plan, I abstained all day Friday, except for a few smokes. But when I woke at five this morning I felt so peculiar that I had no option but to drink half of my emergency wine. I also dropped a 5 mg Diazepam for luck.

Buttercup was awake and excitable. Like he knew she was coming. I fed and exercised him. In the park I made up a bunch of things to say to her. Nothing consistent, just things like, if the mood is right, I mustn't forget to ask if I can call her. Or I could help her pack and remind her of when we moved out of Islington and hope it sparks some kind of upsetting nostalgia. There were also things to say in the event that she hits me with the other Richard. Things that ranged between: 'Hi. Come in. And you are?' with an outstretched hand, and 'Stitch that! You fucker!'

At around nine the wine begins to wear off and I'm feeling viral. Gary threatens. So I begin on the second half. But I'm drinking slowly – a hit whenever Gary murmurs. That way I figure I'll be OK for when she arrives.

I'm too excited to watch the TV so I pace around – face down, like I'm testing for something in the carpets. Finally, the *Saint and Greavsie* music begins and I settle down in the living room. There are four empty wine bottles next to me. It's then that I remember.

It was around a fortnight ago. Giro day – so I'd done solo Indian after kicking-out time. They wouldn't serve me more drink in the restaurant so I came home. Now, although I'd managed to get thoroughly lagged – as was my purpose – I was still full of fear and loneliness and shit. So I telephoned Drink Crisis. Obviously, I hung up when they answered. I mean, I'd made my decision. All I had to do was to stop drinking. And a piece of piss it seemed at the time. I resolved to tip my entire alcohol supply down the khazi – not via me, either. Anyway, I wasted a few cans and felt mighty virtuous. Of course, Pepper was watching – in approval. Next, I cracked the top on a bottle of vodka. But the thought of chucking a full bottle. Exactly – fuck that! So I hid it in the lavatory cistern.

I lift off the cistern lid and, without looking in, place it on the seat. I raise my head. I'm still not looking – after all, it could have all been a dream. You know how things go? I glance down. And there, smiling at me, cool because I recently flushed some puke away, lies the exquisite bottle. The sweet, pellucid virgin – refracting away in invitation.

'Peter Piper picked a peck of pickled pepper. Peter Piper picked a pimple on his pecker. Pepper picked a pimple on Peter Piper's poky, piss-poor pecker.' Sure I'm nine-eighths sober. But I'm still not ready for Pepper. I skull a throatful of vodie and clear away the wine bottles. 'Pepper picked a pink, puss pod of a pimple on Peter Piper's palaeontologist pater's pin-like, pathetic, yet prominently proud . . .'

DONG!

I sign for the parcel. What parcel? I didn't order a fucking parcel.

'What's that?' she asks cheerily, her head peering around the postman. And I remember. Ten fuck films for just £1.99 each.

As I step back to let her in she kisses my cheek.

'She's come to give me a hand. That's alright, isn't it?'

'S'pose. Yeah.'

Obviously, I can't concentrate on *Saint and Greavsie* with my flat being looted – and a pulse of 107. To tell the truth, I'd rather be helping. I glug back another heap of vodka and make a purposeful decision. What I figure is – there's nothing to lose in being nice about things.

Rich is on the landing putting the things Pepper passes her into bin liners. I walk in.

'It smells mighty funny in here, Richard. Did Buttercup do something?'

'Yeah.' I point at the corner.

'I was thinking more of the bed.'

'Well I dropped half a bottle of aftershave on it. Then I tried to get rid of the smell with some of your perfume. But it didn't work.'

'Why didn't you wash it?'

'I don't know how to do pillows and duvets.'

'Daft boy,' she laughs and I raise up my polaroid and start taking pictures of Pepper. I put each one on the bed to materialize. 'Silly boy.' I'm snapping her at all angles. From behind – as she bends into drawers. From the side – as she passes stuff to Rich. Face on – when I deliberately get in her way. She doesn't seem to mind any of this.

'Here. Give it to me,' she says. 'I want one of you.'

'But I look terrible.'

'All the better to remember you.' She snaps me, waits for the colour to come to my face – obviously not much does. Then she goes back into the kitchen to snap Buttercup. 'Is this mine or yours?' she says, holding up a CD.

'What is it?'

'Simply Red.'

'Oh for fuck's sake, woman. It's not mine . . . Pepper?'

'Mmmm.'

'Do me a favour, will you?'

'What.'

'Lift up your top. Let me take one of . . .'

'Don't be so silly.'

'Does this remind you of when we were moving from Islington?'

'No.'

I go to the fridge.

'How about us swapping a CD?' Pepper says, when I return.

'What do you mean?'

'To remember each other by. You pick one of mine and I'll pick one of yours.'

'I don't know. Which one of mine do you want?'

'This one.'

'Oh c'mon, Pepper. That's my favourite all time . . . Mahler's Fifth can cure hangovers. I need it. Besides, I don't want, you . . . you know. It always gets you going. Like Pavlov's fucking dog.' She grins.

'OK. How about this one? You don't play it any more. And it'll remind me of when we first started out.'

I agree. Of late, I've gone off *Mustard and Cressida* by the Plum Jugglers – I mean in the face of *Last of the Church Deacons* and *Peanut Envy*. 'So which one of mine do you want?'

'I don't know. The direness of your musical taste is surpassed only by your dress sense.' She punches me on some burn holes. Then I remember. 'The one that I played you when you were sick. You remember? Bob Dylan.'

'Which one?'

'He looks like a hippy on the front and it's got that song about missing his wife. "Sara".'

'You mean *Desire*. Oh Richard, I can't give you that.'

'Go on. It's the only one of your records that I half like. It's the one that'll remind me most of you.'

'Well, I s'pose I can buy another copy.' She smiles and fishes out the CD for me. Then this happens. She closes the bedroom door and walks over. She reaches out and touches my cheek. The cheerful expression dissolves and single tears, then tears in rapid succession roll out of her. And this, I'm thinking, has been her real expression all along. Her crying intensifies and her face becomes red and animated – like she's a polaroid developing.

Of course, this is my cue to hug her. But I think, 'Fuck that!' Then, obviously, I hug her. It's good that I'm too pissed to cry. Then I cry.

We're on the bed holding each other tightly just saying, 'I love you,' over and over. We've said it perhaps a hundred times. I don't know. The door opens.

'Get out, Rich,' says Pepper.

Yeah, fuck off out of it, mumbles Gary.

I've got my hand in her sweatshirt. I'm caressing the pie crust of her shoulders. But I don't have stiff. It's not like I'm drunk. It's like . . . I can't explain. The bed smells to high fuck.

'I want to just stay like this for ever and ever,' she whispers.

'Yeah, yeah, yeah.'

'But I've got to pack.'

'Pepper, are you shagging someone else?' **More specifically, are you shagging a polo-necked, non-smoking, do-good prick?**

'No.'

You total fucking liar, Pepper. 'Promise?'

'Yes. I've got to pack.'

So how do you explain the envelope I'm going to produce from under the bed in a second? 'Don't pack.' **Or rather,**

195

would produce if I hadn't stuffed it with chuff shots of you – ha, ha, ha.

'I've got to.'

'This isn't begging, you understand?'

'Right.'

'But please, please, please, please, please don't pack.'

'I have to.'

'Why?'

'You understand.'

'I don't. Really I don't.'

'You have to try.'

'Understand what?'

'I don't know. Let me get up.'

When she's up I say, 'Pepper, lift up your top. Let me take a picture.'

'No.'

'Go on.'

'No.'

'Pepper, please.' She cocks her head and gives me one of her *daft boy* looks.

'Nice one, Pepper.' Click. I kiss her once and leave the room.

Richenda's outside. Then fuck knows why I do what I do next. But I don't think the drink's to blame. Besides, I've only had a couple.

'Rich, have a drink,' I command.

'I can't. I'm driving.'

'Have a small one. I want to talk to you.' I pour her a small vodka. She refuses the glass.

'Take it,' I shout. 'And come in here. I've only got a few things to say. It won't take long.'

'Richard. I'm . . .'

'Listen. You barge, uninvited, into my flat. The least you can do is hear me out.' She's in the living room. I release her arm. She looks frightened and it pleases me a little. 'Sit.'

She complies and says, 'What?'

'All I wanted to say is this.' And I'm calm now. 'I think . . . no that's wrong, I know. In fact, I'm fucking positive about this. I hate you more than any other person on this planet. Richenda, you will never know the depths to which my hatred for you runs. It's unfathomable. I hate your hair, I hate your clothes, I hate your hairy legs, I hate your fucking attitude, I hate the whole fucking package. Everything you and your tramp friends stand for. The crap you fill Pepper's head with. Everything. There isn't one single thing about you that I can say I like. Alright?'

'That it?'

'Yeah.'

'Right.'

'Cheers for listening.' Glowing ashes spray from my fist.

Five minutes ago she was Pepper. A slightly better than average-looking mortal with scabby ears and red eyes. A mortal with no dress sense, who said crappy things like 'snugly,' and 'toasty warm' – things that could really get on your tits.

Now, scudding down Holloway Road with her termagant chauffeur, she's turned into some kind of hyperbolic goddess. And I just don't understand it.

In school assembly one day – I must have been ten or so – it was announced that one of the pupils had been killed on the way home from school. He'd stuck his head out of a train window and left it painted across the side of a bridge. The headmaster offered his condolences, then ranted on for the remainder of assembly about what a good bloke he was and how he'd live on in the hearts of everyone that knew him and how it was a new school rule to keep heads in trains. And although no one shed any tears, people were saying things like 'I wouldn't wish that on anyone,' and 'He really wasn't such a bad geezer'. But the fact of the matter was – he was a total cunt. And I'm thinking that maybe this has something in common with my current predicament.

Consequently, I've started to compile a list.

197

Likes hippy music; hippy food; crap in bed; utilitarian underwear; farts in her sleep; has crap friends; has a really crap suitor; sulks a fuck of a lot; drinks slowly; once saw her picking her nose when she thought I wasn't looking; has a fat daft bat mother – who she'll grow up to look like, probably; hates football; hates my music; hates my friends; hates me.

I Blu-tack the list next to my bed and feel satisfied. I go out and buy a magazine to read in the pub.

TALKBACK
Letters

● I hope I haven't missed the boat. But here's a handy tip for smokers wanting to kick the habit. Get yourself pregnant. It worked for me. I haven't had a cigarette in over three years.
   C. Dodder, West Byfleet, Surrey
Peg says: I thought that giving up smoking was supposed to make you put on weight. But you put the weight on first, well done!

● I read your article on bereavement with interest. But I would like to correct you on an important point. You said, 'In time the scars of loss will begin to heal.' I was widowed nearly 46 years ago. Not a day has gone by without me feeling the pain of loss. I don't believe that the scars heal in time. Time merely enables you to live with them.
   M. Russell, Almwch, Anglesey
Peg says: Bereavement is always a sensitive subject. I'm sure all Talk *readers offer their sympathy.*

● I'm 74. But that didn't stop a friend and me travelling down to London to visit the Tate Gallery. It's the first time I've been to a gallery in many years and it was a wonderful day out. I think *Talk* should run a monthly feature on the arts and encourage some of its older readers to get out of their armchairs.
   E. Butler, Milton Keynes
Peg says: Readers, what do you think? Write in and tell us.

● The yuppies who work in advertising must be million-aires judging by all the 'feminine' products advertised in your pages and on television. But they must all be men. If

198

A week later and I know *Desire* word for word. And when 'Sara' comes on or that deranged waltz 'Isis' (which, obviously, is about infidelity not some daft journey), I have to swallow and fight back tears. But they're not 'Oh my fuck, I'm so lonely' tears, they're the same kind of tears I battled with when the Gunners lifted the championship cup. Tears that come because something's so right. Arsenal only lost one game. They did it so right. Some of the things Dylan says are so right. He's been where I am now and it's a lukewarm comfort.

'Isis' – it explains my situation quite precisely. In the song he turns his estranged wife into some sort of goddess, a 'mystical child' who drives him insane. Codswallop. But so right.

Regarding the above. (I'm back in a pub seeing things a deal more clearly) Actually it's crap. 'Careless Whisper' – it's playing on the juke-box now – is having an equally profound effect on me. Letters in shitty women's magazines bring a tear to the eye. I could probably build a heap of significance into the copy on this fucking beer mat.

I get back and re-read the list. It really isn't satisfactory. I scrawl 'Fucking Bitch' across it, then watch porn vids until two to punish her.

This morning, to my delight, I received a postcard.

Richard Darling,
Long time no see. I'd love to see you. You can get me on
XXX XXXX
 Love Becky
 XXX

Now, I don't recall a Becky. But she seemed to know me. I mean, 'X X X'. And if I hadn't been getting my money's worth out of the videos, I'd have probably got an anticipatory rod.

So I waited until I was feeling slightly more horny and dialled the number. I asked for Becky – and guess what? Becky's only part of a fucking debt collection agency. Underhand, or what? So it looks like another move.

But first. A tin or two and a last ditch attempt at salvation. I call my list of contacts. And get this, one actually says that he might have something that could interest me. A slight drop in salary. No problem. Actually, it's for a junior. Well, to be more specific, a placement, expenses and possibly £50 a week tops. Fine. Based quite a long way out of town. Sure. He'll get back to me. Positively, definitely, please today? I'm moving – tonight as it happens. So phone. Definitely. Yes or no, today – promise me. I hang up and scream and jump around and that.

My stereo, rented TV, CDs, (all except two) furniture, and most of my clothes are now up for grabs in various North London hoc shops. First off I call Horace who says he's happy enough to look after my Mahler's Fifth and *Desire* CDs, and Keith Richards' biog but not us. Jeez still has a few weeks to do, besides he has half a dozen or so designer cats. Charlotte has no arguments with the pit bull, she just figures that I won't hit it off with her new boyfriend. This doesn't leave too many people. And I'm thinking that, actually, I never really did have many friends. I arrive home to the sound of my own voice on the answerphone. Excellent.

I run over, scoop up the handset and, panting, greet the caller in my best accent.

'Good news,' says the head-hunter. And finally I feel the straitjacket of my wretched life spring open. At once, all things are so possible. Of course, they always were. And this time, I'm not going to fuck it up. I swear. Watch and see if I don't behave. Then my answerphone tells him to do something unspeakable with a kebab skewer.

10

Just Flesh and Blood and Eczema

I fill up with Extra in the Bass House to stop worrying about where I'm going to stay.

The November night clings to my flesh like a wet blanket. Even Buttercup shivers. I'm deeply regretting not making arrangements before doing the runner. Then again, there was more than a possibility that I'd now be enjoying hospital accommodation – sleeping legs skyward – if I'd stuck around.

It's two a.m. To get warm, Buttercup, myself and my sports bag of belongings board a night bus on Holloway Road. This takes us to Trafalgar Square. By the time I alight, I need a cigarette, a swig or so of vodka and a long think about my next move. We sit down and amass our options. The options come to zero. We must keep warm tonight, then find a cheap flat in the morning. I have nearly £300 in my sky so it's unlikely to be a problem.

'So how long you been out?' a filthy beggar asks.

'Nar dear, yer got it wrong. I'm not homeless.'

'So where d'yer live?'

'Nowhere, just now.'

'So yer 'omeless.'

'Yeah, but I'm not a beggar.'

'Didn't say you were, BA.'

'BA?'

'Bad Attitude.' She pats Buttercup. 'Nice dog. Gi's a smoke, then?' Begrudgingly I give her a cigarette.

202

Liz is fifteen. Been on the streets for a year. Knows every-one. Will show me the cracks tomorrow if I like. 'You'll be alright.'

'It's not like that. I'm going to find a gaff tomorrow. I mean, it's just not like that.'

'Yer got money then?'

'No. But . . . I'll work something out.'

'Course yer will, BA. C'mon, I'll take you to a fire. I'll look after yer, me.'

We walk with Liz round to Lincoln's Inn. And I'm feeling bad. I mean I really would like to give Liz something. Some money, like. Or buy her food. But, I mean you can't, can you? Let on that you've got money. Liz is probably OK. But the rest of these people. Scum of the earth. The sort of people Pepper's into these days.

I sit for a time in this reservation of corrugated metal, wood and cardboard, bonfires and music – yeah, there's music here. I give cigarettes and vodka to Liz and the people who ask, until I run out. No one minds that I don't want to talk much. My mind turns to the red mohawk I saw when I was drinking with Horace that afternoon. And I'm thinking, yeah that's a good way to dress – when you live and sing and share smokes on a fucking reservation. No one here minds Buttercup, who's getting on famously with the other dogs.

But I'll tell you what. I'm feeling mightily uncomfortable here. With Pepper watching and all. Then I remember a line on the CD she gave me and it makes me smile. You see, 'I'm thinking about Isis, and how she thinks I'm so reckless.'

And yeah, I'm feeling guilty as hell. I've got enough money to put us both up in the Hilton for the night and here I am accepting the hospitality of fifteen-year-old Liz – so that I can get a flat in the morning. But it's self-survival, isn't it? You have to think about number one – or you're fucked well and good. Like these people. Drinking Tennents

203

fucking Super on the street. I don't ever want to be one of these people – so help me God.

'I don't let just anyone come in me bash, me.'

'No, thank you. It's certainly much warmer.'

'But I feel right sorry for you. You haven't been out for long. You smell so good.' Liz doesn't smell good. Not heavy duty bad-tramp smell. Just human, you know. Untreated. Not like anyone I've ever been so close to.

'And I like you. You can touch me if you want. I don't mind, me.'

'Just for warmth, eh. Like you said.'

'Yeah.' But I touch her a bit anyway. Because it's what she wants. And she's only fifteen. We kiss. And more.

'No please, I don't want to do it,' I say.

'Why? Why not?' she asks, mightily hurt.

'Listen, Liz. I think I've got a disease. And that's the last thing you need.'

'God. That's so sweet. That's just so sweet of you to tell me. Most blokes . . . never mind,' and she kisses me. And we do it just with hands. Which is good for both of us. I don't sleep much and wish that I had some more drink.

In the morning, I get on a bus back to the Park.

Yeah, I know, I should have slipped Liz something. Left some money in her bash. But, I dunno, she might have felt like some whore or something.

A room the size of an envelope. Two doors – one opening out on to a crappy yard, the other giving me access to the rest of the house. Shared and shit-spattered bathroom. Shit-spattered gas ring, water dripping in, fucked payphone. Ten quid a fortnight to the squat co-operative (I've got my own room, after all). And if I can cough up a month's advance, they'll replace the cardboard with window.

The house is a makeshift conversion on the edge of the Andover Estate – which, if you don't know, is the Broadwater Farm of Finsbury Park. A documentary maker's wet dream, where children are left out all day to rob and play with the dogs. And the only time the police visit is to dig a month-old granny corpse from an armchair. Unlike where I was living before, this is a manor which cannot be described as 'funky'. Obviously, I'll sleep on the carpet. The mattress smells of piss – ironic, eh? Then again the floor smells of mushrooms.

I take a piss in the basin. It stays there. So I sit on my bag for a decent weep. But nothing comes. And although I'm rushing down fast, I feel hard as vodka and codeine.

A knock at the house entrance door. No fear. It's the welcoming committee, Aslan Daniel, with a tin of Super and a lit spleek. Dead touching, or what?

Hashish smoke twists up through Aslan's natural dreads making him resemble a silage heap. Its sweet pinching aroma ignites such a longing in me. But it's clear that he's not going to pass it until it's nearly dead. And I'll bet my apricots he's front loaded it so I won't even get a hit. I'm wrong. He passes it and it's shit pure Skunk. Not a hint of paraffin. And much as I have a healthy tolerance to this stuff – whoa, I'm reeling.

Things in this house are not good, I'm told. Throughout the night there's a cacophony of screams, glass breaking, music, bad plumbing and fucking. Above Aslan and myself live a couple. They're no problem during the week. But on Friday and Saturday nights he rents her out to people from the local for three quid a time. And apparently she's not averse to the arrangement. He's known by folks as Marley. She's known as the Wailer.

To make matters worse there's a crack dealer on the same floor. But to make matters intolerable he fixes guitars and amps in the evenings. And there're a couple of scag queens on the top floor. One is in bad shape.

Apart from that, four students and a handful of doleys inhabit the other rooms. And no one – apart from Aslan, who likes to know what's going on – interferes with one

205

another. Aslan leaves. I put an ear to my bag and my arm around Buttercup and pretend he's Pepper. I fall asleep. Probably sobbing – I don't recall.

Today I headed down to what is affectionately known as the Zippy and Bungle Fan Club, and tried to transfer my dole claim to my new address. I waited for an hour and a half in the enquiries queue. I was told to sit down and they'd call me. An hour passed and they informed me that they'd lost my claim. After a bunch of questions, they assured me that I'd receive my giro on time, or a day late at worst. In the pub at lunchtime I moot that the DSS should be computerized. How un-streetwise of me. Obviously, that would make it harder to fiddle – and as everyone knows, no man can live on Sup Ben alone. I mean, after booze and fags there's fuck all left.

A few ales the better and I head off to St Mary's in Paddington to get my suppurating chap sorted. It's a bit of a hike, but I know the form there. I've been lanced there on a number of occasions. And unlike other places they let you hold it while they dip. I prefer it that way, it's less dangerous – especially if it's a female doing the honours.

Richard is the crack and amp man downstairs. Only he only does amps, and only during the day. Nor does Marley rent out his wife. Apparently Aslan (AKA Nigel Smith) is a bit of a bullshitter. And the estate, far from it being the open prison I'd reckoned, is dead safe. 'A total piece of piss, a fucking community centre. Jus' show yer face a bit. No sweat.' Anyway, Richard's a damned fine geezer. He replaced the lock on my door with a well hard Chubb and rigged up a steel brace on the inside to make it harder to kick in. And we ditched my toilet of a mattress and picked up a virtually odourless one at a secondhand shop on Blackstock Road.

Obviously, I took him to Hornsey Wood Tavern and got us both rat-arsed. What else could I do after such unsolicited human kindness? I beat him nineteen to one at pool – and that was only because I accidentally sliced in the black on the cue-back.

I asked Richard if he would like to come with me to light my old mattress. He declined. And missed a treat.

The thing about bad times is, they're not all that bad. Sure, I can no longer afford to spend every day in the pub. But I get by, with eight or nine tins of Super here in my smelly sack of a room. And each evening Aslan pops down for a nightcap smoke – we buy a quarter of grass, if it's available, alternately when our giros come. And I take it for granted that I dress in a jumper without a shirt, have raucous armpits, wear my boxers inside out three days of the week, that I rob bog roll and light bulbs from pubs and pick up under-par veg when the Stroud Green Road stalls are taken in. The fact that I'm too lazy to wank (besides it still hurts a little) doesn't even bother me. It suffices that Pepper's succubus visits to siphon me once or twice a week.

And listen, I rarely even think of Pepper these days. It's true, I don't need to. She lurks full-time below my other thoughts. Watching my every action like a disdainful phantom. But I'm too far gone to tailor my actions to impress her. I mean, there's a two-bob bit in the front of my chinos that won't wash out. The best I can hope for is a crumb of pity amid the disgust as she regards my decay. And say I did spot her and Richard in a pub one day. It wouldn't faze me in the slightest. They're always on the next table. Laughing at me or ignoring me.

And, of course, there's always my old mate.

Take a look at Buttercup. One solid block of life. Missiling through the bushes after his stick. Firing up and butting my chest so that I nearly lose balance. Buttercup pouncing, so that the little black cushions on his paws nudge my shoulders. Tearing after another dog to say: 'How yer doing? My name's Buttercup and I think life's a fine thing' – scaring shit out of other owners with his misconstrued *joie de vivre*.

'There's so much in the papers about them. But if they're

happy, fed well and exercised regularly, they're good as gold. Bouncer' – his Rottweiler – 'wouldn't harm a fly. You certainly must look after him. I simply can't understand all that talk about putting them down *en masse.*'

And I'm thinking – how could anyone ever be justified in stilling such an overtly wonderful life form? Yeah, and I swallow when I consider that my affectionate beechwood friend panting beside me now trusts me absolutely.

Buttercup *needs* me. It's a fantastic thought. With all his strength, appetite, potential killing ability, Buttercup wouldn't survive without me.

And it strikes me that the important thing here is the interconnectiveness of life. 'With all life's sham, drudgery and broken dreams,' at the end of the day, we're all pulling on the same side. So, yeah fuck, I'll admit it. Maybe I was half responsible for the poor girl's eczema.

What, you may ask, has prompted this rather rosy résumé of my current situation? Let me tell you. It's Christmas Day and we're in one of the finest squats North London has to offer, having a right good time.

This gaff is fantastic. It should be in the fucking Design Museum. This sofa, which is dead comfortable, is made entirely of milk-bottle crates, padlocked together. It turns into a king-sized bed when you pull it away from the wall. Then there are the chests of drawers made out of bread baskets. The bookshelves are wood planks painted tripping colours balanced on coffee jars filled with tripping-coloured water. And, of course, there's our Christmas tree. It's spray-painted silver and decorated with razor blades, barbed wire, chains and broken lightbulbs – and crowned with a plastic dog turd. But best of all is the gas fire. Well, it's not what you'd call a fire, as such. Rather, a big pipe rising in an 'r' shape, straight from the mains. And it's shooting this bloody great blue flame, that tapers up at the end, across the room. You'd think it would burn the place down – but it's safe as houses. I dunno, I'm on perhaps my twentieth Super of the day. And Caroline, who I've just met, is lying across me and I've got my hand in her blouse. Her tits are a bit greasy. But hell, a greasy tit is better than no tit at all and it is Christmas.

But it's no good. Humping Caroline, standing up, in the khazi, that is. It's so fucking cold that half of the old boy won't come out to play. There's a thick ring of rolled up condom round the base. The drink's not contributing. And physiological excuses aside, I just can't do it with Pepper's laughing face up against the frosted glass.

I received my giro today. Consequently I'm back in the raised green section of St Mary's waiting to be told the result of last month's blood test.

And yeah, I did it, I agreed to have my blood tested for HIV. I promised the counsellor that I would inform all traceable partners and remain celibate. I further added that I would probably get full-blown AIDS very quickly due to total lack of positivity in general. The counsellor recommended Transcendental Meditation. But you can't learn it on the NHS.

Like millions of young people before me, I'm waiting to be told whether nature's picked me for the cull. And I'm trying to conceive the sheer volume of terror generated by this, the world's greatest lottery. I'm thinking, without guilt, that God or nature's fascism is infinitely more cruel than anything politics has managed to dream up.

But hell, I'm not worried. Honestly. Obviously, I'd hate to think that I'd injected Pepper's welcoming warmth with a shot of viral cyanide. But I don't worry for me. I mean, I'm in the shadows looking out. I'm really not that fazed about living right now.

My ticket is pulled. And yeah, I literally win the Holiday of a Lifetime. Some grin that is – I mean, what the fuck good is a holiday without spending money? And of course, unlike other *no purchase necessary* draws, this holiday is for one. Last month I won two 150 mg Eradacin – to eat on the premises – and a tub of antibiotic golf balls for my unique cocktail of specific and non-specific urethritis. Yeah, I know I should have taken five days off the lag. But, you know what it's like.

Each night without respite, I dream of being reunited with Pepper. Each morning I wake early, full to the tear ducts with disappointment.

Last week I chanced reading the letter again. It was OK. If anything, it seemed pretty irrelevant. And I've grown sick of the photos. So as the reality of the woman falls back in time, so her spectre increases in its clarity and omnipresence. Man, it's fucking perverse. These days, washed-out ginger hair and skin disease are what I look for in women. But the fact is – and this is what I keep trying to tell myself – I didn't live with a fucking angel. My girlfriend was a human being who shitted and farted and wanked like human beings are supposed to. She really wasn't anything to write home about. What I need is some sort of perspective on things. I need the advice of a third party. And of course, it's been a while, so Jeez – if he's back in circulation – should be good for a few jars and a fistful of pharmaceuticals.

But I'll tell you what's really tipped the balance. Something happened. Something quite bad.

Now, you know me. I drink in pubs. And if I do drink Tennents blue, I do it with some discretion – in my room. I'm definitely not one of those fuckers who drinks it on the street. And, I mean, if I didn't know you or anything, I'd never accost you for money – no way am I one of those. So, when two days ago, I was drinking on the street, there was a thoroughly good reason. I was in between pubs. I'd only had a couple in the Park Tavern and I still had fuck bad **street-fear** and **drink-guilt**. I also figured that my hands weren't quite steady enough for the Worlds End. Yeah, alright, I quite fancy one of the barmaids – she has one of those chins that looks like it's been worked on with a meat tenderizer.

Now, say you didn't know me. You might well get the wrong impression. Sure, my £2 jumble sale overcoat could be construed as trampish. And there's fuck all I can do about my trainers – until my giro arrives. Obviously, haircuts are a thing of the past. But yeah, I suppose I could have combed it. As for shaving – I've been feeling a mite fragile of late and shaving hurts – or at least I think it might. So when she saw me leaning on the railings outside the pub, talking to some of the Super-swilling locals – I only stopped for a brief chat, that's all – she must have got totally the wrong impression.

Now, you'd have thought that seeing her – close up as the car stopped in the traffic – would have done something to convince me of her humanity. No chance. She was only in a black GTi or 205 or something good, with a slick-looking, fuck handsome ad type at the wheel.

And don't even suggest it. I've been over and over that possibility. It was her right enough. Parked right next to me. And of course she recognized me. The look of shock. The disbelief. And if there was at first any doubt in her mind, I put paid to that. Showed her my trade mark, so to speak. Inadvertently, spontaneously, my head fell forward and I disgorged vociferously into the green 'Keep Britain Tidy' bin before me.

So I'm thinking that if – and there is, after all, a faint possibility – she remembered the mainly good things about me, those memories have been shot to shit. Parked up close, as she was, she got a potent lungful of my humanity. She, of course, in neat-as-hell work clothes, in a poncy motor, looked like a fucking goddess. The best I could do in re-taliation was rough her up a bit with one of my looks – hardly revenge, with bilious high-strength raining from my chin.

So it strikes me that the time has come for me to strip

Isis, so to speak. Remember her exactly as she is. Make her human again. Yeah, drop the Memory Cocktail.

'Look at me, man. Just take a fucking look at me. I did five this afternoon, this is my fourth this evening. Look at my hands. I'm totally fucked. I can't even get right any more. I can't even pick up the fucking drink to get fucking right. My pulse is pushing 110. So, really, I don't care.'

'Richard, my friend, don't you feel that you're taking things a tad seriously?'

'Besides, Jeez, like I said. It's not to top myself. It's to work some things out.' Jeez grins.

'You say that, Richard. But judging by the state you're in at present, I'm not entirely convinced. I mean, what in heaven's name have you been doing to your hands and arms? Don't you think you might fare better if I gave you a little money to get yourself back on your feet. I could even rustle up a course of Antabuse to help you get off the sauce?'

'Jeez, I need to do things my way.'

'Richard, you must understand. If you OD, and there's a more than distinct possibility, I can't be responsible. I've got to say "no".'

'"If you were a hardware man and I bought a blade," remember?'

'Yes, but this is quite different . . .'

'Don't insult me, Jeez. Allow me to do this.'

He puts a hand on my shoulder and I get a shiver of homophobia. He pauses there for a time. I'm doing these rigid sort of twitches.

'OK, OK. You win,' he whispers and takes his hand away.

'You fine, fine man, Jeez. And look, no one knows I'm seeing you. No one will suss I scored it off you.'

'No, Horace and Pepper won't have the first clue, will they?'

'Well you won't be culpable. There'll be no proof. And I imagine your gaff's clean after the last run-in.'

'True enough. Drink up, the night is but young.' I down half of the pint in one. My body tells it to fuck off. Luckily, I catch most of it in the glass. I taste it. Seems fine – if a touch warm. Jeez winces.

We're back at Jeez's flat. A small five-roomed affair in Soho – a place he calls his *runaround* – huh. Of course, he tells me that he's never heard of the Memory Cocktail – and yeah, he reckons that I'm enacting the whole drama to get back at Pepper. But if I really am absolutely, one hundred per cent set on it, he has the ingredients. I am.

We drink a bottle of Scotch and crash out in the living room.

When I get back I'm feeling a touch unwell. I drop two Mogadon – what the fuck, eh?

I wake eighteen hours later feeling better than I have in aeons. Yeah, I'm making the right decision. I'm ready for the big one. The disaster. And I'm thinking, if I do check out, all those dreams about trains were a right waste of effort. I've got enough medication to put out a herd of rhino.

Buttercup whines, woofs, sniffs, smiles and does the things that dogs are supposed to do. Pepper's Pepper like she's supposed to be. She may be with Richard. She's probably at work. But she's just flesh and blood and eczema Pepper. And if there is a Richard, he fucks her in the way that people are supposed to fuck. He hasn't got a cucumber of a dick. And, if the truth be known, he probably isn't even a vegetarian. The rat Gary has abandoned ship. There are no more voices. And, as I take Buttercup for our final walk, I am not at all vexed by other people, their dogs, insects, hallucinations or pot holes. And I'm equanimous about the paradox that life really is worth living – provided you're quite serious about probably dying that evening.

'Fancy a pint?'

But Buttercup doesn't say, 'You bet.' Neither do I. So we just go home.

But you know what? I fancy a drink. A cup of tea. With a saucer. So we stop off at the little café opposite the supermarket. My hand is steady as I sip the tea.

Buttercup senses that my desperation has lifted and he's in fine fettle. It's then that I realize that I'm going to have to medicine poor Buttercup too. This vexes me and I take a Diazepam before schedule.

Misty night clambers close around the window. I take two yellow Diazepam biscuits on schedule

I line up the other six and the twelve blue Ativan pills and place the vodka in the centre of the room.

An hour later and I tip out a tumbler of the vodka and sip it with ineffable pleasure. An urge evidences itself. The video of Charlotte. One last time. Obviously, I don't. Sex could so easily turn into a reason to live. Besides, I haven't got a TV or video – the effects are beginning and I'm enjoying the benign confusion. I do another tug of the vodka and skin up.

I float like a hummingbird through a contemplative hour.

Will Pepper or Charlotte or Kat (the first) cry about me? I'm trying to hope so. But the hope so won't come. No, Jeez was wrong. My motives are pure.

Then I remember that a day or so ago I dreamed that Jeez was blowing me. And I enjoyed it. Yeah, I fired off in my sleep. Unless . . . holy fuck! I take a hit from the bottle.

I'm feeling good and pre-operative. I pop three of the Ativan from their tiny display cases and mash them into Buttercup's dinner. Pepper once said, 'This is going to sound really perverse coming from a vegetarian. But in a weird sort of way, I'm turned on by the smell of the food you get him. I mean, I salivate.' Daft cow.

Another conversation comes to mind.

'Richard,' she said, 'do you believe in heaven and hell?'

214

'Hell, I don't know. I hope not. At least, I hope there's not hell. I mean, I'd be a cert.'

'I reckon that our spirits are reincarnated in babies when we die – and we forget everything about our last life. But it's stored on record somewhere.'

'Yeah, well you would think that, wouldn't you?'

'Why would I think that?'

'Because you're so into recycling and that sort of crap.'

I'm wondering how many I should take. I mean, I've got a pretty high tolerance to this junk. But then again, I wouldn't mind pulling through this episode alive. So I drop three Halcyon and sluice them down with another tumbler for good measure.

It's eleven and I snap out of some sort of stupor. I seem to have come in my boxers – then again it could just be regular pus. I really should have laid off the booze when I was on the golf balls. I'm well tired now and seriously nauseous. I snort up half a gram of Billy. It sears up into my cerebral cortex like a frozen wind break and picks me up almost immediately. I do some more vodka and roll a Thai stick. Then I drink more vodka.

Now, this is the most unusual of sensations. I'm doing some fine mental gymnastics. I retire to my mattress to fully appreciate things.

My face has gone numb as hell. In fact all of me is freezing up – I'm totally numb, like my whole body is soaking in a bath of liquid Charlie. I'm utterly paralysed. I can't affect a thing outside my head. I'm out of it – the phenomenal world, I mean. I'm pure noumena.

Just as I'd planned. I'm ceasing to be. All that there is – are the events of my life but no me. No longer the 'I'. The 'I' that caused all the trouble in first place. Just 'i' the passive observer. i – free of my fuck bad adjectives. And it's good. It seems like this is all I've really ever wanted. To be out of the picture. To take an amoral stance in life. No guilt. No fear. Just a life.

11

Double Amyl Rush

I've taken a

Memory Cocktail.

And if i shut my eyes i can create Pepper.

Her water-and-whisky complexion. Her tea-stain hair. Even the wetness and nutty stipple of Her eyes. My cocktail enables me to picture everything, everything about Pepper, exactly as it is. Inch for inch the coastline of Her eczema – Her sad, lip-red rind – and its emotional and lunar vacillation. Even the way Her right foot errs a fraction inward when She walks, how Her left breast is a degree more pendulous than the other as She crawls over me. The mild crab-stick of Her groin, the intimate essence of a post-garlic fart beneath the duvet, the changed scent of illness. Her greeting me, 'Hi-er'.

It's true, i can even get Her to say things. In Her exact voice. Exactly the way She speaks. And what She says is what i make Her say. In fact, with my Memory Cocktail, i can make anyone i've ever heard speak, say just about anything i choose. For instance, if i'd heard You speak, i could make You say things to me. Things You mightn't normally say. I could lie back, just as i'm doing now, and listen as You whine, 'richard, fuck me. Please, please fuck me.' Or say You're a guy – because i'm not gay (except sometimes in dreams – and only just lately) – i could get You to say, 'I really value your friendship rich. You're a diamond.' Here, now, i could recall the disaster in all its forms or play Mahler's Fifth – note for note. With regard to my memory, i'm in utter control.

A fistful of barbs, a nose of pink, a stick and a half of Thai and – if, like me, You can't take being alone at such times – vodka to taste can do this for You. Try it. You'll be surprised at Yourself.

Career down into the epicentre of the chaos of your life. Discover the strange attractor. Make her human.

Reverse the tape and take a look at the video screen. Exit back through the convolutions, the buckles, ribbons and sinews of hot red. Soon enough things will grow more simple. The fiery kaleidoscope contracts. And though tracer lines still materialize and vanish, it's plain to see what it is that's being held before the camera. Yeah, I guess I've known all along – it's the hot, crackling tip of a cigarette.

'Don't sit like that.'
  'Like what?'
'With your legs crossed like that.'
'Why not?'
'Just don't. Mother said I'm in charge . . .'
'Only until we get to Victoria. Then Aunt Sophie is.'
'And give me that comic.'
'Why should I?'
'Because I said so, and I'm in charge. You little git.'

217

'Piss off Seb.' Of course, he leans across the carriage and slaps me hard around the head and snatches the comic. He flicks through it disdainfully, pulls down the train window and lets it flap away.

'Kid's stuff.' He pulls out his cigarettes, puts one in his mouth and offers me one. Obviously, I have to take it.

'Don't hold it like that. Look. That's it. Christ. That's how girls light matches you silly bastard. You're s'posed to strike it inwards. Anyway I'm going to get a lighter with some of my spending money.'

'Yeah?'

'You're not inhaling. Look. Haaa phooo. That's what you're s'posed to do. Go on.' Seb's a far better smoker than I am. In fact he almost looks like a grown-up, the way he holds the cigarette calmly between two fingers and exhales through his nose.

'Inhaling makes me feel sick. I prefer to just blow it out.'

'Well that's the wrong way to do it. It makes you look like a poof. Poof!' I try inhaling but it makes my throat tighten so much I can barely breath. 'Poof.'

'Richard,' Seb leans over. 'Don't flinch. I'm not going to hit you. Why do you always think I'm going to hit you?'

'Because you always do.'

'Mmm. Richard, you know, when we're at home, it seems that you try to avoid me. Do you?'

'Don't know.'

'Well Richard, I'd like to say, that's good. Very good. You see when you don't avoid me, you annoy me. You know that, don't you?'

'S'pose.'

'And when you annoy me, I have to punish you. Do you understand that as well?' I remain silent. 'I mean, Richard, it's only fair. If you annoy me, it's only just that I should seek retribution. Do you know what "retribution" means?'

'Don't tell me. It means you hit me.'

'You see what I mean? "Don't tell me,"' he mocks. 'You

218

*are so fucking disrespectful. So full of yourself for a kid.
And after I went to the trouble of getting us our own carriage
so we could smoke.'*

'Sorry, Seb.'

*'I'm afraid that won't quite do. I think you should get on
your knees and say it.'*

'No, you'll kick me.'

*'I'm in charge, Richard. Now get on your bloody
knees.'*

'No way.'

'Either that or I put my plan into action.'

'What plan?'

'A plan to end my troubles for good. Ho, ho, ho.'

'Oh yeah? What plan.'

*'Well, you remember that careless boy at your school who
had that nasty little accident on his way home on the train?
You see Richard, I was thinking that maybe you could have
a similar one.'*

*'So you want me to stick my head out of the window, do
you?'*

*'Not at all, baby brother. I'm more than happy to do it
for you. "I tried to grab him," I'll tell Aunt Sophie, "but it
happened in an instant." No one will miss you. Mother and
Father hate you. And as for me, I mean Richard, what can
I say? I'm regarded as something of a genius at my school.
Nine O-levels a year early. To have a brother so thick that
he should be at some special school. A brother that has to
visit an educational psychologist, or whoever it is you have
to see. You mental, flid, mongoid git. My God, I hate you
so much, Richard.' Suddenly he launches up, grasps my limp
arms and pins my face against the window.*

*'Fuck off, Seb. Fuck off, you rotten bastard.' He draws
the window down so that the cold brace is on my nose.*

'I'm gonna do it. I'm gonna do it.'

*'Get off. For fuck's sake, you're mad.' He drags the
window down fully. And I actually believe that he's going*

219

to bend me full out of it. That my frail head is going to smash like an egg lobbed against a wall – and that my life will just lollop out.

'Stop screaming, you little bastard. Stop screaming. Look I was only joking Richard, really.' Seb's away from me now leaning against the opposite door. 'Richard, I mean it, take your hand off that cord. Richard, I was only joking. Think about it. I wouldn't really have done it. I just wanted to scare you that's all. Please let go of the emergency cord. We'll be in so much shit if you stop the train.'

'I'm keeping hold of it until we get to Victoria. Or until the train stops at a station and I can get off.'

'Richard, I'm serious. If you accidentally pull it the train could crash.'

'Bollocks. It won't crash. They wouldn't make them on trains if they made them crash, would they?'

'I mean it. It happened only a few months ago. You don't watch the news so you wouldn't know. But it's true. It's going so fast. Then we'll all be killed. And it'll be your fault. Or maybe just the people in the front will be killed and you'll be in so much fucking trouble. You'll go to prison for life. Or be locked in a loony bin, forever. You're too short to hold it. Look, you're on tiptoes. Why don't you let me hold it for you?'

'Huh!'

Seb begins to shout, 'Listen Richard. I'm in charge. I'm sensible. I'm in charge, do you hear? You're going to get such a thrashing when I tell father what you did. And who do you think they'll believe? A fifteen-year-old or a ten-year-old? And you with behavioural problems. Think about it. A little thickie, who bunks off school, shoots animals, sets light to things. No one'll believe a word you say. But if you let go of it now, I promise I won't tell. And I promise I won't hit you. I really promise Richard. And I never break promises. I'm going to count to ten and you've got to let go of it. If you don't, I'm going to tell Father that you tried to crash the train and you'll be locked up. And even if you're not. I'll make your life such a fucking misery.'

'You already do.'

'Yeah, well I won't if you sit down. And Richard, who will they believe? Everyone knows you're bad. A fucking little mental.'

Seb begins to count to ten. I weigh up the consequences of holding on. I'm straining and we're only at Norbury. Besides, I conclude that one way or other Seb will get me. And maybe he was only trying to shit me up. So I sit back down and tense up for the kicking. But Seb remains still and silent.

Then he says calmly, 'Thank you, Richard,' and lights a cigarette.

'And you're not going to hit me? You promised.'

'Of course I'm not,' he smiles. 'C'mon, let's shake hands and enjoy our holiday.' Tentatively I offer him my hand. Grinning amicably he reaches out his. Then snatching my wrist, he places the cigarette in his mouth and forces my other wrist into the same hand. He removes the cigarette from his mouth. And hovering it languidly above my forearms, he says, 'Oh Richard, Richard. We really must get a few things straight.'

A woozy Buttercup woke me, perhaps three days after the self-mortification episode.

I bin the polaroids and letter. I've got what I need. The complete picture. The adjectives. The humanity.

But I soon fish them out again. One should at all times be prepared for relapses.

'Substance needs shadow,' I once said to Horace.

'Yin needs yang,' he replied.

'Good needs evil.' I went on.

'Moderation needs excess,' came next.

'Self needs others,' I went on to say – rather wisely, I consider.

To get to the point. Not even her worst adjectives can help me. Pepper, with her light and dark skin, her black and white moods, her love-and-hate love, is, quite plainly, one of *my* adjectives. A quality more central to my being than my other excesses. Which is to say – quite obviously, I'm totally arse over tit in love with her. And maybe, yeah, I lied a bit. The Cocktail – well did you really think I did it to remember? Did you really think that I didn't leave the door ajar for Aslan? Or position an envelope, with Pepper's work number scrawled on it, casually on the floor?

'Love, love, love, love, you can't give it away,' howls Richard Butler on the juke-box. And he's got a point. You sure as hell can't give love away. You need to go out and flog it. Just like baby clothes, a condom, or a box of washing powder. And it strikes me that one's adjectives are not the qualities that define one – they're the qualities one deserves.

I'll admit that my philosophical mood is largely due to the five strong ones I've managed to down since cashing the giro, but it seems to me that I now have a brief that is eminently solvable.

In short, I need to sort out properly and pitch for an account that I lost some months ago. I need to deserve it back. So that evening I say, 'This, Jeez, is the last session. My last supper, so to speak. Before I crucify myself and become resurrected as an entirely new person.'

'I was of the opinion that you already had crucified yourself. And it is indeed a miraculous resurrection that I'm now witnessing. I can't tell you how relieved I am to see you, Richard. Then again, I must confess that I half believed you were pulling a fast one and were procuring the gear for recreational use.'

'Jeez, I'm a man of my word. But the question is, are you?'

'Naturally, my friend, naturally.'

'Let me get you another.' I buy us both a pint and a chaser with the last of my benefit. I mean, I don't even have enough to get home. He'd better fucking come through.

So I remind Jeez about what he said about lending me money to get sorted. Obviously, he says, 'I must confess that I'm experiencing slight cash-flow difficulties at present. After the enforced vacation and what with other things.'

'Right.'

We drink – in silence. Embarrassed silence from him. Pure huff from me. Then he cracks. 'Oh for fuck's sake Richard. Take it. Take it before I change my mind.' He pulls four nifties from his wallet. Then, with a resigned look, peels off a fifth.

'Cheers Jeez. You're a fucking prince. You really were my last hope. Oh man.'

'I was, was I? When it comes to such matters, most people of your social standing have, somewhere on this green and pleasant land, an estranged father that doubles as a cheque book.'

'Well yes, but he's a total wanker. And there isn't a sorbet's chance in hell that he'd give me a penny.'

'Oh come now. Fathers as a breed are always game for a timely reconciliation. Couldn't the prodigal son hang his tail and return?'

'No chance, man.' So I tell him about things. And yeah, maybe a tear or two hits the table. About Seb's childhood tyranny. About how some of the memories surface periodically. How I eventually freaked and earned five little borstal tattoos. I show him the scars where I dug them out. How I haven't spoken to any member of my family since. And how I'd rather become a pro Special Brew drinker than ask them for wedge.

*   *   *

They should be shut, I know. My eyes I mean. But they're fixed on the nape of her in front. Shit man! – her hair. Neat as wolf fur. That pine slab of neck and her collar crisp and white as cartridge paper. The baby gold butterflies behind her lobes. The taut cotton heart of her touche. The lineament of her spine tight up against the chair brace. Yeah, I'll admit it, I'm pressing down on a famous springer.

The mantra dissolved aeons ago. All I want is to lose the stiffy and fuck off home. Transcendental Meditation is not for me.

Horace O – he's a TM instructor now, and he's letting me learn it for free – informed us that whatever kinds of fucked up demons a person has living upstairs, downstairs, in the basement of their head, TM will exorcise them. However anxious, shallow-breathed or palsied you are, you'll get a decent hit off TM. And – get this – it'll bring your pulse down. But I'm thinking that maybe if you take so many narcotics you get a tolerance to this and can't take the trip. And amidst these and other useless thoughts, the boner melts – like they do.

A telephone at Finsbury Park tube. I'm looking at yesterday's *Standard*.

Break into Advertising

OTE £30K +

If you can communicate at MD level and have the ambition to become a top earner, join our friendly, professional team of advertising sales staff in the West End.

    We don't mind where you've been. It's where you're going that matters!!!

    In the first instance call Amelia Pickle 071 XXX XXXX and sell yourself to me.

Now, hell, there was a time when I could give shit hot phone. But these days my voice is up and down like a bad

TV's. And I'm thinking that using the dog is tantamount to getting up on stage or being the first to cue off for the pub team – sober.

I tell Horace O that TM has no effect on me. He tells me to give it time.

I give it twenty minutes, twice a day, for a week. By the end of the week it's having some effect. Every so often I spontaneously burst into tears.

I tell Horace O that meditation seems to be having a reverse effect. He informs me that this is good. Apparently, I'm pulling the cork on all the shit bottled up in my subconscious. I ask him where all the ethereal shit goes when it's left us meditators, and joke about a celestial sewage system. He tells me it acts as fertilizer, promoting greater psychic health in the community. If one per cent of the citizens of Finsbury Park meditated regularly, there would be a noticeable fall in the local crime rate. House plants would also grow more quickly. Ca ca.

A week later his prognosis is apparent. I have a bad bout of psychic diarrhoea. I swear I can smell the subconscious shit when I enter my room.

A month later I detect a vague sense of well-being. Then again, I always get a mating-season optimism around this time of year. I'm twenty-four soon and full of the spunk of youth.

Listen. Take up Transcendental Meditation. I mean it. It creeps up on you like good health when you quit smoking. (It's a fact, I no longer want cigarettes – besides the offices of Marlborough Publishing are non-smoking.)

And get a load of this. Like I promised, I pulled the communication cord on the Disaster Express, so to speak. I refused point-blank Jeez's final invitation back for a Chaz binge and haven't been on the lag once. Not even a swift tin. Sure, it was a right bitch for the first week or so. Especially between six and eleven – reading sodding library books, and all, declining invitations, passing pub doors (and if I had a newly cashed Giro roll in my sky, I sucked mints to avoid the familiar, inviting smell of opening time), just outright ignoring the deep, deep cravings of my gullet. But listen, I haven't touched a drop for a couple of months. And my arms and hands are almost healed.

But, let me tell you, all in all it hasn't been nearly as hard as I thought it would be. Not with Pepper watching – as she does.

Picture me. Black slicked-back hair. Non-blotchy, well fed face, steady hands, steady voice, regular pulse. I booked in a DPS and three half-pages (a miracle in this recession) this week. Picture me cocked back in my swivel chair at lunchtime speaking into the telephone.

'Yes, that's right, *Pepper Furnival*. Sure, I'll hold.'

Admittedly, it took me a couple of weeks to sell anything. But if I carry on like this I'll be able to shape the debt into something approaching realistic in a couple of years. I've already converted five grand of it into kosher building society loans. 'Yeah, I'll keep holding.' Then took out a new shark loan to pay off the old shark loan. Yeah they . . . 'Sorry? No. Just tell her it's a friend' . . . found me. And they were less than amused. 'Please, just tell her it's a friend . . . So when will she be back?'

Anyway, as soon as I'm a little more sorted, I'm going to rent somewhere proper. Give some money to Liz or something.

Holy fuck! – it's like a double amyl rush – popping in the cranium like a week-old orgasm. And I'm unsure as to whether hearing this voice is doing me good or about to cause sudden incontinence. Instinctively, I grope for a cigarette. I'm enveloped in deep drink craving. But I'm practised. I communicate at MD-level these days. Prolonged sobriety and TM have given me a direct line to Pat. And I say, like she's just a mate or something, 'So where's my birthday card, Miss Furnival . . . Don't be silly, I was only joshing. I just called to see how you were doing . . . You're joking? Entirely gone? . . . Well, that's excellent. So what do they do? Is it a one-off course or do they push needles into you on a regular basis to keep things at bay? . . . That's fucking amazing, Pepper.'

I'm thinking that the bitch without her eczema is going to have a considerably increased pulling ability. A thought which doesn't please me, obviously.

'. . . Listen. I can't talk for long. Things to do. People to rip off, et cetera. Yeah. Yeah? . . .'

Coffee flings itself out of the styrofoam beaker and over my client cards. I suck at the biro, trying for nicotine. I'm playing the mantra on fast forward. I've bitten a half moon in the beaker. And I say it.

'You know it would be good if we could meet up, you know. I mean, I don't mean anything like, you know. Lunch or something. A drink. I don't mean a drink. I don't drink – hardly ever now. Coffee . . .'

I'm sweeping coffee off the desk into the waste bin with a book entitled *Close that Sale*.

'Terrific. Great. When . . . No can do. Client lunch.' I lie.

'Fine. How about that cappuccino place off Wardour Street . . . Fine. Ten past one, Thursday . . .' What do I want? I want you Pepper I want to snort you up, cook you up with sodium bicarbonate and smoke you, skin-spike you, mainline your blood into my neck. 'Don't be silly. Just get me a card.' So I can lick your handwriting, use the card to . . . 'And you can pay for the coffees. Yeah. Look forward to it. Ciao.'

I wait for the tent on my lap to dismantle and sprint out for nicotine. I'm sitting on the wall by the VNU building in Poland Street and smoking to near vomit. This afternoon I shift another DPS, the back cover and a six series of mono halves. I win a three-pack of rubbers for selling the most that day. Obviously, I consider this highly auspicious. Later, I buzz Jeez for some Diazepam to stop me flinging coffee on Pepper and babbling incoherently. At home, I drink a celebration bottle of non-alcoholic wine and masturbate so ferociously that the folk next door pound the wall.

Tuesday. Another successful day at work, accompanied by seven-hour semi at the prospect of seeing Pepper. I'm heading home avoiding pubs – as usual – when this happens.

'RICHARD.' From across Argyle Street. I slice into Little Argyle Street and quicken my step. 'RICHARD!' The voice pursues. I accelerate to *he might be a mugger but I'm not sure* pace. 'Richard, it's me.' Sod it – I decide to run. Then this happens. One of the two cash dispensers ahead packs up. The queue instinctively heads for the other. They see me bounding up, construe me as a queue-jumper and conspire to block my way. And so under some scaffolding on Little Argyle Street, W1, amid a pissed-off cash dispenser queue, after fuck knows how long, I come face to face with my git brother – Seb.

'Richard, Richard. How the devil are you?' He has a hand on my shoulder. I think he wants to embrace. He reaches out to me – and would that I was holding a lit cigarette. 'Richard, how are you?' I take his hand limply and drop it. He's getting none of my sales training, my make-you-feel-good bonhomie. 'So how are you?' And the twat means it.

I feel the comfortable crush of his corduroy collar. His nose is less obliging, but it folds nicely when I nod the weight of my head on to it. He buckles. But not before my knee rises into the enveloping cushion of his genitals.

'Alright, I s'pose,' I mutter.

'Come on mate. We can't let an opportunity like this pass. Let me buy you a beer.'

'Actually, I'm in a bit of a hurry.'

'Richard, I won't take no for an answer. I'm sorry. It's been . . . how long? Five, maybe six years.'

'Honestly, I'm . . .'

'No excuses. I'm big brother.'

I unclip my briefcase, shove his nose in and force it shut.

228

There's much blood. I set the combination and fuck off.

'It's just . . .'

'Come on, Rich. I want to know what you've been doing.'

Amytal, Apisate, Ativan, Bolividon, Buspar, Cocaine, Copixol, Concordin, Diazepam, Dexedrine . . . you name it, I've done it.

'Just the one, eh?'

'No, no, no, no, no. Goodbye Seb.'

'Richard, please. Father and Mother. They'd love to see you. Just write or something.'

'Nothing to write about.'

'Please stop for a chat.'

'You don't understand, do you? How much I absolutely fucking loathe you. I'd rather come into contact with genital herpes than you. And Father and Mother can go fuck themselves. Goodbye, Seb.' Seb grabs me hard by the arm and pushes me up against the wall.

'Look, what you did. I deserved it OK. I fucking deserved it. For fuck's sake Richard. Grow up. What is wrong with you? We're your fucking family. I demand a reconciliation. I demand it. I DEMAND IT, YOU HEAR?' I fling him off and he staggers back into the road. I run through the crowd and escape on to Oxford Street. I'm shaking – like I've been in a fight or something. I would do absolutely anything for a drink. Absolutely anything, I conclude, bar having one. On the tube home I smile. I mean, I really am a quite different person now.

In pre-cognitive dreams it was quite different. All the same, there's something surreal about now. Though I can't say just what. The stench of diarrhoea is real enough. And the zoo-ish shrieks – human klaxons to drown the pain. But there's distance. It's the difference between video and cine film. Like I'm in some American direct response commercial. Maybe the light's wrong. Maybe I did a Nepenthe. Fuck knows.

229

Sliced eyeball, crushed testicle, impacted rib cage, severed ear, arms ablaze. All painless in comparison with the moans and shrieking of Pepper. Of Pepper dying.

Painless compared with the guilt.

I did this, you know? I caused this fucking horrible accident. This disaster.

I'm so sorry, Pepper. Can you die of guilt? Horace, is that you? Listen. I think I've sussed the soundtrack. The Mahler. My personal stereo must still be intact.

'If you pull the chain, the train doesn't crash. It just stops.'

'You don't think it could buckle up when the wheels lock?'

Now, do the wheels lock or does the driver apply the brakes? Plainly a matter I must clear up.

'Pepper, I'm sorry. I think I've pissed myself.'

I wake on Wednesday nervous and distended with hollow loneliness – or is it guilt? And yeah, I've swamped the bed. And I'm remembering the dream. I can't understand it. I didn't even have a fucking drink last night.

Thursday. I'm holding two Diazepam and a glass of water. And I'm thinking that it really is a tribute to Pepper. Me having to load up on barbs before seeing her.

Then, as though her ghost is in my room, I hear her. Speaking softly, as I imagine Isis might. Just telling me that she's human. That she's not out to harm me – nor judge me in any way. Just, it'll be nice to meet. That's all. That really is all.

Well man, apocalyptic nightmares, voices – fuck that! I flush away the pills and head off to work in the fresh and sober morning air.

Make few effective calls all morning. Erectile tissue on standby. Split between playing it cool, cruising up late and arrogant, and arriving early to secure a table. At ten to one

I'm drinking coffee in a small bar in St Anne's Court – checking my hands for shake.

Now get a load of this.

So sorry I missed your birthday. Hope you had a lovely time.
  Lots of love
  Pepper XXX

Lots of love XXX!
'Are you working?' she asks. Her legs are crossed. Cradling her coffee with two hands, as she does, I can't detect hand judder. But I'll tell you what. Her pupils are very much dilated. 'Well, are you creative director of a top-ten agency yet?' she flatters.

'I made a career move. I'm in publishing now. I got disillusioned with the whole business, you know? *Talk* magazine. You know it?.'

'Isn't it a supermarket magazine or a freebie?'

'NO IT'S NOT. It costs forty pee.'

'Whoops, sorry. How's Buttercup? I miss Buttercup.'

'Buttercup's good.'

'And the flat? I bet that's a bomb site.'

'Actually, we moved. Butterballs couldn't keep up his half of the rent.'

'Richard, guess what?'

'What?'

'I'm a suit now.'

And that's it. The newly grown hair confidently pushed behind the scabless ears, the way she looks straight into my eyes, her assured half-smile, her almost amused, 'isn't it odd to see you again' look. A look that says, 'I've been fucking a lot of people since we met and I know that you haven't.' Now her skin's cleared, the condescending bike really reckons she's something. The problem being, of course, she's right.

'Pepper, you're looking really great,' rips out like a sudden fart.

'I was about to say the same about you.' It oozes like a mendacious hisser. 'Shall we have another coffee?'

'Sure. If you . . .'

'Hey Richard, it's really good to see you, you know.'

'Yeah?'

'I mean it. I could almost lean across the table and . . . never mind.' Pepper's hand – and it's made of skin now – takes my hand. I try to get some control by concentrating on the evening when Man United trounced the Gunners by six to two in the Rumbelows Cup. It means my eyes are off her for a moment. 'What are you thinking about, Richard?'

'How much I hate Manchester United.'

'Be serious, please.'

'So what accounts do you handle? Landsdown fucking Megamarts – point of sale, I'll bet.'

'I missed you like hell, you know.'

'Yeah well. You know . . . So your skin's cleared up one hundred per cent?'

'Ninety-nine.'

I'd very much appreciate seeing and touching that skin. 'Through acupuncture? Did it hurt?'

'Richard,' She's holding both hands now and I've given up on the hard-on – I mean, baggy suit trousers sometimes look that way. Don't they? 'I said, I missed you.' And I'm having problems with this. How is it that women can talk like this when they're sober?

'Well maybe you should have called me?'

'Mmm. Maybe. But you'd moved, hadn't you?'

'True.'

'You know what? I was on Stroud Green Road and I could have sworn I saw you. Except, you were talking to this bunch of tramps. So I figured it couldn't be. Then the tramp version of you threw up in a bin and I thought, "So, it is Richard after all." Joke.'

232

'Tramps. Huh. So what would you have done if it was me, then?'

'Oh, I expect I'd have stopped and given you the price of a cup of tea.'

'No really. What if it really was me? And I was totally down and out, like?'

'Don't talk silly.'

'I mean it.'

'So did you miss me?' she urges.

'Stupid bloody question.'

'Answer me, you slag.'

'Like a limb or worse.' The coffees arrive and we break hands.

'Oh Richard,' she grins. 'This is funny. How old do you think Horace O is?'

'Early thirties, I guess. I dunno.'

'I asked him the other day . . .'

'When did you see Horace?'

'Tuesday, I think. We went for a drink. Not that he drinks now, of course.'

'With Horace?'

'Is there a law against it?'

'I thought you didn't like him.'

'He's OK. A bit touched. Besides he's shaved off those smelly dreadlocks.'

'His hair didn't smell.' She laughs.

'He never washed it, Richard.'

'Yeah, but it still didn't smell. I sat in an office with him for years.'

'Well it doesn't matter now. Anyway, I asked him how old he was. And you know what he said?'

'Eh, eh.'

'Fifty-nine.'

'Yeah well he was taking the . . .'

'No, no. I said, "Don't be silly, you can't possibly be fifty-nine." And he said, No, he was born in 1959. It's just

233

he can never remember how old he is so he just says fifty-nine. Don't you think that's funny?'

'Hilarious.'

'You're jealous, aren't you,' she giggles, 'because I went out with Horace O?'

'Of course I'm not.'

'Anyway, maybe if you play your cards right, I'll go out for a drink with you. I mean, we've broken the ice. We can still be friends. There's no law against that, is there?'

'Nothing on the statute books. But you know, I don't drink any more – not at all.'

'Oh yeah, Richard?'

'It's a fact.'

'Hmph. Maybe dinner, then. You still eat, I take it?'

'Tomorrow?' I mouth – like a twat.

'Eh, eh. Got a red-hot date, honey. I can fit you in Saturday, if you get my meaning.' All of this she says in a Mae West accent. And I'm beginning to wonder what happened to the Pepper I used to know and fuck. And, more importantly, whether this one's better.

And though I'm clean – my blood is blood, so to speak – I yet again feel the disorienting bicker of uppers and downers in my system. The upper, of course – the big, half a gram up each nostril upper – is that the re-pitch for the Pepper account has raced from effective call to initial meeting to out and out sales presentation in less than a week. The 100 mg downer is Buttercup.

Now, you know Buttercup. A maximum-contact dog, for sure. Civilized by human devotion. I mean, we'd discuss everything. Naturally, Buttercup didn't offer up many intelligent replies. But he'd pay meticulous attention to my lectures. Smile when I smiled, whine if I was on a low – then pounce over to cheer me up with a few reassuring head-butts. And in my turn, I understood his petitions for food, exercise and male-bonding. Sure, he looked and swaggered around like a right thug. But I'm convinced that he experi-

234

enced some exceptionally complex mental events. For instance, one afternoon we were taking our customary route to the park when Buttercup turned in mid-trot and began to pull me back home. I released him into our room and he fired over to the cupboard and began to whinny. Perplexed, I opened the cupboard and stood back as Buttercup commenced to drag the contents out on to the floor. He shrieked suddenly. He'd found it! His ball. The point being, I didn't even know the ball was there. I figured that it had been lost in the move – two months prior.

So, when I heard that I'd got the job, I figured, I just couldn't abandon him, alone in my fetid cell for five days a week. Watching him, day by day, develop attitude. Get like pit bulls are supposed to.

Obviously, when the receptionist said, 'Put this muzzle on him if you don't mind.'

I replied, 'Well actually I do mind.'

'I'm sorry, I really must insist . . .'

'I mind a lot. He wouldn't hurt anyone. Besides, what if he had something wrong with his mouth?'

'But he hasn't. You want the animal destroyed?'

'That's right,' I say bravely and slip the leather mouth-sandal over Buttercup's snout. I pay the receptionist for the injection and body-disposal, then shuffle out for a bawl.

Striding defiantly back through the Holloway Road shoppers, I'm thinking that it really is for the best. I mean, he didn't contribute too positively to the rancour of my living space. And there's no questioning the fact that he's an expensive non-essential. Besides, I'd have to get him de-balled and tattooed sooner or later – more dosh. I resolve to pour some high-strength into me to maintain this useful state of mind.

I get as far as the bar and ordering, then do a runner and sprint back. I mean, there's got to be something else I can do – someone in London who would be willing to put him up during the daytime. I'd be happy to pay for his food, rent even, and all. You just need to meet him to realize just what a good bloke he is.

'Oy woch it, yer cunt,' I hear bellowed as I barge through a shoulder. Shit, I'm hating myself for my laziness. Obviously, I called the RSPCA and Battersea. Obviously, they told me to get lost. I mean, maybe he could spend his days charging round the estate with the other dogs – then come home at nights. A latch-key dog, so to speak. And I'm sure I'd get used to any bad habits he might pick up on the streets.

So I'm picturing Buttercup in a TV-sized cage, muzzled, like on one of Pepper's anti-vivisection posters. I'm nearly wetting myself at the prospect of seeing his ears prick up, his little flag of a tail flick around when he sees me.

It sounds like a door creaking open. Wrenching the tendon that connects my foot with my leg, that is, as I tumble arse over elbow and roll into the lamp post. A couple of people cheer. An old geezer bends down and asks if I'm OK.

I pull myself up with the lamp post and test the ankle for walkability. Fucked well and good. In an hour it'll be the size of a Scotch egg. So, to the vet's I hobble to reverse the second betrayal I've committed against my best mate.

But no, I'm forced to remain content with the next best thing.

That afternoon, I make the pilgrimage to the park – and pepper one of his favourite urination stops with the ashes.

12

Of Blind Men and Women

Fulham. That's Pepper's sort of place. Golf GTi – her sort of car. But this is insignificant. What is significant is that at eleven o'clock, loquacious and ballsy, big-eyed Pepper just came out with it.

'So are you coming back then?'

'What?'

'You heard.'

The problem, of course, is I'm totally sober. And obviously, I'm scared shitless. I don't think I've done it sober before. At least not with someone new – which she sort of is now. Besides, I'm wondering what she's playing at – I haven't said anything interesting all night. So joking – obviously – I say, 'Be gentle with me Pepper.'

And she says, 'No.'

How can I describe the utter relief, the slaking of holding the naked Pepper, so smooth, alive and obstreperous, after so long? Only, I suppose, as the immediate orgasm that it was. But it was OK – she bust her banks in seconds too. Wailing and shrieking like never before. I say this, but I have heard her ululating in this way. In the fucking train disaster.

Basically, Pepper's turned into a slag since I last knew her. I don't mean this disrespectfully. I mean, I *love* slags.

Yet in Pepper it's, well, disconcerting. But with her thighs reshaping my skull and her hair cowling my groin, I'm sure as hell not filing any complaints.

It's a right novelty for Pepper. Having a body after all

237

this time. And she bounces around her little empire naked but for a small neck chain. Yeah, I thought things were a bit in the balance so I thought I'd weigh the scales with a little 24-carat.

Actually, that's a lie. I'm in love with Pepper and I want her back. Alright?

Now she stands before me, legs astride, like something out of a domination video.

'You're a naughty boy, you know.'

'When he was good he was very, very good but when he was bad he was . . .'

'You made me ill.'

'It's called heartbreak, and you made me ill.'

'No silly. Here.' She points at her ginger nest.

'Sorry. I got it from a toilet seat.'

'I'll give you toilet seat.' And, with this, the excellent slag sits on my head.

We fuck slowly and tenderly. Pepper cries. I lick off her tears and then she says, 'Richard, I'd like you to leave now.'

A sudden and potent emetic it is – unless it's a weep that's on the up. She continues, 'I think it's better if . . . I don't know . . . if we don't see each other for a while. Quite a long while, maybe. If you don't mind.'

'But I do – a lot.'

'Please, get dressed.'

So I got the fix. Obviously, I'm hooked again. And for the rest of the month I undergo the predictable withdrawal symptoms. The technicolour dreams, the flares of hope which, after a second or two, squib into hyperbolic fictions, the stupors of self-pity, and above all the convulsions of white-hot jealousy.

The long and short of it is Pepper Furnival has put in a lot of bed hours of late. But what really gets me is that the one person on this planet who craves a couple of those hours most is the one person that she can't allow herself to see. Oh, and I'm not naive. Yeah, my charismatic, shaven-headed ex-art director – well what do you think? And fuck, does that hurt, or what?

Saturday. I flip a coin and go out to make the call. I tell the hypnotherapist about Pepper. I tell her how it feels like I've been doing bad speed, on my own, for a month. When I get home I bawl for perhaps two hours. After this I feel like eating and sleeping again. Weird eh? I decide to blow the hypnotherapist out.

On Monday morning I receive very powerful messages from my subconscious. The messages say: call in sick, get a haircut, drink five litres of mineral water, eat a bar of Choc-o-lax, meditate. These things I do.

The next day I'm purged and back to work.

And I'm ready to call Pepper. I figure that by anyone's standards it's been *quite a long while*. I change my mind when I discover that I'm sitting on a haemorrhoid the size of a strawberry.

Three days later the bastard still hasn't gone. If I bend over and glance at myself in a mirror, it looks like my arse is giving me the thumbs up. This is unequivocally the worst thing that's ever happened to me. And I'm not even sure exactly what a haemorrhoid is. I fear there's something inside it. I fear it may be blood. I fear what's inside it is trying to escape.

I sell and eat virtually nothing for a week. I don't masturbate, obviously. In fact, the only good thing that can be said of the vicious little balloon is that it has virtually taken my mind off Pepper.

I frequently check the chair to see if it's burst.

I envisage it growing, becoming visible – like a little turd poking out into the seat of my trousers. And imagine. Imagine if it decides to become a permanent fixture – outlawing sex for good. Or worse still – what if it needed to be operated on? 'I won't be in tomorrow, Amelia. I'm having my piles pulled.' Obviously, I'd have to resign. Words like *anal fissure* surface when I meditate (yeah – on a cushion).

But most significantly, it's transformed my warmest hope into my worst fear. Suppose she were to phone and invite me round for a bout of filth?

When I returned from lunch there was a Post-it note stuck to my desk. It read 'Please call Pepper Furnival urgently.'

I saw it this morning. I swear it's grown. I nearly cried – or vommed.

I've sold bugger-all, bar a poxy mono-quarter all fortnight. The ad director, Amelia Pickle, called me into her office and asked me if I had any personal problems. Obviously I didn't tell her about Keith.

She put me on *SUPO alert* – Shape Up or Piss Off.

I'm told that while I was talking with Amelia, a *Pepper Furnival* called. Can I call her back?

The guy who handles the S—Z clients has been made redundant. Scary – but good news all the same. Breathing space. You see, in two months the rag will be running a feature on menstruation and I've inherited S and T. The all important *Sans* and *Tams*. I've already got the *Fems*.

Of course, my glee is short-lived. The cruel symbiosis of good and bad, light and dark, once again conspires to bugger up my life. No Pepper doesn't call again – this happens. I bend down to pick up a pen – no Keith doesn't explode. I lean over my desk to retrieve the biro and what should launch itself out of my inside pocket and land in the central reservation of the archipelago of desks? Only a half-used tube of Anusol. Obviously, I dive under the desk to snatch it back. Obviously, everyone hunches over to see what I've dropped. And I'm considering the feasibility of jamming the biro into my temple and giving it a good stir. You see, everyone except me is female.

'Fibre,' says one of them. 'More fibre in the diet.'

'I once took time off work. Richard, you poor thing.'

'You know,' says Jeannette, the ad manager, 'we ought to run a feature on haemorrhoids. It's a common problem especially after childbirth.'

'Tell me about it.'

'Shall I get you a cushion, Richard? Would that be more comfortable?'

'No, no I'm fine thanks really.' Below me Keith throbs. Keith's got his own fucking pulse these days. No doubt he's working on a brain and a mouth.

'I'm going to have a word with Amelia and Peg. A feature. It's a damn good idea.' Maybe he's not pulsing. Maybe the fucker's laughing.

'Piles of revenue.' Keith's throbbing like he's going to hatch. Like he's the egg of some humourless alien.

'In fact, I'd say we're sitting on a nice little nest egg.' Ticking. Like he's about to blow us all up.

'OK joke's over. Richard, take the bin off your head and go back to your desk. C'mon everybody back on the phone. Pack of three for the first person to get the word *grapes* into a call. Come along, Richard. We're all girls together here.'

Pepper, of course, is in total hysterics throughout the drama.

As Keith gradually melts back into my sphincter, so the spectre of Pepper balloons into my consciousness. And I sell few pages. Obviously, the fact that she called didn't leave my mind for a minute. And after a couple of days I find myself brave enough to call her. I'm told that she's gone on holiday for two weeks.

'Right.'

'Is that Richard?'

'Yeah.'

'How you doing? It's Viv.'

'Vivienne, good grief. You're still there?'

'Yeah. When Pep was promoted I became Basil's secretary.'

'Nice one.'

'Richard. Pepper's been trying to get in touch with you for days.'

'Yeah, that's why I was calling.'

'Oh Richard. Oh Rich. This is going to really piss you off. Oh, I'm loving this. I'm absolutely loving it. Ha, ha, ha.'

'What? What is it?'

'Oh no, this is absolutely brilliant. Guess?'

'Vivienne, you're being a bloody sadist. What is it?'

'Well the reason that Pepper was trying to call you. Oh this is so brilliant. Oh God it is.'

'What. Stop laughing. Tell me.'

'Well Rich, she won a holiday. For two. In Greece. In a competition.'

'Are you sure, Vivienne?'

'Oh yes, she had to write a caption for ClairCare sanitary pads . . . Anyroad, she didn't have anyone to go with.'

'No? No boyfriend?'

'Not as such, I don't think.'

'So who did she go with?'

'A girlfriend, I think. Bad luck.'

'Well I'd have been too busy anyway. But it's a nice thought, I suppose. Talk to yer soon Viv. Ciao.' I've got my head on the desk and my hands round my head. 'FUCK, FUCK, FUCK, FUCK, FUCK, FUCK . . .' Someone hits me with *Close that Sale*. Hard.

Luckily, the pressures of *Talk* deadlines have cracked everyone's resolve and stale cigarette ghosts hang reassuringly amidst us. It means that each time I get given a pickle shot, a porn ECU of Pepper with her Greek fucking waiter, I can fill the hurt with nicotine. The taste of cigarette reminds me of how much I'd like to be in a pub.

I'm twenty-four and (excuse my immodesty for a second) pretty damn fine looking. The West End and Covent Garden are jammed with secretaries, telesales and advertising girls, shop assistants, students and foreigners, using the late evenings and mild weather as an excuse to drink more and consequently step out of their kits for minimal sales pitch.

It's a fact. Whether you're male or female, if you're moderately unrepulsive, drink a bit and make like you and your mate are having a right good time outside one of the more popular pubs in the Covent Garden piazza for a few nights, see if you don't wind up swapping saliva with an American, Swede or pissed-up office worker in the cab home. This is, of course, assuming you're into that sort of thing.

Obviously, I am. So I come to realize that when you're on the wagon and dog paddling against the tide of debt, May, June and July are, without question, the cruelest months.

Late July. Summer's recession being excelled only by the one in the economy. Salary increases have been frozen for a second six-month period. And yeah, redundancy is back in the air at Marlborough Publishing. Working here is like being in one of those fucking hostage scenarios where someone is randomly picked for execution each dawn. Yet, as more and more of us assert our allegiance to Zippy and Bungle and learn of everyday life in Australia, the economy is bowing to no one's demands. And stop me if I'm getting over-political, but it strikes me that the demands are nothing more than basic human rights. The right to work for a living wage, to live under a fairly elected government, to walk the streets free of persecution. Let me explain what has spawned this bitter political lecture.

Imagine. It was my first night out in months. A dinner party, it was. Because I wasn't drinking and I can't afford sherbets, I left in time to tube it home. So I'm heading down Fonthill Road on the way back from the tube, suit on, briefcase in hand, like a total fucking mug victim, when this happens. A car screeches up next to this geezer twenty or so yards in front of me. Two blokes fly out and smash absolute shit out of him with baseball bats. It only takes a couple of seconds and they're back in the car doing a hundred and twenty out of it.

Obviously, I leg it up to the body. And I'm thinking that it's going to be pretty bad news. Brains and shit. Anyway when I reach him, he looks OK – just dead or something. I mean, I know fuck all about first aid, so I just ask if he's OK with the intention of knocking someone up to call an ambulance. Now, I'm bending over, and the body only sits up and head-butts me, then holds a blade against *my* collapsed body and demands the contents of my pockets. Then it runs off to be picked up by the blokes that did him in the first place.

So why the above political conclusions? Well I guess, transcending the affront of the incident is the feeling that things have got to be pretty bad when you make it a categorical imperative never to go to the aid of a stranger.

Anyway, I'm figuring that I'd join some sort of left-wing political movement if I had the membership fee, when this happens to convince me that free markets are actually pretty hip.

Some right good news. Do you remember that darling head-hunter? The one who fixed Horace and me up at RUT. Well, he called me. Head-hunted me so to speak. And I've got an interview at Love.

I visit Horace O to borrow some work samples. It's good. He's lost a deal of his charisma and he smells of alcohol. Obviously, there's no place for TM and long-term temperance in advertising. Leastways, not when you've been promoted to head of art. We go to the Round House. Horace drinks Becks and I drink orange juice and stuff. Try it one night. It's really wild – staying sober and watching someone else grow loud and animated. Especially your old TM instructor. And someone you reckon has been nailing your ex.

Of course, I'm wondering just what sort of an arsehole I must have seemed when I was out on the lag. Women say it and men don't believe it – but it's a fact. Drinking is simply not overly attractive.

Take a look at me. It's eleven. I've spent an evening in a pub without having one. Believe that? Alright, I'll come clean. I gacked down two Becks and a double at last orders. I asked Horace about Pepper. He said he hadn't seen her since she was with me. I accused the fucker of lying. He saw her last February. How the fuck can he remember that far back, etc. and would I like to be kung fu-ed? I let it drop. Five minutes later I asked him how old he was. He said fifty-nine. I bought a beer.

On the way to the tube a homeless person asks me for money. I give him £3 and wish him good luck.

Tomorrow, I have my second interview at Love – the people who make condoms in all shapes, colours and flavours. Obviously, it's a position I want. I don't consider selling advertising space particularly chic and it doesn't pay particularly sheik money at that. It would be a fine step in my sorting out.

Anyway, between you and me, I reckon I've got it in the bag. People still talk about that campaign, you know. And what with my media experience? Piece of piss, wouldn't you say?

Now, as you'll no doubt appreciate, at times I can be a highly shrewd operator. And I'm not above, well, not exactly out and out bribery but, shifting the goal posts, so to speak, to suit my purposes. So when Basil the Bastard says, 'Yer talking aboot a broown envelope, eh?' upstairs in the Star and Garter, over lunch, I reply, 'Basil, I'm not talking about money, bribery, for one moment. I'm not even saying that I can influence things. I mean, I haven't got the job yet. All I'm saying is that if I am offered it, I will take part in certain decisions. Now, it's public knowledge that the account is up for pitch. So, if – and it's a big if – I'm offered the job – one of my first tasks will be to make recommendations for the pitch list.'

'Lemme ge ye anoother.'

'A grapefruit juice.'

'Dooble vodie?'

'Positively no. No thank you.'

245

When he arrived he was limping with a hand in his trouser pocket. And I was reckoning that he'd come here via a peep show.

But he explained, 'Hernia.' How I hate the bloke. 'Straining tee hard on the john, ye know.'

It was only one and he was already pissed and Glasweejan.

He arrives back, slops in his hernia and says, 'Soo wha' yer seying is tha, you'll doo yer best te ge' us on tha' pitch list fur nowt, bu' a slap-up lunch?'

'Not quite. I've worked with you. I know how the agency operates. And as a potential client, I'm in a position to point out what I see might – perhaps – be possible weaknesses in the service you would be offering us.'

'E', ahm no' wi' yer, laddie.'

'Well to put it bluntly, I would expect you to make certain changes to the agency to accommodate a client such as Love.'

'Oh ay? Such as?'

'Well first off, I'd like to see a young team working on the creative. After all it's a young product.'

'Well, ay'm sure tha' can be arranged.'

'Secondly, I'd like to see a young account manager handling the account.' It's then that Basil the Bastard, pissed as he is, cracks on to my reason for calling this meeting.

'Oh ay, Richard? And anyone in particular? Could it possibly be a certain account handler that you were boffing, ba any sleeght chance?'

'Well, I think she'd be ideal for the job. Don't you?'

'Still hoold a candle foor her, eh?'

'Of course not, Basil. I'm getting married in September.'

'Really? Congratulations. Listen. She's no' had enoogh experience. There's folk tha' shoold be promooted afore her. Ah canna even recommend it a' tha' moomeent. Bu' ee'l tall yer wha', eef yer ge' us on tha' pitch lis' ah'll see wha' ah can doo.'

'And it goes without saying that mum's the word.' I shake his hand. 'It's been a pleasure doing business with you.'

Monday. I do good bullshit in a second interview. I suggest that my old agency (but obviously not RUT – the bastards) should be added to the pitch list. They thank me for the suggestion. I do a chessboard on the grid of the psychometric test. I figure that anyone who takes those seriously doesn't deserve a job shovelling shit.

Tuesday. I'm offered marketing manager at a half-decent whack. Am I prepared to do a month's induction in Long Island in the spring? Do fannies fart? I also learn that Basil the Bastard will be pitching to me in a month – ha. I call Pepper and Horace O and arrange a piss-up for Friday. Pepper says she'd love to see me and why didn't I call before?

I consider buying a bottle of champagne to celebrate my mood. The signs are that I've sorted out long term. I decide against it. Then again, a moderately packed reefer or three would hardly be pushing things to much, would it?

Sorted. Sorted long term – that's me. So why, you may ask, am I on my fifth strong one tonight? The answer is, of course, I'm celebrating my new job – with my friends Pepper Furnival and Horace O. And I figure that one night on the razzle won't do me any harm whatsoever.

To be truthful, I did start out on soft drinks. But it became more and more apparent that Horace was making a play for Pepper. Obviously, this pissed me off a lot. It also meant that I had to drum up some decent patter to get into the running. Fuck, how I regret inviting that bastard. Some sodding mate Horace has turned out to be.

But listen. Horace hasn't got an ice cube's chance in hell. With Pepper and me there's history. Pepper has, and always will have – I reckon – a habit for me. Somewhere deep in her blood she's hooked. And when Horace went to the bar, much as we both detest pub snoggers, there was nothing much we could do about it.

She broke and growled, 'Why did you invite him?'

'What's wrong with him?'

'I wish it was just us tonight. Then again, I suppose we'd regret it later.'

'Regret it? Did you regret it last time?'

'Huh.'

Horace is back with the drinks. All evening he's seemed a mite awkward. I mean us, being so obviously nearly a couple again. Then again he's given no hint that he's going to quit before the distance, so we just drink. We talk about Love condoms and Pepper says, 'The coconut-flavoured ones give me thrush.'

Cheers Pepper.

When Pepper goes for a splash, I'm tempted to ask Horace if he wouldn't mind pissing off. Obviously, I don't. He is, after all, my 'best friend'.

When I get back from taking one, Pepper's whispering something to Horace and holding his hand. I'm thinking what a total twat Horace is for letting her use him to get me jealous. Of course, I play it cool.

'I've got to make a phone call,' I tell them.

'Who?' she snaps.

'Won't be a tick.' I go off and pretend to use the phone. On the way back I adopt an ethereal grin – like I've been talking filth with someone infinitely nicer than Pepper. It's hard to maintain in the face of Pepper's hand on Horace's knee. Nonplussed, sweet as pie, I offer to get a round.

'Haven't you had enough, Richard?' blurts Horace.

'No I haven't. Haven't you, Horace?'

'No way, man. No.'

Of course, I'm livid. I've got a far more legitimate claim over her. The bastard. Trying to slide his big black wang where it's not wanted. I drink fast and angrily to subdue my anger. I finger the E in my pocket. The E I was going to spike her drink with if things seemed on. Things seem on, alright. But not necessarily with me. Fuck, how I hate situations like this. I decide to change the unfazed tactic. The tactic I employ is sulking.

248

If only I had the balls just to get up and go. If only I didn't give so much of a toss. If only this situation wasn't totally fucking killing me. I'm reminded of a football game on the village green and Seb saying to me, 'You can't play. It's my ball.' Of course, I was too young to walk on pavements without Seb, so I just had to sit there. For fucking hours, it seemed. Totally excluded. But even at that age you know the rules. You mustn't cry. No way.

And you know what? My best mate fucking Pepper. That would obviously constitute a disaster. Hell, at this moment, I'd rather be liquidizing in a train that entertaining that thought. And yeah sure, it's probably lagered up theory, but I'm thinking that the dreams were saying something of that all along. I mean, maybe all that smashed up pain is metaphorical – like dreams are supposed to be. The rhythmic moaning of Horace and Pepper. Our love-making soundtrack, joyously taking the piss, in the background. Ah, what a fuck bad thought that is.

Christ, I don't know, maybe there *was* something in the way they looked at each other. The way he advised me to dump her. The way she said she disliked him. I never noticed that his hair smelled. I never got that close to him. Oh my fuck. Could he have been the other Richard all along?

Horace O goes to the bar. I'm hoping he has to queue.

'You OK, Richard?' asks Pepper.

'Fine.'

'You seem a bit . . . moody.' Of course, being in such a sulk, there's no way I'm going to say anything useful to her.

'Pepper?'

'Mmm.'

'How about it?'

'How about what?'

'Us.'

'Us what?'

'Tonight.'

'Mmm. Maybe, lovey.' She kisses me. 'Maybe not. We'll

249

see.' Then this happens. She puts an arm behind my head and looks at me in a way I find hard to explain. A kind of half-smile. A nostalgic look. As if to say, 'Yeah, we've got history. Sometimes I might even miss it, you know.' And she kisses me again – for slightly longer this time. I break.

'Pepper, I want you to answer something truthfully. Totally truthfully.'

'Yeah, OK.'

'Have you been fucking with Horace?'

'Richard. Frankly, it's none of your business. But the answer is, of course I have.'

Horace O comes back and plonks the drinks in front of us. I don't rightly know how I must be looking at him. But I figure it ranges somewhere between clinical shock and a murder threat.

'Ha, ha . . . not. You daft, daft boy. Never in a million years.' Then, right there in front of Horace, and all, she plops a huge wet one on my mouth. Good one, Pepper. Good one.

Horace downs his pint in one and says, 'Right, I'm fucking off. See you, Pepper.' He kisses her. With tongues, I suspect. 'See yer, Rich – mate.'

The relief is total. Like falling into the swimming pool when you've been sweating it in the high 80s. Downing the first pint in months. Pouring into someone – unsafely.

I resolve to play it cool. Only I don't. I embrace Pepper and kiss her – lots. All over her face, her head, her hair. And I don't give a fuck that we're in a pub – I've got my hand outside her top, caressing the rise of her breast. I'm about to tell her that I love her. That I'd do anything for her – absolutely fucking anything, when she whines, 'Richard, don't. Not now.'

'Later, yeah? Later, Pepper, yeah?'

Then she swats me totally. 'For fuck sake, go to the loo and have a wank.'

Pepper stares ahead like she's stoned. I glance around the

250

bar and swig like I'm not at all bothered. I buy us more drink to stop Pepper going. I'm counting on the drink making Pepper do something she might regret.

Go on Pepper, say something useful to me. She doesn't. And as I'm sure you'll know from your own experience, it's at times like this when you too can think of sweet bugger all to say.

'Pepper.'

'What?'

'Why are there more blind men than blind women?'

'Is this a joke?'

'No. I just thought that you often see blind men, but rarely blind women. Maybe more men become blind from industrial accidents.'

'What's that got to do with anything? You're weird.'

'I don't know. Shit, forget it.'

'Well it's obvious anyway. There are the same number of blind men and women. It's just that blind women don't go out because they'd get raped by sighted men. It's obvious, isn't it?'

'I suppose . . .'

'Well, you should think before you say things. That's your problem. You don't think before you say things.' Silence – except for the din of the bar.

I was in a pub with Kat (my last long-termer before Pepper) once. She had the hump over something or other. And she just sat there. Purposefully staring at nothing – wasting our lives. Of course, I sat opposite doing just what I'm doing now – fretting. And feeling a right twat into the deal.

Anyway, I vowed, if Kat shames me once more in public, I'm going to walk out and leave her there. Go to another pub. Play pool. Get a party somewhere.

The next time we had a silent row was at a party. It was dead late, I didn't have anywhere to go and I was down the cab fare home, so I let it ride. The time after – the next day

251

as it happened (alright, I went on to disgrace myself at the party) – was in a pub and I did what I'd resolved to. I just walked out and left the bitch to broil in the sour juices of her huff.

Obviously – you're thinking – she left me. Wrong! She came back tearful and repentant. And left me a fortnight later.

'Are you alright, Pepper?'

'Yeah, I'm just thinking.'

'What about?'

'If I wanted you to know I'd be saying it, not thinking it.'

'I'm sorry, Pepper.' I must say this good and pathetically because she kisses me. We snog. I open my eyes to see that her eyes are also open and looking away.

This is Pepper. When it comes to getting a response she's rather like a cat. Scratch it in the wrong place and it gets bored and fucks off. Get it right and it'll be your friend for a bit. Consequently, I'm scouring Pepper's bitter ear with my tongue. Her hand kneads my thigh. Dangerously high. I calculate it's time and break.

'Pepper, you'll be twenty-three soon, won't you? Would you like it if we went out on your birthday?'

'I'll be twenty-three and old enough to know better than to have the likes of you licking my . . . various bits. Swap seats, I need the other one done now.'

'Do you remember when you tried to call me before you went on holiday?'

'Yeah. But it was OK. I picked up something a lot better at the airport.'

'Oh yeah, Pepper. Course you did.'

'Well it was only a crappy polaroid. The films cost the earth. And they're bulky. I treated myself to an Olympus. Go on, start on my other ear – if you want. Go on.'

She grows bored with my tongue and moves her head away. She shoots me an angry look and says, 'Look, Richard. I know what you're trying to do. Alright?'

'What? What am I trying to do? What in the name of all that . . .'

'Listen, I know. So shut up. And it's working. Now your best bet is to get me a large tequila and lime – then start on the back of my neck.' And shit, the look she gives me. It says I've cracked the safe – and there's fucking millions in there. Of course, I'm more that half tempted to fall for this. But there's taking the piss and taking the upper-case piss.

'Yeah. And I know what you're trying to do. In fact, what you're doing rather successfully,' I tell her.

'I'm sorry. What am *I* trying to do?'

'Play me like a fucking pinball machine. And I've just about had enough.'

She says she's going. I tell her to fuck off. She says how dare I row with her when we're not even fucking each other. I apologize and say I'll get her a drink. She says she's still going. I beg.

I break an E and medicine both our drinks. I give Pepper her tequila and she embraces me so as to achieve maximum cheek and ear contact.

'I'm sorry,' she smiles. 'It's funny to see you again. And yeah, I suppose I am in a bit of a strange mood. I'm sorry. I do like you, you know.'

'I'm sorry too. Actually, I more than like you, Pepper.'

'Well I only like you.'

'Right.'

'Lots and lots and lots.'

I caress the back of her neck and she says, 'Actually, that's a bit annoying. And this drink's bloody disgusting.'

We chat around subjects. Pepper looks set for a promotion at work. Her mother still asks about me. Basil was asking about me the other day, too – which she thought odd. Pepper looks at her watch twice. Her legs are crossed.

Then we don't say anything. Like, formalities were really all we had to say from the beginning. Of course, Pat died when I got right. And the more I try to think of interesting things to say the more boring they sound just before I say them. So I don't. Last orders ring. I'm hoping that the Es will take hold fast – thinking maybe I mistimed things. I've just got to keep her with me for the next few minutes. Then everything will change. And I'm considering it a pity that Horace isn't here – to keep her interested until I can go in for the kill, so to speak. Then Pepper shrieks, 'Horace!'

The bastard's only come back.

13

Yours Venomously

Everything's as it should be. The rancour of fear – the shit. The moans and shrieking. And I'm saturated in wet frosty anaesthetic. Yeah, and I'm convinced my friends Horace O and Pepper are somewhere in this disaster. But they come and go like the light and the dark, the shadow and the substance.

I'm considering that the strange attractor of my life has spiralled me into something quite out of my control. How many times have I dreamed of this? How often have I avoided trains? Yet when it came to following Horace O and Pepper into the carriage – I simply had no choice. In all honesty, I'd have cabbed it home if I hadn't reckoned that my not chaperoning them would have led to a far greater disaster.

Obviously, it's necessary to relax here. Allow Mahler to swell around me. Lick the tender crenellations of my body. Pass down into the comfortable trip. Concentrate only on good things. Black out into the light. Shit, the back of my head's bad.

The headphones? I don't even own a fucking personal stereo. Maybe I'm remembering the Mahler, note for note, exactly as it is. Disasters, I'd say, are a fine memory cocktail.

'So, Sebastian, what are you going to do with it?' Father asks, kissing the rim of his champagne glass.

'I haven't quite decided. Perhaps a month or so in the Dordogne to consider matters.'

'On me, of course.'

'Why, thank you, Father.'

'The very least I can do. Richard, open another bottle. It's not every day a member of the family comes home with a first.'

I fetch and unplug a bottle, catching the foam in my mouth – as one does. Then do a couple of neckfuls of the Scotch from the bottle on top of the fridge. When I re-enter the room, my brother's saying, 'Perhaps you should package him off to the army. The discipline would do him good and he might even pick up a useful trade – highly doubtful mind, I'll admit. So Richard, I hear you've decided against a life of the mind.'

'You what?'

'You've left school. No intention of taking O-levels?'

'I got a CSE grade 1 in English and passed Physics, didn't I?'

'Yes, well. I propose a toast. To Richard's blazing academic achievements.' Father laughs. 'You're not concerned about him?'

'Oh there was a time. But, I don't know. It's got beyond that. Visits from the police every few weeks. Finding him asleep on the floor in a pile of vomit most Saturday mornings. Oh, and he only managed to get some fifteen-year-old from Owslebury in the club.'

'So Richard, are you working?'

'I get by.'

'He relieves local farmers of their crows and rats. God help us when he gets a shotgun licence. You're not keeping it here, lad.'

'Shooting. An excellent qualification for the army.'

I turn to leave.

'Where do you think you're going?' demands Father.

'To the pub.'

'You most certainly are not. You will remain here with us and celebrate your brother's achievements.'

'Quite so, little brother.'

'Bollocks.'

'Richard, if you walk out of that door, you walk out of it for good.'

'Fine.'

At around midnight I'm out of money and credit, so I start on the two-mile stagger back. Obviously, I have a few things to pack.

Anyway, you know what it's like. You sober up, begin to rue your actions and try to suss out ways of reversing things some. Well, I have none of those thoughts. I mean, the old man's thrown me out a thousand times, and each time I simply stay at a friend's for a couple of days and he comes to get me, saying, 'This really won't do. We really must talk things over,' and the like. But I'm seventeen and I figure it's time to get a life. So I'm going to pack and fuck right off out of it – for good.

When I arrive back, Seb's still up. Sitting alone, in silence, working on the last of the champagne. I pass the open door and the git calls me in.

'What?'

'Sit down.'

'Why?'

'I want to talk.'

'I don't. I've got to pack.' He rises unsteadily and pushes me into a chair.

'Sit down, you worthless shit. Utterly worthless. Parasite. Richard, answer me this. What is the point of you?'

'What?'

'What point is there in you occupying space on this planet? I mean, you're a stupid, lazy, cruel, drunken, petty criminal. You're a total bloody parasite. Bar an air of malevolence – the prospect of some impending disaster – you contribute nothing to this house.'

'Neither do you.'

He leans over and slaps me hard across the face.

257

'Impudent shit. Go on get out. Go and pack. Get out of my sight.'

So I do.

At least I start to pack. But change my mind.

'Holy fuck. Sweet Jesus. I was only joking. I didn't mean . . . Please Richard. It was the drink talking. Honestly. Please. It's really not worth it. See sense. Oh my God,' sobs Seb when he sees me approaching. 'Please, please, Richard. I beg you. What do you want me to do? Do you want me to get on my knees. Yeah? Shall I, yeah? Or do you want money? Here, here take it. Please, please Richard. You'll get life. You'll never get away with it. Please, p . . . please,' he blubbers. A strange unnatural sight it is indeed. Thoroughly stomach turning.

I lower the rifle.

'Oh thank you. Thank you. Thank you so much.'

Then release one into his thigh.

Seb is on the carpet. Rolling around. Squealing to high heaven. His eyes pouring. And no, I'm not overcome with relief. Nor is any vengeance quelled. No, I'm swathed in hot guilt. Not because I've injured someone. Not because it's the brother I grew up with. No, it's because I've effected something horribly unnatural. Reversed something that was meant to be.

Yeah, yeah. I was rat-arsed. I pulled the chain that crashed the train, and caused the pain and . . . the postal order.

But I've learnt better than to take it to heart, these days. Sure, my cheekbone feels like a smashed cup in a bag. A limb's twisted up beneath me, although I couldn't say which. It could be that ankle again. And, of course, there's the familiar forearm outrage.

But, if the truth be told, it doesn't hurt as much as I'd expected. In fact, I'd say it was a cinch. After all the practice I've had. And though this may sound a trifle flippant – as

I'm being stretchered down the station steps, my greatest concern is to stay awake for a short time. You see, I've never been in an ambulance before.

A rather irritable Pepper said, 'I can't talk now. I'll call you back.' She didn't so I called her. And she said, 'Look, Horace and I have decided to pay for the loo. I mean, it was sort of our fault. I've got to go now.'

I received the letter this morning.

Dear Richard,

I'm drunk. And since I'm not going to send you this anyway, I may as well be blunt. Sorry about the handwriting.

I'm sorry I slept with Horace that night. If it makes you feel any better, I regretted it a lot afterwards. In fact, the more I think about it the more I think what a bitch I must be. I'm sorry we sort of started in front of you. Not terribly sensitive on either of our parts. Especially considering the suicidal state you were in. I mean, it would certainly have been you, if you had been in any kind of state. I just came over all affectionate and happy as we left the pub. Just as you started becoming totally out of it.

Anyway, as I've said, we'll pay for Horace's (antique and bloody expensive) loo. God, looking back, it was so hilarious. You should have been there. I mean, I know you were. But awake I mean. Even the ambulance men were laughing. And the emergency plumber was laughing all the way to the bank. And of course there was you moaning, 'I crashed the train. It's a fuck awful disaster,' the whole time. And then you sat up and said to the ambulance men, 'If I'm a good boy, can I sit in the front?' they nearly dropped you, they were laughing so much. You know, we thought we were going to have to cut the lavatory chain from your hand, you were holding it so tightly.

Anyway, I think you were to blame a little for Horace and me. I mean it was you who insisted that we put the Mahler on. And no, I didn't get him to do what you used to do in that crazy bit before the trumpets and violins make friends. Actually it made me quite sad.

The ambulance men said you could have been electro-cuted by the downstairs electrics. That wouldn't have been too funny.

Do I want to see you again? God I don't know. I'm talking to myself here. But it's OK because there's no way I'll send this when I've read it in the morning. So there. I hope I don't want to see you again. It would be safer for everyone.

Right I've had enough of this crappy letter. Either I'll post it while I'm still pissed or you'll never get it.

Get well soon.

Love and hugs – well a hug,

Yours venomously,

Your wicked slag of an ex-girlfriend,

Pepper.

PS. I've had a piss and some more wine. Hello again.

Actually, I miss you. A hell of a lot sometimes. I cried my eyes out on Saturday. When I thought of what might have happened. And I would have visited you if you hadn't been discharged almost immediately.

You can call me up if you want. But I reserve the right to tell you to piss off. I won't though. Probably.

PPS. God! I'm pissed.

PPPS. Guess what? I'm going to post it.

One minute I was sorted long term. With my tongue in Pepper Furnival's warm mouth on the Hampstead-bound train. Then next, I'm recovering from the cuts and bruises a dislocated jaw and a sprained ankle – courtesy of the total piss-take of a disaster.

And what a piss-take. I mean, as far as I was concerned, I had the situation sorted. Horace O returned to the wine bar at closing time and took me aside.

'Look, Rich my man,' he said, with some sincerity. 'I owe you apologies. I was being a slight arsehole. Too much drink. Too much flirtations with your ex. A drinking man can understand this, can he not?'

'Sure H.'

'So listen. Why not this? My house is fine. Yours is a cess

pit. Both of you come back. We drink some more and numb our noses. Soon . . .' and he nudges me, '. . . it is too late for her to escape. And you two use my spare room?'

'Horace O, you are a total prince.' We do a respect.

And I didn't consider it some sort of conspiracy when Horace O and Pepper argued with me that boarding the North London Light from Camden Road to West Hampstead would be infinitely quicker than taking a cab. For Pepper steadied me to the station – with her hand inside my T-shirt, kissing me periodically – laughing, 'I promise you, you daft boy, it won't crash. Pepper Furnival will look after you.'

Yeah, the Es were doing their stuff good on Pepper. All I had to do was ride the crescent of my poison's rise, get a line up my nose and I'd be sorted. At some point in the not too distant proceedings, I would seek the utility of a decent puke. After several months on the wagon, high-strength in double figures, chasers, Dexedrine and Ecstasy are less than aids to seduction.

The rest is fragments. Heavy petting with Pepper on the train – until I had to break for fear of my stomach's contents drenching her. Her kneeling by me as I lay on the seat, tenderly vowing to look after me. My arms around both of their shoulders as they dragged me to Horace's. Horace's room – fearful looks from him and a bucket before me. A line of Charlie. My Mahler's Fifth CD. Some sort of bastard row. Me chucking my rubbers at Pepper and Horace. Me on Horace's porcelain Armitage Shanks, leaning across into the bath, hot poison firing from my every exit. Thinking I must hasten this, get back to them and avert the disaster. The grotesque soundtrack of the disaster already rising in volume. Feeling empty, less poisonous, ready to act. Ready to stop the train. Stop the mocking rhythm of the disaster train. Turning on the taps to rinse down the puke. Reaching up – still sitting – for the chain. Pulling the chain hard to stop the train. The crash. Then nothing.

TALK**POEM**

We offer a £15 book voucher for each poem we publish. This week's winning poem was written by Stella Evans, a single mother and mature Fine Art student at Preston Polytechnic. Her poem is about her fifteen-year-old daughter.

Misunderstanding

'Mummy, you just don't understand,'
she said.
'I'll admit that he's been a bit underhand,'
I said.
'Not that. Understand how I *feel*'
'About Neil?'
'No inside, inside here.'
'But it's my job to misunderstand,'
I said.
'What! I don't understand,'
She said.
'Who am I to rob you of your delicious despair.
'Of what you feel, deep, deep inside there?'

'Still moping?' Jeez inquires mockingly.

'Nar. I think it's the antibiotics.'

'Of course. Look Richard. I've got something to say to you. Now, don't get me wrong. I'm not for one moment intimating that you're outstaying your welcome. Absolutely not. No, no, in fact the opposite is true. Stay as long as you please. I mean it. No, this house would be intolerable, but for the ebb and flow of my guests. But Richard, how can I quite put this?'

'Spit it out Jeez. I reckon after what's happened, not much can faze me.'

'Well that's exactly it. You're behaving like some bloody martyr. It really isn't the end of the world. I mean, I can pile on the clichés – 'There are other fish in the sea', 'You'll get over it', 'There's nothing new under the sun' – but it really is up to you to pull yourself together. And if it's any consolation, I've spoken to both of them in the last couple of days and it was, unequivocally – unequivocally, Richard – a one-night stand. I mean, in truth I feel that they actually rather dislike each other.'

'Yeah well.'

'And Richard, you acted thoroughly irresponsibly, desperately so. Spiking the poor girl's drink, for God's sake.'

'Yeah, I guess.'

'And I'm not sure that you couldn't be had up for attempted rape, if she got wind.'

'Don't say that.'

'You're a total cad. You know that?'

'Yeah.' I laugh.

'Right the ultimatum is this. You've got a week.'

'That's fine Je . . .'

'A week to say something at least vaguely amusing to me or one of my other house guests or you're out.' We laugh. 'Look at you. What are you reading? Stimulating stuff. Why don't you come and join everybody on the patio. There's still a definite hint of Pimms in the air, wouldn't you say?'

'I can't drink. I've still got another two days of these.' I show him my pill bottle. He reads it.

'Ahh. The cherished little brown bottle that he takes everywhere – like a holy icon. Testimony to the profound significance of his sacred martyrdom.' Jeez lobs the bottle. And we drink Pimms and lemonade and do a modest Cocaine binge until late. At about three, Jeez slinks off with a game couple. And because I'm up and witty I manage to tap off with a filthy Sloane called Veronica who stays my girlfriend for the next fortnight. And when I leave Jeez's hospitality – with a loan for a couple of suits – to reclaim my life, my tumour of an ex is malign. Yeah, sure I'll live.

14

The Slowest Bastard Cab in London

Picture me in my Paul Smith grey single-breasted, Crockett & Jones calf brogues, Calvin Klein white T-shirt – sitting at the boardroom table at Love. Picture Basil the Bastard sitting opposite, smiling, sweating, obsequious and in pain because he can't push his hernia in at a time like this. And, of course (because Basil's no fool), the executive doing what has to be said is a faultless presentation, is account manager Pepper Furnival.

And guess what. The campaign centres around the Beatles song 'All You Need Is Love'. Like the previous three pitches.

Now I'm not sure just how much weight I carry here. I mean if I've got any say, I'm obviously going to recommend these guys. It would mean doing phone with her every day, meeting say twice a week, lunching with her, dinner and, who knows, a bit of product-testing into the deal. It's a short-cut on a stick.

'May I be so bold as to ask for your initial impression? We feel that it meets the brief one hundred per cent, will achieve the desired impact . . .'

'Predictable.' That's Harry the marketing director – my boss.

'Hardly. The visual treatment alone is enough to . . .'

'You are the fourth agency to present to us. And, funnily enough, the fourth to come up with using that particular song.'

'Which suggests,' this is me, 'that there's something in it.'

264

'Richard's got a point,' says Monica, the MD.

Picture Pepper, crimson lipstick, black and dark green eye-paint, green skirt suit, cream blouse, black stockings, green stilettos. Looking good all the same. She's got a slight tan. She's being cool and professional. In total control of the situation. Like I'd never had my dick in her mouth. Like I'd never bent her over the sofa, lowered my head and . . .

'Richard?'

'Sorry?' Harry and Monica are up. Evidently we're going into another room to discuss matters.

'I know this seems terribly rude,' says Monica 'but I'm sure you don't want to be kept waiting.'

'No, no fine, fine,' says the Bastard.

Monica's saying something to her secretary. Harry and I are sitting in her office and he says, 'Well mate. I reckon they win hands down on account managers.' Obviously, I want to say something like, 'Been there, done it.' But Gary's dead.

'Sure.'

'Richard,' says Monica, 'your thoughts – as an ex-agency bod.'

I gesticulate with an unlit cigarette to give my opinion intensity. 'OK. Song's fine, treatment's fine. It'll work. On TV, that is. Which, after all, was the brief. And, in my opinion these guys possibly come out tops. But I'm thinking, how's it all going to translate to thirty-two or forty-eight sheet? I reckon we should tell all the agencies what's happened and get them to re-pitch in a week, say. Show us some poster scamps. Run the race again, so to speak. That's my view.'

'I like it, Richard,' Monica.

'Good thinking,' Harry.

We explain the situation.

'So who should I liaise with?' asks Pepper.

'Well, Richard,' says Monica.

'OK then, Richard, we'll liaise.'

Liaise. Yum.

Obviously, in the week that follows, I can't eat or sleep. And of course, the temptation to kill all this tumbling anticipation with a few jars is ever present. But I don't.

Each evening I just smoke a little hash with Aslan and go to bed, pretending that Pepper's lying next to me. Most nights she winds up giving me a hand-job or two. Usually I say a little prayer as well. Not to God. To Buttercup. Asking him to understand. There always have to be sacrifices. Buttercup says if I get Pepper back it will be worth it. If I don't, he's going to give me a severe mauling in the next life. But there really was no other choice. No one trusts a secondhand pit bull. Buttercup, man, I'm so fucking sorry.

'I'm so sorry.' I've been dreading this call all morning.

Yeah, I couldn't sway it. I argued like hell. Then Monica said, 'Richard, it's plain as hell that you fancy the tits off their account manager. But they simply weren't up to scratch, were they?' I had to concede that, possibly, another agency could do a better job.

'To be honest, Pepper, I thought you had it in the bag too. But Monica thought otherwise. If it's any consolation, you were fantastic . . . I'm not being patronizing . . . Maybe they'll mess it up and you can pitch again . . . So, Pepper, does this mean the end of our liaising?' Obviously, it does.

Bad months follow. I call Pepper and am told that she's left the agency. She just walked out one day and never came back. I call her house in Fulham. Someone else has lives there and they don't know where she is. My trip to Long Island is postponed for a year.

I contemplate calling her mother in Sutton. My bottle fails me. I'm considering the possibility of having a couple of pints one lunchtime for courage. But I don't. Yeah, after my spell with Jeez I was back full-time on the lag – so I kicked it. For good. It's a fact. Besides, the probation officer caught up with me and I have to, well, go to meetings – you know?

After another bastard stretch of **shadow-time** – wasting my life, so to speak – Buttercup tells me, in no uncertain terms, to stop being a wanker and call her mother. And Buttercup's right. I haven't done any fucking since I was at Jeez's. Then again I don't know how to get laid without going out drinking. Do you?

Somewhat warily, I call Mrs Furnival. What a honey. She's delighted to hear from me. Asks me all those motherish questions. And is sure that Pepper would love to hear from me. Pepper lives in Greenwich now. She works in an art gallery. She's living with a lovely man called Rick.

Obviously, I can't do it. Obviously. Rick indeed. Then one morning in early December, this arrives:

Dear Richard,

I don't really know whether this is a good idea or not. Writing to you like this. It's just, Mum said you'd been in touch and, well, I felt like it. That's all. And these days I do the things I feel like. Like getting a tattoo. Oh yes I have.

So, how are you? How's work? I presume you're still there. I hope so. If not, someone else will be reading this. (Hello, someone else, will you please kindly stop reading and send this to Richard like a good chap(ess). Thank you.)

Actually, I don't have very much to say. Except that I don't like losing contact with old friends – and (I suppose) I count you as one of those. Do you think we're grown up enough to be friends? Or do you hate me?

Do you want to be friends? Write to each other occasionally? Maybe even (maybe) 'liaise' once in a while? As friends? Good.

Are you sitting comfortably? Then I'll begin.

I left the agency. Richard, advertising is such utter bullshit. And bad for the skin. I'm working in an art gallery in Greenwich. So, if you ever need a discount painting of the *Cutty Sark*, I'm your woman.

Love life. Are you ready for this? I'm living with a sculptor

– Rick – he's lovely. A bit old and bald, but you can't have everything.

How about you? Fucking anyone interesting? – as you used to say.

Do you still see Horace? He's a funny boy. How about Jeez?

Best wishes

Pepper (far too many brackets) Furnival X

PS. My love to Buttercup

Dear Pepper,

It was one of those mornings. I get flashed at in the park (perhaps it's time I got a haircut – then again I was wearing a suit), the tubes are down, then I get a letter from you.

Seriously, it's great to hear from you. I guess I could handle friends. And I'm glad you seem so happy.

Let me deal with instances of nosiness one by one.

How am I? Healthy – I run each morning, do weights three times a week. I've given up smoking and drinking. Honestly – the last drink I had was months ago.

Yes, I am at the same place. Sitting comfortably. I'm marketing director now.

Love life. Mmmm. Make sure you're sitting down. Have you seen the latest Love commercial 'Stop In the Name of Love' (a far better idea – why didn't anyone think of it during the pitch?) Well the brunette model in that and myself, how shall I put it? We're not an item but things are torrid, if you know what I mean.

Horace O is married (how the mighty fall), two months ago I was best man.

Please write again.

Kind Regards,

Richard X

Dear Richard,

Thank you so much for replying. You seem really sorted.

Well, well. Old Horace.

So you're going out with Cathy Shelton. Lucky you. I

read an article about her a few weeks ago. It said she's set to become the next super model.

And marketing director in three months. Richard, I'm so happy for you.

Guess what. Rick's been commissioned to do a sculpture for the Holiday Tower in the Docklands. He reckons that, as the rooms are mostly used by businessmen knocking off their mistresses, he should do something erotic for a joke. Each time I go into the studio, he's photographing another orgiastic scene. But I don't mind. A woman must suffer in the name of art.

Hey listen. I'm going to ask you something. However you answer I still want us to remain friends, OK. But it's something that's been sort of bugging me. It's silly but it's something I want to clear up in my head. Do you remember that message on your answerphone? Were you really having an affair when we were going out? I know it's silly but I'd like to know. I mean, it won't hurt me or anything. I'd just like to know.

Love Pepper X

PS. How's Buttercup? I miss him.

PPS. How about meeting up sometime?

Dear Pepper,

What do you take me for? Of course I didn't touch any other women. No, it was like I said – a less-than-successful ploy to get you jealous – because you were being such a bitch, remember? On my word.

Now, Pepper, I've got some bad news. Buttercup bit someone in Finsbury Park and I had to have him destroyed. It was more of a friendly nip really. I think the woman had something against pit bull terriers and she reported it to the police. God, I tried everything. I offered her money. Then I tried to hide Buttercup from the police. But it was no good.

I'm feeling a bit low at the moment. Cathy and I had a bit of a row last night. But she'll be round this evening, tearful and apologetic as ever.

Oh I didn't tell you, I took up flying. I may be banned from the roads but not the skies. Anyway last weekend I got my full pilot's licence. Maybe I'll take you for a loop the loop when we finally 'liaise'.

Pepper, you know how that question about Charlotte bugged you. Well, there's something about the past that's been on my mind. Will you answer me a question, please? I mean it's not something that's been gnawing away at me – but I'd like to know, all the same. When we were living together, or before that – were you having an affair? And was his name Richard, or Horace, for that matter?

Look forward to hearing from you.

Richard X

Dear Richard,

I'm so sorry about Buttercup. I can't imagine him biting anyone. He must have been being over-playful, poor thing. Besides, I thought he was a Staffordshire.

And in answer to your question, yes!

Bet that shocked you.

Yes, I will tell you about my steamy affair with the other Richard and the one with Horace. It all happened in the confines of your suspicious mind.

There never was another Richard. Never. I had two boy-friends at University. In the first year, there was Adam, it lasted ten weeks, then he decided he was gay. Then in the second and third years there was Mark – he ditched me for someone else.

I made up the other Richard to slow you down, if you remember. It was just the first name that came to mind.

And as for Horace. Well, in truth he did try it on a few times – especially when we split. And that night. Richard, I really don't know what came over me. It was so weird. I'd never thought of him in that way before. I truly wish that night hadn't happened.

Richard, if you think I'd get in an aeroplane with you, you can think again. You're scary enough on tarmac.

Guess what? I've turned carnivore. I started with fish. Graduated to a sausage. Now I binge on it. I can't get enough. I think I'm going to have a coronary. Do you remember those gross 'meat harmonica' kebabs that used to be your staple diet? Aren't they just gorgeous?

Richard, why do you always write your office address at the top of your letters, then post them in N4? Don't you want me to write at your home address? Would Cathy get jealous?

Let's meet up soon. For a doner kebab binge.

Got to go now,

Love and hugs Pepper XXX

Dear Pepper,

I'll get straight to the point. I think you're lying. About the other Richard, that is.

OK, it's time for a confession. I was messing around on Sidney one day and I happened to find myself in your personal files. And I'm sorry, I grew a little curious. I know it's unforgivable – but at least I've admitted it. Anyway in one letter to Marianne, you tell her all about what slob I am and that you feel guilty about Newcastle Richard.

Now, do you remember when you got back from Newcastle, and I took the day off work because I'd just got Buttercup? Well, in the morning, I thought it would be nice to unpack your gear for you – I was doing some washing anyway. And what should fall out? A three-pack of condoms with two gone.

And yeah, I'll admit it. And you'll hate me forever. I read a letter you'd been sent. A pathetic love letter. Postmarked Newcastle, signed Richard. Explain that!

I'm sorry I did those things. I'm also sorry that you still feel the need to lie to me.

Yes Cathy is a very jealous person.

And yes we should meet up. But I don't eat kebabs any more. Not good for the fitness programme.

Lots of love,

Richard X X X

Richard,

Don't you ever, ever talk to me (write to me rather) like that again. I've never lied to you. Never, ever. (Well except about the other Richard – in the beginning.) I've got a good mind to stop writing.

So you accidentally found yourself in my files. Huh. What you didn't figure was that, as file server, I got a daily access report. It told me that every day, User Seven (you) was entering certain files of mine. So I concocted a letter to let you know, in no uncertain terms, that yeah, we were on, but what a shit you were to boot (not that it had any effect, mind). I also mentioned the other Richard for reasons I've explained. And, ever since, you've thought that I was having an affair. Ha.

Oh, and in case you're interested, if you had pressed 'view' instead of 'enter' when you were doing your spying, it wouldn't have appeared on the access report. Of course, I kept my proper personal letters in the office documents directory – but you wouldn't have thought of looking there, would you?

And you had a good old rummage through my personal things. (Washing indeed!) You found a lone condom and assumed I'd used the other two? Tut. When I was in New-castle, Marianne bought them for a joke. Yes, a girlie joke. She took one, gave one to Richenda and gave the third to me – in the box. A condom box isn't the sort of thing you want to leave in a nightclub ashtray, is it?

And the letter from Newcastle. Obviously a pathetic bluff on your behalf – to get me to admit my terrible secret. I've never heard so much complete crap.

Oh and talking of lying. How's Cathy Shelton? You must be terribly upset that she's getting married to that Crystal Palace player (who she's been engaged to for over a year now). The piloting going well? How's your physique? And why does your company stationery still say that Harry Evans is marketing director?

I don't know if I want to see you. Or continue writing.
P.

Dear Pepper,

I'm sorry that I told you those porkies. I'm sorry I accused you of lying.

Let me try and explain why I lied.

My life is a piece of 24-carat shit. I've got so much debt. I owe a fucking telephone number. It's like I've got a mortgage but no house. I spend much less than I used to, but I simply don't earn enough to make the repayments. And I've been getting all sorts of threats. I've already got three County Court Judgements against me.

And yeah, I'll admit it, I've got a very slight drink problem. I mean I'm in control, but, you know, it means I can't really go out at all. I'm not much fun on the orange juice. And I can't give up cigarettes or puff, obviously.

And I miss Buttercup a lot.

I've even contemplated suicide. You know, I tried to OD a while back? It's true. Obviously, I know that's not the answer. But when I stop and think about things, it sometimes seems the obvious conclusion. Pepper, I'm so fucking pissed off with things.

Some nights when I'm sitting alone in my khazi of a room, I think that I'd be better off doing a stretch. At least everyone would be in the same boat as me. Yeah, and sometimes I think, 'What the fuck is the point?' I'd be better off banging on and going back on the lag.

And my career. You're right. Advertising, marketing, it's all shit. I mean, spending your day trying to sell things to people who don't want them. If I wasn't so much in debt, I'd pack it in and do something worthwhile. I'd like to help the homeless. I know you'll think that's shit. But I promise it isn't. I know I always told beggars to fuck off before – but never now. I always buy the *Big Issue*.

Anyway, please don't stop writing. Please. I am very, very sorry. Your letters are really all I've got. And if we could meet up over Christmas, it would be an unbelievable lift. I'm going to be alone over the whole of Christmas. My best hope is that the office is open for most of it.

Richard X

Dear Richard,

Your last letter upset me a lot. Then again I've been having a rough time lately – with Rick. You know, the white hot has cooled to ice blue and the arguments don't seem to stop. I'm sorry I was so hard on you. I was just – well, bloody cross. Don't you dare ever think about suicide. Do you hear me?

And listen, you're not useless. Think about it. You have a fantastic talent. You can sell condoms. Sure, it doesn't sound like much. But it's brilliant. You could have saved the lives of thousands of people. Saved thousands of terminated pregnancies or unwanted babies. So Richard, you do have a purpose. I was so proud of you when you did those commercials. I still am.

Yes, let's meet up. I need cheering up too. And it would be good to get away from Rick for an evening. Let's do junk food. I'm going back to Sutton on the 23rd so call me at the shop before that.

Lots of love
Pepper X X X X

Listen, I could have saved the lives of thousands of people. Nice one, eh? And I'm seeing Pepper tomorrow night. Albeit in my dog-shit of a flat. Obviously, she'll have to feel sorry for me. She's rowing with her prick boyfriend – which is good. And to top it all, I scored over 100 million on the *Terminator II* machine in the arcade at lunchtime. Consequently, I'm thinking that here, now, it's all going rather well.

Anticipation is surely one of the finest things. But it's fragile. And so, much as I'm smiles, jokes and generally a fine fellow today, I'm fuck frightened that something beyond my control is about to happen to demolish it all. That ironic bastard who holds the joy stick in my life is going to balls things up – like he usually does when things are looking half up. I mean, there's loads that could go wrong. Barring natural and man-made disasters, Pepper and Rick could make up, she could bottle out or – the worst possible thing – I could talk a load of crap and blow it for good. So when the phone goes, my infallible prescience tells me it's not good.

But it's cool. Just wanker debt collectors getting stroppy – yeah, they've found out where I live and work. I promise I'll wedge them some after Christmas. The truth of it is, I'm going to have to go home at Christmas and get some dosh from the old man. Either that or move again.

Phone rings a second time – it's Pepper cancelling. Only it's not. Just business.

Take a long lunch. I'm trying to find Liz. I have something for her. But I end up in an arcade on Old Compton Street feeding £1 nuggets into thankless pinball machines.

Call Pepper to confirm. She's cool. Obviously, I can't work. Besides things are slow at the moment.

TALK EXPOSÉ – **PEPPER**

HOT NEWS –

Pepper: Can it really be an addictive drug?

Last year it was salt that we all had to avoid. Now it's the turn of pepper. Melanie Abdul reports on the disturbing findings of a Zurich research team.

You're enjoying a romantic meal at your favourite Italian restaurant. Everything's as it should be. Your partner's charming as ever and the Chianti is perfect. Your main dish arrives, tender pasta steaming with lashings of the sauce of your choice. The waiter heaps on a spoon of tasty parmesan. Then he asks the sixty-four-thousand-dollar question . . . 'Pepper Madam?'

Experts have told us for a long time to cut down on our salt intake if we want to live longer. But now it seems that our harmless, if spicy, friend pepper is heading for the same treatment. Within the innocuous black peppercorn *piper nigrum* lurks a hallucinogenic chemical, myristicin, which experts say could be psychologically addictive.

But that's not all. It has long been known that certain varieties of the soft pepper are addictive. Red and green chili peppers, especially if eaten raw, increase blood pressure and can produce a 'cocaine-like rush' as the pulse soars and blood surges into the brain. (Raw chili pepper eaters in Mexico have been known to suffer heart failure.) Zurich scientists now claim that the same is true (although to a lesser degree) of our humble table-top pepper . . .

At five thirty the phone goes. My bowel shifts – audibly. It's Harry. Can I hang on until he gets back? He'll be an hour at the latest. It's dead important. Dead important.

At six thirty Harry hasn't shown. I'm chain-smoking. I'm balling sheets of paper. I'm stretching out paperclips and descaling my teeth with them. The second hand on the clock has sped right up. It's six thirty-five in no time. Fuck! – I hit a filling. At six forty I can still feel the shock – a streak of outrage, running from the root of the tooth into my right eye. Pepper will have left. My heart works like it's amylled up. Like it's going to burst out of my throat. I light a cigarette from my dog end and do a pulse count. Ninety-eight. Not good. Oh yeah, and when Harry arrives he'll probably only want to do an hour of *quality dialogue*. Yeah, a nice long meeting – just to really fuck me up. Cheers Harry. Cheers God. But people are like that aren't they? Right bastards. They totally slow up when you look anxious and need to shoot. Especially when they suss you're on a promise – and they don't have any fluffy at present. Like Harry doesn't. Ugly bastard.

'Look Harry, I really, really have to dash,' I say at ten to seven.

'Yeah, I'm sorry I took so long. Christmas shoppers. Bastards, the lot of them. Look all I wanted was to give you this.' He hands me a bottle of Jamesons. 'And say thank you for all your efforts during the year. And have a damn good Christmas.'

'Cheers Harry. I would crack it now. But I really have to run.' We shake hands and I fly out of the building.

I'm using the cash dispenser on Wardour Street – saying,

'Hurry up you fucker, hurry up you thick tin bastard.' The woman behind me with the little girl is tutting loudly and deliberately.

'Don't fucking tut at me.'

'I didn't. I didn't. I didn't,' she squawks. She's shitless – thinks I'm going to belt her or something. I fucking should.

'I'm terribly sorry,' I tell her. 'Hard day. Happy Christmas.'

Then this happens.

'BA! BA. Is that you?' from behind me.

'Fuck me! Liz. How's it going?'

'OK. You look . . . fuckin' 'ell. Fuckin' suit – or what?'

'Liz, look. I'm sorry. I've really got to run. But, like, I've got something for you.'

'Something. What?'

'Somewhere to live.'

'Huh?'

'Yeah. A squat. North London. It's good. It's fine. And you can bang on and everything. I can even wedge you a bit to get you sorted. But I've gotta burn. I really have. Look, can I meet you tomorrow?'

'I dunno. Dunno what I'll be up to, me.'

'Oh for fuck's sake. Look, I'm in such a rush.'

'Why?'

'Not now. Look. Come with me. Come back with me in a cab.'

'No way, guy.'

'Look, you helped me out, yeah? Now it's my turn. Trust me Liz. Liz. Liz. Trust me. Trust me.' And here I'm using my eyes and voice to achieve maximum powers of hypnotic persuasion. A technique I picked up on an intensive three-day course on the 'Art of Persuasion', in Boston. A technique that I'd hitherto considered a waste of Basil's money. 'Liz. Liz. You can trust me,' I coax.

'Bollocks.' Quite obviously, she misconstrues my growing desperation.

'For fuck's sake you've got to believe me. There's a room free in this squat. I've kept it for you for a month – 'till I could find you.'

'Yeah well I've been in 'ospital, me.'

'Right. But you've got to believe me. You've got to come back now.'

'Buy me a drink?'

'You don't understand. I *have* to go. *Now*. So, are you coming?'

'No funny stuff?'

'Absolutely. Absolutely not. Promise. Total word of honour. Coming?'

'Nar.'

'Right, well it's up to you. You can either have a room of your own or you can freeze. I gotta go.' I land a cab and get in. Liz stays put. Then changes her mind, sprawls in and says, 'Don't fuckin' try anything, guy. I've got hepatitis. Bin in hospital, me.' Then, 'Fuck me! Good in 'ere, or what? I've never been in one of these before.'

I'm trying to communicate with Pepper telepathically. 'Be a bit late, Pepper. It's only polite to be slightly late.' Maybe if I'm not there she'll wait for a bit. She'll wait – won't she? On the Andover Estate? In the dark? She'd be out of her fucking mind.

Obviously, this is the slowest bastard cab in London. And obviously, it being Christmas, Oxford Street and Tottenham Court Road are seriously constipated. Come on. Come on, you fucker.

Liz prattles relentlessly. Nudging me and pointing in horror at the clock as each twenty pee clicks up. Obviously, I've got better things to concentrate on. But when she says, 'What I said before. Well, it's alright,' and she takes my hand and drops it on to her leg, I reiterate the nature of the offer and she shuts up for a bit. Yeah, I know I should be trying to figure just what sort of shit she's been through out there. Feel guilty about it in some sort of way – though fuck

278

knows why, I mean, it's not *my* fault, is it? But all I can think of to say is, 'I always buy the *Big Issue*, you know?'

It's seven fifteen before we get to Camden. And I'm watching every move the driver makes. Thinking, 'I just bet that this bastard's going to take me the long route through Islington and get us fucked up in the jam on the one-way.' Of course, he'll say, 'Six of one and half a dozen of the other.'

Liz is trying to relate the story about how there's a gang of blokes who are torching homeless people as they sleep. And I'm thinking I'd like to set fire to Liz. I mean, how the fuck can I practise what I'm going to say to Pepper – yeah, explain Liz, and all – with her gobbing on so? It's seven forty-five and we're not even near the Seven Sisters Road.

15

A Rather Hackneyed Metaphor

Pepper Furnival, hands in pockets, shivering a little is standing on my door step. It's seven fifty-five. And get this. Next to her is an overnight bag.

'Hi-er.'

'Pepper, I'm so sorry I'm late. Pepper, this is Liz.'

'Rr-ight,' she says glancing at Liz and looking back at me – mouth falling open a fraction.

'I'll explain everything. Let's get inside.'

'You're sure, I'm not . . . er, well . . .'

'No, no. I'll explain.'

'Alright?' says Liz cheerily.

'Hello.' Pepper's hands remain in her pockets.

'I'm sorry there's nowhere much to sit. Why don't you two sit on the bed.' Pepper looks mortified. Yeah, Liz looks pretty rough in the light. Contagious even.

'S'alright. I'll go on the floor.' Doubtless respectful of our contamination fears. And she's about to say something – 'hepatitis' or 'fleas', I'd hazard – when I heartily announce, 'A drink. And then I'll show Liz to her new home.'

'Home. Oh what?'

Of course, I don't have to explain. Liz, knocking back Pepper's wine like a pro, tells her everything – yeah, including 'keeping me warm' in her bash. I merely fill in details. Like the ads I placed in the *Big Issue*, the lunchtime searches, paying to keep the room empty for a month. And Pepper, her mouth tight and her eyes bulging, stares at us both alternately and she doesn't utter a single word.

I want to say things like, 'You do believe it, don't you?',
'You don't really reckon I've been . . . ?' You see, I don't
reckon Pepper's ever heard anyone quite like Liz before.
Someone so young, so together, yet so young all the same.
It must all sound so concocted, so practised. Like a major
pitch when one of the directors, perfectly and impassively,
reads his contribution from a pile of dog-eared notes. I
interrupt.

'Liz, I reckon it's time I introduce you and you get settled
in. Yeah?' She nods. A bit sadly, like she's being thrown out
of a party – which she is. 'Here Liz, take the rest of the
bottle.'

On the way out Liz squawks, 'What's happened to that
nice dog you 'ad?' Yeah, it's spontaneous. Just-remembered.
It's perfect. And Pepper smiles.

'Well, well,' says Pepper when I'm back. 'Well, well.'
And she laughs. Takes a gulp of wine. 'Well, well.'

She's right, we are old friends. Her perfume is an old
friend when we do our little embrace. Everything about her
is, I don't know, so good and familiar. Like that first pint after
a couple of days on the wagon. Pepper's just so comfortable.

'So how are things with Rick?'

'I don't want to talk about that now.'

'Sure.'

'Tell me more about Liz.'

'There's nothing more to tell. She said it all.'

'But were you two ever, you know?'

'Christ no. I was homeless for one night. She saw I was
OK and I haven't seen her since then. Honest.'

I'm reckoning that Pepper's considering all this mighty
strange. I bet she's never been in a gaff this bad. And I'd
be surprised if she's ever had such close and prolonged contact with someone as ragamuffin and street-sussed as Liz.
Sure, her friends did their best to be like Liz but they never
quite pulled it off. Their phoney accents. Phoney scents.
Phoney views.

281

'Do you still see Rich and that bunch?' She shakes her head. She pulls a two-litre bottle from her bag, pours another tumbler – it's her fourth of the evening – and says, 'He's taking things badly, Rick. Very badly. He's meant to be moving out after Christmas but I don't reckon he's going to go. The commission fell through and that's really finished him.'

'Poor sod.'

'Huh. You don't mean that, do you?'

'Nope.'

'Anyway it's poor me. He's turned into a right bastard. He's even started selling some of my things. To get money. So he can get more drunk and morose. Huh, why do I always attract drunkards? I've taken to carrying my valuables on me. Hence the bag.'

'Is he safe? I mean, is it safe for you to be there?'

'Oh yeah, it's safe enough. Just uncomfortable.' I tip myself my second – half a glass of wine topped up with warm mineral water.

'Richard, you've had a woman in here recently.'

'Sorry?'

'I can smell her. Just below the dope.' But she's wrong. It's Aslan's strange Egyptian perfume. 'Long-term prospect, eh?'

'Yeah, some model from a chocolate bar commercial.' I joke. 'But she just comes round for the incredible sex.'

She smiles.

Now under normal circumstances, after four tumblers of wine, Pepper would be game. But now, she seems kind of distant. Not like she's bored – no, she seems fascinated with the circumstances she's found me in – almost like there's no one home. I weigh up the equation. The speed drinking, the taciturnity. Yeah, after so long, after all that shit with Horace, Pepper's just a little shy. I mean, she wouldn't be here, on my bed with me, telling me about what a shit Rick is if she didn't want . . . exactly. So I lean towards her slightly. And yeah, of course she reciprocates. We kiss. My tongue is met by unyielding lips. How embarrassing. She's kind enough to ignore it. My best bet is to play it cool. Stay good friends. And worm in – like a gentleman.

There's a long, long pause.

'So what do you want to eat?'

'What are my options?

'Kebabs, Indian, fish and . . .'

'Indian. Yeah? I fancy that. Like old times.'

I have to confess that the evening is not going particularly amazingly. The conversation, well, it's all made up to fill spaces, there's no Pat between us. So I go out for the food and try to think of some useful things to say.

The obvious course of action is to drop a couple of high strengths in the Tandoori to improve my conversation. But these days I no longer follow the obvious course. Instead, I dive into a pub, have a couple and lose a quick game of pool. The more I delay, the more agitated she'll get. And agitated people with bottles of wine drink them – ha. The prospect of another couple is subliminal. But fuck that! I've got Pepper Furnival in my room. Yeah, the real, living Pepper Furnival in *my* room.

True to plan, Pepper's doing well with the wine. Still I only cop a half-smile when I re-enter.

Now, I know why I'm only picking at the food, that's obvious. But what's wrong with her? Maybe the state of my room's putting her off. Maybe it's because I'm displaying all the wit and charm of a train-spotter. Anyway, it's not like she's being deliberately off. I guess she's trying.

'Nice curry . . . Do you order takeaways often? You always used to . . . Do you remember that time that I threw up all night after curry? The best tandoori I know is on Holloway Road. Their tandoori king prawns are the size of fists . . .' Utter shit it is.

Then this happens.

There's a loud and violent hammering at the back door. Holy Fuck!

'Oh my God. It's Rick. He must have followed me.' Undoubtedly the worst thing that could possibly happen, I consider.

But I'm wrong.

Face tattoos, earrings, ringed fingers and baseball bats. These two guys I've just let into my room are the worst thing that could possibly happen. They shut the door behind them and close the chink in the curtains. And I'm whizzing through the database of people I've fucked off. No one this badly – surely?

'Right son, first I'm going to ask nicely. If the answer's *no*, I'm not going to be quite so nice.'

'Richard, what's going on?' Pepper's crying.

'Would the young lady like to leave?'

'What do you want? What do you want?' she screams at them.

'I'm about to get on to that. It's a small matter of twenty grand. Have you got it son? Or do we close your account in a slightly less polite way?'

'After Christmas. Yesterday on the phone. I said. You said. C'mon be reasonable . . . I've got a tenner. That's it.'

'OK, let's get it over with.' He lifts the bat and moves in. I fling myself off the bed, into the corner and roll up like a king prawn. The disaster. It's honed in. Searched me out and come to visit. And because one's thoughts are perspicuous and in slo-mo at such times, I'm thinking, 'See Richard, I told you, you were going to die in a real disaster. I knew you were cut out for greater things than pulling that sodding khazi down on yourself.

'Stop it,' Pepper shrieks. She's up now and standing between us.

'Out of the way, darling or you'll get one. I mean it.'

'Listen, listen. I'll pay. I'll pay you. Just don't touch him. Leave him alone.'

284

'You got twenty grand on you, love?'

'Well maybe not that much. But I've got quite a lot. Honestly,' she weeps. 'Just believe me. In my bag.' I look up warily. Disbelieving. Why is it that some people can affect things on this planet and other's can't? She's emptied her bag on to the mattress. Then she hands them a building society book. 'Here, here, take it. Please. Take it all.'

'Patricia Margaret Furnival – eleven grand, two hundred and twenty-six pounds, forty-two pee.'

'There's more. There's interest on it too.'

'What am I supposed to do with this? Besides it's well short.'

'Look, here's my bank card as well, take it. It's got my signature on it. It matches the invisible one in the book. They'll accept it for identification. You can withdraw it first thing tomorrow. I can't close the account tonight. Or even, if you want, I'll meet you and withdraw the money. It's instant access. You can take it all out.'

'I'm not sure.'

'Please, please. Look it's got my address in it. If anything goes wrong . . .'

'I still don't know.'

'Well, I'll come with you then. In the morning. Like I said. Oh please, please take it.'

'You still at that address then?' She goes to her bag and fishes something out. 'Look take that. It's where I work. I'm there in the daytimes.'

'You realize, of course, that this little exchange falls under the official secrets act.' He slowly wanks his bat. 'Any funny stuff. Anything. You. You down there. You understand?'

'Yes. Yes. Of course.'

'You got a good bird there, mate. Right, we'll be back for the rest in a couple of days. And if I have any problems – any – you'll hear. It's been a pleasure doing business with you madam, sir. Let's go.'

Pepper and I are on the mattress. We're both crying a lot.

Her out of fear and shock. Me, I guess, out of shame. Bad behaviour, or what? I reach for the wine.

'No, no. Stay,' she whimpers. So I do. And I reckon it's a good half-hour before we speak.

'Richard, I keep thinking they're going to come back.'

'Not tonight. It's alright.'

'They might change they're minds about the book.'

'They know what they're doing. C'mon, Pepper. I need a drink.' We pass the wine bottle back and forth until it's empty. I get the Irish.

'Oh Pepper, Pepper. What can I possibly say? Thank you so much. You were so brave. I'll repay you. I promise. Oh my God. I swear.'

'It's only money.'

'It was what your father gave you for a house, yeah?'

'Yeah.'

'Look, I'll call the police. We can stop it.'

'And then what? You get killed. Killed.' And she starts to cry again.

'Thank you. Thank you. Thank you . . .'

She puts a finger over my lips.

'Shhh.' We're both still shaking and need more drink. Pepper drinks willingly from the whisky bottle.

After some more time of intermittent crying from Pepper and holding each other, I say, 'Why did you do it, Pepper?'

'Daft fucking question.'

'Not really. Your life's savings.'

'Because I love you. Satisfied?' We tighten our hold.

'I love you too, you know?'

'Yeah.'

'All the time you were gone . . .'

'Shhh.' We kiss. And this time she allows my tongue in. I check. Her eyes are closed. When we break from kissing, I notice the familiar sight of fucked up carpet. 'Do you think I ought to do a bit of clearing up?'

'No, stay here.'

'OK.'

She starts sobbing again. Between sobs, she says, 'Richard, please don't drink any more. Please, I really want you to be OK. Please, don't drink any more, for me.' I put the bottle down.

It's one a.m. and the carpet's bugging me a lot.

'Richard, you can't sweep it.'

'What do you suggest?'

'You'll have to wash it.'

It has minimal effect – my scrubbing effort. And I'm about to resort to bleach (the carpet is, after all, a creamy, shitty sort of colour) when Pepper breaks down again. Not sobbing like she was before, but really bawling. So I stop and attend to her.

'Come on now. They've gone. It all happened four hours ago. They won't come back now.'

'It's not that.'

'What is it then? The money? Pepper, I will pay you back. I promise.'

'No, no. It's nothing. Just hold me.' I do this and she begins to calm down. She lets go of me and, cool and totally together, says this, 'I'm so confused, Richard. Rick and me. You. Just holding you like this it's so . . . so . . . I don't know.' I reach down for the bottle. But change my mind.

'Pepper I need to tell you some things. Some things about me. Will you listen?' She nods.

So I tell her about getting right. Getting right for her. About how she watched over me getting right. Encouraging me.

'I was?'

'Does that sound dumb?'

'No. When I was ill that time, lying on Rich's smelly couch. It was like you were there saying it's OK for me to come home. Saying you'd look after me.'

'And it was true.'

'Yeah,' she grins.

'But, like if you'd have known what I was doing. Would you have wanted me to do it? Been encouraging me?'

'You know I would have.'

'But you'd have wanted me to do it for myself – not for you. Right?'

'I suppose.'

'Did you think about me much, Pepper?'

'No, never. Of course I bloody did.'

'No, I mean a real lot. Sort of all the time on and off.' Her eyes grow wide. She puts a hand over her mouth and turns her head away. 'Pepper. Did you?' I ease her head back round. Her eyes are glassy. And she nods ever so slightly – like a kid owning up to some crime.

'Yes,' she sighs.

'Did you dream about me at nights often? Actually like, most nights?' Her eyes squeeze shut and tears bubble out. She clenches her mouth and gives a slightly more purposeful nod.

'I'm sorry Pepper. Is this conversation upsetting you?' Pepper exhales deeply, like she's resigned to something. Something she's not entirely sure she's happy about.

'No, Richard. It's not,' she sobs – as her arms go around my neck and cool tears run down inside the back of my shirt collar. And so I just hold her. Happy to have her leak down my back. And I'm telling her things. Not things like how much I've been missing her. Nor begging. I just state the facts. I tell her just how excellent she is. Give her back some of the adjectives I'd taken. The adjectives she deserves.

Her hands are in my hair and her warm mouth is on mine. I lift my hand into her top and she sighs.

There's a gentle knock at the door.

'Oh my God.'

'Don't worry. It's Aslan. A friend.' I explain to Aslan that I have company and he goes. Much cold rushes into the room. I shut the door and turn back. Pepper opens her arms for me.

288

'Indian food, my bed in Sutton, Granny Furnival's cinnamon cake, Nevile Furnival – my family's cat, icy spritzers,..'

'What are you on about?'

'I'm trying to add up how good this feels. Skiing fast, Buttercup smiling, the smell of suntan oil.'

'Twit.'

She urges my hand back to where it was and whispers. 'Go on. Please carry on with what you were saying. All those nice things about me.'

'Since when did flattery ever get me anywhere with you? Besides it's your turn. Granny Furnival's cake indeed.'

'Well, you drink too much, have horrible habits, smell of cigarettes, swear all the time, wet the bed . . .'

'Not any more.'

She touches my face. 'Now me, again. Go on. You're far better with words.' I pause, and regard her thoughtfully – then say, 'Aw Pepper. You know? You're nothing to write home about. A bit dippy.' She slaps the back of my arm. And laughs, 'Yaow!' when my hand squelches across her tit. Her hands rise into my shirt and we kiss more. 'Hey, smooth boy, let's fuck.' 'And then what?'

'Maybe some more, and more. A bit of sleep. And wake up together in the morning. Aren't you curious about my tattoo?'

'Yes I am, actually. But then what? Fuck more? Or will you go back to that tosser Rick?'

'You have to pitch for this account first. And don't call Rick that.'

'Shit, Pepper. Are you putting me through some sort of a test? Why is everything so bloody complicated with you?'

'Oh hell, Richard. Don't get heavy with me. I just really need to make love – with you. Don't spoil things.'

'Yeah, but I'll get hooked again. Then in the morning you'll go and get cold turkey.'

'What's wrong with you, Richard? Isn't it plain? What do you think I'm trying to say to you? Oh yeah, I've been living with a guy for six months, things are going a little awkwardly at the moment so why don't I pop around see my ex, with a bag full of gear, give him my all my money and have a quick fuck while I'm there? Then piss off back?'

'Well I don't know. I mean. You are funny – sometimes. Aren't you, Pepper?'

'Yes well.'

'Yes well what?' She presses her face against mine and gives a long frustrated growl.

'Just – yes well.' Pepper begins to undress and I get up. 'Where are you going *now*?'

'To get something.'

'Oh right. How responsible. I suppose you get them for free, ha.' And it's true. I am being responsible. I'm not pitching for a one-off job here, I want the whole account. And, sure, what I'm about to do next may shoot everything to shit. But certain matters must be cleared up. I open the drawer, lift out the envelope and surreptitiously remove the polaroids. I walk over to her with the envelope.

'Actually, Pepper, it's not what you think. It's a letter. And I think it might upset you a little.'

'Oh dear.' I take one last look at the cardiac arrest of a post-mark before I hand it to her. Yeah, there it is in plain red and white: 'Rocastle Upton Tyrone. London WC2'. And, of course. Oh my fuck. I retch as it comes back to me. And as the realization takes hold, cigarettes stab my ears. My eyes try to push their way out. My cheeks are being steam-ironed. And I feel an old-style vom on the way up.

'Well, show it to me then. What is it?'

'No, no, Pepper. I've changed my mind.'

'Go on, Richard. You can't wind me up like that.' She dives up and snatches the envelope.

'It's something I wrote to you. One afternoon at work. But when it arrived we were getting on so badly that I decided not to let you see it. I was a little drunk at the time and, well, it's a bit silly, actually.' She reads it and tears fill her eyes.

'I don't think it's silly at all. Can I keep it, please?'

'I guess.'

'I wish I'd got it then. It's the sort of thing that could have made all the . . . never mind.'

Pepper says the most excellent things. Quite simply the best things ever. Things like: 'I love you so much,' and 'You'll never know how much I missed you, how much I cried after the last time. Don't ever go.' Sure they sound like lines from shitty pop songs when *I* say them. But with her mouth at my ear, her words metered by gasps, groans and squeaks – her little speech really is spot on. And, to use a rather hackneyed metaphor, this really is very much like downing that first pint after so, so, so long on the wagon.

As I cradle her here, soothing away the post-climactic tears, I'm thinking that maybe, just maybe, the pitch is finally over and I've won the account.

flamingo

ORIGINAL

Ray Shell

Iced

'The book is a powerhouse, Ray Shell writes beautifully. The story is heartbreaking, I kept putting it down and picking it up again – it won't let me go.'   MAYA ANGELOU

This extraordinary, immensely powerful debut novel takes the form of a diary written by Cornelius Washington – a forty-four-year-old crack addict. The diary, rendered in a rhythmic and gripping stream of consciousness, charts both the harsh realities of Cornelius's grim present and the upheavals and excitements of his colourful past. During his life he has moved up and down the East Coast of America, encountering a host of startling, enlightening and sometimes terrifying characters along the way. Once brimming with ambition, Cornelius dabbles with drugs as a young man before gradually becoming hooked. Finally, he becomes what he most fears, a 'Vampire-Zombie', one of the lost dead souls at the end of the addiction line.

Iced is at once a shocking account of the horrors of the addict's life, and a compelling and often uplifting tale of human love and loss.

flamingo

ORIGINAL

Jane Smiley

A Thousand Acres

Winner of the Pulitzer Prize for Fiction
and the
US National Book Critics' Circle Award

Larry Cook's farm is the largest in Zebulon County, Iowa, and a tribute to his hard work and single-mindedness. Proud and possessive, his sudden decision to retire and hand over the farm to his three daughters, is disarmingly uncharacteristic. Ginny and Rose, the two eldest, are startled yet eager to accept, but Caroline, the youngest daughter, has misgivings. Immediately, her father cuts her out.

In *A Thousand Acres* Jane Smiley transposes the *King Lear* story to the modern day, and in so doing at once illuminates Shakespeare's original and subtly transforms it.

'*A Thousand Acres* is a strong, gnarled shocker of a novel . . . superb. Its success is down to Smiley's ambitious gusto, her intuitive handling of the relationship between character and landscape, and her willingness to haul genuine moral freight across the panorama she has so expertly painted.'   *Sunday Times*

'*A Thousand Acres* is a superlative, extraordinary, amazing new novel . . . a great American tragedy about the failure of a family's land and the failure of its love. There may have been better novels than *A Thousand Acres*, but I fear I didn't read them . . . a haunting inquisition into the decline and fall of a family.'   Anthony Quinn, *Observer*

'Her singular gift is the grace with which she can move up through the literary gears to imbue her long, gripping, multi-layered narrative with real grandeur and moral seriousness. The novel's emotional power comes from the accretion of piercingly good small things.'   *Independent on Sunday*

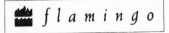 *flamingo*

Robert O'Connor

Buffalo Soldiers

'When there is peace, the warlike man attacks himself.'

NIETZSCHE
Epigraph to *Buffalo Soldiers*

For the US army, peace is the continuation of war by other means. For the GI, every day is a struggle – even more so the night.

Set in Mannheim, Germany, *Buffalo Soldiers* is the story of Elwood, clerk to the Battalion Commander of the 'fighting 57th' and major-league drug dealer. For Elwood, life is a search for supremacy, drugs both his weapon and, inevitably, his weakness. Attempting to run a smooth operation in the face of frequent outbursts of ferocious violence, much of it racial, Elwood manages to stay a hair's breadth ahead of the game – at least until rival dealer Sergeant Saad and the military police begin to put on a double squeeze . . .

'One of the best novels I've read in a long time. Robert O'Connor skilfully blends the hilarious satire of *Catch-22* with the knuckle-hard realism of *From Here to Eternity*. Hugely entertaining.'

J. G. BALLARD

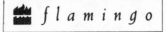 *flamingo*

Dorothy Allison

Bastard Out of Carolina

'Resonant, emotionally complex and strong as hell'
Mary Gaitskill, author of *Bad Behaviour*

'Compulsively readable, *Bastard Out of Carolina* is filled with juicy writing and full-blooded characters. Alison can make an ordinary moment transcendent with her sensuous mix of kitchen-sink realism and down-home drawl'   *San Francisco Chronicle*

This astonishing first novel tells the story of the Boatwrights of Greenville County, South Carolina, a 'white-trash' family of hard-drinking men and indomitable women. Proudest of them all is Anney's illegitimate daughter, Ruth Anne, known as Bone. With little hope of employment beyond the textile mills and roadside diners, Bone dreams of a life not only away from Greenville but also far away from Daddy Glen, her stepfather, whose sly coldness and dangerous fury will test the love of them all.

Written in a mesmerizing voice that mingles the languid rhythms of country music with raw, unsparing descriptions of emotional and physical violence, *Bastard Out of Carolina* marks the emergence of an extraordinarily gifted writer.

'*Bastard*'s success is in its emotional precision and irrepressible lyricism, forcefully combined. Allison relates the difficulty of Bone's struggles with intensity and humour . . . An irresistible cast of characters, Allison renders their every look and touch with absolute precision and discernment'
San Francisco Review of Books

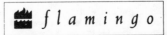 flamingo

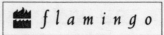
flamingo

Flamingo is a quality imprint publishing both fiction and non-fiction. Below are some recent titles.

Fiction

- ☐ Life Force *Fay Weldon* £5.99
- ☐ The Kitchen God's Wife *Amy Tan* £4.99
- ☐ A Thousand Acres *Jane Smiley* £5.99
- ☐ The Quick *Agnes Rossi* £4.99
- ☐ Ordinary Decent Criminals *Lionel Shriver* £5.99
- ☐ Iced *Ray Shell* £5.99
- ☐ Dreaming in Cuban *Cristina Garcia* £5.99
- ☐ The Republic of Love *Carol Shields* £5.99
- ☐ Pepper *Tristan Hawkins* £5.99
- ☐ Bastard Out of Carolina *Dorothy Allison* £5.99

Non-fiction

- ☐ The Gates of Paradise *Alberto Manguel* £9.99
- ☐ Long Ago in France *M. F. K. Fisher* £5.99
- ☐ Ford Madox Ford *Alan Judd* £6.99
- ☐ C. S. Lewis *A. N. Wilson* £5.99
- ☐ Into the Badlands *John Williams* £5.99
- ☐ Dame Edna Everage *John Lahr* £5.99
- ☐ Number *John McLeish* £5.99
- ☐ What the Traveller Saw *Eric Newby* £5.99

You can buy Flamingo paperbacks at your local bookshop or newsagent. Or you can order them from Fontana Paperbacks, Cash Sales Department, Box 29, Douglas, Isle of Man. Please send a cheque, postal or money order (not currency) worth the purchase price plus 24p per book (maximum postage required is £3.00 for orders within the UK).

NAME (Block letters)_____

ADDRESS_____

_____

_____